Lightning in a Drought Year

Lightning in a Drought Year

Michelle Black

WinterSun Press

Published by
WinterSun Press
P.O. Box 2626
Frisco, CO 80443

ISBN 0-9658014-2-X (cloth)
ISBN 1-929705-00-X (trade paperback)

LCCN 99-63575

All events and characters portrayed in this story are fictitious and references to real persons, places or events are used fictitiously. Any other similarities to actual persons, either living or dead, are purely coincidental.

Cover art by Ann T. Weaver

This book is also available in electronic format
published by Hard Shell Word Factory
ISBN 1-58200-542-7

For my mother,
Virginia Black

Chapter One

The prairie once formed the floor of an ancient ocean–an immense, prehistoric inland sea. Over the course of countless centuries, air replaced water, but the vast, rolling character of the seabed remained.

On cloudless days in the Flint Hills, visions of the ancient ocean persisted. The incessant prairie winds whipped and whispered through the switch grass and roared in the ears of the plains dwellers like memories of the primeval ocean currents.

1886

The south wind washed over Laurel McBryde like an epiphany on that April morning of her twenty-first birthday. The south wind was a fair wind, always the harbinger of good weather to come. Moist and gusty post-dawn breezes sent the peach-tinged cumulus clouds rolling wildly across the newly green plains. The sensuous sound, the feel, the very taste of the blustering wind entranced her as she walked along lugging her heavy camera and its spindly-legged wooden tripod. The scent of wet soil and new growth permeated the air.

Rapidly changing splashes of light and dark raced across the stark, tallgrass prairie. The huge, puffy clouds and their dancing shadows performed a vivid ballet for her on the treeless expanse of earth left fresh and shimmering from a pre-dawn cloudburst.

Laurel was certain such a landscape could give rise to dreams and prophesies. Her father's hired hand, Old Michael Touching Ground, spoke often of visions and vision quests, but she sensed no dark foreboding in the clearing skies.

Her goal was self-portraiture that morning. She wanted to memorialize her twenty-first birthday with a picture she could give to her father. He said he wanted one to frame and set on the desk in his study.

She carefully placed her boxy camera down on the black fringed shawl she used for a dark cloth to free her hands to set up her tripod. She paused a moment to pick some prairie violets and place them together with her bundle of blue-eyed grass in the pocket of her smock. She favored milkweed, but it would not bloom until mid-summer at least. She grabbed a handful of her long, dark hair and braided it loosely to keep the breezes from blowing it in her face.

The blustering wind died down for a moment, just long enough for her to catch the sound of her name being called. She whirled around to scan the surrounding plains and immediately saw Old Michael limping in an awkward half-run towards her.

"Meez Laurel, Meez Laurel," he shouted in his fractured English. "Come quickly–your fadder...hurry, hurry."

She knew by the tone of his voice something calamitous had happened. She grabbed her beloved camera by its leather handle and took off running towards home, afraid of what she would find there.

She arrived at the house and dashed into her father's study. He sat in his favorite reading chair, surrounded by his cherished books. He sat so still and silent, he could have been sleeping, but when Laurel saw his eyes staring cold and fixed at the far wall as though he were gazing at the portrait of her mother which hung there, she knew he was dead.

She stood for a long time observing him, heavy camera still in hand. She had not experienced death since she lost her mother at the age of six. But she had been carefully sheltered from that loss. This one was hers to face alone.

Old Michael arrived at the door of the study, breathless and still agitated.

"What now, Meez Laurel? What now we do?"

"I must summon the Hartmoors," Laurel whispered with a plaintive formality, her eyes still fastened on the lifeless form in the familiar chair.

Thus, the Hartmoor family re-entered Laurel McBryde's life for the first time in the fifteen years since her mother's death.

"The Flint Hills. How could anyone live here and hang on to their sanity?" said Cassandra Hartmoor, Laurel's maiden aunt.

"It's so bleak and eerie," commented Alice Hartmoor, Laurel's aunt-by-marriage.

"There's nothing for the eye to catch onto," said Margaret Hartmoor, Laurel's grandmother, as she fanned herself vigorously.

"Laurel called the scenery 'mystical,'" offered Alice.

"*Mystical*? What on earth did she mean by that?" asked Margaret.

"Who knows? She says such odd things," Cassandra complained in a tired voice.

"That's an understatement, my dear," said Margaret.

Fools, thought Laurel from behind closed eyes. She barely knew her traveling companions in the hot, crowded carriage well enough to fully distinguish the speakers by their voices, though all were her female relations by either blood or marriage.

They presumed she slept, and nearly she did but for the swaying and bouncing of the airless compartment that carried them south across the Kansas prairie. The grinding complaint of the wooden wheels against the rocky suggestion of a road played in rhythmic harmony with the ceaseless prairie wind outside.

The dusty, uncomfortable stagecoach carried Laurel and the Hartmoor family south from the McBryde ranch, called Windrift, to Chisholm, a small town just outside of Wichita.

"I suppose Laurel was happy at Windrift simply because she had nothing else to compare it with," Cassandra Hartmoor remarked.

"I tried to take her away from there fifteen years ago," said Margaret Hartmoor.

"When Sarah died?" asked Alice.

"Andrew wouldn't hear of it, the fool," Margaret grumbled. "A man trying to raise up a little girl out here in the middle of nowhere. The idea was absurd."

"What did he do for a living?" Alice persisted.

"He practiced law before he married Sarah," answered Margaret.

"But how could he maintain a practice out in this kind of isolation?" queried Alice.

"Didn't he ride the circuit as a judge for awhile?" asked Cassandra of her mother.

"Yes, but not after Sarah's death," replied Margaret. "He didn't seem to be interested in much of anything after that. Just kept on living in that big, old house. To this day I can't imagine what Sarah saw in him–a man older than her own father."

Laurel inwardly burned with this criticism of her father. She longed to defend him, yet was too embarrassed to let the women know she secretly eavesdropped on their conversation.

"How did Sarah meet Andrew?" Alice pursued.

Laurel didn't know whether to be flattered or irritated by her Aunt Alice's interest in her family history.

"He came to Chisholm when it was just a sprout of a town. Helped Gregory set up the Hartmoor Bank. Saw to all the legal details."

"Laurel must have been awfully devoted to her father, keeping house for him all these years," murmured Alice.

"He spoiled her quite thoroughly," Margaret pronounced with finality. "All that is going to change, I'm afraid."

"A shame he had to die on her birthday," said Cassandra.

This statement rankled Laurel even more. Her Aunt Cassandra made it sound like her father had picked the day on purpose. It wasn't his fault he suffered a fatal heart attack on her twenty-first birthday. His health had been failing throughout the winter. Though over seventy years of age, Andrew McBryde had enjoyed robust health until this last winter.

He tried to hide his shortness of breath from his daughter, yet she was a keen observer. She saw how frequently he gasped for air after climbing the stairs and how often he massaged the throbbing pains in his shoulder and arm. She didn't know what these signs meant, but she knew something was wrong. She begged him to see a doctor, though the closest one was a five hour wagon ride away. He dismissed his problems with a casual wave and a brave face.

"I was impressed with the manner in which Laurel handled all the arrangements," said Alice.

"Yes, admirable," agreed Margaret, her mother-in-law. "She seems reasonably intelligent."

"Yet she never attended school of any sort, did she?" Alice mused. "Jack said the nearest town would be Killdeer and there's no school there."

"There's hardly a town there!" laughed Cassandra.

The other women chuckled.

"Her father tutored her, I'm sure," said Margaret.

"Did you ever see a house more cluttered with books?" Alice whispered in a conspiratorial tone.

"Did you ever see a house more cluttered?" Cassandra offered another jibe.

Once again Laurel mentally winced at their laughter. Didn't the Hartmoors realize that books were her only friends? Books were her only outlet, her only window to the world beyond the vast, empty hills surrounding Windrift.

"Windrift will soon be a memory for our Laurel," said Margaret, the only one who had not laughed at Cassandra's joke. "She will find life far more interesting in Chisholm, back in the bosom of her family." She paused a moment and Laurel heard the old woman sigh. "And even if it's not, we have our work cut out for us."

"What do you mean, Mother Hartmoor?" asked Alice.

"Marriage, of course. At her age, we have no time to waste. Still, I'm sure a suitable match can be found. She has her mother's looks."

Laurel preened at the notion she resembled her mother. She had only limited memories of her, but had spent many an hour studying her mother's portrait, the one that hung in her father's study. She'd been surprised by the resemblance her Aunt Cassandra bore to her late sister, though where Sarah Hartmoor's features had been heir to a distinctive grace of line, her younger sister Cassandra's face remained as stubbornly plain as an unfrosted cake.

"She has the lovely dark Hartmoor hair," Alice commented helpfully.

"She doesn't know how to wear it," Cassandra drily observed.

"I sometimes wish my Christine had inherited the Hartmoor hair," Alice continued, ignoring her sister-in-law.

"But Jack's hair isn't dark," countered Cassandra.

"Christine's hair is very attractive, Alice," Margaret said.

Laurel thought her grandmother must be trying to be kind. She couldn't imagine anyone liking little, five-year-old Christine's riotous mass of carroty red hair.

"And Laurel's eyes," Alice continued. "Such a dark shade of blue in contrast to her fairness. Blue eyes with black lashes–I've always thought that to be one of the loveliest combinations."

Laurel remembered how her father used to tell her she had eyes "as blue as the October sky." She held her breath to keep the tears at bay.

"Did you notice her clothes?" Cassandra continued to snipe. "At least ten or twenty years out of fashion."

"They're Sarah's clothes," said Margaret curtly.

A chilled silence fell upon the coach momentarily. Laurel sensed another reproach in the ladies' silence. Why did they consider it odd that she wore her dead mother's clothing? She had thought herself thrifty to make use of the garments, in addition to their sentimental value to her.

"She's had a strange upbringing, to be sure," Margaret continued. "Living on this Godforsaken, treeless plain. You probably don't remember, but Chisholm was once this empty. Back in the Sixties, the Government used to pay you to plant trees. Gave you title to land by the quarter section if you'd plant trees."

"Thank heaven they did," sighed Alice.

"Civilization," intoned Margaret. "We wrested civilization from this barren land. Civilizing our little Laurel shouldn't be much of a task compared to that."

"We hope!" laughed her daughter.

The stagecoach wheels rolled over a large rock, jolting its occupants in their seats. Laurel's head bumped against the frame of the window and she could no longer pretend to doze.

"Sorry about that, ladies," the driver shouted.

"Everyone all right?" called Jack Hartmoor, Alice's husband. He rode outside the coach next to the driver, disdaining the all-female entourage within.

Little Christine, who sat wedged between her mother and Laurel, now also awakened from her afternoon nap. She squirmed in her uncomfortable position between the two women and sighed with childish annoyance.

"Is mama's darling alright?" Alice asked her little girl. "The wheels went bump. That's all."

"How much longer, do you think?" Laurel inquired, as politely as possible. She attempted to stretch herself as best she could, given the cramped environment.

Her grandmother glanced at the small watch pinned to the lapel of her traveling jacket.

"It's nearly three," Margaret announced. "We'll be home before dark."

Laurel nodded and looked out the window at the prairie miles rolling past. She wondered when and if she would ever see Windrift again. Her lip trembled with another sudden urge to cry. She took a deep breath and shut her eyes tight to regain her composure.

"Were you able to get some rest, Laurel?" asked Alice, smiling benignly over the head of her little daughter.

"Yes, ma'am."

"Oh, my goodness, don't call me 'ma'am.' We're family, you and I."

"By marriage," Cassandra interjected.

"Are you looking forward to living in Chisholm, dear?" asked Laurel's grandmother.

"Oh, very much. Might I inquire when Chisholm's next city elections are held?"

"Planning on running?" asked her Aunt Cassandra, with barely concealed sarcasm.

"Oh, no–voting. Everyone says the legislature is going to pass female suffrage for municipal elections next session. I can't wait."

"Uh-oh." Cassandra rolled her eyes and laughed. "Don't let my brother hear you say that. We'll never get him to shut up."

To answer Laurel's blank expression, Alice, with a complacent smile, jumped in to explain. "My husband is a very prominent member of the Republican Party in Chisholm, Laurel. Unlike some of the more radical members of the party, we don't care for the idea of woman's suffrage. I mean, election days are so rowdy. The very thought of a decent woman going out on such a day is so...unseemly."

This response astounded Laurel to such a degree, she didn't know what to say next. Her father had been a committed supporter of political equality for women, so she assumed all educated and right-thinking individuals naturally agreed.

"Oh, please, it's too hot in here to discuss politics," complained Margaret. She mopped her brow with her handkerchief.

"Tell us more about *you*, Laurel," Alice asked to change the subject. "We're all so anxious to get to know you better."

"Yes, do tell," mumbled Cassandra, with less sincerity. This remark caused Margaret to glance at her daughter with a warning look, which Cassandra deliberately ignored.

"Well...there's not a lot to tell," Laurel replied cautiously. Her companions smiled, taking this answer as a sign of Laurel's modesty. Actually, Laurel felt profoundly intimidated by the discussion she had just surreptitiously overheard, not to mention the shock of learning her new family's political persuasions.

"Tell us what you used to do all day," prompted Cassandra.

"Well, I'm fond of reading," Laurel asserted, suddenly intent on reproaching her Hartmoor relatives on the still-sensitive issue of leaving most of her favorite books behind. Her audience exchanged various glances in response to this, but said nothing. Feeling guilty for creating this awkward silence, Laurel added, "I like to make photographs."

"You can make photographs with a camera?" Cassandra asked in stunned disbelief. The other women also leaned forward, their curiosity piqued.

"Yes." Laurel smiled with new-found confidence at the interest she'd aroused.

"So where is your camera?" Cassandra pressed on.

"In my trunk."

Margaret's bright, dark eyes crinkled with amusement. "Jack swore you had the heaviest clothes imaginable when he and the driver loaded that trunk on the coach!"

Laurel had kept the existence of her camera a secret from the Hartmoors after the disagreement over the books. She didn't want to risk them forcing her to leave her beloved camera behind. She had carefully wrapped the lens, the camera body, the dismantled tripod, the glass plates, and all her other gear in her dresses and blouses and linens and placed them securely within the one trunk she was allowed to bring.

"Do you think you might photograph my Christine?" asked Alice eagerly.

"I'd be happy to. I can't just yet, though. I'm waiting for a new order of photographic chemicals to arrive from a firm in Chicago. Now I wonder if they'll find their way to me in Chisholm."

"Did you inform the postmaster in Killdeer of your new address?"

"We don't exactly have a postmaster in Killdeer."

Cassandra snickered.

Laurel ignored this, but did not wish to explain that the provisioner in Killdeer served unofficially in that function. He handled the job reasonably well–at least when he was sober.

Alice prodded Laurel with more questions about her hobby and Laurel, encouraged on her favorite topic, chattered on nervously for half an hour about lens settings and silver salts while the hapless Alice nodded and smiled politely.

Margaret studied Laurel with a penetrating frown as Laurel spoke with more animation than she had shown during the somber preceding week. Laurel caught her disapproving glance from the corner of her eye and wondered what was wrong.

The sea floor lost its rolling quality the farther south they traveled. More trees were seen on the flattening horizon. A town appeared in the distance. Laurel watched it grow in size with much anticipation. The Plains Transit coach pulled into Chisholm just before supper time, as Margaret had predicted. Jack fetched the wagon and horses from the livery while several men unloaded the baggage and carried it to their wagon.

On the short trip from Chisholm to the Hartmoor farm, Laurel watched the sun setting on the flat western horizon. As Jack guided the team off the main road and onto Hartmoor land, Laurel caught sight of a young man working in the adjacent field. She squinted her eyes to see what he was doing. As they neared, she realized he was mending a fence on the far side of a growing stand of winter wheat.

The Chisholm afternoon must have been as warm and sticky as the one they left at Windrift since the young man had removed his shirt and tied it around his waist.

The fair skin of his back, crisscrossed by suspenders, had reddened under the prairie sun's punishing veil. His tousled blond hair clung in wet curls to the back of his neck. The slanting rays of dying sunlight played upon the handsome, muscular lines of his shoulders and back.

As they drew closer still, she studied the lean, attractive figure he made as he worked so diligently in the early evening heat.

He heard the sounds of their wagon approach and immediately untied the shirt from his waist. He turned in the direction of their wagon and, with a broad grin, held the faded cotton shirt across his chest with an exaggerated pretense of modesty.

Laurel found his face to be no less attractive than his physique. Sweat-drenched, blond curls framed his fine-boned features in a pleasingly boyish way. Pale eyes shown from his face, even in the failing light.

"Don't look!" he shouted gaily as they passed him on the dusty path.

Cassandra waved to him.

Jack urged the horses into a faster gait while his wife, seated next to him, turned to her sister-in-law with a scandalized frown.

"Cassie! How could you wave at him?" scolded Alice. "He was...only...only half-attired."

"I've seen him in less." Cassandra laughed. "Well, not since he was five. But I'll wave at him if I please, Alice, thank you very much."

"We've all had a long day," sighed Margaret. "Let's get home and get some supper into us quickly."

"Laurel's enjoying the view," Cassandra archly observed.

Laurel snapped back into a forward facing position, flustered to have been caught so blatantly staring.

"I...I'm sorry," Laurel stammered. "It's just that he was so...so extraordinary looking. With his blond hair and muscular shoulders, he looked like a young Adonis. And—"

Laurel's innocent enthusiasm gave way to an awareness that everyone in the wagon now stared at her. An awkward silence followed in which Cassandra stifled a giggle into her handkerchief. Alice discreetly busied herself re-arranging her daughter on her lap and Jack glanced back uncomfortably to his mother to take charge of the situation.

"Laurel—" Margaret's voice carried a hard edge to it that made Laurel's hands instantly go cold. "It is inappropriate for a young lady to observe, much less comment upon, a young man's...physical appearance."

Laurel dropped her gaze into her lap, her cheeks burning with embarrassment. Her father had raised her to speak her mind and that was what she had done. In her artist's eye, she had found the young farmer's careless grace an attractive sight–just to look at, nothing more. She hadn't intended the innuendo assumed by her relatives. She wanted to explain this. She wanted to ask who the young man was and why Alice didn't think they should speak to him, but she couldn't.

The wagon jerked to a halt in front of the Hartmoor home and everyone jumped down as quickly as possible. All except Margaret, who sat quietly for a moment as her family withdrew into the house. Laurel heard her grandmother take a deep breath and murmur, "Our work is cut out for us."

Laurel now keenly sensed that in joining the Hartmoor household, she would be called upon to play the game of life by a new set of rules and she hadn't the slightest inkling what these rules might be. She retreated into the Hartmoor house to hide her homesick tears from the rest of the family. She was ashamed to be crying like a baby. She hated showing such weakness. She hated feeling publicly embarrassed. She hated being reprimanded for some infraction she didn't even know she had committed.

She hated the Hartmoors.

Chapter Two

The Hartmoors buzzed around the house in a noisy swirl of industry, everyone unpacking and chattering and calling orders to everyone else. No one called to Laurel so she wiped her wet face on her sleeve and began to wander about, exploring her new home.

The Hartmoor house was considerably larger than her house at Windrift and she grudgingly had to admit she found it impressive on first viewing. Painted sky blue, with generous white millwork trimming every available eave and overhang, the Hartmoor house stood pompous and tall over the surrounding Kansas wheatfields. A large, carved letter "H" proudly emblazoned the front door. "H" for "Hartmoor?" Laurel wondered, or "Headache" or "Homesick," both of which she felt at the moment.

A covered porch, which Alice called the "veranda," completely encircled the two-story frame dwelling. A parlor, a dining room, a large kitchen and an enormous pantry occupied the main floor with four bedrooms on the second. Graceful white picket fencing divided the large yard into quadrants, separating the stables from the storage sheds, the smokehouse from the kitchen garden, and the tidy front lawn from everything else.

Most wondrous of all–gas lights illuminated every room. One had only to turn a small knob on the fixture to adjust the brightness. This innovation startled Laurel the first time she watched her grandmother light the kitchen to prepare supper.

"Did you grow up in a tent, Laurel?" Cassandra laughed when she noticed Laurel's amazed expression.

"Don't mind Cassie," clucked Margaret when her daughter left the kitchen. "She just doesn't know what to do with you yet."

Laurel had no idea what her grandmother was talking about, but didn't pursue it. She answered simply, "Yes, Ma'am."

Margaret looked up from the ham she was slicing to smile wryly at her granddaughter. "What are we going to have to do to get you to stop calling us all 'ma'am,' child? We're your family." Margaret sighed and continued her preparations.

"I'm sorry," Laurel answered, hoping the irritation she felt did not creep into her voice.

"You don't have to be sorry. I know we're all strangers to you. But that won't last long, now will it?" Margaret looked up again, a warm smile creasing her sixty-five-year-old face.

Laurel returned her grandmother's smile, relaxing a little for the first time since leaving Windrift hours before.

Supper was eaten quickly, as everyone seemed anxious to retire after the long journey. Laurel retreated to her new quarters, a large bedroom she was to share with little Christine. The lilac-sprigged wallpaper lent a cheery air and the large window that separated the two small beds would no doubt brighten it further.

Christine proudly showed her grown-up cousin her impressive doll collection and a lavishly decorated two-story doll's house that Christine gravely informed Laurel quartered both the Queen of England and the President of the United States.

Laurel was not used to sharing a room and did not really look forward to having a five-year-old roommate. Laurel's only other option would have been to share a room with the acerbic Cassandra, which couldn't have been an improvement.

Yet another dilemma presented itself when she looked all over the Hartmoor yard to find the privy. Too embarrassed to ask her grandmother or any other adult, she finally queried little Christine on the location of the "necessary" only to be led, not outside, but to a room the little girl called the water closet. She escorted her big cousin over to an ornately carved wooden box. She opened the lid to display a water-filled porcelain bowl. When Christine casually yanked on a chain to demonstrate how to flush the device, Laurel's jaw dropped in downright awe. Even more impressive was the supply of hot water to the bath tub, piped directly to the tub from a water heater next to the kitchen stove.

Once she got over her chagrin at being such a bumpkin, she decided she liked the modern household conveniences the Hartmoors enjoyed. If living with them would not be fun, it would at least be comfortable.

Amid the bombardment of sights and sounds and circumstances, Laurel soon learned the rhythm of the Hartmoor house and its inhabitants. Her Uncle Jack disappeared into Chisholm each morning after breakfast to attend to the running of the First National Bank of Chisholm, informally called "the Hartmoor Bank" by everyone in town.

Cassandra presided over the cleaning of the house and the care of the garden and stables, while Margaret and Alice busied themselves in the kitchen most of every day, when not engaged in a sewing project.

Laurel's only employment within the household seemed to be as a full-time playmate for the tiny terror, Christine. Though Laurel appreciated Alice's many grateful acknowledgments of her help with Christine, she really had no experience with children and found the little girl a difficult commodity.

The problem was not that Christine did not like her new roommate, but rather that she liked her too well. She demanded Laurel's attention every waking minute. Her good moods proved as irritating and exhausting as her tantrums which habitually punctuated her tumultuous little day like rolling thunder pausing to crackle with lightening every so often.

Day after day of Christine's oppressive affection began to wear on Laurel. She now realized Alice's effusive gratefulness probably sprung from relief. Laurel longed for her chemicals to arrive from Chicago. Then she could at least pursue her photography.

One warm afternoon, after her charge drifted off into a rare nap on the porch swing while listening to a story read aloud, Laurel decided to make a brief bid for freedom.

She managed to extricate herself from the swing without disturbing the little girl and silently stepped off the porch. Once she reached the grass of the lawn, she started running. When she lost sight of the house, she stopped to catch her breath. Then she laughed at herself, feeling ridiculous at having assumed it necessary to *escape* from a five-year-old.

As she continued on her walk, she soon wished she had remembered a hat. The weather was unusually warm for April and her black taffeta dress clung to her limbs, while pinching her at every other point–waist, elbows, shoulders, neck. The dress was on loan from Cassandra since Laurel had no proper mourning clothes of her own. She and her thirty-seven-year-old aunt were the same height, but of markedly different build. Cassandra's thin form contrasted sharply with Laurel's more rounded shape. Laurel's full breasts ached against the constraining fabric, making it nearly impossible to take a deep breath.

She pulled the pins and combs from her hair and let it fall in a thick cascade down her back. "The Hartmoor Hair," she smirked as she lifted it off her shoulder to fly in the cooling breeze. She loved the sensuous release of wearing her hair loose and free.

She wandered across the wheat field, yanking her skirts and petticoats along as they caught in the underbrush. She saw in the distance a grove of poplar trees unexpectedly towering into the bald prairie sky. Seeking the slim shade they might offer, she made her way towards them as fast as the dense wheat stalks would permit her.

She stopped suddenly about twenty yards from her goal when she caught sight of a man leaning against one of the poplars. She caught her breath, afraid he would hear her approach. She recognized him immediately–he was the young farmer she had seen the afternoon she arrived.

The young man stood drinking from a canteen. Then he tilted his head back and poured water over his face. He shook his tousled blond hair like a wet dog, then wiped his dripping face on his shirt tail. When he looked up, he saw Laurel.

Once again, his pale eyes amazed her. So light in color they contrasted sharply with his tanned face. Piercing, good-humored eyes. She could not look away. She had never seen anyone with eyes lighter than the complexion of their face.

He smiled and opened his mouth to speak, but Laurel turned and briskly walked in the opposite direction, pretending she hadn't seen him. She still didn't know why she was not supposed to speak to this young man, who looked to be near her own age, but she did not wish to risk her grandmother's disapproval at this point in time.

She had thought about the young man often. The visual impression he had made on her was not one to be easily shaken off. She had particularly liked the joking way he had held up his shirt, pretending a modesty he obviously didn't feel.

She thought she heard him call to her as she hurried away, panting for breath in her borrowed mourning clothes, but she did not turn back. She didn't fear that he would harm her. She just didn't know what behavior the Hartmoors would consider correct.

Soon the Hartmoor house was in sight. Christine ran to Laurel as soon as she saw her approach.

"Cousin Laurel, Cousin Laurel, where you been? I missed you!" She grabbed Laurel's wrists, demanding to be swung in a circle–their latest game. "You're supposed to play with me!"

"Yes, I know," Laurel groaned.

&

"Cassie, wasn't there something you were going to ask Laurel this morning?" Margaret prodded her daughter in a tone she might have used when Cassandra was seven rather than thirty-seven.

Cassandra glanced up from her morning paper blankly. She had been lost in study of the classified ads, searching for a new horse to add to her growing collection of breeding stock.

Laurel looked warily across the breakfast table, still chewing a large mouthful of toast.

Cassandra turned to her mother, imploring her for some clue to jog her memory.

Her mother frowned and said through clenched teeth, "The matter we discussed last night."

"Oh, yes, of course. Would you like to come riding with me, Laurel?"

Alice hid a smile behind her napkin, then busied herself washing jam from Christine's sticky little face.

"Uh...well, yes. I mean..actually, I don't know how to ride. I mean, actually, I've never ridden."

"Never?" Cassandra was incredulous. "I can't imagine a Hartmoor never having ridden a horse."

Laurel shifted in her seat uncomfortably, aware once again she was not meeting Hartmoor expectations. "My father wouldn't let me."

"Then your father was very foolish."

"Cassie!" Margaret and Alice reacted in unison.

"I'm sorry," Cassandra backed off. "It's just that–"

"Given what happened to Sarah, I think it's perfectly understandable Laurel's father would be protective of her," Alice defended.

Cassandra frowned at her sister-in-law. "What happened to Sarah was a freak accident. Sarah was the most gifted horsewoman I've ever known. I wish I were only half so good."

"You're very gifted yourself, Cassie," said Alice in an almost patronizing tone.

"Thank you," mumbled Cassandra, surprised to receive a compliment from Alice, however half-hearted.

"Horses were the ruling passion of your mother's life, Laurel. Did you know that?" asked Margaret with a benevolent smile. The faraway look in Margaret's eye told Laurel her grandmother's thoughts were drifting back to a reminiscence of her elder daughter, now fifteen years gone. She seemed both melancholy and warmed by the memory.

"Yes, I did," Laurel answered, almost afraid to interrupt her grandmother's recollection. "My father used to talk about her often. And I have some memories, too. I was six, you remember."

"Your mother would have a fit to think her only daughter had never been on a horse," persisted Cassandra.

"Perhaps Laurel's father took the position that if a skilled horsewoman like Sarah could get herself killed, think what could happen to someone less experienced."

Laurel smiled inwardly to hear Alice defend her father.

"Sarah was trying to break a green mare at the time and–"

"Could we not change the subject?" Alice interrupted. "Laurel, dear, you needn't apologize for not wanting to ride."

"But I *do*...want to," said Laurel with an enthusiasm that surprised everyone. "I would *love* to learn to ride. I would appreciate a lesson, Aunt Cassie."

"See, there," said Cassandra triumphantly to Alice.

Margaret chuckled and shook her head as all the women rose to clear the breakfast table.

Cassandra led Laurel upstairs to find her some riding clothes. Laurel hoped she could keep secret from her aunt the fact that she actually loathed horses. She didn't like touching them, smelling them, or even standing near them.

The thought of riding terrified her, but she saw this opportunity as an excellent entry into the Hartmoor good graces. She would give this challenge her best effort, no matter what. Besides, her father always told her that to overcome a fear builds character and, failing that, her first riding lesson meant a whole morning away from Christine. She decided this was her lucky day.

"You're sure you're not afraid?" Cassandra asked skeptically as she marched Laurel out to the stables.

"Oh, I'm just fine," Laurel lied. The riding habit, like the mourning clothes, fit too tightly in the bodice and hips. Laurel fidgeted as she hurried to keep up with her energetic aunt. She had never worn this sort of skirt before, draping as it did in a manner not unlike a pair of men's trousers. The stiff, black wool fabric chafed between her legs. Previously, nothing but plain cotton drawers had separated Laurel's soft, slender thighs. On the other hand, the freedom of movement the riding habit presented intrigued Laurel a great deal. If she owned one of her own that actually fit, she might grow to like it.

Cassandra glanced back over her shoulder and noticed her niece was not keeping up her brisk pace.

"What's the matter? Boots too small?"

"They're alright."

"You're limping."

"They're a little small," Laurel confessed. Her aunt's extra riding boots were actually pinching her curled toes with exquisite pain, but Laurel refused to show weakness in the face of Cassandra's previously constant stream of criticism.

"We'll take you into town soon and have a new pair made for you."

"Uh...thank you." Her aunt's sudden generosity stunned Laurel, reinforcing her belief that these riding lessons might turn matters around for her in her new home.

"I'm going to start you out on old Mona."

"Old Mona," Laurel repeated.

"What?"

"Nothing."

"You and Mona are about the same age–that makes you a good match."

"A twenty-one-year-old horse?" Laurel could not believe it.

"She's a sweet old thing. Don't sell her short. You don't want a young, frisky one. Not yet, anyway."

Cassandra entered the stable and quickly returned, leading a sleepy-looking mare out and securing the rope of her halter to a fence post.

Laurel reluctantly approached old Mona to pat her long neck with a gloved hand. The docile mare's once-chestnut coat now showed gray with age. Laurel's pulse quickened with a tiny kernel of fear as she touched the animal. *My mother loved horses, my mother loved horses*, she chanted inside her head for courage.

"She's already been groomed by the stableboy. You'll find her saddle and bridle hanging in the tack room. It's the darkest one, just inside to the left."

Laurel stepped into the little shed. The room was cool and dark, lit by only one small window. The overwhelming odor of oiled leather burned Laurel's nostrils. As her eyes grew accustomed to the limited light, she lingered to examine the room in detail.

Her thoughts dwelled not on horses and tack, but on photography. The shed would make a splendid dark room. The size and dimension were adequate and the wooden workbench along the right side of the shed was a perfect height to hold trays of developing chemicals and fixing baths. The light from the small window could easily be blocked and if daylight should leak in around the door, a blanket could be hung against it. "Laurel? Can't you find them? I'm sure they're there on the left. Don't forget to bring one of those blankets."

"Coming."

Laurel carried out the saddle, bridle, and horse blanket, then held them dumbly as she watched her aunt skillfully saddle her own horse, a fine bay gelding.

Laurel placed the blanket on old Mona's back, then the saddle. She carefully buckled the saddle under Mona's furry, graying belly, then stood aside to wait for further instructions.

Cassandra picked up Mona's bridle and walked over to Laurel and her mount.

"First, slip the halter off her nose–but always keep it around her neck until you're ready to lead her away."

"Why is that?"

"So you don't have to go off chasing her across the county."

Laurel shrugged. Old Mona did not look interested in running across the yard, much less the county.

Cassandra slipped a portion of the bridle over the horse's ears, leaving the bit resting against Mona's dark gray lips.

"Now, to get her to accept the bit, you've got to stick your finger in and tickle the roof of her mouth."

Laurel grimaced.

"She won't bite you! You'll be putting your finger in the *corner* of her mouth where she doesn't have any teeth."

Laurel's fear turned to disgust at the thought of sticking her finger, gloved though it was, in this enormous creature's slimy mouth. She steeled herself–*my mother loved horses, my mother loved horses*–and did as she was told.

When Mona dutifully opened her mouth, Laurel was so surprised she forgot to pull the bridle into place. After three more unsuccessful attempts, each time banging the metal bit painfully against Mona's yellowed front teeth, Cassandra intervened in exasperation.

"There," said Cassandra, the task completed in a matter of seconds. "Now it's time to mount up. Watch me."

Cassandra placed her left foot in the stirrup and her left hand on the saddle horn. In a single, graceful maneuver, she swept herself up into the saddle, locking her right knee around the special pommel of a lady's side saddle.

Laurel tentatively slipped her own foot in her stirrup, then grabbed the saddle and pulled with all her might–only to have the saddle slide right under the horse's belly taking Laurel and her stirrup-tangled foot with it.

"Help," Laurel squeaked in tiny, embarrassed voice from under the horse. Mona whinnied. Laurel was fairly certain the old nag was laughing at her.

Cassandra immediately dismounted and came to her niece's rescue.

"I forgot to tell you," Cassandra laughed. "Mona always takes a deep breath when you saddle her. You have to cinch the girth twice to compensate. It's one of Mona's little jokes."

Laurel made a put-upon face to Mona and growled, "Ha-ha."

With the saddle properly cinched, Cassandra boosted Laurel onto her horse. Laurel found the sensation of being so high off the ground surprisingly pleasant, even exhilarating.

"Afraid?" Cassandra asked again.

"No, I'm fine."

By Cassandra's expression, Laurel knew her aunt did not fully believe her bravado. She proceeded to give Laurel basic instruction in reining as they made their way slowly north from the house in the direction of the large wheat field.

In the distance, Laurel saw the grove of tall, slender trees she had passed on her walk the day before and, once again they caught her attention. The small, shiny leaves reflected the sunlight and trembled wildly at the slightest breeze. The glittering display fascinated her.

Laurel scanned the vast fields of wheat as well as the grove of poplars for some sign of the young farmer. She secretly wanted to see him again, though not while in the company of her Aunt Cassandra. That would prove embarrassing.

They rode along in silence for awhile, then Laurel felt comfortable enough in the saddle to attempt some small talk.

"Have the Hartmoors always lived here, Aunt Cassie?"

"Oh, no. We were all born in Indiana. My father and brothers were posted here during the war–"

"The War between the States?"

"No, the War for Independence!" Cassandra tossed a comical frown over her shoulder and, for once, Laurel understood her aunt was teasing and not trying to be cruel.

"Which side?"

"The *right* side, of course!"

Laurel felt foolish and stupid once again. She actually still wanted to ask "Which side?" but didn't. She assumed her Hartmoor relatives sided with the Union, just as her father had done.

"Anyway," Cassandra continued, "They spent most of the war fighting Indians rather than Rebels. They were garrisoned at Fort Clearwater–that's at the junction of the Arkansas and the Little Arkansas. My father actually knew Jesse Chisholm."

Laurel smiled at the obvious pride in Cassandra's voice. Every girl, no matter what their age, must enjoy boasting a little bit about her father, she thought. The two women had at least that much in common.

"I assume Jesse Chisholm is the man Chisholm was named after?"

"Of course. He was a half-breed scout. He started a trading post that eventually turned into the town. The Chisholm Trail was named after him, too. You've heard of the Chisholm Trail, I hope."

"Oh, yes."

"Anyway, Papa knew there was a lot of promise out here and he moved Mama and the rest of us out right after he and my brothers were discharged from the army." Cassandra turned to Laurel with a curiously sullen expression. "You know, Chisholm would have ended up growing bigger than Wichita if only the Prairie and Western Railroad had picked it for its railhead. Oh, well, I guess we've done alright."

Laurel felt the Hartmoors had done more than "alright." Though they were not wealthy by the standards of the East, in the small town milieu of Chisholm, Laurel knew her inherited family was one of the most comfortably off in the county. She picked up on this fact almost as soon as she arrived when she observed the differential way the shopkeepers and delivery men treated her grandmother and aunts.

"Were you ever attacked by Indians?"

"Oh, heavens, no. They signed a peace treaty with the local tribes the same year we moved here. After the Homestead Act, people poured into the area. Most of the Indian trouble was farther west by then. Are you hungry? It must be gone to noon by now."

Laurel dutifully turned her horse around to follow her aunt. Though skinny as a flagpole, Cassandra never missed a meal and seldom missed a second helping. The day was further embellished by sitting through the noon meal listening to her aunt praise her incipient expertise at horsemanship.

In a strange way, Laurel felt as though her mother just might be smiling down on her.

Chapter Three

"I think Mary Carmichael's birthday tea on Sunday might prove an excellent opportunity to introduce Laurel to our circle of friends."

Laurel overheard her grandmother's remark before entering the dining room where Alice and Cassandra labored in the midday heat to hang new wallpaper.

"Don't you think it still too soon after her bereavement to ask her to participate in social engagements, Mother Hartmoor?"

Laurel peeked into the dining room. All the women had their backs to her, intent upon their task. All three had their sleeves rolled up, aprons on, and kerchiefs tied around their heads.

Tall, slender Alice, the tallest in the family, strained to reach the ceiling with the dripping paper. Laurel envied Alice her height. She made a commanding presence, but for the slouch she adopted whenever she stood next to her husband. The pair had been of equal height on their wedding day, ten years before, but as a twenty-year-old bride, Alice had not yet stopped growing. She ended up two inches taller than her husband, a man who had no surplus sense of humor about himself. Laurel learned this and other tidbits of family gossip from Cassandra every morning during their riding lessons.

"If you ask me, she doesn't act all that bereaved," said Cassandra. "Watch it–you're dripping on my head!"

"Laurel is just very controlled, that's all. You're not holding it straight. I think Laurel's self-restraint shows an admirable strength of character. Mother Hartmoor, I read a very informative article on modern mourning etiquette last month in Harper's Bazaar. They were unequivocal on the appropriate length of mourning for a parent. One year, no less."

"One year for the wearing of mourning, surely," said Margaret. "But one can attend social engagements of a quiet nature sooner than that, I'll be bound."

"Three months," Alice insisted with authority. "One must not attend social gatherings for at least three months."

"Well, proper etiquette or no, she's got to start making contact with society, Alice. She needs practice being with people. She lacks the social graces–not too surprising considering she was raised up like a savage."

"But she speaks Latin and Greek, Mother Hartmoor."

"Latin and Greek are not going to get her a husband. As I've said, at her age, there's no time to waste. Where is she anyway?"

"I haven't seen her since noon–Alice, it's slipping again."

"It's not my fault. I assume she's with Christine. At least she promised me she would look after her so we could–"

"Christine is napping, Aunt Alice. Do you need any help?"

"Try not to sound so enthusiastic," Cassandra laughed. She wiped a splatter of wallpaper paste from her cheek, only to smear it into the wispy tendrils of hair that escaped her tight, dark topknot and clung to her wet face in the oppressive midday heat of the dining room.

"We can manage, Laurel," said Margaret. "In fact, we're nearly done. I'm going to go start cooking. Chicken tonight, I think."

Laurel carefully backed out of the room and headed upstairs to change into her riding clothes. She successfully changed skirts without waking Christine and slipped out of the house before anyone could notice or stop her.

She had already decided today was the day she would attempt to ride solo. Riding provided her with a wonderful new outlet since her photographic chemicals had still not arrived. She had written letters to the supply house in Chicago twice, but had not heard from them yet on her overdue order.

She saddled old Mona with some help from Arthur, the stable hand, and rode north. The scenic little poplar grove was her destination, but before she could reach it the sudden movement of a jackrabbit in the tall, waving stand of wheat startled Mona who jerked and reared in an attempt to reverse direction. Laurel lost her stirrup and her balance as well. She slid off Mona's back and fell to the ground with a thud.

"Are you alright?" called a man's voice.

Laurel quickly sat up and tried to see through the surrounding thicket of green wheat who had witnessed her unplanned and ungraceful dismount. A figure ran towards her, but the late afternoon sun shining behind him obscured the man's identity.

The figure reached her and leaned over to see what was the matter. When his shadow fell upon her, she recognized the elusive young farmer with the striking, pale eyes.

"Are you injured?" he demanded with concern.

"Only in dignity." She tried to smile to cover her embarrassment, but struggled to regain her breath. The young man also breathed hard from his short sprint to her side.

The tumble had caused much of her hair to fall loose from its pins and combs. She glanced about to locate them and brushed the twigs and dust from her tangled curls with her fingers, self-conscious of her disheveled appearance. The "Hartmoor hair" was a complete mess at the moment.

The young man offered her a hand and pulled her to her feet.

"Actually, I'm new to riding," she said between gasps. "Actually, I don't even like horses and I feel like a complete fool!"

"You only look like a partial fool."

She turned to him in surprise as he led her to the poplar grove, but saw only uncritical humor in his face.

"I'm sorry, I'm sorry," he laughed. "I couldn't resist."

Laurel shared his joke at her expense.

"Here, you sit down and I'll go catch your mare. Would you like some water?"

"Oh, yes, please." The fall had shaken her more than she realized. She noticed her hands were trembling as she seated herself on an outcropping of limestone.

He handed her his canteen, an old army issue, then dashed off in chase after Mona, who had wandered some hundred yards distant and now busily nibbled at the growing young wheat.

Laurel took a sip of the warm water. Not too refreshing, but still it helped to calm her nerves. She looked about her, pleased by the unaccustomed shade the stand of poplars presented. A small knot of trees in varying stages of maturity formed the grove. Most of the trunks were no thicker in circumference than the breadth of Laurel's hand. Leafy branches sprouted from the ground up on such young trees, giving the grove a luxuriant sense of seclusion from the broad plains that surrounded it. The more mature specimens towered thirty feet overhead.

The small spade-shaped leaves shimmered with waxy brittleness. They fluttered and flapped incessantly, at peril to every breeze. The world outside the shelter of the poplar grove now seemed to Laurel unbearably bright and sun-drenched in comparison to the cylinder of dense foliage in which she now sat. No wonder the young man employed the shade for respite from the May afternoon's heat.

Growing at the base of the limestone outcropping stood a tall spray of wild, white indigo. The sturdy sprigs of the prairie wildflower pleasantly scented the humid air.

The young man returned soon with Mona in tow. He tied the mare to a tree on the outside edge of the grove.

"I can hardly believe a Hartmoor woman not being crazy about horses," he observed, seating himself on the ground across from her. He took back the canteen and helped himself to a drink.

"My name is McBryde," she corrected him.

"But you're Mrs. Hartmoor's granddaughter, aren't you?"

Laurel nodded, surprised he knew this.

"I know a lot about you," he boasted good-naturedly. "You come from up in the Flint Hills. You've moved in with the Hartmoors because your father died. The Hartmoors think you read too much and don't talk enough and you claim to know how to make photographs." He finally paused for breath after reaching the end of his catalog. "Sorry. It's a small town. Having someone new to talk about is a big thrill."

Laurel smiled self-consciously. "You have me at a disadvantage. I don't even know your name."

"If I were Rumpelstiltskin, I'd make you guess."

Laurel teasingly pretended to give this challenge thoughtful consideration. "Let me see...is your name William Shakespeare?"

"Nope."

"Julius Caesar?"

"Doubt it."

"Thomas Jefferson?"

"I think you'd better give up," he grinned.

"I guess I'll have to." Laurel thought the tone in his voice was odd when answering her joking questions–almost as if he hadn't known the names she guessed. But that was ridiculous, she had named the most famous men in history. She continued the Rumpelstiltskin tease. "Does this mean I have to give you my first born child?"

"Suppose so, don't you think? But I hate to walk off with somebody's first born child before we've even been properly introduced." He rose and walked deliberately to where Laurel sat and extended his hand to her with exaggerated formality. "Carington Fairchild, at your service, Miss McBryde."

She shook his hand, smiling broadly. "How do you do, Mr. Fairchild?"

"Very well, thank you, Miss McBryde."

Shaking hands afforded her the opportunity to study his remarkable features in detail. She almost forgot to let go of his hand, so amazed was she by his clear brow, his finely cut jaw, and those eyes–large green eyes the color of a new-made promise.

They held each other's glance too long. Both looked away in awkwardness. Laurel demurely dropped her gaze.

"Is Carington a family name?" she asked to make conversation.

"Reckon so. Seems pretty cruel to inflict a name like that on a kid without good reason, don't it?"

Laurel didn't know how she was supposed to answer. She feared she had innocently insulted this nice man.

"It was my mother's maiden name," he explained, reading the confusion in her face. "But nobody ever calls me that. I'm just plain 'Carey' to God and everybody."

Mona whinnied loudly as if to say, *Did you forget about me?*

"Do you want me to see you home?" he asked.

"Oh, no, That's alright."

"I could lead you back...or ride with you, if that would make you feel better."

"I couldn't impose–"

"I wouldn't have offered if I didn't want to."

"Well..." She began to weaken. The thought of getting home alone grew less appealing by the second. "Are you certain you wouldn't mind?"

"Come on."

He laced his fingers together and held them out for her. She awkwardly placed her boot in his hands and he boosted her into her side saddle in a single motion. He then hoisted himself up, behind her. He placed his arms around her to take charge of the reins and dug his heels in Mona's sides to urge her into a trot. He made it all seem so easy.

Laurel bounced up and down as they crossed the field. She held on to the horse's mane with both hands. She shut her eyes tight and prayed she wouldn't fly off again. They arrived quickly within sight of the Hartmoor's perfectly symmetrical blue house with its elaborate white millwork and proudly carved "H."

Laurel felt suddenly ill-at-ease, worried the Hartmoors might not approve of such an unorthodox riding arrangement. After all, Alice had disapproved of Cassandra even saying hello to this man for reasons that still remained mysterious to Laurel. Fortunately, he solved the dilemma for her by bringing the horse to an abrupt halt.

"This is as far as I go. Can you get on from here?"

"Oh, yes, surely."

He effortlessly slid off the horse, leaving Laurel alone on old Mona and not feeling any too confident. He saw her unease and motioned for her to dismount as well.

She carefully unhooked her knee from the saddle and placed her hands on his shoulders. He grabbed her waist with both his hands and she was back on her feet in a swift motion.

"There, now," he grinned down at her.

She tipped her head up and studied his face one last time. Those amazing, pale green eyes. He was only five or six inches taller than she was. Her forehead reached his chin.

She had not spent her girlhood daydreaming about love or concocting romantic fantasies, yet for one exhilarating moment, she thought he might lower his face to hers and kiss her.

But he did not. He simply released her waist and handed her Mona's reins.

"Good day, then, Miss McBryde." He turned and headed back in the direction from which they had come.

"Good day...and thank you," she called after him.

He turned, gave her a playful salute, and was off again.

The following Sunday, Laurel rode to church with her grandmother and uncle. Jack drove their buggy while Margaret and Laurel rode behind him. Alice stayed at home, nursing Christine through an early summer cold. Ten years of marriage had produced only one child for Jack and Alice, so Alice fiercely defended Christine from every danger, whether real or imagined.

Cassandra had already gone over to Mary Carmichael's house to help with the preparations for the afternoon birthday tea Laurel was slated to attend. Cassandra was the best friend of Mary's older sister, Hazel.

The trio rode along in silence, each in his or her own way enjoying the lovely May morning with its fresh south wind and blooming flowers. The white steeple of the Presbyterian Church rose in sight when the Hartmoor carriage passed another family on their way to church. A man, a woman, and two little girls, walked along the roadside.

"Good morning," called Margaret, as they passed.

Laurel craned her neck to see around her grandmother to learn the identity of the young family.

"That's Carey Fairchild," Margaret informed her granddaughter. "Carey is one of our tenant farmers."

The whole family waved to the Hartmoor carriage in return to Margaret's greeting. The young man was indeed Carey Fairchild, Laurel's rescuer and new-found friend. On his shoulders rode a little girl of about two years of age. Next to him walked a blond young woman holding the hand of a girl who looked near Christine's age. The woman appeared attractive in a winsome way with doll-like features and large blue eyes, though a look of fatigue marred her superficial beauty and aged her youthful face. Her pretty eyes bore dark circles under them and the bow lips pressed themselves firmly in a worried frown. The raised waistline of her simple cotton dress displayed the unmistakable swell of pregnancy on her slender frame.

"And that is his wife...and family?" Laurel asked, crestfallen, but at pains not to show it.

Chapter Four

"I know some may criticize me for asking my granddaughter to attend a social gathering so soon after her bereavement, but it is my firm opinion that nothing could be more beneficial to her than getting out and meeting some young women her own age."

Young men, you mean, thought Laurel sourly. She closed her eyes to the embarrassment of the situation she now faced and wished she could close her ears as well. The afternoon steadily declined in enjoyment from that point on for her, though everyone else seemed to be having a good time.

The birthday girl, Mary Carmichael, did not display any noticeable cordiality toward Laurel when Margaret introduced them. Mary pushed her auburn ringlets back from her plump face and said she was glad Laurel was able to attend, then turned and greeted another girl before Laurel could even thank her.

Before Laurel was introduced to Mary's sister, Hazel, Margaret warned Laurel that the young woman was not at all well. Rumor had it that she suffered from consumption, but the family refused to confirm it.

"Be gracious, but don't get too close," Margaret whispered.

Hazel was much friendlier than her younger sister, but did not look well. Her wan face betrayed a fatigue her cheerful smile could not mask. A coughing fit soon sent her running to her bedroom, not to be seen the remainder of the afternoon.

Margaret embarrassed Laurel still more by pointedly introducing her to every unmarried male in attendance, whatever his age.

Laurel finally sought refuge in the Carmichael kitchen.

"Laurel, what are you doing in here?" Cassandra demanded as she refilled a silver serving tray with small sandwiches. "Why aren't you in there talking to people and making new friends?"

Laurel shrugged. She wanted to tell her aunt that she wasn't used to meeting so many people at once and that she felt the invisible isolation of being the only member of an ensemble who had not been intimately acquainted with each other for years.

"I don't have anything to talk about," Laurel confessed.

"Well, stay by me or mother. We'll get the conversations going."

Laurel crossed the room to the settee where Margaret sat busily chatting with several other women of her own generation. Two of the women exclaimed over Laurel's resemblance to her mother, Sarah. Laurel took this as a compliment. She thought about how her mother would have probably felt completely at her ease in these situations and would no doubt have said lots of clever things to delight her listeners.

Instead, Laurel stood behind Margaret and merely listened to the conversation, pretending rather than actually taking part in it.

Every so often, she searched the room for the Fairchild family before she realized that they would not travel in this comfortable group.

On the ride home, Laurel's head throbbed from the exhaustion of nervous anxiety. Her cheeks ached from the long afternoon of polite smiling.

"Hazel did not look at all well," Margaret observed.

"She's going to be fine," Cassandra insisted.

"At least one member of our family refused to attend the party out of fear of Hazel. Isn't that right, Jack?" Margaret leaned in the direction of her middle-aged son, who drove the carriage, as usual.

"You'll have to ask *her*, Mother," Jack answered, refusing to be drawn into the women's conversation.

"Stuff and nonsense," Cassandra sniffed. "Alice is afraid of her own shadow."

"You would do well to be careful, Miss," answered her mother.

Cassandra's defense of her friend impressed Laurel. She had to respect someone who would face down a fear of the dreaded consumption to stick by a girlhood friend.

"Oh, Mother, you're being silly," Cassandra countered. Then she leaned closer to Laurel and Margaret to confide something she did not wish to share with her brother. "Hazel told me something strange today. She said her monthlies have stopped all together."

"Oh, dear, that can't be a good sign," Margaret whispered back. "I didn't know the consumption caused that effect."

Her daughter shrugged. The humid air began to cool as the sun disappeared.

"Grandmother, are the Fairchilds our neighbors?"

"I suppose you could call them our neighbors. They live on our land." She turned to Cassandra to add, "We saw the family on their way to church this morning."

"Have they lived there a long time?"

"Carey's lived in that old sod house nearly all his life," said Cassandra. "How old do you suppose he was when Lizzie showed up that day?"

"No more than four or five, I'm guessing." Margaret squinted her eyes into the distance, searching her memory.

"Lizzie?" Laurel questioned.

"Carey's mother," Margaret continued. "She appeared out of nowhere on my doorstep one day with Carey in tow and asked if she could stay the night in the old soddy out by the West Jane. I told her she could, of course. How could I turn my back on the poor thing?"

"But where was Mr. Fairchild's father?"

Cassandra snickered wickedly. "Don't we all wonder?"

Laurel didn't understand her aunt's amusement.

"Lizzie claimed to be a war widow. And perhaps she was, for all we knew. It was common enough in those days."

Laurel wanted to mention that Carey's mother must have been married since Carey Fairchild had told her that Carington was his mother's maiden name, but she kept silent, not wanting to reveal her meeting with Mr. Fairchild.

"If she were really a widow," Cassandra reasoned. "Why didn't she have any family to take her in?"

"We don't know and she wasn't saying, so we should be obliged to take her word for it," said Margaret.

Cassandra rolled her eyes, then leaned near Laurel. "She no doubt got herself into trouble and her family threw her out on the street."

Laurel listened agog. She'd never heard scandalous stories and gossip before.

"I doubt that she got *herself* into trouble," Margaret smirked, then hid her amusement behind her lacy, embroidered Sunday handkerchief.

Cassandra laughed out loud at her mother's little joke.

"What's so funny?" Jack asked, turning in his seat to face his family.

"Oh, nothing," Cassandra giggled.

Margaret hushed her. "Regardless of Lizzie's past, I would have helped her in any case. A good Christian does not turn his or her back on someone in need."

"I take it she didn't come from around here."

"Oh, no," said Margaret. "She was always a bit mysterious about where she came from–about anything to do with her life before she came to Chisholm. I heard her mention Douglas County more than once, but I don't know. Jack was posted there for part of the war and he never heard of her family. She seemed to have a little money coming in from somewhere. And she sent Carey out to do odd jobs as soon as he was old enough to manage."

"Lizzie was so odd," Cassandra mused, now serious again.

"But so pretty, beautiful even. How strange for a woman so refined and obviously educated to turn out the way she did. A very sad thing."

"She went mad," Cassandra whispered to Laurel.

Laurel's eyes widened at this information. She thought about the mad woman in "Jane Eyre." She assumed the mad were confined to asylums. She tried to imagine a mad woman alone on the prairie raising a little boy.

"How did you know she was mad?" Laurel asked.

"Mad is too strong a word, really," said Margaret. "She was just terribly odd. And sad. She cried a lot. At the most inappropriate times."

"And sang," Cassandra chuckled. "She was always singing."

"Lovely voice," Margaret remarked. She sighed with the memory. "She seemed to slip a little farther off the leash every year."

"She took her own life–that's how we knew she was mad."

"She committed suicide?" Laurel was completely enthralled by this story.

Cassandra nodded.

"How old was Mr. Fairchild when his mother...?

"Carey was just fourteen or so," said Cassandra. "Poor thing. All alone in the world."

"I tried to get him to come live with us," said Margaret. "But he insisted on staying in that old soddy. Took care of himself. 'Course, he'd been doing that all his life. I think he took care of Lizzie more than she ever took care of him. Never saw a cuter little boy. Impossible to scold."

"Did you know that Mae is in a family way again?" Cassandra mentioned.

"Yes," sighed Margaret with disapproval. "Just what they need–another mouth to feed. Can't afford the two they have already."

"Carey should never have married that Mae–she's a real piece of work."

"I don't believe Mae's family gave Carey much of a choice," said Margaret.

Jack pulled the wagon into the yard. Laurel was sorry to be home before this interesting conversation could be ended. She hoped her aunt and grandmother might continue it during supper or after, but they did not.

❧

Laurel announced she would take a walk after supper, saying she wished to make use of the long spring evening. She left her uncle, aunt, and grandmother on the porch sipping lemonade and marched off in the direction of a creek called the West Jane.

She now possessed a consuming curiosity about the Fairchild family and decided to play spy. She found the soddy with no difficulty by following the West Jane north from the Hartmoor house. The small creek gully produced enough in the way of trees and undergrowth to cloak her approach.

Cassandra had informed Laurel on one of their morning rides that the West Jane was one of the three streams crossing the Hartmoor property. It ran from a common source south into the Little Arkansas. An Army cartographer first charted the area in the late 'Forties and, with a notable lack of originality named all three springs after his wife, hence the names East Jane, West Jane, and Middle Jane. Close to the Fairchild house, the West Jane and Middle Jane joined briefly to form a small pond. They then split off again and ran south, angling towards the east and west boundaries of the Hartmoor land. The East Jane had run dry the summer before signaling the beginning of another drought cycle.

The Fairchild house itself was a small rectangular dwelling with a single frame window. The sod-covered tar paper roof carried a rounded shape of the box car design, rather than a peaked roof like a frame house would have. A large, natural limestone fireplace served as the home's only distinguishing feature. This lent a certain rustic grace to its otherwise spare and unaesthetic appearance. Laurel thought it obvious from the condition of the place that Carey Fairchild was no craftsman or woodworker.

The yard of the house contained the accumulated trappings of years of living on the raw edge of existence. A dilapidated chicken coup was present, though no chickens could be heard or seen. A wagon sat in so run-down a state as to give the impression it had not been moved in more than a decade. All of its wheels were missing. Then Laurel reasoned that as the Fairchilds did not own a horse, of what value was a wagon?

Between the house and the pond stood a well-tended garden, not as large as the Hartmoor kitchen garden, but probably adequate for a small family. Laurel could see corn and cabbage growing and an undergrowth that looked like strawberries.

Viewing the Fairchild home made Laurel's heart ache for her new friend's poverty and chafe at the convenience she so took for granted at the Hartmoor house with its leaded-glass windows and Battenberg lace curtains, its marble-topped vanities, and maroon velvet portieres.

Still, the sod house possessed an honesty about it in that it pretended to be nothing more than it was. The same could not be said for the Hartmoor house where much of its finery was essentially counterfeit. Machines, not hands, carved the ornate walnut furniture legs. No human hands crocheted the delicate doily head rests on the parlor chairs and settee. The wainscoting that lined the dining room walls below the chair rail was not leather, but rather pressed paper stained to give the appearance of embossed leather.

If the occupants of the little sod house found its circumstances as pathetic as Laurel, they did not show it that humid May evening.

The lively shrieks of little girls' laughter filled the air. Laurel strained for a better view. Carey seemed to be engaged in some sort of game of tag with the girls. He would chase one and then the other, then swing them high in the air whenever he caught them.

Finally, he collapsed exhausted on the ground and the girls pounced on top of him as he shouted in mock protest and called to heaven for rescue.

Carey's wife appeared at the open door of the soddy to announce that supper was ready. The happy group made their way towards her.

"I've told you again and again not to get them so excited before mealtimes," she scolded her husband sharply as he passed her in the doorway.

Instead of answering, he brushed her with a light kiss on the forehead, then disappeared into the house. A look of disgust briefly twisted Mae Fairchild's pretty features, then she, too, went in the house.

Laurel walked home feeling depressed and guilty over her reconnaissance activities. The domestic interlude she had just witnessed disturbed her, but she didn't know why.

By the time she reached the Hartmoor house, the sky was nearly dark. She saw her Uncle Jack on the front porch. Rather she saw the glow of his cigarette in the gathering dark. Margaret did not allow him to smoke in the house, so every evening after supper, he stepped out onto the porch and smoked in silence.

He looked lonely sitting out there. Laurel wondered what he thought about. His day at the bank? His family? His youth? The War? Did he have secrets no one could even guess at?

Laurel bounded up the porch steps. She thought she caught the scent of whiskey as she passed him, but surely this was impossible. Prohibition was the law of the state, written directly into the Kansas constitution. The sale of all alcoholic beverages was legally forbidden. Laurel was quite certain her grandmother would never permit the consumption of a prohibited substance on her premises. Although the "wets" and the "drys" still tilted at one another in public debate and many a saloon still flourished in open contravention of the law, the legality of the situation was not in doubt.

"Good evening, Uncle Jack," she called as she slipped through the door beneath the big, carved "H." She thought perhaps the "H" stood for "Hermit," for that is the word she decided most befit the isolation and solitude her uncle seemed to crave.

A barely audible "hmmph" was his only reply.

Chapter Five

Every Monday afternoon, after the laundry was hung to dry, the Hartmoor women went calling. Laurel was invited to accompany them for the first time since joining the household because they now concluded she was out of deep mourning and into a transitional period in which their friends would deem it acceptable to socialize to a limited extent.

But Laurel had other plans. She was not anxious to revisit all the people she had met at Mary Carmichael's birthday party the day before. She decided she could not stand two afternoons in a row of non-stop smiling and nodding and having nothing to say. She pleaded a headache and told her grandmother she needed to lie down.

From her bedroom, she watched Cassandra drive the other women–little Christine included–away in the family buggy. She smiled with the notion that she had the whole house to herself.

Laurel had been surprised when she first moved in that the Hartmoor family had no household servants. Her father had led her to believe the Hartmoors were quite wealthy so she had naturally assumed they were waited on hand and foot by a battalion of servants like the families she had read about in English novels.

Wealth or no wealth, the Hartmoors lacked pretension, despite their social prominence. A part-time stable boy, a couple of hired hands who tended to the general maintenance of the grounds, and an elderly widow who helped with the mending were the only staff the Hartmoors employed.

Jack Hartmoor, who lacked pretension decidedly less than the rest of the family in Laurel's estimation, often suggested adding a housekeeper or a cook to the ensemble, but his mother always firmly rejected such ideas. "The notion of a strange person wandering around my house–I couldn't abide it!" Margaret would say.

She never bothered to ask the opinion of her daughter or daughter-in-law on the subject and, in deference to her, they offered none.

Laurel reveled in the quiet solitude of the empty house. She was used to being alone and had actually come to miss it since moving to Chisholm.

She wandered about the silent house, but soon grew bored and picked up a book to read. The warmth of the still afternoon eventually drove her to the porch, then for a walk in the yard.

Finally, she found herself heading for the poplar grove to enjoy her reading. By the time she reached it, she had grown so uncomfortably warm her sleeves stuck to her arms in wet patches and her small starched collar chaffed the delicate skin of her throat.

She sat down on a huge outcropping of limestone in the twinkling shade of the dense, quivering poplars and began to read again. The constantly varying patterns of light and dark at play upon the page made reading a challenge, but the tranquility the grove provided made the idea of returning to the house unthinkable. She closed her eyes to inhale the scent of the wild white indigo that grew near the base of the limestone.

"If you read aloud, we could both enjoy the book."

Laurel jumped at the unexpected voice.

She looked up to see Carey Fairchild standing less than ten feet away.

"I'm sorry," he smiled as he approached her. "I didn't mean to startle you."

She smiled back somewhat shyly.

"Well? How about it?" He took a seat on the ground a discreet distance away yet close enough to carry on a conversation. He wore a faded, oft-mended pair of overalls and a thin cotton shirt rolled up at the sleeves. Laurel's eyes fell upon his bare feet, dirty and callused.

"I'm not used to performing for strangers," she said awkwardly.

"Are we still strangers?"

"I...suppose not."

"I'm serious. I'd enjoy listening. You really don't mind, do you?"

His attention flattered her, but made her shy at the same time.

"Well?" he demanded like a petulant child, but smiled at her so winningly she couldn't help but smile back.

She opened her book to the page she had been reading and cleared her throat. Before she could utter a word, self-consciousness overwhelmed her and she giggled instead. She tried again and still no words came. The giggling turned to laughter and the harder she tried to regain her composure the harder she laughed.

Carey laughed too, enjoying her plight.

"I'm waiting," he teased. He folded his arms across his chest in pretended impatience.

"I'm sorry," she managed to say as she wiped a tear from the corner of her eye.

"Is the book that funny?" he asked with mock gravity. "Let me see." He snatched the book from her grasp and pretended to skim it. "No jokes here–please begin."

Laurel's laughing fit now bordered on convulsion. The muscles of her face were so inclined to smiling they resisted her every effort to relax them. She drew a deep breath and held it.

"Miss McBryde, I think you need to work on this shyness problem."

"I'm not shy. Not really," she gasped, at last starting to contain herself.

"Then why are you blushing?"

"I'm not blushing," she protested, trying not to laugh anymore. She placed her palm to her face only to find her fair cheek on fire.

"I'm gonna give you one more chance. I'm gonna come back here tomorrow at this very hour and if you're here, I'm gonna expect to be read to."

"I'm under no obligation to read to you, sir." She smiled broadly, enjoying this banter.

"'Sir?' I've been called a lot of things in my time, but never 'sir' before. I'll let that pass for now, but I don't agree with you. You're trespassing on my acreage. You owe me something."

"My grandmother owns this land!"

"And *I* lease this quarter section. If you're gonna sit under my trees and make use of my shade, you're gonna read aloud to me. That's my offer, take it or leave it."

"I have an idea. This is a book of Shakespeare. I was reading the sonnets, but we could read the plays together."

His expression altered radically at the mention of the word "together." He shook his head.

"Now who's being shy? It'll be fun. My father and I used to do this almost every evening in the winter. We'll each take–"

"No," he interrupted. He suddenly rose and walked a few paces away. "I'd rather listen."

"Don't be silly. I can't read a play by myself. I promise you'll enjoy it."

"No. I can't," he mumbled with his back to her.

"Yes, we can."

"I can't...read."

"Not at all?"

"Not enough. I never went to school."

Carey braced his arm against one of the trees, still refusing to face her. She hadn't meant to embarrass him. She didn't know what to say or do. She hugged her book of Shakespeare to her bodice and closed her eyes to concentrate. She worried that she had just ruined the only friendship she'd managed to make in the two months since leaving Windrift.

Just when she nearly thought she would cry or he would leave and never come back, an idea occurred to her.

"Would you like to learn?" she asked in a small voice. She didn't dare look up.

"What?" He turned to face her.

"To read. Would you like to learn?"

He frowned. "I think I'm a little too old to go to school. Don't you?"

"I could teach you," she said in a voice barely above a whisper.

"What?"

"Oh, nothing. Never mind. I didn't mean to be so presumptuous."

"You'd teach me. Is that what you said?"

Laurel looked him in the eye and nodded.

"Are you sure about this?" he pressed.

She nodded more vigorously. What am I getting myself into? said a voice in the back of her head. Her heart pounded with anxious excitement.

To her relief, he began to smile. "Reading lessons...hmm. I've been thinking of raising the rent on this grove."

She laughed with relief and delight. He offered her his hand and pulled her to her feet. They shook on the bargain and agreed to meet the following afternoon. Laurel promised to bring a book easier to master than Shakespeare.

Laurel walked home humming to herself. For the first time since her father died, she had a reason to look forward to tomorrow.

✤

The following afternoon found Laurel and Carey in the shade of the poplar grove undertaking their first reading lesson together. Carey proved himself an unself-conscious and eager student. Laurel was delighted to find out his skills were not so limited as she had feared.

He knew the fundamentals of reading, but lacked the guidance, experience, and practice needed to mature his ability to an adequate and useful level. He told her his mother had given him early training, but her instruction had been too sporadic and discontinuous, thus undermining any real progress. All he needed was an interested tutor, a position left vacant until now.

The pair met every afternoon and by the end of the following week, both teacher and student were impressed with the progress they had made. Carey flattered Laurel at every opportunity, unrestrained in his praise of her patience and her teaching abilities.

"This is the key," he said one day with a sincere enthusiasm.

"To what, in particular?"

"To freedom. My freedom."

"From what?"

"Farming, of course. Nobody can make a living on a farm these days."

"But you look so good at it." Her thoughts were drawn, as they often were, to the afternoon she first arrived at the Hartmoor home and saw Carey working so diligently in the late day sun, mending a fence. The perfect picture he made there that day had never left her.

"I don't know about that," he laughed.

"What would you rather do?"

He shrugged. "Anything else. Just a job, a regular job in town. Regular hours, regular pay, never at the mercy of the railroads and the bankers and the blasted changing weather."

"I didn't know it was so hard."

"That's because you've never had to farm! Times are bad for everyone now, Miss McBryde. But especially for farmers. Something's wrong with a world where an honest man can't feed his family. Once these lessons are done, once I can read and cipher good enough to get along–there'll be no stopping me."

"I think I hear a man of ambition talking." His passion on this topic caught her off guard.

"I just might surprise you, Miss McBryde." He raised his eyebrows for emphasis and they both laughed.

"Actually," he continued, "I'm hoping to get some type of job in the fall, after the fall planting's done."

The very mention of autumn excited Laurel.

"I love the fall. Especially October. It's my favorite month. Sometimes I think I spend the entire year just waiting for October to return."

"What's so special about October?" He grinned at her enthusiasm.

"Well, I love the weather, the cool, crisp days and the chilly, clear nights. The hills around Windrift turn a thousand shades of beige and brown."

"Most people are sad to lose the green of summer."

"Not me. I know this will sound perverse, but I like to watch nature dying each year. There's a beauty to the dying as well as the growing. And the sky, the October sky. Have you ever noticed just how incredibly blue an October sky can be?"

"I guess I'll have to look up more often."

"It' so vivid it almost seems to vibrate against your eyes. My father used to say–"

"What?"

"Oh, nothing." Laurel looked down into her lap and nervously fidgeted with the reader.

"Why are you blushing?"

"It's silly, it's nothing." She sighed in her embarrassment. "It's just that my father used to tell me my eyes were as blue as the October sky." She shrugged and smiled to derail any attempts he might make to mock her. Her voice almost caught when she mentioned her father. She hadn't had the opportunity to speak about him to anyone. The Hartmoors made their feelings clear–they had liked and respected him up until the moment their elder daughter chose him for a husband. Almost as a reflex, she clutched the silver locket holding her parents' pictures.

"Your father was right."

Laurel looked up into Carey's face as he stood near her spot on the limestone outcropping. His clear green eyes bore no trace of mockery. No smirk twisted his full lips. No humor marked his handsome face.

"Anything can happen in October." She paused and drew a deep breath for dramatic effect and carefully announced with narrowed eyes: "There are moments in October so perfect that if you had to live your whole life just to experience that one moment, it would have been worth it. Do you know what I mean?"

He cocked a skeptical eyebrow. "You're kinda odd, Miss McBryde. Has anyone ever told you this?"

"Only the Hartmoors–*constantly.*" She grinned, knowing he was just teasing her again.

"Well, lucky for you, I consider 'odd' to be a virtue."

"Oh, Mr. Fairchild," she laughed.

"You can call me Carey. Everyone else does."

"Oh, and please call me Laurel. We needn't be so formal, do you think?"

He considered this for a moment. "I don't imagine your family would approve of us being on a first name basis. We'd better stay 'Mr. and Miss' outside this place."

She nodded in solemn agreement.

"You don't tell them about these lessons, do you?" he asked with apprehension. "They wouldn't approve, you know."

"No, I haven't told them, but why should they disapprove?"

"They wouldn't think it looked right. A man and a woman alone together, no chaperon. People around here would talk. I don't want to harm your reputation."

"But that's so silly. I'm not afraid of you."

Carey laughed. "God help me if you need to be!"

"God help us both!"

"I'm serious, Laurel." His smile faded. "No one would approve of this–me being alone with you. And they're probably right. To me, you're like lightning in a drought year."

"Like what?"

He raised his fair eyebrows provocatively and the faintest smile returned. "You're a dangerous commodity, Miss McBryde. You have no idea."

Laurel frowned her utter lack of comprehension. Then a new thought occurred to her. "Have you told your wife about these meetings?"

"Lord, no. She'd be the worst one to tell."

"But, we're not doing anything wrong, Mr. Fair–Carey."

"She just wouldn't understand. Mae...don't...I mean, she...never mind, nothing." Carey shook his head and smiled to indicate they should drop the subject.

Laurel searched for something to say to break the mood.

"Oh, I nearly forgot the surprise I brought for us."

"More strawberries?" He sat back down and lounged at her feet.

"Birthday cake!" She pulled a napkin-wrapped parcel from the pocket of her smock. She carefully unwrapped the cake only to discover that the afternoon heat had melted the icing. She handed Carey a large, messy piece which he eagerly accepted. She guessed his limited financial circumstances did not often afford the luxury of confections.

"*Almost* as good as strawberries," he winked as he took a large bite.

Laurel smiled and blushed as she always did when he flirted with her.

"Whose birthday?" he asked with his mouth still full.

"My Uncle Jack's. It was yesterday. We had a big celebration last night."

The moment Laurel uttered the words "Uncle Jack," she saw Carey stop chewing and stare at the rest of the uneaten piece of cake as though she had just told him it was rat poison. When he realized she saw the face he made, he smiled self-consciously and took another large bite.

"Uncle Jack was in a terrible mood all during the dinner."

"I wouldn't think a banker charging 24 percent interest would have much to fret over."

"Interest rates *are* high right now," Laurel agreed. "But he worries about the decline of the cattle trade from Texas."

"Decline? I'd say it's pretty well over. Been several years since I've seen a herd come through Chisholm." Carey laughed as he thought back. "I can remember the days when I was a kid and the cowboys came to town. A wilder, smellier bunch of human beings, you couldn't imagine."

"When you were a little boy, did you dream of growing up to be a cowboy?"

"Oh, Lord, no." He grew serious. "I always wanted to be a professional baseball player."

"I've never seen a baseball game."

"Well, you better start coming when our season starts, next week. Your uncle's bank sponsors the team–we're the Chisholm Cyclones. I play first base."

"Oh, my. I've heard the family talking about 'the cyclones,' but I thought...I thought they were commenting on the weather!"

"Ah, baseball–for three hours every Saturday, I'm in heaven."

"Mr. Thoreau said,'That man is richest whose pleasures are cheapest.'"

"Well then, I guess, by this Mr. Thoreau's standards, I'm downright wealthy."

They both laughed as they finished their cake and licked their sticky fingers like two children. Then they laughed at each other and the silly picture they made.

"Hold still," Carey said.

"What is it?"

He untied the red handkerchief he wore knotted around his neck and leaned close. She looked at him uncertainly.

"Frosting on your chin." He licked the corner of the handkerchief and lightly brushed her chin. He leaned so closed she could feel the radiating warmth of his skin and sense his moist, cake-scented breath on her face. She met his pale green eyes for only an instant, afraid of what might happen if she held his gaze.

The awkward tension returned to the grove like an uninvited guest.

"Oh, dear, it's nearly supper time," she said.

"You're right." He jumped to his feet. "Mae'll have my hide if I'm late for supper." He turned and walked off in the direction of his house and wife and children.

Chapter Six

The brightly colored uniforms of the Chisholm Cyclones dazzled Laurel as she sat with Cassandra and Alice in the bleachers of the baseball diamond on a broiling hot Saturday afternoon. White flannel shirts, knee pants, and caps all trimmed in bright blue, blue stockings, and white canvas hobnailed shoes set the team apart from their adversaries, the Red Stockings, a club from Wichita.

Laurel struggled to make out which player was Carey. They all seemed to look alike in their uniforms. When the game began and the players took their positions on the field, Laurel asked Cassandra what first base was, then where first base was.

She finally located Carey and watched eagerly as play commenced. Cassandra gave her a running commentary on the action which only served to confuse Laurel more.

Carey won a cheer from the crowd by tagging out a runner at first base during the opening inning. He struck out his first time at bat, but got base hits in three other innings.

Laurel found the game's rules hopelessly complicated and couldn't tell when to cheer. She had to take her cues from the crowd.

Near the end of the seventh inning, Jack Hartmoor brought a young man by to meet Laurel. The two men had spent most of the game down near the field with the team. The gentleman was one Martin Simpson, a twenty-seven-year-old clerk at the Hartmoor Bank.

"I hope you are enjoying your first baseball game, Miss McBryde," Martin Simpson cordially began after introductions were completed.

"I'll enjoy it more if the Cyclones win," Laurel responded. The Cyclones were behind by two runs.

"Might I have the pleasure of calling on you, Miss McBryde? Perhaps tomorrow afternoon?"

Alice Hartmoor snapped to attention at this request. Smiling at her husband for performing his duty so admirably.

"I...uh...I suppose–" Laurel stammered, nonplused by this sudden attention.

"Miss McBryde would be delighted to receive you, Mr. Simpson," Alice deftly intervened.

Thus Laurel was to accept her first gentleman caller. She was so astonished by this development, she could barely concentrate on the remainder of the game. The Cyclones ended up winning, 11-10, and a large post-game celebration was held in their honor on the field, but the Hartmoor women did not stay for it. Alice was too excited to get home and tell Margaret of Laurel's good news.

ℰ𝒶

Martin Simpson was known to have ambitions at the bank so his motives were somewhat suspect, but this mattered little to the Hartmoors. Alice nervously fussed over Laurel's hair on Sunday and whispered words of advice and encouragement prior to Laurel's entrance into the parlor.

Jack excused himself after making the appropriate introductions. He left to open the Saturday mail still waiting for him on the dining room china cupboard.

"Hello, Mr. Simpson." Laurel smiled demurely, as Alice had instructed and offered the young man her hand.

"Good afternoon, Miss McBryde." He shook her hand gently.

The perspiration from his hand left hers feeling clammy, but she pretended not to notice. They seated themselves opposite each other in the two chairs that sat on either side of the hearth.

"Would you like some lemonade?" Laurel asked, also on instructions from Alice, who now hovered just out of sight in the dining room.

Laurel was secretly glad Cassandra had gone home from church with Hazel Carmichael, who had looked remarkably well for a change. Laurel was nervous enough without having to worry about teasing or criticism from her aunt.

"Lemonade would be delightful," replied Mr. Simpson. The afternoon was warm and he drew his handkerchief out of his pocket and mopped his perspiring brow. He was a portly young man with thinning black hair slicked back from his forehead. He wore a drooping mustache, also jet black, trimmed in the same style as Jack Hartmoor. Laurel noticed the similarity at once and wondered if Mr. Simpson were consciously imitating his employer.

Laurel started to rise to fetch the lemonade, but Alice beat her to it. She returned to the parlor with a tray containing a pitcher of lemonade, two glasses, and a small plate of sugar cookies.

"Do sit and stay with us, Aunt Alice."

"Oh, perhaps in a little while. I am helping your grandmother in the kitchen at the moment."

With dismay, Laurel watched Alice scurry back into the dining room.

"A lovely day," Martin observed, after taking a sip of lemonade. He stuffed a cookie into his mouth.

"A little warm. This seems awfully warm for May, don't you think?"

"Your uncle tells me you're fond of horses."

"He did?"

"Well, yes. He says you go riding every morning with your aunt, Miss Hartmoor."

"We ride occasionally, I guess."

"A gifted horsewoman, your aunt. I hear your mother was much the same."

"So I'm told." A roaring silence followed that threatened to break Laurel's eardrums. She searched her mind for some topic of conversation that might impress Mr. Simpson. He, meanwhile, stuffed several more cookies into his mouth.

"Are you familiar with the works of Plato, Mr. Simpson?"

"Umm...somewhat," he answered through a mouthful of cookie.

"Did you know that 'Plato' was not his real name?"

"No, I suppose I didn't." He squinted at Laurel uncertainly.

"His real name was Aristocles. Plato was just a nickname. It meant 'broad-shouldered.' He was supposedly built like a wrestler."

"How interesting." Another hard silence followed.

"I've read the *Commentaries* of Julius Caesar," Martin offered.

"So have I."

"That's awfully heavy reading for a young lady such as yourself. I would expect you to prefer a romance novel to a ponderous history tome."

"I read novels, too. I read all kinds of things."

"Wouldn't want to spoil those pretty eyes with too much reading, now."

Laurel cringed at Martin's clumsy attempt to flatter her. "I personally don't think much of Julius Caesar."

"Surely you will agree that Julius Caesar was as great a man as Plato, Miss McBryde."

"Julius Caesar was the greatest criminal in human history."

"And what, pray tell, was his crime?" Martin asked with condescending bemusement.

"He destroyed the great library at Alexandria."

Martin laughed. "Destroying a building? That's not much of a crime to label him the greatest criminal in history."

"All the knowledge of the ancient world was collected in that 'building' as you call it. All the succeeding generations of humankind are his victims. The destruction of knowledge is the most barbaric, unforgivable–"

Jack Hartmoor rescued his young clerk by choosing that moment to enter the parlor with a package under his arm.

"This box is addressed to your father, Laurel. It somehow found its way here."

Laurel jumped up eagerly. She recognized the company name on the return address immediately. "My chemicals–they've come at last."

She beamed at the befuddled Mr. Simpson. "I've been waiting two months for these to arrive. I'd almost given up."

She glanced around for some instrument with which to tear open the box.

"Chemicals, Miss McBryde? Are you a chemist?"

"No, a photographer."

Alice entered the room upon hearing the word, "photographer." She and little Christine watched anxiously as Jack offered Laurel his pocket knife to cut off the string wrapped around the package.

"You can make photographs?" Martin asked, somewhat incredulously.

"Where can I set up my darkroom?" Laurel demanded of her grandmother, who had now joined the group in the parlor to find out what all the commotion was about.

Martin tried to swallow the embarrassment of being ignored.

"Mother Hartmoor, Laurel's photographic chemicals have arrived. Now she can start making photographs. You'll start with my little Christine, won't you, Laurel?"

"I'd be happy to, Aunt Alice. But first I'll need to get my darkroom up and running."

"How much space do you need?" Margaret asked.

"That little shed near the stables would be perfect if–"

"That's Cassie's tack room. You won't talk her out of that, I'm afraid."

"There's that large closet at the end of the hall upstairs," Alice suggested.

"That's awfully small–Christine, put that down!"

Christine stuck out her tongue at Laurel and dropped the vial she had picked out of the box. Laurel deftly caught it before it hit the floor. She gave Christine such a fierce warning look, Christine hid behind her mother's skirts.

"Yes, the closet...that will have to do," Margaret pronounced and returned to the kitchen.

"I'll go begin to clear it out," Alice volunteered.

"Thank you, Aunt Alice," Laurel called after her as she sat on the floor counting and examining the various supplies that had arrived.

"Well, if you'll not be needing me further...." Martin now perceived himself to be thoroughly forgotten in the excitement.

"Oh." Laurel glanced up and reminded herself to be polite. "Thank you for coming, Mr. Simpson." As an afterthought, she added, "Do come again."

"He won't be back," Jack Hartmoor announced flatly at supper.

"What happened?" asked Cassandra, wanting all the details of Laurel's first call by a potential suitor.

"She was rude to him," answered her brother. He carefully wiped his dark blond mustache on his napkin. Jack was the only Hartmoor who did not have the "Hartmoor hair" that his wife so admired. The only blond in a family of brunettes, his honey-colored hair, darkened though it was with heavy pomade, set him apart in the family, like an outsider.

Laurel stared down at the tablecloth, furious at this brusque assessment.

Alice struggled with a rebellious Christine. "Sit down, Mama says sit down now." She looked over the table to Laurel. "Laurel, dear, you did seem a trifle short with Mr. Simpson."

"I don't know what you're all talking about. I made polite conversation with him and fed him cookies and lemonade. What else was required?"

"Your conversation was the oddest I've ever heard for a young man and woman in nearly a courting circumstance."

Laurel wanted to remark that Alice should not have been eavesdropping, but bit her tongue. She knew Alice meant well, however irritating her manner of going about it.

"I spoke about things that interested me."

"But Laurel, you need to speak of things that interest *him*." Alice turned to her husband. "Isn't that right, dear?"

Jack glanced up from the evening paper he had been idly perusing since finishing the meal. He shrugged and returned to his reading.

"Laurel, perhaps we need to discuss this situation." Margaret was trying to be kind, but her irritation over Laurel's slipshod treatment of her first marriage prospect showed through.

"I did everything you told me to do," Laurel insisted. "Should I balance a ball on my nose like a trained bear?"

"I saw a dancing bear at the circus," Christine offered.

"Laurel, don't you want to have suitors and be popular?" asked Margaret in an almost rhetorical tone. "A young woman's pretty years don't last forever. You don't want to waste them."

Jack rose from the table and left to finish his paper on the front porch. He seemed to feel himself above the conversation of women and seldom participated to any great degree.

Alice cleaned the table around Christine's place as the little girl ran off to follow her father. Cassandra cleared the dishes and Laurel rose to help her, but her grandmother sat her down with a stern look that said their conversation was not over yet. When the others had left the table, Margaret continued.

"Laurel, don't you want to be happy? Don't you want to be married?"

"Does the former depend upon the latter?"

"I believe it does."

"Then I suppose I do. But I want to fall in love and won't that just happen when the time is right?"

"You are terribly naive for a girl your age." Margaret leaned close with a conspiratorial smile. "Sometimes fate needs a push."

Laurel looked back at her grandmother blankly.

"*Men* need a push. They don't always know what's best for them. We womenfolk have to lead them in the right direction. And frankly, Laurel, sometimes you have to make certain concessions to your pride."

"Concessions?" Laurel grew apprehensive. She feared her circus bear analogy might prove too close to the mark.

"A woman needs to go out of her way to make a man feel good about himself. Do you understand?"

Laurel propped her head upon her elbow and stared at the table cloth. She did not answer.

"I'm just asking you to be a little bit more friendly, more outgoing, more mindful of what you say to folks." Margaret drew herself up tall in her chair at the head of the Hartmoor family table. "You're a pretty girl, Laurel. Don't squander your opportunities fighting battles that don't really matter."

"I'll try to do better in the future, Grandmother." Laurel's voice betrayed her humiliation and lack of enthusiasm.

Margaret frowned, fearing she had been too hard on her obviously ignorant and stubborn granddaughter. "We have several social occasions to look forward to in the coming weeks. There's the Fourth of July picnic we always host for all our bank employees and tenant farmers." She patted Laurel's hand. "You'll get used to meeting people. I know you could be quite a success if you set your mind to it."

Laurel lifted her sulky head and managed a half-hearted smile. Margaret returned her smile, then rose to see how the clean-up was progressing in the kitchen.

A picnic for all the tenant farmers. That would mean Carey and his family would be invited. Laurel drew a deep breath and began to smile in earnest.

Chapter Seven

June promised to be the hottest and driest on record. According to Carey, such weather was good for the coming winter wheat harvest. Rain at a late date could ruin the crop, causing it to break down and rot in the fields. All good farmers of Turkey Red winter wheat had their crop in by the Fourth of July.

Still, the heat and the drought had everyone on edge. With June this unforgiving, what could be in store for July and August?

But Laurel bore the heat with a minimum of complaint. Most of her days were agreeably divided between her photography in the morning and her reading lessons with Carey in the afternoon.

She spent most of her photographic time making the numerous tests and experiments necessary to adapt her camera and darkroom chemistry to the new surroundings. Re-establishing a reliable formula for shooting, developing and printing was time consuming and painstaking work.

"What made you want to become a photographer?" Alice asked as she watched Laurel set up for her first portrait subject: the uncooperative Christine.

"I wanted to stop time," Laurel answered as she measured the distance between the chair she and Alice had lugged from the front porch to a spot under the broad cottonwood tree in the yard.

"To do what?" Alice laughed, then turned to see where Christine had run off to.

Christine took refuge in the swing that hung from the other large cottonwood in the side yard.

"Chrissie-belle, don't stand up on the swing. Sit down now or Mama will scold. Don't make me come over there!"

Laurel paused her work after adjusting the legs of her wooden tripod to the correct height. "I feel like whenever I've photographed someone, I've somehow captured a piece of them. When the light strikes the features of my sitter, it somehow belongs less exclusively to them once I capture it in the gelatin and transfer the image to the paper."

"I have no idea what you mean," Alice smiled, still glancing at the mischievous Christine out of the corner of her eye.

"Think about it," Laurel continued as she now placed her heavy view camera on the pinnacle of the tripod, and screwed it on securely. "I freeze the moment and save it forever. The beautiful face stays unlined and youthful, the child's eyes never blink, the lover's smile never fades."

"I never thought of it that way before," Alice mused. "Do you need my help?"

"Just with Christine." Laurel was almost ready and pulled out the film holder.

Christine was wrestled into position, sitting atop a pillow in the big porch chair. Laurel carefully adjusted the focus of her lens on the upside down, mirror image present on the back plate of her camera.

"Why do photographers have to hide under a cape?" Alice called as she attempted to smooth Christine's wild red locks. She licked her fingers and pressed the little girl's unruly bangs back from her forehead.

"To block the light," Laurel shouted back from underneath the hot, black fringed wool shawl. She deftly moved the black leather bellows back and forth on its little track until she was satisfied she had obtained the best focus possible. She re-emerged from the cloth and set the aperture of the lense.

"Is she ready, Aunt Alice?"

"I guess so." Alice straightened Christine's skirt two more times before ducking out of the camera's range.

"I'm hungry," shouted Christine.

"One more minute, precious."

"Actually, four more seconds," Laurel whispered, smiling, showing off, proud of herself and her accomplishments.

Alice beamed at Laurel, who now held the shutter release at the ready.

But before she could squeeze it, a huge gust of wind swept down the prairie and toppled Laurel's huge camera on its spindly tripod legs.

Laurel and Alice simultaneously dove for the camera and caught it before it crashed to the ground, but not before both fell and landed on the dry, dusty earth.

Christine climbed down from her uncomfortable seat and trotted over to see the action close up. She stood over her mother and cousin and stared down at them with impatience.

"I said I was hungry!"

Laurel and Alice lay on their backs looking up at Christine and the relentless prairie sky above. They began to chuckle, then laugh at the ridiculous position they found themselves in. Both sat up.

"I've always thought this spot would be the perfect place to build a gazebo," Alice remarked, half to herself.

"A gazebo?" Laurel had never heard the word.

"A gazebo, a summerhouse. It's a little ornamental structure with a roof and a floor, but no real sides. We had one in our yard in St. Louis where I grew up." Alice smiled dreamily. "Your Uncle Jack and I courted in that summerhouse. It was so romantic. There is something positively *magical* about them. You have the oddest, most wonderful sense of privacy, even though none actually exists. A dazzling enchantment. Jack promised to build me one here." Alice sighed. "But he's never gotten around to it."

As Alice spoke, Laurel inspected her beloved camera, which now rested in her lap like a great, big mechanical baby.

"Is your camera alright?" Alice pulled herself to her feet and shook the dust from her skirts and petticoats.

"Seems to be. Are you alright?" She grinned up at Alice, shielding her eyes from the noonday sun with her hand.

"Perhaps we could try again tomorrow?"

The Hartmoors remained undaunted in their efforts to launch Laurel into the social scene of Chisholm. Two weeks after the less than agreeable visit of Martin Simpson, one Jeffrey Shaw, the oldest son of a rancher who owned considerable acreage south of Chisholm, was invited. Laurel gleaned from breakfast table comments that the Shaws were not quite so prosperous or polished as the Hartmoors, but were regarded by Jack as having potential. Jack, as president of the only bank in Chisholm knew the financial particulars of nearly everyone in town. He knew who was prudent and who lived closer to the edge.

"He's only nineteen, according to Jack," said Alice as she fussed over Laurel's hair.

Laurel sat stiffly in a wooden chair next to the kitchen stove while Margaret watched Alice curl Laurel's hair.

"Has anyone in the family divulged Laurel's age, do you suppose?" Margaret asked, obviously concerned about the two-year age difference.

"I don't think so, Mother Hartmoor. I'm certain Jack wouldn't have had cause to mention it when meeting with Mr. Shaw or any of his sons."

"Well, then we're probably in the clear."

"I'm supposed to lie about my age?"

"Don't move, Laurel. I might burn you. I'll take the curling iron out in a minute. Until then, hold perfectly still."

"I'm not ashamed of my age. Why should I lie about it?"

"A man doesn't want to court a woman older than himself, child." Margaret shook her head. Laurel could be so bright about some things and so dim about others.

"You mean, I'm supposed to *deceive* this Mr. Jeffery Shaw?"

"'Deceive' is much too strong a word, Laurel," said Alice.

"We're just asking you to be discreet," said Margaret firmly.

"I think you're asking her to lie," announced Cassandra, who entered the kitchen in time to catch the last of the age discussion. She had just come in from the stables where she and Arthur, the stable hand, had presided over a mare giving birth to a foal.

"We didn't ask for your opinion, Cassie," said her mother. "And I don't think you're in a position to be giving advice on the subject of finding a husband, do you?"

Cassandra threw her bloody gloves down on the kitchen table and angrily stomped out of the room.

"Oh, dear," groaned Margaret and pulled off her apron. She followed her middle-aged daughter upstairs.

"What's wrong with Aunt Cassie?"

"Don't move, dear. I'm afraid Mother Hartmoor was somewhat tactless. I'm quite sure Cassandra's spinsterhood is not her fault. I think, though, Mother Hartmoor may see it as a poor reflection on her own mothering skills–the fact that Cassandra failed to marry."

"But what's so terrible about not being married?"

"Don't be silly, Laurel. All women would be married if they could. To be a wife and mother is the...ultimate fulfillment of a woman's role. Everyone knows that."

Laurel said nothing. She knew she would not be able to argue Alice out of her beliefs on marriage. Still, Laurel felt so demeaned by the process.

"Did you hear that Lydia is coming up from Wichita to stay with us over the Fourth of July holiday?" Alice asked as she made yet another long curl from Laurel's top knot. "I know she's anxious to meet you."

"I received a letter from her last month. I'm not exactly sure how we're related."

"She was married to Marcus Hartmoor. The eldest Hartmoor son. He passed on about nine or ten years ago. Just after your uncle and I were married."

"Did they live here in Chisholm before that?"

"They did for a time, I believe. Then Lydia's father became ill and they moved to Wichita to keep his dry goods store open. Marcus actually resigned his position as senior vice-president of the Hartmoor Bank to go off and run his wife's silly little dry goods store. Can you imagine? Your grandfather was livid, according to Jack."

"What became of the store after Uncle Marcus died?"

"Oh, Lydia runs it all by herself, poor thing. A shame they never had any children. She could have used the help. I'm sure you'll enjoy your acquaintance with Lydia. At least the two of you share the same view on suffrage."

"I don't understand why you and Uncle Jack are so opposed to the idea of women voting, Aunt Alice." Laurel was excited by the prospect of casting her first-ever vote when municipal elections were held the following year. Her father had been certain the measure was close on the political horizon.

"Now, Laurel, you must know how prominent your Uncle Jack is in this community. And how he is very well thought of in the local Republican Party. You just might see your uncle running for elective office in the future."

"Oh, my."

"Well, you must also understand that equal suffrage is only espoused by persons who, well, are on the fringes of polite society. They do not understand how the sphere of politics is meant for men exclusively. No decent woman would want to go out and vote. You know what election days are like."

"No, I guess I don't."

"Well, they are days of complete misrule, I'm sorry to report. Perfectly decent, upstanding men use it as an excuse to drink immoderately and conduct themselves in the most rowdy and illiberal manner."

"Why doesn't the local sheriff do something?"

Alice shook her head with a tsk-tsk. "But really there is a much more fundamental reason to oppose women's suffrage, Laurel. If women were voting as well as men, it could cause dissension within a family–between the husband and the wife. It might lead to the wholesale destruction of the family unit itself and society as we know it."

"Aunt Alice–I smell something burning!"

"Oh, dear!" Alice released a lock of Laurel's now-smoldering hair from the curling iron.

ℰ𝒶

Jeffery Shaw arrived punctually at six. Laurel still felt silently humiliated by the fact he'd been invited at all. The purpose of the invitation was so utterly transparent, she thought everyone acted a little uncomfortable.

Jeffery was an affable sort who tried to be light and pleasant despite the tension in the room.

Laurel, on the other hand, was not so generous. She refused to participate in the event beyond monosyllabic responses. As Margaret and Alice set the main course, a roast of beef, on the table, Jack turned the conversation to a topic he knew to be near to his young guest's heart: hunting.

Jeffery warmed to the subject as Jack hoped he would. The two enthusiastically discussed rifles, weather, hunting dogs, and clean shots until Laurel could stand it no longer.

"Do you enjoy killing things, Mr. Shaw?"

Everyone at the table tensed at this unexpected question. The hapless guest shifted uncertainly in his seat.

"Well," Jeffery began slowly, "hunting is a sport. It's an enjoyable pastime."

"Killing little animals with explosive weapons–that's a sport?"

Jeffery shrugged and glanced over to Jack for support.

"Hunting's an excellent sport. A true man's game. Right, Jeff?"

"Yes, sir."

"Do you favor killing some animals over others or do you kill all with equal pleasure?"

"It depends on the season," Jeffery murmured, not quick enough to follow Laurel's game. "Joe and me, we went rabbit hunting last week." Jeffery directed this remark to Jack. Cassandra leaned over to Laurel to whisper that Joe was Jeffery's younger brother.

"Rabbits?" Laurel persisted. "Rabbits?"

"Yes, ma'am."

"Little bunnies? They certainly had a sporting chance, didn't they?"

"*Laurel,*" Margaret warned.

"I just don't understand why people enjoy killing things, that's all."

"This may come as a terrible shock to you, Laurel," said Jack with a malicious gleam in his eye, "but we had to *kill* the cow that put the meat on your plate."

Everyone laughed at Jack's joke–except Laurel.

"Maybe we would all be better off if we stopped eating dead flesh."

"This is lovely dinner conversation," Margaret remarked, ruefully glancing at the ceiling.

"Pythagoras was a vegetarian," Laurel continued. "He compared the eating of–"

Jack interrupted irritably. "We're not interested in what Pythagoras had to say, Laurel."

"Who?" asked Jeffery in confusion.

"I think it's time we all went out onto the porch to serve up some of the ice cream we worked so hard on this afternoon," said Alice.

The entire group rose, grateful for this suggestion even though not all had finished their main course. Everyone promptly adjourned to the porch. Laurel did not speak the remainder of the evening, nor was she spoken to. The young man left as early as he could politely do so. The moment he and his horse were out of sight, the onslaught of criticism began.

"I have never been so humiliated in my own home in my entire life, young lady!" Jack's voice shook with anger.

His wife placed a soothing hand upon his shoulder. "What got into you, Laurel? You did everything within your power to drive that poor young man away."

Laurel shrugged and hung her head.

Margaret sat quietly rocking in her porch chair, but Laurel could tell from the firm set of her mouth that she was as angry as the rest of the family. Only Cassandra found the situation amusing. She sat on the porch railing and snickered at the proceedings.

"You know, news of this will spread, Little Miss Too-Good-For-This-World," Jack continued. "In a month, there won't be a man in the county who'll come near this house."

"Oh, Laurel, he's right," said Alice. She shook her head in frustration. "And after all that trouble I took with your hair."

"I'm sorry," Laurel mumbled, feeling guilty now. "I don't know what comes over me."

"If you expect to live on my charity for the rest of your days, you've got another thing coming!"

"Jack, that's enough," snapped his mother.

Jack and Alice left the porch and entered the house to prepare for bed. Cassandra reluctantly followed, leaving Laurel alone in the darkness of the late evening twilight with her grandmother.

"What are we going to do with you, child?"

"A sacrificial lamb on the Almighty Altar of Marriage," Laurel droned, under her breath.

Margaret sighed, but continued to rock.

∞

Laurel couldn't wait to tell Carey about her horrible evening. She didn't know how she ever got by without a confidant like Carey.

"It's a pity that slavery is outlawed," she announced teasingly. "Then they could just hold an auction and sell me to the highest bidder!"

Carey hooted with laughter at this suggestion. "You'd be a bargain at any price!"

"I overheard Uncle Jack call me a 'damned, spoiled misfit.'" Laurel had never said the word "damned" out loud before and it felt surprisingly good, like she'd invaded some exclusively male preserve. "Their bedroom's next to mine, I can hear everything that goes on there."

"That must be entertaining," Carey grinned.

"What do you mean?"

"Nothing, go on."

"Uncle Jack seems to hate me and I don't know why."

"Well, he hates me, too, so we have that in common."

"Why does Uncle Jack hate you?"

Carey shrugged. "No idea, but he always has. You can tell when a person doesn't like you. They don't have to put it into words."

"Oh, let's forget about them. Shall you read or shall I, today?"

He sighed. "I'm so tired, would you mind?"

"Farming *is* hard work, isn't it?" She felt sorry for Carey. She could tell he often hadn't felt like coming to the grove for the reading lessons since the wheat harvest began, but came anyway, exhausted or not. Twice, he'd fallen asleep while she read to him. She'd watched him doze and studied the curve of his jaw, the line of his brow, the delicate arch of his upper lip with its faint suggestion of blond whiskers only slightly darker than his sun-bleached hair.

His quickness to learn still amazed her. His grasp of numbers was even more astounding than his hunger for the written word. He had memorized the entire multiplication tables to the twelves in a single weekend. He could calculate sums in his head that Laurel was forced to scratch out on the little chalk board she had "borrowed" from her tiny roommate, Christine.

What a tragedy he never attended school. Such a waste. If his mother, Lizzie Fairchild were alive this minute, Laurel would have given her such a talking-to.

They sat in their usual places, with Laurel perched upon the limestone outcropping, her legs tucked up under her and her long black skirts trailing to the ground. Carey lay on his back on the ground with his head pillowed against the limestone by the hem of Laurel's skirts and petticoats.

Carey raised himself on one elbow and turned to look up at Laurel. "Do you mind my saying that you have a really odd smell about you today."

"You don't rival the rose yourself," she teased. "Oh, I'm just joking. It's the chemicals, the photographic chemicals. I didn't have time to change clothes before coming here. Sorry."

"Are you making pictures yet?"

"Nothing worth looking at, I'm afraid. The Hartmoors give me nothing but trouble. They want to see the end product, but they all complain about the equipment and the chemicals. Uncle Jack claims the smell of the chemicals ruins his appetite. Aunt Cassie says they burn her eyes and nostrils. Grandmother says the house will never be the same. Oh–are you going to attend the July Fourth picnic? I'm going to take a photograph of the gathering and make a print for every family there."

"Oh, we never miss it. You'll get to meet Mae and the girls. I'll introduce you."

"Have you ever told Mae about these reading lessons?"

"Well, I...not exactly. I mean, it's not that we're doing anything wrong. She just wouldn't understand."

"But doesn't she know how much you want to leave off farming and get a job in town? I mean, after all, she's the one you're doing this for, right?"

"I've tried to tell her. She just...I don't know. Whenever I want to improve myself–which would help the whole family–she accuses me of thinking I'm better than her. Or that I'm ashamed of her or something." Carey shook his head in frustration.

Laurel decided to change the subject. Discussions of Mae always made her uneasy. "I brought my favorite today, Shakespeare–*The Complete Works*. I'll pick one of the sonnets. You know, I think Mr. Shakespeare thought every single thought worth thinking at least once."

He sat up and playfully snatched the book from her.

She tried to retrieve it but he held it just out of her grasp.

"Let me keep it," he insisted, grinning.

"No, Carey, not my Shakespeare."

"But *I* want to think every single thought worth thinking."

"Don't mock me. Give it back." She loved her *Complete Works* like a devoted Christian loves his Bible. Not having it near was unthinkable. "It's my favorite."

"I know." He smiled at her, but defiantly.

She didn't understand this game. She frowned, then feigned disinterest. "Do as you please."

Chapter Eight

The Fourth of July sun baked the tired landscape and sent heat shimmers across the horizon. The day of the big Hartmoor family picnic had arrived at last.

Several of the local farmers, Carey among them, erected a large canopy on the side lawn. Jack Hartmoor directed the operation with limited enthusiasm. He made it clear to his family in every way he could that this annual event, begun by his father and continued by his older brother, was nothing more to him than a boring obligation, not to mention a frivolous waste of money.

Meanwhile, the Hartmoor women fussed in the kitchen, culminating a week's worth of cooking. Laurel was set to the task of making pie crust for the three dozen peach and strawberry pies to be baked for the feast. Margaret made her scrub her hands until they were raw, so fearful was she of Laurel contaminating the pie dough with her photographic chemicals.

Sore hands aside, Laurel enjoyed the preparations. She became quite proficient in cutting the lard into the flour. Even Cassandra saw fit to compliment her at one point, though her comment carried the unspoken hint that Laurel had at last found some domestic chore at which she was not hopeless.

Four large hogs were slaughtered, dressed, and placed over a pit of fiery coals to cook all night and through the morning of the Fourth. Margaret walked in nervous circles around the barbecue pit countless times to determine if the fire was exactly the correct temperature. She gave endless instructions to Arthur, the stable hand, who had been assigned the thankless job of tending the fire all night.

Laurel watched with an amused eye as her grandmother, hands firmly planted on hips, barked out orders to anyone within shouting distance. By sticking her head out the kitchen window, Laurel could not only gain a breath of less steamy, if not refreshing air, but also see the men working to erect the canopy.

She grinned to see Carey, his shirt undone in the morning heat, labor with the group. She could see him and the other farmers talk and joke among themselves. She wondered what Mae Fairchild, Carey's wife, would be like. Perhaps she would be a friend for her.

"Laurel! What's burning?" shouted Alice, as she swished into the kitchen wearing a new dove gray summer frock.

"Oh, dear! My biscuits!" Laurel flew to the smoking oven, grabbed a kitchen towel and pulled out the smoldering remains of two dozen buttermilk biscuits. She surveyed them with dismay, then held them out to her aunt. "A treat for Uncle Jack's hunting dogs?"

Alice laughed in spite of herself. "Oh, Laurel, we can't leave you alone for a minute."

Laurel managed to laugh at herself for once as she scraped the burned biscuits into the scrap bucket for later feeding to some of the animals about the farm.

"Laurel, why don't I finish up in here, while you go upstairs and get dressed for the picnic?" Alice grabbed an apron from the hook behind the door and Laurel hastily left the heat of the kitchen.

She stepped out onto the side porch, but only in time to see Carey walking towards home, no doubt to fetch his family for the picnic. In the distance, she spotted Cassandra driving the family buggy home from town with their weekend guest, Mrs. Lydia Hartmoor, seated beside her.

Laurel eagerly ran out into the front lawn to greet them.

"You must be Laurel," Lydia Hartmoor called from the buggy as Cassandra guided it toward the stables. She pulled the horses to a brief stop so that Lydia could climb down and unload her traveling bag in front of the house.

"I'm so happy to meet you," Laurel offered politely as she picked up Lydia's bag and carried it up the porch stairs for her.

"And I must say the same," answered Lydia with gracious enthusiasm.

Laurel's high hopes for meeting her Aunt Lydia Hartmoor were not disappointed. At forty, Lydia's still-youthful face carried strong features so sharply cut as to look exquisitely beautiful one moment and shockingly ill-arranged the next. Her hair, as blond as a Valkyrie, showed her Swedish heritage on her mother's side. Her elegant dress and demeanor reminded Laurel of the fashionable ladies she'd seen on the pages of the many newspapers and magazines to which her father had subscribed.

"The Plains Transit Coach was late," Lydia complained. "I don't think the driver cared to work on a holiday. I feared I would miss the picnic altogether."

"Oh, no, it's not for another hour, at least," said Laurel. "It's a fine day for a picnic, don't you think?"

"A bit warm for my taste, but at least no rain. Your grandmother tells me you're a photographer, Laurel."

"Yes, ma'am."

"And that you're going to make a photograph of this afternoon's gathering."

"Yes, ma'am." Laurel beamed with hard-to-disguise pride.

"How wonderful. I think–Oh, hello, Alice. How are you?"

The two women embraced as Lydia and Laurel entered the front hall. "Where is that darling little girl of yours, Alice?"

"I can't seem to find her at the moment." Alice's long, thin face carried a perplexed frown.

"I'll go look for her," Laurel offered, disappointed to break away from Lydia so soon.

"Oh, thank you, Laurel. But do allow enough time to dress for the picnic."

Laurel mentally groaned. She felt Alice implied that she looked like such a mess she would scare all the potential suitors away. She sat Lydia's traveling bag at the bottom of the stairs and trudged off in search of her little cousin.

At the stroke of noon, carriages, wagons, and families on foot began arriving. The sight of so many people descending on the Hartmoor farm both excited and intimidated Laurel. She nervously watched from her bedroom window as she enjoyed the rare comfort of sitting in nothing but her camisole and drawers before putting on yet another stiff black dress. She felt like an old black crow compared to everyone else clad in bright calicoes and summer stripes like blooming prairie flowers. She reminded herself with a sigh that she wore the mourning clothes out of respect for her father. She clutched the silver locket, gave it a quick kiss, then let it drop back to its usual resting place, banging back and forth between her breasts where she assumed her heart must lay deep in her chest.

Laurel caught sight of her grandmother. Margaret stood in the yard staring up at her with a disgruntled expression. She impatiently motioned for Laurel to both cover herself and come join the gathering. Laurel jumped into action and soon joined the noisy festivities.

She glided through the throngs of bank employees, tenant farmers, wives, children, Hartmoor family friends, fellow church members, and business associates and wondered if the entire population of Chisholm was in attendance. She smiled shyly at faces she recognized, but no one called to her or asked her to join them. She couldn't help but notice the distinct difference in dress between the families of the bank employees and the tenant farmers. The townsfolk wore fashionable clothing befitting the middle class to which they belonged, whereas the farmers and their wives wore shabby, faded garments, twice-turned, homespun, and graceless. Their children ran barefoot and hatless in the July heat.

Laurel caught sight of Carey. He and his older daughter stood in the long line outside the canopy where the food was being served. He squatted on the ground to be eye level with five-year-old Rachel. A lively conversation engaged the pair.

Laurel found herself too nervous to think of eating, though the roasting hogs sent out a delightful aroma. She was both anxious and terrified of taking center stage to photograph the picnic. She decided to go ahead and set up her equipment. Staying busy would distract her from her nerves. A small crowd of interested onlookers formed about her as she set her tripod up in the middle of the front yard. The group photograph was to be staged upon the wide front porch of the house. The cluster of gawking neighbors pressed Laurel for details about her hobby, flattering her a great deal.

Laurel's task was nearly complete when her attention was distracted by the sound of Carey's voice, raised in anger. Both she and the others near her camera turned to seek the source of the loud exchange now taking place nearby.

"All I'm saying is, if the government were in charge of the money supply instead of the banks, maybe an honest man could afford to make a living without the banker holding the mortgage on his land taking the food out of his children's mouths."

Laurel strained to see Carey over the heads of the other picnic-goers. She could catch only part of his face in the crowd, but could tell it was flushed with emotion.

"Fairchild's right," Jud Amberly, another farmer joined in. "I can't afford to own my own land at the price of borrowing money today."

"You farmers are better at squawking about your problems than solving them," snorted Martin Simpson, the bank teller who had unsuccessfully tried to court Laurel.

"Well, the rough fact is, we got plenty to squawk about," Carey rejoined.

"What do you think you know about it?" continued Martin, in a scornful tone.

"I know I'm sick and tired of a legislature bought and paid for with railroad money," Carey shot back. "I'm sick and tired of investors back East being able to speculate on the future prices of my wheat, when all I get for it is the going rate at harvest time when the market's glutted."

"You sound like a dang radical, Fairchild," Dave Taylor, another tenant farmer, put in good-naturedly.

"I don't think it's radical to want a fair playing field, a fair chance to make a living," Carey insisted, his voice growing tighter as his emotions rose. "The way I see it, the world's divided into two groups–the producers...and the parasites!"

This brought murmurs of support from the farmers and their wives, but stony silence from the bank employees who knew his "parasite" remark was pointedly directed at them.

Laurel felt thrilled by Carey's enthusiasm at standing up for his beliefs, but cast a nervous glance through the crowd, afraid of her uncle's reaction to this slap in the face. She saw Jack standing on the porch, watching the debate uneasily. Margaret stood near him, also observing the tense exchange.

"Better a 'parasite' than a hayseed!" spat out a viciously grinning Martin Simpson.

With this insult flung into the hot afternoon breeze, Carey rushed at Martin.

Large Jud Amberly deftly intercepted Carey before his fist could reach its target. Joe Taylor and his grown son, Dave, helped subdue the furious Carey, while several bank employees closed ranks with Martin Simpson.

Laurel looked back at Jack Hartmoor, praying he would defuse the situation before it could get out of control. She saw her grandmother whisper something into her son's ear before he dashed down from the porch and headed into the incipient fray.

"Boys, boys, let's settle down," Jack shouted with a forced-sounding joviality. "This heat will steal all our good humor if we let it."

"I'm sorry, Mr. Hartmoor," Carey immediately offered. At this conciliatory remark, Carey's friends released him. "You're right."

Carey walked directly over to a glowering Martin Simpson with his hand extended. Martin glanced at Jack, his boss, for guidance.

Jack forced a smile and nodded to Martin. Martin, somewhat grudgingly, took Carey's hand and shook it briefly.

The crowd audibly sighed their relief, though tension still hung in the humid air.

"How about a baseball game?" Jack suggested. "Bank employees versus the tenant farmers?"

"City versus country?" Carey grinned mischievously at Martin Simpson. Clearly, he relished the opportunity to work out the smoldering resentments of their differing professions and cultures on the acceptable playing field of sport. "Up to the challenge, bankers?"

The young farmers, all members of the Chisholm Cyclones shared Carey's enthusiasm, and quickly joined with him.

The bank employees, only a few of whom played on the local team rose to the invitation and backed Martin by removing their jackets and rolling up their sleeves.

Jack hurried off with two other men to fetch the baseball equipment while the crowd formed themselves loosely into an audience. The two makeshift teams huddled together to decide who would play which position.

Laurel smiled at Jack, though he didn't see her. His tactful handling of the situation impressed her. She made a place to sit and watch the game near her camera. She feared to leave it unattended to watch the game from a better perspective. She hovered around it like an anxious mother protecting her child. She felt, for an irreverent moment, like Alice.

A toss of a coin brought the farmers up to bat first. They easily scored two runs, while the bankers struck out on their first three times at bat.

Laurel stood up to watch Carey at bat for the first time in the top of the second inning. Martin Simpson, the bankers' pitcher threw a pitch that bounced two feet from the plate, inviting derisive laughter from the crowd. Carey's arrogant smile and Martin's furious frown told everyone in attendance that the hostility between the two men had not abated in the least.

Martin's second pitch flew over the heads of Carey and the catcher. More laughter from the crowd, more anger and tautness on the face of Martin. Laurel saw Mae Fairchild seated with a group of farmers' wives behind the improvised home plate. Mae laughed and clapped with everyone else as Martin, obviously nervous and still agitated from his near-fistfight with Carey, threw yet another wild pitch.

"Thanks, Simpson," Carey called out to taunt Martin. "You're making this too easy for me." Carey seemed destined to take a base without so much as swinging his bat.

Martin narrowed his eyes and threw the ball with all his might. The pitch hit Carey in the side just under his elbow and sent him crashing into the catcher.

The crowd lunged forward, with the farmers diving onto the field to attack the bankers. Laurel rushed to where Carey lay stunned on the dusty ground. When she reached him, she found his wife, Mae, placing a delicate hand on his forehead to brush his blond curls out of his eyes.

"Just got the wind knocked out of me," Carey said to those standing over him. He held his aching side with both his hands while his two little daughters gave him kisses.

The two opposing baseball teams did considerable shouting, shoving, and name-calling, but no punches were thrown. Jack Hartmoor waded into the melee and announced loudly that a wagonload of oysters had just arrived.

An excited hooray rose from the assembled crowd and all proceeded to the wagon piled high with oysters packed in ice and straw.

Laurel's head spun from the alternating temper of the gathering, moods that seemed to change faster than the prairie weather on a spring day. She glanced back to find Carey. He still sat on the ground where he'd fallen. Dr. Parnell knelt next to him. Carey pulled up the long tails of his cotton shirt to reveal a large, red swelling on his side, just below his rib cage. He winced silently as Parnell examined the bruise.

Laurel saw Jack draw Martin Simpson aside from the throng now mobbing the oyster wagon. At Jack's prodding no doubt, Martin Simpson approached Carey and appeared to offer his apologies.

Laurel watched Carey nod to Martin and the two men shook hands, then Martin helped Carey to his feet. Carey, supported by his wife and daughters, walked slowly towards the oysters. He still held his side and looked as though breathing pained him. With relief, Laurel presumed the fracas was over for the day.

ℰ𝒮

After everyone had finished their oysters, Jack Hartmoor made a general announcement for all to assemble on the porch for the photograph. Laurel took a deep breath and wiped her sweating palms on her apron. She was on stage at last. She hurriedly made final adjustments for exposure as the crowd of picnic attendees shuffled into position amid a great deal of noise, confusion, laughing children, barking dogs, and crying babies.

Laurel placed the photographic plate in the back of the camera, made the final adjustments to the aperture of the lens, and prayed the light wouldn't change before she could release the shutter.

"I'll count to three, then everyone must be perfectly still," she shouted to the crowd as they jammed themselves upon and in front of the porch. "One, two," she held her breath and closed her eyes, "Three!"

A cheer soared from the crowd when she waved to indicate the photo was complete. Being the center of attention nearly overwhelmed her. She busied herself with her plates and camera, avoiding eye contact with the crowd. She hoped she didn't look foolish.

She hurried into the house with her equipment as soon as she had it disassembled and remained in her room until the dessert was served under the big canopy just after six. Cassandra called up to her to help serve the pie.

The setting sun on the western horizon cast brilliant orange rays over the yard. The warmth of the day abated only slightly.

Laurel washed her face with tepid water and walked downstairs to serve her time on the dessert line. A dance was scheduled to follow the fireworks display. Jack and several of his bank employees made final preparations for the show in the fading light. Laurel watched them set up the impressive and fearsome-looking set of missiles for nearly an hour, then she wandered back over to the lawn to sit alone. From where she sat, she could discreetly survey the picnic scene and had an unobstructed view of the Fairchild family.

Mae Fairchild sat on a blanket conversing with two other young matrons. All looked similar in dress, plain white cotton blouses and dark, unfashionable skirts. All had young children nearby. Their talk appeared animated and serious.

They paid no attention to the presence of Carey who now lay next to his wife on the blanket as he played with his younger daughter. He held the blond-haired toddler above him and pretended to toss her in the air, but never actually let go. The little girl shrieked with delight.

Laurel had not spoken to Carey yet today and wondered when he would introduce her to his family, as he had promised. Carey finally sat up and leaned near his wife to hand the toddler back to her mother. Mae did not speak to her husband, but took the child into her lap and began a game of peek-a-boo with a handkerchief. When the little girl laughed, her mother smiled with delight. The smile transformed Mae's features in a way that astonished Laurel. Suddenly,

Mae was young again and pretty. No wonder Carey loved her. A dazzling smile, dimples, doll-like features, blond ringlets–what man could resist her?

Laurel felt profoundly plain by comparison. She sat with a sour face and watched the rest of the crowd milling about, lounging on the grass, talking, chasing children. Soon the darkness would swallow up the yard. Laurel's boredom and loneliness returned, but only for a short time.

The fireworks display began with an explosion louder than any sound she had ever heard before. A yelp of surprised fear escaped her before she could contain her amazement at the gaudy display that filled the enormous dome of the prairie sky. The last rays of the setting sun still warmed the western horizon, but did not interfere with the exploding bombs of sparkling light that showered down over the Hartmoor farm to the "oohs" and "ahs" of the onlookers. A roar of approval from the crowd greeted each new burst.

The annual fireworks display was the one aspect of the picnic in which Jack Hartmoor took a serious interest and he had managed to develop a certain expertise in its presentation. One colorful umbrella of sparks followed the next and competed with the veil of stars in the summer night sky. The display built to a grand and noisy conclusion as the small group of local musicians tuned up for the dance.

Large torches illuminated the flat, grassy area set aside to become the dance floor. Laurel watched as couples, young and old, drifted onto the lawn to begin the first dance. The torchlight lent a magical beauty to the scene. Laurel wished she could capture it with her camera, but nighttime shots were out of the question due to the need for bright light. The exposure time required for a dimly lit scene would not wait for human participation.

"May I have this dance, Miss McBryde?"

Laurel gasped to look up and discover Carey standing over her. He laughed at her startled expression and pulled her to her feet.

"I...well...I–" she sputtered.

He grinned at her confusion. "Is that a 'yes' or a 'no'?"

"Umm, wouldn't you rather dance with Mae?"

Carey shrugged with a vaguely distasteful glance backward to where Mae and their two daughters sat. "Mae doesn't want to dance with me. She's still mad."

"About what?"

"Let's see, where to begin?" Carey pretended to count on his fingers. "I shot my mouth off in public about my radical political views, I insulted my hosts,

I picked a fight with Martin Simpson, who Mae thinks is the finest gentleman ever to walk on God's earth, and–what else? Oh, yes, Martin hitting me with that pitch–that was somehow my fault, too. Anyway, I told her I would invite one of my hostesses to dance to be polite before leaving. So here I am."

He took her reluctant hand and began to lead her towards the dance floor. She resisted after a few steps. He turned to her, confused.

"You really don't want to?"

"Well, yes, but...no." She beckoned him closer to whisper, "I don't dance."

"Are you a Methodist?" he laughed.

Laurel didn't understand his joke. "It's not funny. I don't know how. And I don't want anyone to find out, especially the Hartmoors. They already think I'm strange and unfeminine. If they find out I can't dance, they'll give up on me for sure."

Laurel and Carey exchanged knowing smiles. Her problems with the Hartmoors were a secret joke they shared.

"There's only one solution to your problem, Miss McBryde," he announced with mock seriousness.

She waited.

"I'll have to show you how to dance."

"No, please, I'd rather not."

"It won't hurt a bit," he teased.

"You may think differently after I've trod upon your poor feet, Mr. Fairchild."

"I'll risk it. It'd have to hurt less than that wild pitch today."

"Are you feeling better?"

"Oh, sure. Come on. They're starting a slow tune. No one will notice us way over here."

But several persons noticed, among them, Mae Fairchild and Jack Hartmoor. Neither of whom were pleased by the sight.

Carey took Laurel's hand in his, then placed her other hand upon his shoulder. Haltingly, they moved in time to the music. Laurel giggled nervously. She felt the warmth of his hand at the back of her waist, even through her many layers of clothing and corset. He led her gently back and forth, now pushing, now pulling her in the proper direction.

"Do you think Martin Simpson hit you on purpose?"

"Of course, he did. He claims he didn't, but you saw it. What do you think?"

"Well, he was a pretty poor pitcher to begin with–oh, sorry!" Laurel had stepped on his foot again. She had never possessed exceptional coordination or grace and had to often grasp his shoulder tightly for balance. Every couple of steps, the dancers collapsed against each other in defeat. They laughed at their efforts and did not see the approach of Jack Hartmoor.

"Get your hands off my niece!" Jack grabbed Carey's shoulder and roughly shoved him apart from Laurel.

"Uncle Jack!" Laurel cried in surprise. She wondered what new sin against propriety she had committed now. "Mr. Fairchild was just showing me a few dance steps. That's all."

"I believe Mr. Fairchild has a *wife* he could be dancing with."

Carey's pale green eyes narrowed, his thin nostrils twitched. "I'll dance with your niece if she wishes, Mr. Hartmoor."

"Oh, no, you won't."

"But Uncle Jack–"

"Go in the house, Laurel." Jack barked the words. Laurel could see his fists clenching and unclenching as though he were preparing for a fight.

"Is a poor dirt farmer not *good enough* to dance with your niece?" challenged Carey with a firmly set jaw.

"Uncle Jack, please." Laurel placed a conciliatory hand on Jack's elbow, but he shook it off.

"Laurel, go in the house!"

Mae Fairchild joined the action, with both her young daughters in tow. Though she glared angrily at Laurel, her sudden appearance was secretly welcomed. Surely the two men would not start a fight in the presence of the children.

"Carey," she began.

"Stay out of this, Mae," Carey whispered fiercely without looking at his wife. His intense gaze towards Jack Hartmoor would not waver.

Laurel's heart pounded. She did not want to be the cause of trouble, especially between the Hartmoors and her only real friend in the world. She had never seen this contentious side of Carey's nature before . He was like a different person around other people.

"Carey, it's time to go home," said Mae. She held the youngest girl in her arms. The toddler dozed against her shoulder, not awakened by the tension of the moment.

Rachel, the older girl, peeked out from behind her mother's skirts. "I'm sleepy, Daddy. I wanna go home," she said.

Carey turned to his daughter immediately. "Of course, honey." He knelt down and reached for the girl.

"Thank you and your family for your hospitality, Mr. Hartmoor," Mae offered cautiously.

Carey picked up little Rachel and braced her against his hip. The Fairchild family turned as a group and walked away from the festivities.

"I'm sorry, Uncle Jack." Laurel didn't know what she was apologizing for, but she couldn't think of anything else to say.

"Go in the house," Jack replied coldly. He watched the Fairchild family retreat into the darkness of the recently harvested wheat fields that lay beyond the Hartmoor yard.

Meekly, Laurel did as she was told.

Laurel tossed and turned all through the humid night, unable to erase the unpleasant confrontation between Carey and Jack from her thoughts. Christine slept soundly, though she kicked the covers off her bed in her sleep.

Laurel decided to go down to the kitchen and drink a glass of water, or perhaps milk. Maybe that would relax her. She pulled on her wrapper for decency's sake, though the house was still as warm as an oven baking steamy bread. She eased down the stairs, hoping not to wake anyone or get one of her uncle's hunting dogs barking. If one started, they all chimed in.

She stopped abruptly at the bottom of the stairs when she noticed the gasolier was turned on to a low level in the dining room. Apparently she was not the only family member having trouble finding sleep. Jack was awake as well.

She watched him kneel before the lower portion of the china closet. He drew a key from the pocket of his dark red dressing gown and unlocked the ornately carved walnut doors. She studied his clandestine actions with interest as she saw him remove a glass bottle from the little cupboard. He yanked a cork from the bottle and poured an amber colored liquid into a glass that he had pulled down from the shelf of the hutch above the cabinet. He quickly tossed the drink down his throat.

She stared dumbly in scandalized amazement to realize her uncle flaunted the temperance laws with such abandon. She wondered if her grandmother knew about the contents of the china cabinet. She remembered the night earlier in the summer when she had thought he smelled of whiskey when she passed him on the porch.

Jack replaced the bottle after refilling his glass once more and re-locked the cabinet. All the plates and glasses clattered when he firmly shut the carved doors. As he stood up again, he turned and his pale eyes met Laurel's for half an instant. He frowned, then furtively turned away. He extinguished the gaslight in the dining room and took his glass of proscribed pleasure out onto the porch with him.

Chapter Nine

Before Laurel could enter the dining room the following morning, she cringed to overhear herself once again be the topic of breakfast table conversation.

"She doesn't seem to fit in well with our friends," Alice said delicately.

"It's not that she can't, it's that she won't," Cassandra stated flatly.

"She has a bit too high an opinion of herself, if you ask me," Jack put in.

Laurel caught her breath, wondering what Jack may have told his mother about the incident with the Fairchild family.

"She doesn't seem to know quite how to get people to like her. Especially men," Alice remarked.

"She scares them away," Jack snorted.

"Perhaps she doesn't understand the subtleties involved," Lydia Hartmoor interjected. "With her isolated upbringing, she never *had* to make friends, so she probably never learned how."

"There has to be some explanation for this problem," Margaret commented. "Her looks don't stand in her way."

"I think Laurel is quite attractive, really," said Alice. "She just needs–"

"And she is a member of this family," Margaret continued as though Alice had not spoken. To Margaret Hartmoor, membership in a family as established and prosperous as the Hartmoor clan ought to have been an unparalleled asset in a town as small as Chisholm. As dwellers in the comfortable circle of natural conformity, the Hartmoors were certain outsiders somehow chose their fate. In the smothering embrace of small town existence, the trait of individuality was not well received. The assertion of personal preference over societal norms was to be regarded with a mixture of suspicion and contempt.

Social acceptance was a virtue to be valued. Any behavior calculated or misdirected toward any other goal was not to be genteelly tolerated, let alone understood.

"And this photographic hobby of hers," said Jack. "Why can't she do something more ordinary with her time?"

"More feminine," Alice clarified.

"Perhaps the photograph of the picnic was a bad idea," Margaret mused.

"At least it put her in the spotlight," offered Lydia.

"Everyone was talking about her, that's for certain," said Cassandra.

"But what were they saying, I wonder?" Margaret worried aloud.

"Did anyone see her after the dance began?" asked Alice.

Laurel tensed, waiting for Uncle Jack to tell about the Fairchild incident.

"No, I didn't see her after the fireworks," said Cassandra.

"I didn't either," said Lydia. "And I looked for her. I was hoping we'd get the chance to talk and get to know each other a bit. But I'm afraid I was so caught up in renewing old acquaintances. I really must visit Chisholm more often."

Jack said nothing. Laurel mentally breathed a sigh of relief.

"Good morning." Laurel entered the dining room and took her usual place at the table with a forced smile.

"Did you enjoy the picnic, Laurel?" Margaret asked in noncommittal tones.

"Yes, ma'am." Laurel dished up some now-cold scrambled eggs. "I'm sorry I overslept. Could you please pass the salt, Aunt Lydia?"

Jack tossed his napkin onto the table with a sigh. "Well, I'm off."

"Why are you going into town on a Saturday, Jack?" asked his mother. Alice, too, waited for his reply as he rose from the table.

"Firemen's Ball. First meeting of the planning committee. I'll be home by noon, but if I'm not, don't wait dinner on me. You know those boys."

Everyone chuckled as Jack left the room.

"Uncle Jack is a fireman?" Laurel asked in surprise.

"Nearly all the gentlemen in Chisholm are members of the Volunteers," Alice explained.

"The association is far more social than the name implies," Cassandra snickered.

Alice bristled at this remark. "Just because the Firemen enjoy each other's company does not diminish the importance of their service to the community."

"Most civic duties don't require a two hundred dollar initiation fee," Cassandra sniped.

Laurel could tell by the way Cassandra said the words "two hundred dollars" that she must have considered the sum not only to be exorbitant, but unnecessary.

"The initiation fee serves only to–"

"Let us not revisit this old argument," Margaret interrupted Alice. "I will not have money matters discussed at my breakfast table."

"If the Volunteer Firemen are a social organization, who actually fights the fires?" Laurel asked. She felt greatly relieved the conversation now centered on a topic other than the picnic or her lack of social success.

Lydia laughed merrily at Laurel's observation. "Laurel, aren't you the perceptive one!"

Laurel smiled at this compliment, pleased and flattered to bask in the good opinion of her Aunt Lydia.

"The Volunteers fight fires," Alice insisted.

"Since when?" asked Cassandra.

Alice audibly huffed at her sister-in-law, but Christine chose this moment to spill the remainder of her glass of milk. Alice jumped up and pulled Christine to her feet on her chair to wipe her smock.

"I'm sure the Volunteers would rise to the occasion, should one occur," Lydia smiled diplomatically.

"Let's just hope they're not put to the test any time soon. It might interfere with preparations for the annual Firemen's Ball," said Cassandra.

"Enough, enough," Margaret shook her head. She asked the other women at the table to excuse themselves as she wished to speak with Laurel privately.

Oh, dear, here it comes, thought Laurel with mild dread as she took a sip of cold coffee.

"Laurel, what went wrong at the picnic?" Margaret asked when everyone else had finally left the room.

"How am I to explain a fistfight between the bank employees and the farmers?"

"I'm talking about you, dear. What went wrong?"

"Nothing," Laurel answered carefully. "I had a good time. I especially enjoyed the fireworks. Uncle Jack did a marvelous job."

"Laurel, social occasions are for socializing. Every time I looked for you, you were either dragging about the house or sitting by yourself. I'm sorry that I was too busy to help you find friends–"

"It's not that, Grandmother. It's not your fault–or anyone's. I just don't have anything in common with anyone here."

"Why do you say that?"

Laurel shrugged. "No one wants to talk to me. No one thinks the things I like to talk about are interesting."

"What sort of things?"

"Oh, books I've read, photography, the law–"

"The law!" Margaret shook her head from side to side in disbelief and amusement. "Oh, dear girl, dear girl–don't tell me you talk to young men about the law."

Laurel frowned. She did not appreciate being the focal point of humor she did not understand. "My father and I often talked about the law. It's a fascinating subject. Why doesn't anyone here think so?"

The mention of Andrew McBryde brought matters into focus for Margaret. "Your father did you a great disservice in the manner in which he brought you up, Laurel." She raised her hand to silence Laurel's incipient retort. "I know he loved you. But the fact remains that he failed to teach you the essence of getting on with others in society. He raised you without the social graces necessary to a young girl's life. I don't mean to criticize him unduly. He was a man and these matters are best handled by women. You should have been brought to live with us when your mother died–but that's an old controversy."

Laurel shifted uncomfortably in her chair and twisted the white linen tablecloth in her lap under the table. Margaret leaned closer.

"I'm going to ask you a simple question and I want a well-considered answer from you, dear. Are you willing to try and change your ways enough to improve your prospects for marriage?"

Laurel stared at the remains of her breakfast in front of her. She was confused by her own emotions and embarrassed by her grandmother's blunt assessment of her shortcomings. She twisted the tablecloth more furiously under the table until the plate jiggled.

"I suppose," she finally mumbled.

"I must warn you that such an undertaking may require a considerable amendment of your outlook."

"I want to do what's best. I want to be happy."

"Will you accept our help and trust our judgment?"

Laurel sullenly nodded.

"Will you at least try our suggestions?"

Laurel looked up to face her grandmother and nodded again.

"Don't look so mournful, child. I'm not inviting you to your own funeral."

Laurel smiled in spite of herself and rose from the table. Before she could leave, though, her grandmother caught her sleeve and bade her sit down again. Margaret's smile faded and Laurel wondered what new direction the discussion was about to take.

"I want to speak to you about one more thing, Laurel."

"Yes, Grandmother?"

"Jack mentioned to me this morning before breakfast that he saw you dancing with one of our tenant farmers last night."

"Yes, ma'am. Mr. Fairchild."

"Why on earth did you do that?"

"He asked me?"

"There's no need to be impertinent."

"I wasn't being–"

"Don't sass me, young lady. You're too old for that."

"I'm sorry." Laurel dropped her head and stared at the eggs drying on her plate once again.

"Laurel, married men and unmarried women do not dance together. Now, I'm not necessarily blaming you. I'm certain you had no appreciation of just how unseemly and improper it was."

A knot tightened in Laurel's stomach. Unseemly, unseemly, everything she did or said was *unseemly*.

"Young Mr. Fairchild ought to have been more concerned with your reputation, even though he never has been with his own."

Laurel glanced up from the table to face her grandmother once again. She thought it odd that Carey would knowingly tempt her to do something that others considered obviously wrong. She refused to believe this of him. "I'm quite sure Mr. Fairchild didn't know it was wrong."

"He undoubtedly knew, but didn't care. If he didn't know, then he's even wilder and more uncivilized than I imagined–and I've known him all his life."

"But he seemed very nice," Laurel protested quietly.

"Laurel, it is incumbent upon you to guard your reputation."

Laurel wanted to respond that she didn't care what the citizenry of Chisholm thought of her, but wisely kept quiet.

"All a woman has is her reputation," Margaret continued ominously. "If she loses it, she is despised."

"Life at the Hartmoor house is intolerable!" Laurel ranted to Carey as they sat in the grove that afternoon.

Laurel perched on the outcropping of limestone as always and Carey reclined on the ground at her feet, leaning against the stone with his back to her.

"All they can think of is how quickly I can be married off!"

Carey laughed at this and picked up the hem of Laurel's skirt that had fallen across his shoulder. He absentmindedly played with it.

"The subject seems to tantalize their every waking hour," Laurel continued. "It consumes all their energy. Why can't they just leave me alone?" Laurel sighed dejectedly. "They're right, though. I'm not popular. I don't have any friends."

"You have me," Carey murmured into Laurel's hem, but she didn't hear him.

"Nobody likes me. Everyone thinks I'm strange."

"I think you're wonderful." Carey was addressing Laurel's hem once again and again, she remained oblivious to his remarks.

"What's wrong with me? I want to fit in. They accuse me of not even trying and I know I haven't always been cooperative, but I have tried at times. Really, I have."

"You don't need to convince me," Carey whispered as Laurel's outburst continued. He stroked the stiff black silk fabric of Laurel's hem over his face slowly, sensuously, as though lost in another world. The silk taffeta caught against the stubble of his afternoon beard which, because it was so fair, could not yet be seen, only felt.

"How can I behave the way my Grandmother says I have to and still be true to myself? I don't want to become one of those false women that I see around me–no thoughts or opinions of their own, always deferring to everyone. They seem so foolish and yet, they're the ones who make quite the social success."

Laurel had Mary Carmichael in mind as she said this. She both envied and despised the plump and haughty Mary, whose engagement had just been announced the week before the Hartmoor picnic. Mary was the center of attention at the gathering. Everyone rushed to congratulate the happy couple and all the other young girls squealed with delight over Mary's news.

Laurel stared into the sun-drenched distance beyond the shade of poplar grove with narrowed eyes. "I guess I'm supposed to behave like Mary Carmichael."

"Mary Carmichael is an idiot," Carey whispered dreamily. The texture of the stiff black silk against the sensitive skin of his face and throat aroused him.

"I just don't know if I can bear to act like that. I promised my grandmother this morning that I would, but it just strikes me as so...so *demeaning*!" She pounded her fist against her knee for emphasis and glanced down at her audience to catch his reaction just as he mumbled something into her hem.

"Did you say something?" she asked in surprise.

"No." He grinned sheepishly up at her, tilting his chin up to see her upside down. He immediately dropped the hem of her skirt, feeling as foolish as he undoubtedly looked. "I was just agreeing with you. Are you in trouble with your Uncle Jack?"

"Oh, no, I don't think so. He didn't mention the matter to anyone but my grandmother, who, by the way, thought we'd committed the greatest crime imaginable."

"I suppose, in your family's view, we did. Can't have their own kin being seen in the company of their scum-of-the-earth tenant farmers, much less have them dare to ask you to dance." Carey sat up straight and casually hugged his knees to his chest, pillowing his chin upon his knees as he did so. He, too, stared into the bright distance with a discordant frown souring his youthful, handsome features.

"Oh, Carey." Laurel wanted to object to his grim assessment, yet she knew her family and the world of Chisholm well enough by now to realize he spoke at least an echo of the truth. She now knew without being told that Mae Fairchild would never receive a social call from the Hartmoor ladies on their calling rounds. The Fairchild family would never be invited to dine at the Hartmoor table. Receiving the charity of an invitation to the annual Fourth of July picnic, a symbolic act to honor those employed by the Hartmoor family rather than an extension of friendship, was the only civility the Fairchilds could expect of the prosperous owners of the land they worked.

"How is your injury?" Laurel inquired, embarrassed to be talking only about her own problems.

"Oh, fine. Want to see?"

Before Laurel could answer in the negative, he had already slipped off the shoulder of his overalls and yanked up his shirt tail. "It's a beaut," he boasted.

"It looks awful," she whispered as she stared at the grotesquely bruised flesh below his ribs. Then she thought how Margaret would react if she caught Laurel looking at Carey's bare torso. She would probably die. Still, Laurel couldn't bring herself to look away. She found herself perversely fascinated. A twinging sense of danger enveloped her. *Lightning in a drought year?* she wondered.

Carey seemed inordinately proud of his injury as he displayed it and pressed gingerly around its edges. Laurel fought the urge to touch the swollen, purple skin herself. And she saw more than just the bruise. Also exposed was Carey's taut waist. She could see his navel and curling dark blond hair around and below it disappearing into the waist of his under drawers. Finally, he dropped his shirt and pulled his overall back into position.

"I know what you can do," Carey announced abruptly with a mischievous grin.

"What?" She still stared at where the bruise lay, though it was no longer on view.

"Dancing lessons." He jumped to his feet and assumed the stance of a man asking a partner to dance.

"What?" Laurel repeated more forcefully.

"The key to social success," he continued with mock authority. "Come on, get up. I'll teach you to dance."

"Here? Now?" Laurel gave Carey a dubious frown. She was fairly certain he was teasing her.

"You taught me to read. I'll teach you to dance. Lessons for lessons–it's a fair exchange."

"Oh, I couldn't." Laurel blushed now that she realized he was serious.

"There you go again–still too shy. That won't do at all, Miss McBryde. If you're gonna replace Mary Carmichael as the belle of the county, you're gonna have to lose that shyness."

She giggled in spite of herself.

"I'm waiting."

"Oh, alright. Just don't make fun of me." She reluctantly stood up and took her partner's offered hand and placed her other hand awkwardly on his shoulder.

"This wallflower's gonna bloom yet," Carey said with a wink. He slowly led Laurel in the basic box step of a waltz. "One, two, three, and ...one, two, three, and–"

Laurel half-stumbled several times as she struggled to imitate his steps in reverse.

"Perhaps I should practice by myself," she suggested in frustration after stepping on Carey's foot for the second time in as many minutes.

"Oh, no. This is much more fun, don't you think?"

She glanced up from their grassy dance floor for the first time since they began the lesson. She smiled uneasily. Dancing with him was fun–more fun than it should be.

She returned her concentration to the movement of their feet. At times, she grasped his hand and shoulder so tightly to keep from losing her balance, she caused him to wince.

"Holding on for dear life, Miss McBryde?" he laughed with good-natured amusement.

"Oh, sorry." She immediately relaxed her grip. She sighed and pulled away. "Maybe I'm just not ready for civilization yet."

"I think civilization just isn't quite ready for you." He put his hands on his hips as he surveyed her with a kindly eye.

"But what's wrong with me?"

"There's nothing wrong with you. The world's what's wrong. It don't make a place for people who're different. People like you and me."

"I don't understand." She shook her head sadly.

He held out his arms once again to resume their dance. She complied, enjoying the closeness of him, the warm strength of his hand, the hard, lean muscles of his shoulder beneath his thin, homemade cotton shirt. He held her closer than before. This time her bosom touched his chest occasionally. A drop of perspiration tracked down the side of his tanned face and splashed against Laurel's cheek. He didn't notice, so she said nothing and laid her cheek against the soft cotton of his shirt to dry it. She tucked her head beneath his chin as they swayed in the afternoon heat, oblivious to their prairie surroundings in the preternatural seclusion of their poplar grove.

This must be what Alice was talking about when she tried to describe the magic of a summerhouse, Laurel thought. She decided right then and there that Alice was not quite the dimwit she had taken her for. She would have to pay more attention to her in future.

"Oh, Laurel," Carey breathed. His hand dropped from her back to encircle her waist.

She felt his arm tighten and looked up at him.

He lowered his face to hers and gave her a sensuous, lingering kiss. Laurel's first. She was surprised but she did not resist, she did not pull away. She felt a strange detachment, as though she were an observer as well as a participant. She acutely sensed the warmth of his face, the faint, scratchy stubble of his beard, the soft pressure of his lips against hers, the scent of his skin. For her, the whole world was reduced to his kiss in that instant. Nothing else mattered.

When their lips finally parted, Laurel saw a look on Carey's face she did not recognize. He was a stranger to her with his eyes half-closed and his breathing so heavy. She had never observed the look of fever-pitch desire on a man's face before and did not immediately comprehend it.

Reality struck her like a wave crashing against a jagged coast when she realized what they had just done. Angrily, she broke their embrace.

"*How could you*?" she whispered harshly.

"I...I'm sorry," he stammered, confused by her contradictory response. "Forgive me, I–"

"We had a perfect friendship. Why did you have to spoil it?"

"I couldn't help it, Laurel. What did you expect?"

"Do you think I'm some loose woman you can use as you please?" Laurel's face flushed with anger and disappointment.

"Hell, no!"

"Don't swear at me!"

"I just...I thought...I thought you were feeling the same things I was." His pale green eyes pleaded with her for reasoning, not reckoning.

"Don't presume anything," she shouted and turned her back on him. She shook her head fretfully. "This friendship meant so much to me."

"And to me."

"Now it's ruined, don't you see that? It's ruined."

"Laurel, I'm sorry. It's just that when I kissed you, you kissed me, too. You kissed me back, Laurel."

Laurel did not wish to be reminded of her complicity in their transgression. She turned to him and said coldly, "I do not wish to see you anymore."

"Laurel, I said I was sorry–"

"You should be!" She turned and stomped off in the direction of the Hartmoor house. She walked as briskly as she could, but with every step fought the urge to look back.

"Laurel. Come back. We'll talk."

Laurel ignored Carey's entreaty and marched even faster.

"Laurel, come back. *Please*."

The prairie wind erased whatever else he called. She wiped the tears that rolled down her hot cheeks. She stayed true to her resolve and did not look back.

"*Laurel*."

ꝭ

Two unpleasant days later found Laurel sitting in the porch swing with bored disinterest, staring out at the vast fields of the Hartmoor land.

"A package came for you, Laurel," Jack said as he mounted the porch steps. He casually dropped the small parcel into her lap as he passed her where she sat.

Laurel stared at the flat, rectangular object which was wrapped in brown mailing paper and carried no return address. Before Jack entered the house, he paused and turned.

"Are you going to be ready to leave after lunch?"

"My bag is in the upstairs hall."

"Taking any of your photographic nonsense with you?"

"No," she replied curtly as he left the porch. The question of her photographic equipment had already been raised and answered by Margaret two days before when Laurel had burst into the house, fresh from her regrettable meeting with Carey, and had demanded that Margaret contact Lydia immediately to ask if Laurel could visit her as soon as possible.

Margaret had met Laurel's request with less suspicion than Laurel had anticipated and had actually shown some enthusiasm for the idea. Lydia responded with similar interest by return post and Laurel was to leave in the afternoon for Wichita. Jack would drive her there and see to a business matter as well.

Laurel examined the package carefully and guessed what was contained inside by the familiar weight and shape. She carried the package upstairs to her room to open it in privacy. When she tore the paper off she found just what she expected: the volume of Shakespeare she had given to Carey weeks before.

Well, now it is really over, she thought as she sourly stared at the book. In sudden anger, she threw the book to the floor. She immediately felt foolish for such a childish gesture. Such a display of emotion was more fitting to Christine, not a grown woman like herself.

She stooped down and picked it up. It was only then that she discovered the true reason for the book's return. The inside front cover contained a brief message that was not there before she loaned the copy to Carey. Pencilled in carefully measured block printing were the words:

"*Frends, still? Pleese.*"

The sentiment in the short message found its way through the poor spelling. She sighed in exasperation. She desperately wished to resolve the matter somehow, but now it was too late. She did not know what to do. When her anger melted away enough to review the incident more carefully in her mind, she had stopped blaming him totally for what happened. The fact remained, she had not only returned his kiss, but had enjoyed it. She was as guilty as he was.

She doubted she could ever see him as merely a friend again after that. And yet she already missed him so terribly. The day she left him calling after her in the poplar grove she was convinced she should never see him again.

Now her resolve had retreated slightly. Was there a possibility their friendship could recover?

Her mind whirled. She debated whether to tell the Hartmoors she had suffered second thoughts about leaving, but quickly discounted the idea. To turn down Lydia's invitation–after she had initiated the visit herself–would be unforgivably rude. Perhaps some weeks apart would put better perspective on her unresolved feelings for Carey.

Whatever she decided, she would need to act quickly. Without further delay, she penned the words: "Maybe. August 1," into the inside cover of the book, just below Carey's message.

The first day of August had been tentatively set as her return from Wichita. She hoped Carey would understand the brief message to be an appointment of sorts. She feared to be more explicit lest someone else find the book before Carey.

She ran down the stairs with a clatter of her boots upon the wooden treads and the swish of her cotton petticoats against the rail.

"Where are you going?" Margaret called from the dining room as she heard Laurel pass in a rush.

"Out. Need to run an errand before I leave."

"But dinner will be ready in a dash. Come back."

"Sorry, this can't wait," Laurel called back as the screened porch door slammed shut behind her.

"Laurel!"

But Laurel was off at a run down the steps and across the yard before her grandmother's reprimand could be heard or answered.

Before arriving at the grove, she stopped to catch her breath in the hot noon sun. She squinted to determine if it was deserted. She wished to avoid seeing him again so soon.

Satisfied she was alone, she entered the grove and placed the book on the familiar outcropping of limestone.

A sudden breeze rattled through the poplar leaves. She jumped at the sound. Then she laughed. I'm as nervous as a thief, she thought. She hurried back to the house so as not to be too late for the meal and risk her grandmother's further displeasure.

Chapter Ten

"Aunt Lydia, why isn't it possible for men and women to be friends?"

Laurel's question broke the silence of nearly half an hour as the two women sat quietly rocking in the wooden swing which hung from the roof of the small back porch of Lydia's house. The house was not so much a house as a living quarters built behind and over the dry goods store.

The back porch faced the alley, not a scenic view, but clean and quiet after business hours. Pale yellow light from the gas street lamp at the mouth of the alley fell across their laps.

Even at ten in the evening, the air lay still and oppressively warm. Each day of July grew hotter than the last. By the third week of the heat wave, the inhabitants of the sun-baked plains began to lose their taste for recording the details of the thermal siege.

"I have the distinct impression that question sprung from a much longer train of thought to which I have not been privy, Laurel." Lydia smiled indulgently in the darkness at her niece.

The pair rocked silently to stir the humid air. Laurel, beneath her furrowed brow did not see her aunt's amusement. She struggled with just how much of her dilemma with Carey to reveal. Over the course of her three week stay, she had grown to not only like her Aunt Lydia, but value her opinion. If anyone could counsel her, it would have to be Lydia, who didn't know Carey and would not pre-judge him.

She would be returning to Chisholm soon and knew she would miss these quiet evenings on Lydia's back porch. She liked the comfortable silence Lydia allowed in her house. In the homes of Chisholm, conversation was expected and silences were tense and unpleasant. Even at Windrift with her father, Laurel had been expected to converse on some notable topic or read aloud. With Lydia, talk was never forced unnaturally by motives as superficial as courtesy.

Laurel liked her aunt's house as well. Though it was small and not particularly comfortable, it was funny and unique like its owner. The rooms were cluttered with newspapers and newspaper clippings, cut out and then abandoned. Pieces of clothing that wanted mending were strewn about, forgotten and waiting. Books lay scattered everywhere, sitting open to the last page read or stuffed with whatever happened to have been near when a book mark was needed.

Lydia's house reminded Laurel of her old home at Windrift. The careless disarray of Lydia's living quarters sat squarely at odds with the spotless order of the Chisholm Hartmoors where an almost antiseptic cleanliness prevailed.

"House cleaning is the work of menials," Lydia was heard to say on several occasions during Laurel's stay, though Laurel observed that Lydia spent countless hours keeping her little store as neat and well-groomed as any Hartmoor could wish.

The order of Lydia's house might have been so awry as to disturb even Laurel's unrefined sensibilities, but Lydia's shop–Guire's Dry Goods–did not know a poorly rolled bolt of cloth nor a misplaced pair of scissors. The areas of Lydia's life held most dear to her were clearly revealed, even to the most casual observer.

"What's really on your mind, Laurel?"

"Well...I know a person. And that person is a man."

"Sounds interesting already."

"It's not really funny."

"Forgive me."

"Anyway, we're friends. He's a better friend than I've ever had before–except for my father. But a family member doesn't count as a friend. Anyway, I was always happy when I was with him and–" Laurel paused and looked over at her aunt intently. "If I told you something, would you promise not to tell Grandmother, or anyone else?"

Lydia nodded uncertainly, so Laurel continued.

"Now there's a problem–I think he might be in love with me."

"That's an odd problem," Lydia laughed. She sobered when she perceived the pain in Laurel's face. "Don't you love him back?"

"Oh, no, ma'am. But I do *like* him severely."

Lydia laughed again. "Did he tell you he loved you?"

"No, but he tried to kiss me." Laurel was not ready to admit to Lydia or any other living soul that more had occurred than that.

"Oh, my."

"But we have to be friends. Nothing more. I want it to stay that way."

"That will disappoint your grandmother."

"You don't understand. He's my best friend in the world, but love is out of the question."

"But why?"

"There...there are...complications." Laurel did not feel comfortable enough with Lydia to reveal that the "complication" had a name and a title, specifically Mae Fairchild, Carey's wife. She sighed with piquant melodrama. "I guess men and women are not supposed to be friends. I mean, not the way men are friends and women are friends. It's as though there were a rule that there can only be love between men and women or nothing at all."

"Love is seldom logical enough to follow rules, Laurel." The tone of Lydia's voice was amused, but not unkind.

"But *society* has rules. Great heaps of them. And Grandmother knows them all."

"And you're certain society has a rule?"

"Oh, yes."

"Then maybe society is wrong."

Laurel cocked her head with interest. She liked debating and discussing with Lydia almost as much as she enjoyed the comfortable silences.

She liked everything about her visit to Wichita, so far. During the days, while Lydia busied herself minding the store, Laurel went out on her own to explore the city. Each day brought some new experience. The flood of fresh images made her ache to record them. Many times she longed to lug her camera equipment about with her on her excursions.

She had even been tempted to buy an amateur snapshot camera. The amazing portability of its small size and simplicity of operation intrigued her, but economic pressures curbed her extravagance. The camera, with its 100-shot roll of film, cost a whopping $25.00. The tiny allowance Jack gave her did not allow for such whims.

Evenings had included visits to ice cream parlors and roller skating emporiums and other such exotic amusements. She enjoyed reading the morning and evening newspapers from cover to cover. Chisholm had only one daily paper and local gossip filled its pages. Jack received the Wichita morning paper at the bank and often brought it home with him, but to have a fresh paper delivered to one's doorstep, morning and evening, as well as twice daily mail deliveries, struck Laurel as the height of civilization.

One portion of the paper she read with extra attention was the local help-wanted ads in the classified section. Each day she eagerly scanned the "Positions for Hire" only to be disappointed by the lack of occupations open to women. Laundresses, wet nurses, waitresses, and housekeepers predominated the "female" listings.

Laurel had already tried unsuccessfully to secure a job at Jack's bank. She had cautiously approached him on the porch after supper one evening when he seemed to be in a rare good mood. She knew she was interrupting his usual post-dinner retreat to the porch to smoke a cigarette or small cigar, but this seemed to be the only time she could have a private word with him.

"What kind of job do you think you are qualified for?" her uncle had asked, seemingly amused by her very presumption.

Laurel had shrugged. "I'm quick with figures. Perhaps I could be a teller." She sat down across from him in Margaret's usual seat, trying to place herself upwind from his cigarette smoke.

"All our tellers are *men*, Laurel." Uncle Jack's tone had implied this fact was so obvious, he didn't know why he needed to point it out to her.

"Why can't a teller be a woman?"

Jack frowned at Laurel's ignorance, afraid she might be trying to bait him into yet another debate on the tiresome issue of women's suffrage. "My customers would not feel comfortable transacting business with a woman. They would take their funds elsewhere before they would deal with so unprofessional an enterprise as one hiring young girls to handle their monetary concerns. I have enough trouble convincing people to trust banks at all with their money. It's a relationship built on trust. I spend half of every day explaining to people why they should put their money in my bank rather than stuffing their mattress with it."

Laurel giggled.

"I'm entirely serious on this point. Many around here still remember the Panic of '73."

Laurel shrugged blankly.

"Well, you're too young to remember, but I assure you it gave every member of the financial community an unwarranted black eye. And then there's all this current nonsense going around about abolishing national banks."

"The Farmer's Alliance?"

"Ridiculous anarchists."

"The farmers just want fairness, Uncle Jack."

"The farmers want a handout at my expense. Those radicals don't know what they're talking about. And let me point out that *women* are foremost in their ranks."

Laurel had sighed, defeated, and rose to leave.

Jack raised his eyebrows and ended the discussion with a shake of his head and a mumbled, "Female bank tellers."

Laurel had almost given up hope of finding an occupation to call her own. She now pursued the discussion with her aunt, enlivened by the prospect of a good debate that warm summer evening. The previous months of simply being told she was wrong about everything by the Hartmoors had worn her down.

"How can society be right or wrong?" she asked after turning her aunt's statement over in her mind several times. "It just exists. It's not a person."

"I'm speaking more about...the general consensus of opinion. An attitude the majority shares."

"And shouldn't I share it? I mean if I want to be happy?"

"I think my point is that you should share it only if it *makes* you happy. You needn't be too influenced by the opinions of others."

Laurel grinned at the essential anarchy of this line of thought. "Does my grandmother know you think this way?"

Lydia chuckled. "I doubt Margaret would share my views on everything. She certainly disapproves of my work for the Equal Suffrage Association."

"Oh, Aunt Lydia, I think it's exciting. Why is it you never mentioned it during your visit? Perhaps I could do some work for the cause in Chisholm."

"The Hartmoors forgive me my radical leanings as long as I don't bring them to the dinner table. In fact, I'm afraid I was under orders not to mention such matters to you."

"Don't worry–I won't tell Grandmother." Laurel giggled conspiratorially. "But you must promise to tell me more."

"Only if I can hear more about this mysterious suitor of yours."

"He's not a suitor, Aunt Lydia." Laurel turned abruptly serious. "You mustn't call him that and you must never breathe a word of this to the other Hartmoors."

"Now, Laurel, I promised, didn't I?"

"What was it you meant earlier when you said I need not be influenced by society's rules? Is that why you're a suffragist?"

"I suppose, in a way."

Laurel studied her aunt's strong features in the dim gas light as she continued to speak. She admired Lydia's independent, sometimes irreverent, outlook. She found a kindness and a wisdom there, but a hard, steely shell as well. Her voice possessed a timbre and her words a cadence that made people listen to her carefully.

"The problem with society, as I see it," Lydia continued, "is that these rules we live by aren't necessarily based on truth. They don't allow people to simply be themselves. Look at the ridiculous presumptions society makes about women, for example. The rights of married women–"

"Absolutely. Married women don't have any rights. That's why my father advised me never to marry."

"I suppose he envisioned you keeping house for him indefinitely."

"I guess so. I'm so confused. Grandmother and Aunt Alice keep telling me how every woman wants to be married, how that's the fulfillment of their destiny, and that God designed them to be mothers–"

Lydia chuckled.

"It's not funny, Aunt Lydia. It scares me, in fact. And in order to catch a husband, they expect me to *demean* myself. They keep telling me I speak too freely and too directly. They say I have to pretend to be silly and empty-headed in order to attract male attention." This was not exactly how Margaret and Alice had attempted to explain the art of flirtation, but it was certainly the way Laurel had come to understand it. "I refuse to act like a fool, just so some stupid oaf can feel good about himself!"

"I'm sure no one is suggesting you demean yourself, Laurel. You must be comfortable with your actions or they will never be right."

Laurel sighed and kicked out her skirts to stir the heavy night air. She thought over her situation for several minutes more.

"If men and women were friends, then perhaps..." Laurel could not think of how to finish her sentence.

"I don't see friendship and love as mutually exclusive. Can't you 'love' a friend?"

"No."

"Do what you feel is right, Laurel. Don't worry so much about other people. Don't throw away something special on a matter of definition."

"Other people just wouldn't understand," Laurel mumbled. She would love to have taken Lydia's advice, yet she knew her aunt had offered it without full knowledge of the facts. Her emotions and logic remained tangled in confusion.

Lydia smiled at Laurel's seriousness and fondly put her arm around her shoulder. The two women left the back porch to prepare for bed.

"Laurel, would you really like to know more about my political activities?" Lydia asked before Laurel put her lamp out.

Laurel nodded vigorously.

"Well, then I think I should perhaps introduce you to a new friend of mine. She's become active in a number of women's groups that I attend here in Wichita and she's quite the most arresting speaker I've ever heard, male or female. Yes, you'll have to meet Mrs. Lease."

On the following Tuesday evening, Laurel and Lydia closed her shop early and headed for the social hall of the Congregational Church. The hall, located in the basement of the church, was only marginally cooler than the street level rooms. Ladies' fans swooshed up a roar to rival a flock of geese in the crowded hall filled with middle-class men and women in wilting cotton summer clothes.

A Mrs. Randolph called the meeting to order and everyone seated themselves on wooden chairs that squeaked and clattered against the polished oak flooring.

"Tonight, let us welcome a speaker of resonance and renown," said Mrs. Randolph. "Her name is Mrs. Mary Ellen Lease. You may know her husband, Mr. Charles Lease. He owns the pharmacy just a few blocks off Market Street. Mrs. Lease has been kind enough to speak to our group here tonight. Please give her a warm welcome."

Lydia squeezed Laurel's hand and the pair exchanged smiles as Mrs. Lease stepped up to the podium. Nearly six feet in height, she made a commanding figure, and, with her hair swept up in a prim psyche knot, she appeared taller still.

"I am pleased to speak to this wonderful group," began Mrs. Lease in a voice so strong and rich, Laurel could feel gooseflesh prickle her clammy skin. "There can be no finer endeavor than assuring that women are accorded the franchise which is their right if we are truly to call America a democracy..."

For the next hour and forty-five minutes, Laurel sat dazzled and enchanted by Mrs. Lease's stirring rhetoric. She spoke on a variety of issues beyond just women's suffrage. She addressed the subject of reform on many levels, citing current economic woes and the hardships the farmers seemed to bear in disproportion to the population at large. Laurel listened intently as Mrs. Lease enumerated with such acute clarity the problems Carey had so often lamented in simpler language.

Laurel envied Mrs. Lease's composure and her passion. To stand up in front of so large a group and utterly take control–what must that kind of power feel like?

At the end of an extensive question and answer period, during which a local newspaper reporter made several rude and uncalled for remarks relating to Mrs. Lease's appearance rather than her politics, the meeting concluded with the singing of a suffrage song, written to the tune of "Battle Hymn of the Republic."

There's a wave of indignation
Rolling round and round the land,
And it's meaning is so mighty
And its mission is so grand,
That none but knaves and cowards
Dare deny its just demand,
As we go marching on.
    Men and brothers, dare you do it?
    Men and brothers, dare you do it?
    Men and brothers, dare you do it,
    As we go marching on?
Whence came your foolish notion
Now so greatly overgrown,
That a woman's sober judgment
Is not equal to your own?
Has God ordained that suffrage
Is a gift to you alone,
    While life goes marching on?

Chapter Eleven

When the first day of August arrived, Jack Hartmoor ventured to Wichita to bring Laurel home. After seeing to a business matter at the Fourth National Bank, he called for Laurel at Lydia's store. As uncle and niece rode along in the open buggy, a fierce hot wind whipped across the prairie.

Each blistering gust singed Laurel's face and forced her to shield her eyes with the edge of her plain black bonnet. She silently cursed the incessant south wind and was growing to hate it as much as the rest of the Hartmoors.

She had never hated the south wind when she lived at Windrift. It blew just as constantly there, but at Windrift no conversations were rendered inaudible–there was no one to talk to. No embarrassment was occasioned when skirts were tossed high or hair was pulled from combs–there was no one to see.

In Chisholm, the only time Laurel liked the south wind was at night when it caused the house to rattle and creak. Some nights she imagined the stolid Hartmoor house magically swaying in the fierce breezes. Unfortunately, such nights usually ended up with little Christine running to Laurel's bed for protection from all the noisy bogey men she imagined were outside creating the woeful din.

"My guess is these winds will bring in a thunderstorm," Jack observed as another wave of dust caused them both to flinch.

"I hope so," murmured Laurel as an appropriate reply. The parched land needed rain so desperately. She squinted her eyes towards the southwestern horizon. A dark haze grew, barely visible, in the distance, perhaps confirming her uncle's prediction. Though she knew the land needed rain, she worried a storm might interfere with the appointment she had made for this afternoon.

"Did you enjoy your visit to Wichita?" Jack seemed to be making a rare, but sincere effort at conversation.

"Oh, very much. I rode in an electric trolley car and I ate my noon meal in restaurants every day."

"My sister-in-law is not famous for her cooking." Jack smiled into the distance.

Laurel was forced to share his little joke at Lydia's expense. "When it came to food, I was pretty much on my own!"

Jack laughed out loud. "Is her kitchen still the nightmare it always used to be?"

"Once a week a little German girl comes in and cleans it up for her."

"Poor little German girl!" They both laughed together. "My brother Marcus used to say...." Jack's voice trailed off and his humor faded.

"Oh, I also talked on a telephone."

Jack smiled at this. "Amazing, isn't it? I plan to bring telephone service to Chisholm soon."

"Uncle Jack, that would be grand."

"Well, glad you approve," Jack murmured with a slight hint of condescension. "No one else in town seems to understand the importance of the issue."

"Would we have our own telephone at the house?"

"Not initially. But at the bank, of course. And at other businesses around town. Eventually lines could extend to our home." Jack sighed. "Of course, I'll have to line up more investors before that day comes."

"It's very expensive, I suppose?" Laurel was not really so interested in the business of telephones as she pretended. She was so surprised to have stumbled upon a topic of conversation her uncle actually seemed to enjoy, she was loathe to let it go.

"I've set aside roughly $10,000 for my own share, but I'll have to find several more like-minded persons with investment capital before I can see this plan through."

Laurel nodded silently, impressed with her uncle's willingness to invest in the future. If only he were more forward-thinking in his politics, she might learn to like him.

She tried to think of additional questions to ask about telephone service, but could not, so the conversation drifted away once more. As they rode along in silence, Laurel shifted in her seat again and again, never quite finding a comfortable position.

"I learned how to roller skate," she finally volunteered to break the awkward silence. When he didn't respond immediately, she continued. "Have you ever skated, Uncle Jack?"

"Once...when I was courting your Aunt Alice. It's not something I'll ever be tempted to try again, I assure you."

Laurel looked away and smiled. The thought of her serious uncle attempting something as frivolous as roller skating was funny. Had he done it just to please Alice? That was hard to imagine. He never seemed to go out of his way to please her now that they were married. He had never built her the summerhouse she longed for. Laurel hoped the man she married–if she ever married–would not feel that the wedding completely ended his initiative to please.

Jack proved right about the weather. By the time they reached home, the hot winds changed to cool ones. The temperature dropped nearly twenty degrees in the space of time it took them to cover the distance between Chisholm and the Hartmoor farm.

As the family sat down to their noonday meal, roasted beef with rich gravy, turnips, and mashed potatoes, the windows of the dining room shook with the force of the thunderstorm about to commence. Massive anvil heads formed angry white towers in the sky. They moved closer and closer together, and soon filled up the blue corridors between them. Thunder echoed down the fields surrounding the house.

Christine wailed as each new roar of thunder rattled the windows. Finally, Alice gave up trying to talk her daughter out of her fears and took her upstairs to bed to distract her through the storm with stories and games. Laurel secretly sighed with relief that she was not asked to take this duty.

Not only was she hungry from her journey–and her grandmother's cooking was so infinitely superior to her Aunt Lydia's–she wanted to be free to keep her afternoon appointment. She anxiously glanced out the window many times during the meal, wondering if the wild weather would make her decision for her. Nagging doubts about the proposed meeting with Carey had plagued her throughout her visit with Lydia. Ultimately she had decided to keep the meeting and was thus prevented from accepting her aunt's generous offer to stay on in Wichita until fall.

Her anticipation of meeting with Carey again made dinner table conversation with her family difficult. While Cassandra peppered her with questions about her experiences in Wichita, Margaret quietly studied her granddaughter. At the end of the meal, she finally spoke.

"How do you intend to spend your time now that you've returned to us, Laurel?"

"Well, first off, I thought I'd go to work in my darkroom and get all the prints made of the picnic."

"A good idea. Several of our friends have made polite inquiries about your abilities as a photographer, since no pictures have been forthcoming."

"Did you explain that I was out of town?"

"Don't worry about it, Laurel," said Cassandra. "Most of the folks around here have never seen a photograph of themselves, much less seen a *female* photographer."

"Speaking of which," added Margaret, "I overheard quite a discussion of you, Laurel, at the ice cream social after church two weeks ago."

"And who is so lost for conversational topics that they are forced to discuss me behind my back?"

Margaret's gaze and voice sharpened as she apparently neared the true focus of her remarks. "Several young men of the neighborhood were expressing opinions about you. The general consensus seemed to be that they felt photography to be an unfeminine pursuit. One young man, however, came staunchly to your defense."

Alice reappeared in the dining room to announce that Christine had fallen asleep. "I hope the thunder doesn't wake her up," she murmured as she sat down to finish the cold remains of her meal.

"Who would that be?" asked Laurel of Margaret. Tension electrified her as she perceived her grandmother's disapproval.

"One of our tenant farmers, Carey Fairchild."

"Just like Fairchild," snorted Jack from behind his newspaper. "Loves to be different."

"You could do no wrong in his book, Laurel," Margaret continued. "You've apparently made quite an impression on him."

Laurel's cheeks burned with chagrin.

"Well, see there, Laurel," Cassandra jibed. "The feeling is mutual between you and Carey."

Laurel now thought she would die of embarrassment. Being reminded of the humiliation she had felt after openly admiring Carey's physical attributes the day she arrived seemed to come back to haunt her endlessly.

"Oh, Cassie, don't tease poor Laurel about a careless remark she made months ago."

Laurel smiled gratefully over the table to Alice to thank her for taking her defense.

"Laurel can take a joke," insisted Cassandra.

"Since when?" asked Jack.

"*Husband*, that remark was unkind."

"*Wife*, I did not intend any unkindness."

Of course, you didn't, thought Laurel bitterly.

"I reckon we all could stand to take ourselves a little less seriously," Margaret intoned. She looked directly at her son as she spoke.

"Too bad Carey's married," Cassandra continued mischievously. "I mean, seeing as how he and Laurel are sweet on each other."

Jack threw down his paper. "I don't think any kin of mine would stoop to marrying a field hand."

"He's not a field hand, he's one of our tenants," Cassandra persisted, never shrinking from a fight with either her brother or her sister-in-law.

"He's a good first baseman," Jack observed. "But hardly someone we'd invite to enter our home, much less our family."

"Jack is right, Cassandra," Margaret announced as she rose from her seat and began to collect the dishes. "No Hartmoor woman would be so desperate as to marry *that* far beneath her."

"Excuse me, please," Laurel mumbled and hurried out of the room instead of helping with the dishes as was usual. She dashed out to the front porch to sit in the porch swing. She felt like her grandmother had just slapped her in the face. A strong wave of dust stung her face and eyes. Large drops of rain began to fall in the dry, cracked yard.

By mid-afternoon, the thunderstorm raged full-force. Rain poured down in heavy sheets, slapping the sides of the house like waves. Laurel watched the storm with nervous intensity. At three o'clock, she decided to venture out, despite the weather. Feeling foolish and foolhardy, she wrapped a rain cape around her shoulders, located a large, black umbrella behind the front hall coat tree, and slipped out the back door, hoping her absence would not be noticed.

The stormy winds blew so strongly, she could barely walk against them. When she finally neared the grove, she squinted against the pelting rain. The tall, slender trees waved madly with each torrential gust. She could not keep her eyes fixed on her target long enough to make out enough detail.

She stopped, suddenly filled with doubts. No one would come out in weather like this. Perhaps he had never even gotten her return message. Perhaps he hadn't understood its intended meaning. Perhaps he had totally forgotten her–or worse, lost interest in her once he understood they were only to be friends.

Just as she was about to soundly curse herself for being so ridiculous and stupid to have come out at all, she reached the edge of the grove and there, sitting on the familiar outcropping of limestone, entirely wrapped in a large gray tarpaulin, sat Carey, the author of all her foolish distress.

"I'm glad to see you're as crazy as I am. Welcome home." He lifted the tarp to beckon her to sit next to him. She closed her umbrella and warily joined him under the makeshift rain shelter.

She giggled nervously at their close proximity. Fortunately, he made no move to kiss her now. She could feel the heat of his body in their humid tent of treated canvas. The scent of his wet hair and skin mixed with the smell of her muddy skirt hems and made for a heady, sensual stew.

They both stopped smiling simultaneously and stared at the wall of awkwardness that stood between them. Nothing would ever be quite as free and easy as it had been before.

"Laurel...I wouldn't have blamed you if you'd never wanted to see me again. Just let me say I'm terrible sorry about what happened last time we was here and–"

She raised her hand to silence him. "It's alright. I accept your apology and if I'm to blame in any way–"

"No, no...it's not your fault at all. I don't know what got into me. I'd bite my own tongue off before I'd insult you. It won't happen again, I swear it. I'll swear it on the heads of my children if I have to."

Laurel smiled. "I don't think that will be necessary." His declaration flattered her. His words carried the ring of preparation to them. "Just promise we'll be friends forever."

"I thought that was mighty obvious by now."

"Good," she said primly. She looked into her lap and stretched out the hopelessly wrinkled fabric of her skirt.

"So, how was Wichita?"

"Amazing." She launched into a litany of all her many activities of the last few weeks, concluding with the shocking revelation of her Aunt Lydia's affiliation with the Equal Suffrage Association. "By the way, you do support the cause of women's suffrage, don't you?"

"Women's suffering?"

"Women getting the right to vote."

Carey grinned. "It sounds like I better say yes."

"How do you feel? We've never really discussed this before." She would never have admitted it to Carey, but she had harbored a secret resentment of the fact that Carey, a man who, prior to her teaching could not read or write, had the ability to vote and she did not.

"I never really thought about it. I guess I don't mind one way or the other."

Laurel was mildly disappointed by this lukewarm endorsement, but at least he was not opposed to the idea, like her uncle and aunt. She wondered how Cassandra felt on the issue. Not that Cassandra gave a hoot about anything that did not involve horse flesh.

"The most amazing aspect of my whole visit was getting to hear Mrs. Lease speak. She said the most interesting things about the farm situation."

"Mary Ellen Lease? I've heard of her–they call her 'Yellin' Ellen,' don't they?" Carey grinned.

"I hope they don't mean any disrespect by it," worried Laurel. "She's quite the most dynamic speaker I've ever heard in my life. She gave me gooseflesh with her speech. Do you know what she says?" Laurel leaned close to Carey, scandalized to repeat Mrs. Lease's exhortation. "She says Kansas farmers should raise less corn and more hell!"

"Good for her! I like her already."

The sun came out just in time to set. Carey shook out the tarp and Laurel pulled off her sodden rain cape. Lateral orange rays stretched out between the heavy clouds that formed the leftover remnants of the afternoon cloud burst. The world of the prairie bloomed green-tinged and steamy.

"How have the Cyclones been doing in my absence?"

"Not our best summer. Three wins, three losses. But last week I hit a home run in the eighth inning."

"And that's good?"

Carey laughed. "Yes, that's good."

"Congratulations, then."

Carey extended his hand to her for a proper handshake.

"Since all other forms of contact shall be strictly forbidden," he explained with grand formality, mocking her good-naturedly once again.

She blithely curtsied as she gave him her hand. "I'm glad to be home." Then she realized that this was the first time she had ever referred to Chisholm as home. Still, she would not allow the big, carved "H" over the Hartmoor door to stand for "home" just yet. "Harmony," perhaps. She would at least grudgingly go that far.

"Tomorrow?" he asked casually as they parted.

"Of course."

Chapter Twelve

Each morning, after the breakfast dishes were done, Laurel retreated to her darkroom in the upstairs hall closet. Mornings were the only time of day cool enough for her to bear the stifling atmosphere of the tiny windowless room. Even then, the room lacked sufficient ventilation and occasionally caused her to swoon from the fumes of her developing chemicals.

For a week, she worked diligently printing the numerous copies of the Fourth of July picnic group–one print for each family in the picture. She proudly displayed them at the breakfast table when she had completed the project.

"These are wonderful," exclaimed Margaret as she examined Laurel's work.

"Everyone will be so impressed," chimed in Cassandra.

Even Jack gave an approving nod.

Laurel glowed with pride. So rarely was she showered with compliments by the Hartmoors, the experience felt strange.

"We shall wrap each one in a tissue covering and place each family's name on it–just like a present," said Alice with enthusiasm. "Won't that make a nice impression?"

She and Alice set to work on the wrapping project immediately. By early afternoon all the pictures were ready, save the one Christine tore in two during one of several tantrums she threw over not being allowed to help her mother and Cousin Laurel with their work.

Alice, embarrassed by Christine's destructive temper, apologized profusely to Laurel.

"It's alright," Laurel responded. "I'll stay home and reprint the last one and deliver it myself while you and Grandmother deliver the rest."

"But Laurel, you must come with us on our round of calls. That's the whole point. I mean...um...that's not what I meant to say. We just thought it would be nice for you to have an opportunity to visit with our neighbors and–"

"Aunt Alice, I couldn't. I would feel...too self-conscious."

"Oh, oh, well, I don't know how your grandmother will feel about this." Alice's long thin hands fluttered with anxiety. She seemed to live in fear of upsetting her mother-in-law in any way.

"She'll understand," Laurel tossed off confidently as she left to return to her darkroom and reprint the last shot. She dashed up the stairs and retreated into her suffocating womb of a work space before anyone could stop her. She smiled to herself that Christine's bratty action had accomplished two goals for Laurel simultaneously: She had an excuse to avoid the much dreaded round of social calls and she was able to make sure that the Fairchild family's was the copy to be reprinted, thus giving her an excuse to pay a call of her own on Carey's house and meet his family.

She had just donned her oil cloth apron and heavy rubber gloves when Margaret jerked the door of her darkroom wide open.

"Grandmother! I've told you–I've *begged* you–never open this door without knocking. You could have spoiled a print or worse, a negative. I must have total darkness."

"What's this Alice has told me about your not coming with us to deliver the photographs."

"I'm busy," Laurel replied.

"Doing what, may I ask?"

"Didn't Aunt Alice tell you? Christine tore up one of the prints. I've got to make a new one or one family will feel left out."

"And you can't finish this tomorrow?"

Laurel thought quickly. "Uh...the chemicals are still fresh and I can get two uses out of them and...and...I wouldn't want the one family to find out that they were...uh...neglected or second best."

Margaret frowned at Laurel's bizarre explanation. She turned to leave, then turned back again. "Laurel, just what, pray, occupies all your spare time? You manage to disappear completely every afternoon."

Laurel stiffened. "I walk. I read. Sometimes I make photographs. I just like to be alone, that's all." A knot formed in Laurel's stomach from so much bold-faced lying. She knew well enough that spending time alone with Carey, no matter how innocent–indeed, spending time with any male without the protection of a proper chaperon–would not meet with Margaret's approval.

"Most ordinary people don't like to be alone, leastways not as much as you do, child."

Laurel shrugged and tried to look hurt, though she actually was not insulted by her grandmother's remarks at all. "I can't help it if I'm not ordinary."

Margaret gave up with an irritated sigh and left Laurel alone with her chemicals.

Laurel chose her moment to visit the Fairchild family with care. She wanted to meet Mae, but did not want to meet her alone. She hurried out the back door immediately following supper to catch the family in the evening before the children were in bed.

She ran most of the way, but slowed her pace to catch her breath once the Fairchild house was in sight. Seeing the small sod house again depressed her. Simplicity may have had its virtues, but there was nothing simple about the raw life offered by the grim little homestead.

She reached the door and listened for a moment. She heard Carey's voice above the chatter of the two little girls and decided to knock. Her sharp rap upon the door produced an uproar inside the house, suggesting to Laurel that visitors were a rare occurrence.

Five-year-old Rachel Fairchild opened the door a crack. As soon as Carey saw who stood on his porch, he immediately dashed out to greet her. The large flat slab of limestone that served as the porch could only accommodate two adults comfortably, so the moment Mae Fairchild appeared, carrying two-year-old Caroline on her hip, Carey ushered everyone into the yard.

Laurel thought it odd that he did not invite her inside. She wondered if he were ashamed of where he lived. Such vanity seemed out of character for him.

"Forgive me for arriving unannounced. I just stopped by to bring you this photograph," Laurel stammered with a nervous smile. She hastily added, "I made one for every family in the picture."

Carey pulled the print carefully from its tissue wrapping and all the Fairchilds strained to find their faces in the small picture. "Why look, Mae, there we all are."

"Where? Where?" demanded little Rachel.

He knelt to Rachel's level and pointed. "Right here. See? There's Mama and Daddy and Sister and you."

"That's me?" Rachel grinned up at Laurel.

"This is extraordinary," Carey enthused.

"*Extraordinary*?" Mae mocked her husband. "Where did you get a word like *extraordinary*?"

Carey ignored his wife's remark and instead introduced everyone. "Mae, this is Miss McBryde. She's Mrs. Hartmoor's grand–"

"We've met," Mae curtly interrupted.

"Why, of course, at the picnic." Laurel tried to sound friendly.

"Yes, yes, foolish of me," Carey laughed and waved the photograph. "Thank you for this, Miss McBryde. I don't reckon this family's ever had our picture taken before. Have we, Mae?"

Mae was in the process of shifting Caroline from one hip to the other and either did not hear her husband's question or pretended not to.

Laurel regarded Mae's waistline, swollen with six or seven months of pregnancy beneath Mae's loose, ill-fitting cotton dress. Mae and the rest of the family were barefoot.

"If you'd like, I could take a family portrait of you all," ventured Laurel. "I'd enjoy–"

"No, thank you, Miss." Mae's cool tone caused Laurel to instantly regret her offer.

"But Mae, I think it's a wonderful idea," Carey said as Rachel pulled the photograph from his hand.

"No, *thank you*," Mae repeated, more rudely than before. Setting down the toddler, Mae turned and went back in the house.

Carey flashed an embarrassed frown in Laurel's direction, then followed his wife inside, slamming the door behind him.

Laurel and the two little girls stared dumbly after them as the sound of angry voices sifted through the door. The words were blurred, but the topic of their argument was not hard to guess.

In a few moments, the little girls lost interest in their parents' quarrel and found other amusements in the yard. Laurel stood alone, feeling ridiculous and sorry she had come. She picked up the photograph which Rachel had dropped on the ground and placed it on the porch before turning to leave.

The following afternoon Laurel ventured to the grove, uncertain whether Carey would meet her there or not. She was surprised to find him waiting for her when she arrived.

"I'm sorry about last night," he blurted out as soon as she entered the circle of trees.

"No, *I'm* sorry. It was rude of me to come without an invitation."

"It's not that. Mae just...Mae don't like you."

"She doesn't even know me."

"She's still mad that I asked you to dance at the picnic. I guess she's jealous or something. I don't know. Let's start reading."

Laurel was satisfied to let the embarrassing subject of last night drop and they assumed their customary positions, Laurel seated on the outcropping of limestone and Carey lying at her feet. He opened the book she had brought, "Great Expectations," by Mr. Dickens, and haltingly began to read.

The late August afternoon stretched out still and humid. The waxy leaves of the towering poplars hung silent with not even the hint of a breeze to stir them. Laurel idly fanned herself with a piece of folded newspaper she had been using as a bookmark. Teasingly, she fanned Carey now and then.

"Thank you," he said, pausing to take a drink from his canteen. He wiped his mouth on his forearm and offered her the canteen.

She took a sip, then paused, thinking about how the canteen had just touched Carey's lips. She remembered his kiss, the taste and feel of it. She blushed when she opened her eyes to realize he was watching her. She quickly handed back the canteen.

"Carey, can I ask you a personal question?"

"Always."

"How did you and Mae first meet?"

He smiled and shrugged. "I never really 'met' her. I knew her all my life. Her folks had a place just east of here."

"Still?"

"They moved away not long after we was married. Their name was Brock. Haven't heard from them in years."

"Doesn't that make Mae sad? I mean, I didn't see the Hartmoors for years, but we stayed in touch. Letters, birthday presents–"

"Mae can't read, Laurel," Carey interrupted. "Besides, there was never much love lost between Mae and her family. Mae's just so–" Carey stopped short, as though he realized he was about to say too much.

"My aunt said Mae's parents forced you to marry her," Laurel whispered solemnly.

"Thank you for gossiping about me."

Laurel grinned and blushed.

"Well, if you must know, your aunt was right."

Laurel bit her lip with nervous excitement, both anxious and afraid to pursue this conversation.

"But you're looking at an innocent man. I swear that before God and everybody."

"You mean you didn't–" Laurel lowered her voice again–"compromise her reputation?"

"Miss McBryde!" Carey cried in mock outrage. "Such personal questions!"

Laurel giggled.

"Mae told her ma I had. Swore I had. But I never more than kissed her, though I did do plenty of that. We'd been sweethearts since we was kids."

"But why would she lie?"

Carey shrugged. "All I know is, one day her two older brothers showed up on my doorstep and said I was gonna make an honest woman of Mae before the day was out or else."

"Oh, my." Laurel abruptly stopped smiling.

"Then, of course, they had to have their fun."

"They attacked you?" Laurel asked in a horrified whisper.

"Did they! I made a pretty sight at the altar: a broken nose, eyes swole shut, a lip so split I couldn't have kissed the bride if I'd wanted to. It was a week before I could stand up without getting dizzy."

"Oh, Carey." Laurel reached down and patted his shoulder. "Why would Mae lie? Why would she tell her parents you seduced her if it wasn't true?"

He stared into the distance with his green eyes narrowed in bitterness. "Somebody seduced her, but it weren't me."

"How do you know?" Laurel knew she should not ask such intensely personal questions, but her curiosity could not halt her wayward tongue.

Carey paused a long time before answering, as though once again weighing how much of his family history to reveal. "She was...already in a family way," he answered delicately.

This disclosure scandalized Laurel thoroughly. "Little Rachel?"

Carey vigorously shook his head. He lowered his voice as though he were afraid the wind itself would overhear the secrets he told. "Rachel didn't come along 'til more than a year later. She lost the first one a month after we was wed."

Laurel felt strangely relieved and yet not surprised. Rachel was the living image of Carey. The younger daughter, Caroline, favored her mother in looks. "Did you ask Mae who...who was responsible?"

"'Course I did. I'm as human as the next. One night I got so mad I nearly hit her when she wouldn't say. But...she cried so hard. She started screaming like a crazy woman, 'Don't ask me that, don't ask me that, please don't ever ask me that.' She was near out of her head. I never saw the like of it. I was afraid she would go off the way my mama did. I suppose you've heard that story too."

Laurel nodded solemnly, hating to make Carey recall his mother's suicide.

"So I never asked again."

Laurel shivered. She could sense she should not venture any farther down the avenues of Carey's troubled marriage.

"I sometimes wish she'd just come to me and told me her trouble. I would've married her anyway. Laurel, I would have, truly." He sat up suddenly. "Oh, well. Can't change the past, only the future."

Laurel witnessed his abrupt mood-change and knew he wanted to drop the present subject. She searched her mind for a new, less personal topic.

"Oh, Carey, did I tell you what happened with Christine?"

With a confused laugh and shake of his head, he told her "no."

"I truly believe the little demon lays awake nights plotting new ways to destroy my peace of mind!"

"She's only a little girl. Everything she does makes perfect sense in *her* little head."

"Don't you defend her to me. You don't have to live with her. I don't know what I'm going to do. Aunt Alice seems to have appointed me the unofficial baby nurse. They expect me to watch her whenever they have something better to do."

"Well, it don't seem like you have much else in the way of chores around the Hartmoor house."

"If they expect me to earn my keep, frankly I'd rather scrub the floors than take care of that little monster."

"You're just not patient enough. I feel sorry for Christine. From what you tell me and what I've seen, she's got a father who ignores her and a mother who's afraid she'll break. I think she just needs a firmer hand."

"That's what I gave her this morning. That's what got me in trouble with Aunt Alice and Uncle Jack."

"What happened?" Carey sounded like he was rapidly losing interest in the conversation. Laurel sensed a tension growing between them whenever she talked about the Hartmoors.

"She got into my darkroom. That is sacred territory as far as I'm concerned."

"Queen Laurel of Hartmoor."

Laurel playfully slugged his shoulder and continued her tale of woe and outrage. "She opened and spilled bottles of chemicals, exposed a new box of film and almost opened up plate holders I had just shot yesterday. When I tried to grab the holders away from her, she bit me! Look." Laurel displayed her hand which still bore a small pink arc in the shape of Christine's incisors.

Carey laughed and shook his head.

"That's when I swatted her on the backside. She started screaming though I know I didn't hurt her. Aunt Alice rushed up and threw a fit. Her precious baby can do no wrong, of course."

"Of course."

"Then Uncle Jack came home for lunch and heard the whole story and gave me a huge lecture on how this was *his* house and I was living on *his* charity and how if I ever raised a hand to his child again I'd regret it." Laurel paused for breath.

"You live on his charity?"

"Well, only in a manner of speaking. My father left me what little he had in trust until I'm twenty-five. Uncle Jack is my trustee, so he's kind of like my guardian until then. It's all so medieval. I'm perfectly capable of handling my own affairs."

"You don't need the likes of Jack Hartmoor running your life."

"Well, anyway, I had the proverbial last laugh."

Carey gave her an upside down questioning glance from his seat at her feet.

"I told them how terribly dangerous the chemicals were–how poisonous. The chemical I use to fix the image is potassium cyanide–that's a very serious poison. I told them my darkroom really shouldn't be in the house at all–that it should be moved outside to the little shed Aunt Cassie uses as a tack room. I've had my eye on that tack room ever since I arrived...and now it's mine!"

Carey looked back up at her, still puzzled.

"I should have realized ages ago that Alice would go to any length to protect her precious Christine," Laurel explained. "Once I made it clear to them what a danger the darkroom presented, they were only too happy to move me out."

"Why is Mrs. Hartmoor so over-protective of Christine?"

"Christine's the only child she'll ever have. She can't have anymore. It's a family secret–don't tell anyone. I'm not even supposed to know, but Aunt Cassie loves to gossip about Aunt Alice and Jack. She's been to visit doctors as far away as St. Louis–that's where Alice is from–and all of them tell her the same thing. She can't bear any more children. It's sad, I guess, though I'd count it a blessing, if I were her. Better too few than too many."

Carey said nothing to this, so Laurel veered back to her original story. "I can't wait to set up my new darkroom. It's going to be such an improvement on that miserable old closet."

"Laurel's day ends well," Carey murmured sarcastically.

"I suppose my problems seem quite trivial to you," Laurel pouted.

With an immediate shift of mood, he sat up and turned to face her. "Never, Miss McBryde. Never. These afternoons are the only thing I have to look forward to each day. If it weren't for you–and baseball–I'd have no reason for living."

"Oh, stop." Whenever he called her "Miss McBryde" she knew he was teasing her.

"I'm serious. It's not like I have anyone else to talk to."

"You have Mae."

"Oh, Laurel, Mae and I don't talk."

"How can two people who live under the same roof–" and a small roof it was, too "–not ever talk?"

"You've never been married. You wouldn't understand."

"You and Mae are just having a tiff." Laurel had picked up the word 'tiff' from Alice. Alice never used the word argument when referring to a disagreement or fight she had with Jack.

"A tiff that's lasted six years. Well, I've got to go home now so we can 'tiff' some more–whatever 'tiff' means."

He lifted his arms and placed his hands behind his head in a languorous stretch. Laurel's eyes followed the sensuous movement of his arms. She marveled once again at the beautiful interplay of muscle that defined them. The afternoon sun glinted off the blond hair of his forearms. When he finally finished stretching, he stood up, then pulled Laurel upright.

He held her hands in his long seconds after she reached her feet. Laurel felt a chill of anticipation, fearing he would try to kiss her again. She tried to pull her hands away, but he would not release them.

"Carey..." Laurel warned.

He gazed at her with a strange, mischievous defiance.

She glanced away, to the sun setting hot and golden in the western sky. The days were growing shorter as the end of August neared. She looked back into his large, clear eyes, eyes as green as a new-made promise. She tried to speak, but found no words. She felt the chill again, the tiny twitch of fear at being drawn into a spiral of unspeakable wickedness.

Lightning in a drought year.

She continued to stare into his eyes. She almost hated them for their beauty and their growing power over her. Slowly, as one in a dream, she pulled her right hand from his and gently brushed a stray lock of blond hair from his forehead.

The earth stood unnaturally silent at that moment as though caught in the same chilling liquid that surrounded Laurel, slowing her movements and lengthening time itself. She ran her fingers across his suntanned brow, down his temple, and along his angular jaw. He placed his hand over hers and pressed his lips to the sensitive skin of her palm.

So intense was the sensation this simple act evoked in her that she jerked her hand away in surprise. Then, embarrassed by her hasty reflex, she spoke quickly in a silly, unnatural voice. "Tomorrow...tomorrow I would like to take your photograph."

"Tomorrow is Saturday."

"Oh, right," Laurel stammered. She drew a deep breath to regain her composure.

"Will the Hartmoors cut you loose on a Sunday morning?"

"Don't you have to walk Mae and the girls to church?"

"Not this week. The walk was getting too much for her, so the Taylors volunteered to drive her and the girls with them."

Laurel was surprised the Taylors had a wagon big enough to accommodate the Fairchilds in addition to their own nine children, but didn't say this.

"Sunday, then."

Chapter Thirteen

"This will be the first picture I develop in my new darkroom," Laurel announced as she set up her equipment on Sunday morning to take Carey's portrait.

"The last baseball game of the season is coming up. You ought to take a picture of the Cyclones, Laurel," Carey suggested as he sat patiently for his portrait.

"I already offered to shoot a team picture," Laurel answered. "Uncle Jack informed me that the whole town thinks I'm too unfeminine when I make photographs, so he told me 'no.'"

"That son-of-a–" Carey glanced away rather than finish his sentence. "Did you enjoy the game yesterday?"

"Oh, yes. Very much." Laurel busied herself to raise the tripod to the perfect height, then cranked the camera itself into a perfectly level plane of focus. She hummed as she worked, pleased to have so cooperative a subject for a change. Carey had heard her complain of the ineptness of the Hartmoor models often enough, so he knew what was expected of him.

She noticed he had dressed carefully for his portrait. His blue cotton shirt, though worn, was washed and neatly pressed. He'd slicked his hair back from his forehead, causing him to look much more mature.

She could not forget the content of their conversation the previous Friday afternoon. All during the sweltering baseball game on Saturday, she had stared at Mae Fairchild and wondered what had transpired prior to her marriage to Carey. Why had she claimed Carey as her lover, when there had actually been someone else? A married man, perhaps, or some cad who had abandoned her. Her motivations must have been tragic, Laurel concluded in her romantic imagination, but she still didn't feel this justified the wrong Mae had done to

Carey. To gain a husband through deception was outrageous. She fumed with the injustice of the situation for Carey's sake. That he claimed he would have married Mae anyway, had she just confessed her dilemma in a forthright way, ennobled him in Laurel's mind.

Laurel pulled the dark cloth over her head and shoulders to carefully focus Carey's upside-down image on the ground glass.

"Hold still, please." She completed the adjustments, then placed the negative holder into position and removed the dark slide. She emerged from her dark cloth with tousled hair as usual. The mess the dark cloth always made of her hair had been one of the Hartmoors' many complaints against her making photographs in public.

"A lady would not wish to be seen with her hair in so disheveled a state," her grandmother had remarked. The beautiful, dark "Hartmoor hair" must be perfectly coifed at all times. Laurel felt tempted to cut it all off.

"Carey, I just can't stop thinking about what you told me about Mae."

A look of panic crossed Carey's handsome face. "Laurel, I should never have told you that. I don't know why I did. I've never talked about it with anyone in all these years. Promise me you won't ever tell anybody what I told you." He shook his head as though exasperated at himself. "I don't know what it is about our friendship that makes me tell you things I never say to anyone else. Do you feel that way, too?"

"Of course." She squeezed the shutter release in her hand and sealed the moment in the silver salts just as a flattered smile crossed his face.

He helped her disassemble her equipment and place it back in the large pack she carried it in.

"What did you tell the Hartmoors about not going to church this morning?" He swung the tripod over his shoulder and they began the walk to Laurel's house.

"I lied and said I had a terrible headache," Laurel confessed.

"I hate the fact we have to lie just to see each other. Maybe we should stop–"

"No, you can't mean that. Please don't stop meeting me at the grove. Please, Carey. We're not doing anything wrong."

"I never said that. In fact, meeting you was about the luckiest thing ever happened to me. Your lessons have brought me a job, Laurel."

Laurel stopped still in surprise. "What?"

Carey turned to her with a proud smile. "Mr. Kellerman, the man with the Farmer's Alliance up from Texas, he offered me a job with them, once the fall planting's done. This'll be the first winter I can remember that I'll have regular money coming in."

"Oh, Carey, that's wonderful!" If they both had not been so burdened down with equipment, she would have hugged him. "What sort of job?"

"Going out and talking to other farmers like myself. Trying to convince them to join the Alliance. You know, organize sub-alliances and so forth. Just found it out yesterday after the game. Somebody told him what I'd said at that blasted Fourth of July picnic at your place and they recommended me to Kellerman. He gave me a whole packet of pamphlets and papers to study." Carey's expression changed suddenly.

"And?" Laurel prodded.

Carey frowned. "Mae tore 'em all up. Said I got no business sticking my nose into other folks' affairs. She hates politics."

"But doesn't she understand that the Farmer's Alliance is just trying to help her and all the farm families?"

"Mae, well, it don't matter cause I'm taking the job whether she likes it or not. I'm pretty excited about it, too."

"Oh, Carey, I'm so proud. Maybe Mae will come around in time."

Carey was about to reply when both heard a sound in the light south wind. Somewhere, a woman's voice cried out.

Carey's head jerked in the direction of home. His sod house stood about a half mile in the distance.

"Was it Mae?" Laurel asked, reading the alarm in his face.

"She was going to church. She–"

The cry sounded again. It might even have been Carey's name being called.

He set Laurel's tripod on the ground and ran towards his house. Without pausing to think, Laurel set down her camera and followed him.

By the time she reached the Fairchild home, Carey was already inside. The door stood half-way open and she stepped up onto the porch to peer inside.

Carey knelt next to Mae, who sat doubled-over on the floor.

"I don't understand it," Mae cried. "It's too soon. Way too soon. And I'm bleeding. I don't understand it."

"Where are the girls?" Carey asked as he tried to help Mae to her feet.

Bright red blood covered the back of Mae's loose-fitting smock.

"I sent them on to church with Mrs. Taylor. I didn't feel so good, so I stayed home to rest. Where, in the name of God, have you been?"

"I'll go for the doctor."

"You know we can't afford the doctor. Go get Mrs. Taylor. She'll do fine."

"But something's wrong. You need a doctor, Mae."

"We don't have the money," Mae whined.

"I don't care. You're in trouble."

"Don't leave me alone. I'm afraid." Mae's face contorted with pain and she groaned loudly, grabbing Carey's shoulders.

"Mae, I've got to go now!"

Carey nearly crashed into Laurel as he bolted out the door.

He spun around. "Laurel, thank God you're here. Something's wrong. I'm going for Dr. Parnell. Could you stay with her until I come back? I'm just afraid that–just in case–can you stay?"

Laurel's expression twisted in confusion. She managed to nod as he turned and took off running out of the yard.

"Borrow a horse from the Hartmoors!" she called after him.

"Thank you," he shouted back.

"Who's out there?" Mae's voice demanded from inside the sod house. A gust of wind had blown the door open wider.

A lump of fear caught in Laurel's throat and prevented her from immediately answering. Uncertainly, she stepped up onto the little stone porch.

"You!" Mae still knelt on the floor in an expanding puddle of blood. "I might have known he was with you."

"Hello, Mrs. Fairchild." Laurel smiled unevenly and stepped in.

"Get out of my house, you miserable whore!"

Laurel blanched. No one had ever called her names before.

"Don't you think you should get into bed, Mrs. Fairchild?" Laurel's voice came out much higher and weaker than she intended.

"Don't even speak to me, you filthy slut!" Mae tried to raise herself, but her pregnant belly made grace difficult.

"Oh, Mae, let me help you." Laurel closed the door and ran to Mae's side.

"I don't need your–" A distracting pain overcame Mae's resistance and she could not stop Laurel from half-lifting, half-dragging her to the bed. Once there, she lashed out with another string of curses and insults, some which Laurel, in her sheltered upbringing, had never heard before.

"I think, for the sake of your health, you should calm yourself," Laurel interrupted primly.

"You shut up, you dirty harlot." Mae struggled to remove the tattered smock that she wore over her nightgown. The tie at the neck was tangled in a knot and she could not undo it.

"Why are you calling me all these terrible names?"

"You think I don't know what's been goin' on?" Mae yanked in frustration at the knotted tie.

"I don't know what you're talking about. Here, let me help you with that."

Mae slapped Laurel's hands away. "You and my husband–that's what's been goin' on."

"I'm acquainted with Mr. Fairchild, but I can assure you that nothing untoward–"

"Oh, shut up with your fancy talk! Just leave me alone and get out of my house."

"Alright, alright. I'm going. I'm sorry." Laurel made for the door.

"No, wait–" Mae gasped, then turned her face away with another fierce contraction.

Laurel realized in that instant that Mae was afraid to be alone. Laurel's own dread doubled. If Mae was so fearful of being alone in her labor that she was forced into the ignominy of asking Laurel–whom she obviously despised–to stay with her, events must be going very wrong indeed.

Laurel nervously glanced out the small front window of the dark, little house. She tried to mentally calculate how long it would take Carey to get into town, locate Dr. Parnell, and return.

She walked back over to Mae's bed and once more attempted to help her reluctant patient untie the knotted housecoat.

"Don't," Mae whined weakly, yet she surrendered the tie to Laurel's steadier fingers when another spasm of pain racked her small frame. Laurel had to pity her. Mae was entirely helpless and she knew it. Words were her only weapon now.

"How I hate you, you miserable whore," she spat out as the contraction ended.

"Oh, stop it, Mae, you're getting repetitious."

Mae rolled over on her side, away from Laurel. She started crying. Whether the tears sprung from pain or unhappiness, Laurel could not tell.

"We were happy until you came," Mae whimpered.

Laurel pulled a simple, homemade wooden chair over from the dining table to Mae's bedside. Was Mae telling the truth? Had she and Carey been happy before he met her? Had she, Laurel, interfered with their marriage without even knowing it? She remembered the kiss Carey gave her with a guilty vengeance now. Did Mae know about the kiss? Surely not. But Carey had told her Mae was angry he had asked her to dance at the picnic.

"I'm simply a friend to your husband. I don't mean you any harm."

"Married men don't have *women* for friends." Mae turned on Laurel with renewed vigor, having perceived a twinge of weakness in her adversary. "I didn't want to expose myself and my children to the scandal of an adulterous husband, but you don't leave me no choice."

Laurel sat straight and still, as wooden as the chair she sat in. "I think you need to rest and when–"

"You will hear me out!" Mae shouted as yet another contraction caused her to arch her back and moan in spite of herself.

Did childbirth involve this much blood? The sheets of the bed and Mae's nightgown were soaked in scarlet. Laurel had seen a cow and a mare give birth, but nothing like this had happened.

When the worst of the spasm passed, Mae relaxed and renewed her verbal assault. "Just you wait," she hissed. Mae's face flushed with an eerie glow that made Laurel shudder. "I'll tell everyone what you've been up to. Everyone! I won't stop until you're ruined in this town. We'll see if that fine family of yours stands behind you when they know the truth about you. That you've been sneaking around with my husband."

"That's not true," Laurel pleaded, though she knew that reasoning with a madwoman was probably a waste of breath. She frantically glanced out the little window again. She squinted her eyes to see into the distance, hoping she could make out the shape of the doctor's buggy racing toward the house. How long would it take? How long?

"You're a fool. He'll ruin you. He has nothing to lose and you have everything. Can't you see–Oh, damn this pain!" The contraction's severity gripped and twisted Mae until she screamed, unable to stop herself.

Laurel watched helplessly, unable to think what to do. The bleeding continued unabated, soaking the mattress of the bed thoroughly. This much bleeding couldn't be normal. Mae seemed oblivious to this situation, dividing her time between enduring the pain of childbirth and verbally attacking her imagined rival.

Mae reopened her eyes, only to glare up at Laurel with such a fury, it almost took Laurel's breath away. "Just you wait, Miss High and Mighty. Soon everyone will see you for the harlot you are–"

Laurel's temper finally gave way. "I find it strange a woman with your past should be so anxious to toss around names like 'harlot' and 'whore.'"

This remark stopped Mae cold. "What are you talking about?"

"I know the circumstances of your marriage. I know how you lied to your parents about Carey so they would force him to marry you. I know you had another lover before your marriage, so don't pretend such moral superiority with me, *Mrs.* Fairchild. I know better!"

Laurel regretted the angry words almost as soon as they left her mouth. Mae's stricken look told her she had just hurt her more than any contraction on earth.

"He told you? He told you?" Mae whispered, incredulous. Before she could say anything else, another fierce pain gripped her.

Laurel bit her knuckle in frustration. Why had she said it? No matter what the provocation, she couldn't believe she had just attacked a woman who might very well be dying. The awful spell was broken by the sound of commotion in the yard. Laurel ran towards the door only to have it flung open in her face by Carey and Dr. Parnell. She jumped out of their way, thanking heaven they arrived when they did.

"Miss McBryde, isn't it?" Dr. Parnell inquired as he quickly pulled off his hat and coat. He casually tossed them on the kitchen table.

Laurel meekly nodded as she edged closer to the door. Still dazed by her bitter exchange with the small blonde stranger who now writhed in the bed, she couldn't wait to make her escape. She could almost feel the freedom from the suffocating hostility of the cluttered little room. She pressed her icy fingers against her hot brow to stem the pounding flow of blood that caused her head to throb.

She watched Carey dash to his wife's bedside. He gasped aloud when he saw how bloody the bedclothes were.

The doctor set his black leather bag next to the bed. As he rolled up his shirt sleeves he caught sight of Laurel, her hand on the doorknob.

"Miss McBryde, surely you're not leaving us?" barked Dr. Parnell. "I'll be needing assistance here."

"What can I do?" Carey shouted over one of Mae's screams.

"Not much right now. Fathers have already done their worst by this pass. Why don't you wait outside?"

Mae stopped screaming long enough to frantically grab Carey's arm. "Don't leave me. Don't leave me. I want to talk to you!"

"Not now, Mae. The doctor's here." Carey disengaged Mae's grasp and rose from the bed, clearly frightened by the situation.

Dr. Parnell rapidly laid out a gruesome array of medical instruments, the very sight of which caused Laurel to shudder.

He looks like an old general, Laurel thought, well-practiced in the arts of battle and looking forward to the fray. She knew her grandmother considered Emory Parnell something of a frontier relic, left-over from a previous time. Like Margaret's husband, he had first come out to the Kansas plains with the army and had stayed on after the war, settling in Chisholm before it had a name.

Twenty-five years later, he still looked the part of the Civil War surgeon–long hair swept back from his forehead and hanging past his collar, sweeping handlebar mustache, out-dated clothing–as though he were permanently stranded in the era of his youth.

"Come on, girl, I need your help," he snapped at Laurel. Clearly, he expected no insubordination in the ranks.

Laurel swallowed hard and moved slowly back towards the bed. She exchanged an unreadable glance with Carey as he left the house to wait on the front porch.

"Oh, Mrs. Fairchild," said the doctor as he deftly rolled up Mae's nightgown, exposing her bloody limbs and hard, round belly. "We must get this bleeding under control."

"Is it normal to bleed so much during childbirth, Doctor?" Laurel whispered.

"Not this much. Looks like we may have a torn placenta."

Laurel didn't know what a placenta was, but watched with horrified fascination as the doctor pressed his hands over Mae's abdomen. She almost gasped aloud when he plunged his hands between Mae's thighs for a more intimate examination. Mae cried piteously at this new invasion. Laurel turned her face away, embarrassed for Mae's sake. Her eye caught sight of Carey peeking in the window, his face a mask of worry.

Laurel snapped to attention as the doctor began to order her about. She followed every command without hesitation, reacting to the crisis with a mechanical detachment.

She watched, mesmerized, as a tiny head emerged between Mae's thighs. First the head, then one shoulder, then the other were expelled in successive contractions, with the rest of the little body sliding out in a final rush.

Mae's cries subsided into exhausted panting.

Laurel stood ready to take the baby from the doctor and wrap it in a soft cotton blanket as she had been told to do. Long seconds passed, but no sound came from the baby, a tiny, wrinkled seven-months child. Laurel couldn't yet see if the child were male or female.

Mae looked up in alarm. She, too, obviously wondered why the child remained silent. The doctor listened to the infant's heart.

"I'm sorry, Mrs. Fairchild. This little one didn't have a chance. Born too soon." He held out the dead child for Laurel to wrap it in its blanket.

Mae whined weakly, unable to manage a cry. She tried to reach out for her baby, but her arms had no strength. Laurel, after a nod from the doctor, placed the child next to its mother. Mae no longer seemed to notice Laurel's hated presence. She focused her attention entirely on the stillborn baby, surveying its tiny features mournfully.

Dr. Parnell quickly ushered Laurel outside so as to speak to her and Carey together.

Carey tried to enter the house as soon as the doctor opened the door, but Dr. Parnell barred his entry by catching hold of his shoulder.

"What's wrong? What's happened?" Carey asked.

"The baby didn't make it, Fairchild. But that's not our most immediate concern."

Carey and Laurel stood still in fearful anticipation of the doctor's diagnosis.

"Your wife has hemorrhaged severely." Then Parnell translated into simpler terms. "She's lost a great deal of blood."

Carey once again tried to break free of the doctor's grasp to rush to his wife's side, but the doctor prevented him with a severe look.

"I want to try a blood transfusion. It's risky, but it's the only chance we have. I'll need the help of you both. Are you willing?"

"I'll do anything. Anything," Carey said with passion. He raked his hand through his hair, as though trying to calm himself.

Laurel nodded her assent.

"Good. Now let's get on with it."

When the trio reentered the house, they found Mae lying motionless, still holding the baby.

Carey's eyes widened in panic. "Is she–?"

The doctor placed a hand on Mae's throat to check her pulse. "She's just unconscious. Roll up your sleeve and sit there at the table."

The doctor pulled more equipment out of his bag.

"Doctor Parnell, should I...uh?" Laurel motioned to the baby still tucked into the crook of Mae's arm.

"Wrap it up and place it somewhere," the doctor replied brusquely. He quickly returned to his work at hand, tying a tourniquet around Carey's upper arm.

Laurel picked up the stillborn infant, so light in weight it felt like one of Christine's dolls, and realized with a shock the little body was already growing cold. The child's face bore a waxy, gray appearance. A thin covering of dark hair stuck to the bloody little scalp.

She glanced at Carey as she passed the kitchen table. He watched miserably as she carried the baby to a handmade wooden cradle near the limestone fireplace.

Laurel could not bear to look as the doctor introduced the large needle into a vein in Carey's arm. She was forced to participate when Parnell required her to hold a length of rubber tubing that ran from the needle and quickly filled with Carey's blood.

Carey watched intently while the doctor poked Mae's arm with a similar needle. Laurel found she grew light-headed every time she looked at the dark blood in the yellow tubing. She struggled to maintain her senses, knowing the doctor did not need two patients to contend with at this critical juncture.

The doctor rose from Mae's bed and told Carey to lie down next to his wife. Laurel walked next to him, still gingerly holding the tubing to be used for the transfusion. Carey lay down as gently as he could so as not to disturb either needle.

"Sit up in the bed just a little. You need to be higher," said Parnell as he completed his connection of the two rubber tubes with a squeeze bulb very similar in appearance to Laurel's shutter release. Soon Carey's blood flowed directly into his ailing wife.

"When will we know if this works?" Carey whispered. His eyes never left Mae's pale face.

"Hard to say. Sometimes these transfusions work beautifully and sometimes they kill the patient outright. We don't know why."

Both Carey and Laurel flinched at the word 'kill.' Parnell's bedside manner had not softened much from his days as an army surgeon. Laurel could now understand comments she had heard Alice and Margaret exchange concerning his brusque and, to the more delicate souls, offensive manner. According to Margaret, his methods were technically correct and skillfully employed, but fragile sensibilities and female modesty were not his concern. Human flesh was but the raw material of his trade and he would never see it otherwise.

Parnell scrubbed his bloody hands in a wash basin at the dry sink in the portion of the house that served as the kitchen. He hummed to himself as he washed, emotionally detached from the life and death struggle just waged in his presence. Laurel looked down at the dried blood on her own hands and cuffs. The sight caused a flush of nausea.

"I need some air," she whispered and bolted from the house. She ran out into the yard, breathing hard, fighting the urge to vomit. She leaned against the pump handle to steady herself. Gradually, her head cleared and she pumped some water into the trough to rinse her hands and splash on her face.

A cloud bank rose in the southwestern sky, promising rain. What time was it? Well past noon. That was certain. She looked back at the sod house with dread, but knew she must return. She had just reached the doorstep when she heard the sound of a horse and buggy in the distance.

She made out the unmistakable sight of her grandmother driving toward the house at a good pace. Fear clutched Laurel–what if Mae regained consciousness and carried out her threats to destroy Laurel's reputation? Laurel tried to banish these selfish thoughts. After all, the mad young woman in the little sod house lay on the point of death. Still, Laurel could not quiet her guilty conscience.

Mae's bitter accusations had forced Laurel to admit a truth she had previously refused to acknowledge until this very afternoon: That her feelings for Carey were something more than friendship. The sight of Carey's worried, caring face as he watched over Mae during the blood transfusion had caused Laurel her first, exquisite pang of jealousy and she knew she would never feel the same way about him again.

"Laurel," called Margaret as she pulled into the yard. "Whatever is going on here, child?"

Laurel ran to her grandmother's rig to help her down. "Oh, Grandmother, how did you know where to find me?"

"Arthur, the stable hand–he told us Carey came by in a terrible fright and borrowed a horse to fetch the doctor. He said you told him to."

"It's Mrs. Fairchild. She's had her baby too soon and it died and she bled something awful and–"

"Hush, now, calm yourself. Let's see what's going on."

The two women entered the Fairchild house and were warmly greeted by Emory Parnell. He had just completed the transfusion and had removed the needles from Mae and Carey's arms. Carey held a rag to his arm and stood up shakily. Parnell steadied him and sat him back down in the chair next to the bed.

"Maggie, you couldn't have come at a better time." Dr. Parnell extended his hand in a gallant handshake.

"What's the story here, Emory?" Margaret threw her hat and gloves on a chair by the door and walked over to the foot of the bed.

Carey sat leaning his elbows against his knees. He held Mae's hand pressed to his cheek. Laurel watched this tender gesture with another agonizing stab of jealousy. Mae's eyelids fluttered open, but she didn't seem too aware of her surroundings.

"Our Mrs. Fairchild's had a rough go of it, I'm afraid," said Dr. Parnell. He now packed up his gruesome instruments.

Margaret surveyed the situation and went straight to work. She unfastened her cuffs, turned them up, and told Carey to help roll Mae onto her side. She efficiently stripped the bloody bed linens from one side, then the other, and deftly replaced them with clean ones without ever moving Mae off the bed itself.

"Laurel, heat up some water," Margaret ordered. "She'll need the comfort of some warm towels to ease the pain. Carey, bring in some wood to help Laurel start a fire in that stove."

Laurel and Carey did as they were told, like obedient children in the presence of a stern parent. Laurel marveled at her grandmother's ability to take charge of a situation in an instant.

Carey said nothing to Laurel as they worked together to build a fire and heat the water. Laurel sensed he was avoiding even looking at her.

Margaret and Dr. Parnell chatted about Mae's condition, then he left saying he still had a man waiting with a boil to be lanced back in town. After his departure, Carey resumed his vigil at Mae's bedside while Laurel and Margaret focused their attention on the tiny corpse in the cradle.

Laurel followed Margaret outside into the yard. Margaret placed the infant's body in the trough and sponged it clean. For the first time, Laurel determined the baby's sex. As Margaret rinsed the child's skinny limbs, Laurel saw the tiny bud of a penis together with a small scrotum between the baby's thighs. Carey had a son, or would have had one in two months' time.

"Emory tells me you made an admirable assistant, Laurel. I'm proud of you."

"I just did whatever he told me to do," Laurel answered modestly. She had more troubling questions on her mind. "Grandmother, Mrs. Fairchild said some things to me. Some really bad things."

To Laurel's utter astonishment, Margaret laughed out loud. "Oh, child, never listen to what a woman says in labor."

"Why is that?"

"Because a woman in that condition is so out of her head with the pain, she's liable to say anything. Trust me, some of the finest ladies on the face of this earth have been known to curse a blue streak when they're in their time."

"Ladies? Using curse words?"

"You'd be amazed."

Margaret carefully wrapped the infant in a fresh blanket and carried it inside. "How is Mae doing, Carey?"

Carey looked up from Mae's bedside. "Sleeping, I think. Her breathing's pretty regular."

"Where are your girls?"

"With Mrs. Taylor."

"I'll stop at the Taylors on the way home and tell Imogene what's happened. No doubt, she'll be over straight away. And I'll leave that horse you borrowed. Just in case."

"I'm obliged, Ma'am."

"Carey, would you like us to take the baby to Mr. Swallow's?"

Carey turned a painful face on Margaret and said quietly, "I'm afraid I can't afford the luxury of an undertaker, Ma'am."

"Don't worry about the expense, Carey. I'll help out."

"No, Mrs. Hartmoor. I can't accept your charity. I thank you for the offer, just the same."

Margaret sighed, but did not press the issue further. She picked up her hat and gloves and motioned for Laurel to prepare to leave.

Laurel walked over to the bed one last time. She whispered to Carey, "I'm sorry for your loss."

Carey glanced up briefly and nodded.

Before Laurel could turn to leave, Mae opened her eyes and looked up to see Laurel standing over her. With her parched lips, she uttered the single word.

"*Monster.*"

Laurel felt like she had been physically struck. She looked over in Margaret's direction to see if she had heard this strange epithet. Fortunately, her grandmother was almost out the door.

Then she looked at Carey, who likewise seemed stunned by his wife's remark. He looked up at Laurel in a confusion of emotion. Grief? Guilt? Fear? Hatred? Laurel couldn't tell.

She hurried to the door and stepped out on the porch. Margaret sat waiting for her in the buggy. Laurel tried to take a deep breath. She focused her eyes on Margaret in the buggy, only ten paces away. She heard a crack of thunder from the approaching storm. She could smell rain in the air.

Laurel looked at Margaret again, but the world turned red, then spun, then went black.

Chapter Fourteen

If Laurel slept at all that night, she did not notice it. Her grandmother had put her straight to bed after a dose of bread soaked in warm milk–Margaret's prescription for any and all types of emotional upset.

"Poor Laurel," Margaret told Alice and Cassandra as they got her undressed and ready for bed. "She's learned more about life and death in one day than any young girl ought to have to know."

"I'm just tired and I haven't eaten all day, Grandmother. That's why I fainted. There's nothing wrong with me."

Still, she enjoyed the pampering and being allowed to go to bed at seven in the evening. Best of all, Alice announced that Christine would be sleeping in her and Jack's room, ostensibly to give Laurel a chance to rest in solitude to recover from her ordeal, but everyone in the family knew Alice's motives were much more likely that she feared Laurel had been exposed to some dreadful illness at the Fairchild house that she might communicate to little Christine.

Whatever the reason, Laurel was grateful to be left alone. So many dire thoughts swam in her head–Mae's threats, Mae's frightening labor and stillborn baby, Laurel's own guilt that she had innocently intruded on Carey's marriage.

Heaviest on her conscience was her betrayal of Carey's secret concerning the circumstances of his marriage to Mae. He had just that morning begged her never to reveal what he had told her and instead, what had she done hardly an hour later?

She felt like a criminal. Carey would undoubtedly disavow their friendship the moment Mae told him what she had said. She couldn't blame him. She didn't deserve his friendship after a betrayal of that magnitude.

And what would happen if Mae, presuming she lived, carried out her threats to ruin Laurel's reputation? She was on thin ice with the Hartmoors already.

Would they stand up for her? Would Mae's word be taken over hers? Mae Fairchild didn't hold much standing in the community, but she had lived here all her life, whereas Laurel was still a newcomer, a stranger in Chisholm society. Strangers were always more suspect.

Sometime before dawn, Laurel decided on a course of action. She would run away–return to her old house at Windrift and figure out a future from there. She technically owned the house and the 200 acres of property on which it sat, though her father had left it to her in trust, with Jack Hartmoor named as her guardian, until she reached the age of twenty-five. Four long years to wait. What could her father been thinking to have chosen the age of twenty-five? If only he had set down twenty-one as Laurel's age of majority, she could be free of the Hartmoors this moment.

Leaving was the best all-around solution. Even if Laurel could imagine a future in which Mae did not carry out her threats *and* by some miracle, Carey did not hate her for breaking his trust, she would still be left with the most unsolvable problem of all: the scary, doomed feeling that she might actually be in love with Carey.

Seeing him, knowing that, not seeing him, knowing that–either way, she was going to be miserable.

She lay in bed plotting her departure. She could not manage the trunk she originally brought with her. She would have to borrow a valise. She knew one was stored in the closet that had previously served as her darkroom.

The thought of her photography caused her to weep. Her camera and tripod, together with the newly shot portrait of Carey now lay abandoned in the field near his house. What effect would the morning dew have on all of it? If condensation seeped into the lenses or the plate holders, they would surely be ruined. And her brand new darkroom–she would be giving up that as well. I've made a terrible ruin of my life, she thought in self-pity.

She must have dozed off at some point, for nightmares of Mae's childbirth ordeal came to her in and out of the darkness of the stuffy room. Mae's screams, Mae's blood, the tiny dead baby's gray, waxy face, the blood-soaked sheets, and Mae snarling the word, *Monster*–all reverberated through Laurel's subconscious in a swirl of torment.

As soon as pre-dawn light began to filter into the bedroom, Laurel rose and dressed. She slipped out of the house and made her way back to where she was certain she had dropped her photographic equipment when she and Carey first heard Mae's cries the day before.

She searched the area again and again, but no trace of the camera or tripod remained. She couldn't understand it. Had someone stolen it? Had animals carried it off? She was practically certain she had retraced her path of the morning before.

As the sun broke over the eastern horizon, she gave up and returned home. If she spent any more time looking, she would miss her opportunity to leave the Hartmoor house undetected on her flight to Windrift.

By the time she returned, she realized with dismay that the family was already up. She saw movement in the kitchen, probably Margaret who was usually the first one in the household to rise. She slipped in the front door and tried to make it to the stairs without arousing notice, but her grandmother stepped out of the kitchen just as she entered.

"Oh, Laurel, you couldn't sleep either, I see. Come into the kitchen and sit down. I have some bad news."

Laurel swallowed hard and did as she was told. She sat at the kitchen table, nervously tapping the toe of her boot, wet from her walk in the dew-laden grasses. Her hems were soaked as well.

"I'm sorry to say all your good nursing work yesterday came to naught. Mae Fairchild passed on just after ten last night."

"Oh, dear Lord." Laurel's hand flew to her gaping mouth in shock.

"Laurel, let's not take the Lord's name in vain. I know when one is severely tested by circumstance the need to vent our emotions verbally is almost uncontrollable, but the mark of true breeding is to resist such course urges."

"I'm sorry, Grandmother. But it's so awful, the thought of it. She was so young, so near my age...to think that now she's just...gone."

"Well, Emory told me yesterday she had only the faintest chance of survival. He didn't want to tell you and poor Carey."

"That's so sad. Poor Mr. Fairchild. And those little girls. Those poor little girls. I know what it's like to lose a mother."

"Yes, of course you do, dear. Try to calm yourself. You did all you could."

Laurel did not wish to feign a love for Mae Fairchild that she did not feel. She did not wish to be a hypocrite, even within the confines of her own mind, yet the enormous wrong she felt she had done could now never be reconciled. Most of all, her heart silently broke for Carey's sake. His pain was hers, no matter what the cause. "How did you find out the news?"

"Cassie rode over there last evening after we put you to bed. She stayed until...well, until the end came. I'm putting together some food for Carey's breakfast. Cassie's taking it over to him as soon as she's dressed. Would you like to go along?"

"Yes, ma'am. I would."

Laurel rode alongside Cassandra in the Hartmoor buggy to Carey's house. She sat silently trying to digest the fact that Mae Fairchild was dead. She barely heard Cassandra's constant stream of chatter.

"So I said to Carey, 'You've got to let Mr. Swallow come over this very night and get Mae ready for the funeral,' and he answers that he's got no money for a funeral and I said not to bother his head about that–that's what friends are for, after all. Then he gets his back up and I lose my temper with him and talk to him like he's a little boy again. 'Carey,' I say, 'Don't let your pride talk louder than your good sense.' So he finally says 'Yes,' and I sent Arthur into town at daybreak to fetch Mr. Swallow."

"When will they hold the funeral?"

"Don't know. In a couple of days, I imagine. I wonder if the Brocks are coming in from Dodge? They might wait the funeral on them."

"The Brocks are Mrs. Fairchild's parents?"

"Yes. I frankly never cared for them. Oh, look, Carey's outside."

Cassandra skillfully guided the buggy into the yard and pulled the horse to a stop. Laurel saw Carey, still wearing the same clothes from the day before, bloodstained shirt sleeves and all, tossing a baseball against the side of his house.

"Carey, we've brought you some breakfast," Cassandra called as she jumped down from the buggy.

"Not hungry," Carey mumbled without missing a catch of his baseball. He threw the ball rhythmically against the side of his sod house, slowly wearing an indentation into the packed dirt wall. Toss–thunk–bounce–catch.

Cassandra marched over to where he stood. "You need to eat whether you feel like it or not, Carey. You need to keep your strength up. Has Mr. Swallow come yet?"

Toss–thunk–bounce–catch. "Come and gone."

"Carey, Laurel and I have brought you biscuits and gravy and a nice slice of ham. At least try to eat it. The next few days aren't going to be easy ones, you know. Folks'll start coming round to visit as soon as the news spreads."

When Carey refused to answer further, Cassandra took the food basket from the buggy and carried it inside.

Laurel hesitantly made her way toward Carey while Cassandra was occupied in the house.

"I'm so sorry, Carey."

Toss–thunk–bounce–catch.

Laurel twisted her hands, one in the other, not knowing what else to say. What had Mae told him? Was he angry? Was this the grief of a young husband or was it the hostility of a man who knew she had not only betrayed his trust but had said cruel things to his dying wife? She had no way to know.

Without missing a single toss, Carey finally spoke. "I went for a walk last night after..." He swallowed hard and turned his face away. When he had recovered himself sufficiently to speak, he said unemotionally in a low voice, "I found your camera. I didn't want it to get stolen so I brought it back here. It's in that shed over there. You can pick it up sometime else if you'd rather your aunt didn't know about yesterday."

"Thank you. Yes, some other time perhaps."

She stood awhile longer and watched him toss the baseball over and over. She wondered if such a monotonous activity were somehow therapeutic. Never in the months she had known Carey had they been at such a loss for words.

Cassandra finally emerged from the sod house. "I've straightened up in there for you, Carey. You're all set to receive callers. Everyone will be bringing more food, no doubt. I trust your girls are still at the Taylors."

Toss-thunk-bounce-catch.

"Yeah."

"Carey, I took the liberty of dropping off a couple of Christine's outgrown frocks. I thought little Caroline and Rachel might want new dresses for the...services."

Carey shrugged without looking up.

Cassandra turned to Laurel with a somewhat exasperated, What-else-can-we-do? look.

Laurel shrugged back and the two women departed.

Laurel returned to Carey's house late that evening to retrieve her camera equipment. No callers were present, so Laurel confidently approached the house only to find Carey still engaged in his solitary game of catch.

"I've come for my camera, Carey."

Carey glanced up from his baseball game long enough to jerk his head in the direction of the little shed he had earlier indicated he had stored it.

Uneasily, she walked over to the shed, found her tripod and bag full of equipment. With the tripod over one shoulder and the large equipment bag over the other, she returned to the side of Carey's house to attempt to engage him in some sort of conversation.

She stood for many seconds, waiting for him to stop tossing the baseball long enough to acknowledge her presence. When he refused to even look at her, much less speak to her, she turned and began the long, heavily burdened walk home, crying every step of the way.

ﻌ

Carey did not look Laurel in face even once during the funeral and burial. He made a sad, but stoic sight at Mae's graveside, standing there holding the hand of his older daughter, Rachel. Both Rachel and her little sister Caroline wore the dresses Cassandra had brought for them, Christine's castoffs.

The turnout included nearly half of those in attendance at the Hartmoor's Fourth of July picnic. All the Hartmoor tenant farmers and all the players on the Chisholm Cyclones came with their families.

The many crying babies in the crowd disrupted the solemnity of the occasion, yet also served as a doleful reminder that a baby's birth had caused this tragedy.

Laurel's heart had never been heavier. She no longer planned to run away, but staying in Chisholm with the knowledge Carey hated her, was not a pleasant alternative.

ﻌ

Many times during the first two weeks of September, Laurel slipped out to the poplar grove just on the off chance Carey might be there. She wanted so desperately to apologize for what she had said to Mae. But how could he forgive her? She couldn't even forgive herself. She finally ceased her afternoon vigils.

She had many distractions to ease the pain of losing Carey. Life at the Hartmoor house hummed with autumn activity. September was canning month and the Hartmoor women involved Laurel in their labors. Cucumbers were transformed into pickles, tomatoes into relish, strawberries into jam, peaches into marmalade. Yams, corn, okra, and green beans were all carefully preserved in glass jars with decorative labels.

Laurel's favorite new skill involved the transformation of apples into apple butter. She happily took over the chore of grinding the peeled apples into mush in the machine designed for that purpose, then stirring the mixture for hours over a wood fire behind the house until it had cooked down into the delicious, cinnamon-tinged treat to spread on toast and biscuits.

Laurel found her new darkroom a positive joy to work in. Though Cassandra still occasionally griped about losing her tack room, even she had to admit Laurel's pictures were better than ever for the new and more spacious working quarters.

By the end of the month, just when Laurel had almost gotten used to the absence of Carey in her life, he appeared one evening in the front yard.

Laurel had just finished her usual evening task of drying the dishes and had stepped outside the kitchen door on the east side of the house to escape the muggy heat of the kitchen. She jumped at the sound of his voice, but he was not addressing her. He stood in the yard with his hat in his hand speaking to Jack Hartmoor, who sat rocking lazily in the front porch swing.

Laurel silently approached, but hung back unnoticed at the corner of the house.

"I'm here to give my notice, Mr. Hartmoor."

"Notice?"

"I'll be vacating my land tomorrow, the first of October, sir."

"Hell of time to tell me, Fairchild. I'll never get another tenant before the fall planting."

"Not a problem, sir. Joe Taylor and Jud Amberly want to split my acreage between them."

"Oh, well, that's different."

"Can I tell them it's alright with you?"

"Certainly. Tell them to come round and I'll have the papers redrawn. Where will you be off to, Fairchild?"

"Dodge City, at first."

Dodge City! Over one hundred miles away. Laurel got a sick pain in the pit of her stomach. She would never see him again.

"What sends you to Dodge?"

"My wife's parents live out there now. They've offered to take care of my daughters so I can take a new job."

"A new job?"

Carey paused. "I'm gonna work for the Farmers Alliance. Recruit new members out in the western part of the state."

"I suppose you can't be talked out of this damn, fool enterprise?"

"Not likely, Mr. Hartmoor. I didn't come asking for your blessing."

"Nor will you get it. Don't you realize you're dealing with a bunch of radicals? Hardly a step above anarchists?"

Carey did not answer. Laurel guessed he was refusing to be drawn into a political debate.

"The Cyclones will miss you next season," Jack offered as perhaps a conciliatory gesture.

"I'll miss them, too."

"Well, good luck anyway, Fairchild."

"Thank you, Mr. Hartmoor."

The words exchanged between Carey and her uncle were polite enough, but the tone was flat. Both were feigning a cordiality neither felt.

Carey replaced his hat and turned to walk away. Seeing him leave her yard made her feel like the breath had been sucked out of her body.

In a stroke of impossible luck, Jack got up and went in the house. When he was safely out of sight, Laurel took off running after Carey.

"Carey, wait," she called, breathless from running a quarter of a mile.

He stopped and waited for her to catch up.

"Hello, Carey."

"Hello, Laurel." He did not smile, but for once did not look away either. With a pang, Laurel remembered how he used to break into the most dazzling smile the moment he caught sight of her.

"Carey, you can't leave."

"I'm afraid that's just what I plan to do. Tomorrow afternoon, in fact."

"But you don't want to leave Chisholm, do you?"

"It's not a question of what I want to do. The Alliance needs me and Mae's parents made me a good offer."

"But I could help you. I could look after your girls while you worked."

Carey smirked. "You enjoy your nursemaid job so much with Christine–"

"Don't tease me, Carey. I'm serious. I could do a good job."

"I'm doing what Mae would've wanted. She'd want her folks looking after her children."

Laurel read his unspoken message. Laurel would be the last woman on earth Mae would have wanted to replace her.

"Oh, Carey, you can't leave without saying goodbye."

"Well, I guess that's now."

"No, in the grove. Please Carey. Meet me there tomorrow. I need to talk to you." She never imagined herself a woman who would use tears to get her way and yet, there she was, begging him with tears in her eyes.

Carey ran his hand through his hair and looked away uncertainly. "Maybe I could leave the next morning. I was thinking about that."

Laurel held her breath.

"Alright. I'll be at the grove in the late afternoon. I suppose Mrs. Taylor will keep the girls one more night."

"Oh, Carey, thank you." Laurel raced home, so grateful for Carey's change of heart. She was losing him, but at least she could try and make things right between them before he left. Maybe he would even consent to a correspondence.

Special things always happened in October.

Chapter Fifteen

The first day of October began as beautifully as an October morning could. Though Laurel had lain awake much of the night rehearsing in her mind what she would say to Carey, she jumped out of bed with a burst of enthusiasm.

She dashed down to her darkroom without bothering to stop for breakfast. She set her mind to printing the portrait of Carey to give to him as a parting gift. She wanted him to remember her and a photograph would be the perfect choice.

She sat on a wooden stool in her new darkroom and carefully examined the single plate holding Carey's image in reverse. She frowned to learn that the plate holder had leaked a small amount of light that damaged the edge of the image, though not Carey's face itself. Artful printing would be necessary to minimize the defect.

She hummed as she measured and poured her developing chemicals. She loved her new quarters, so much more spacious and convenient. By ten, she had one good print made. She took down the heavy curtain she used to block the light from the little glassless window to study the print. She couldn't decide if she liked the picture or not.

Carey's face appeared as handsome as always, but his pale green, promise-colored eyes faded to an even paler gray in the photograph, giving them a strange, ghostly appearance that Laurel found disturbing. She then remembered that at the moment the photograph was taken, his wife was only hours from death, though he did not know this. Was there a premonition of the tragedy in the haunted look to his eyes? Laurel shook off the eerie notion as superstitious foolishness.

When she had carefully rinsed the last traces of chemicals from the print she took it up to her room to dry it between the pages of a book. She decided to leave the chemicals in the trays in case, after examining the print in better light, she decided she needed to do further work.

She lay on her bed looking at the wet print and felt the cool October breeze from the window pour over her face. The moment delighted her. She closed her eyes and relaxed contentedly. The lack of sleep from the night before caught up with her.

She knew nothing until the sound of Alice's voice, calling Christine to wash for lunch, jarred her from her delicious late morning nap. She sat up, startled. The photograph she still held against her chest now curled in all directions. She quickly placed it in her large dictionary to flatten it.

She was about to join the family downstairs in the dining room when one more blissfully cool breeze from the window beckoned her to sit down a moment longer. At last the long heat wave of the summer had broken. She gazed out at the flat prairie and the deep blue October sky and felt such a profound serenity wash over her.

"Laurel, have you seen Christine?"

"No, Aunt Alice. Sorry."

Alice left and Laurel sauntered down to the dining room.

Jack and Cassandra soon joined Laurel and Margaret at the table. They quietly waited for the remaining two members of the family to complete the ensemble.

A slightly breathless Alice poked her head in the dining room window. "I can't find her anywhere."

"The duck is getting cold," grumbled Jack. Duck was his favorite.

Laurel sighed with a frown and rose from the table. "I'll help you look."

She had no sooner spoken than all heard a distant sound of Christine screaming. Instantly, everyone dashed for the back door, simultaneously struck by the same fear. They headed directly towards Laurel's darkroom.

Christine sat on the floor of the little shed, drenched in an unknown chemical which she had overturned upon herself from one of Laurel's developing trays. Christine held her eyes, screaming.

"My baby's been poisoned!" shouted Alice.

"Get her to the kitchen," Margaret ordered. "We'll make her vomit it up with salt water."

Jack struggled to pick up Christine, who fought and kicked wildly.

"We don't know that she drank any," Laurel offered helplessly. "Maybe she just got some in her eyes."

"Shut up!" snapped Jack. He nearly knocked Laurel down as he swept Christine to the kitchen. The rest of the Hartmoor women followed in haste.

"They're not all poisonous," Laurel called after them. "I sort of exaggerated the danger." No one heard her as they disappeared into the house.

Laurel felt dazed and sick with fear. She knelt down and touched her hand to the spilled wetness. She sniffed it to identify the chemical. It was not the potassium cyanide. She jumped up to convey the happy news to the rest of the family.

By the time she reached the kitchen, she was already too late. Alice and Cassandra had forced Christine to drink salt water and Christine had begun to vomit.

"It's not poison," Laurel called triumphantly as she burst into the kitchen. Margaret bade her be quiet.

Somehow, Christine started choking on her own vomit. She coughed and coughed, then she could not cough. Her blue-green eyes stared wide and frantic as convulsions shook her tiny frame.

Jack and Alice held their daughter and glared at each other powerlessly as Christine's contorted face turned from red to purple to gray. In minutes, Christine silently slipped away as the family watched in horror.

Alice broke down first, sobbing hysterically. She refused to let go of her daughter. Margaret finally convinced her to carry the child upstairs.

Laurel did not join the family in her bedroom. She sat at the bottom of the stairs and buried her face in her hands. When the din of sobbing subsided slightly, she heard heavy footsteps behind her. She turned to see her uncle rush past her, his face contorted with an angry despair.

"You and your damned photography! This is all your fault," he snarled.

"I'm sorry," she whispered, but he was already out the front door. She shut her eyes tightly as she realized in an instant what would happened next. Her camera sat out on the porch on its spindly wooden tripod.

With the sound of a terrible crash, Laurel knew her camera had just been thrown off the porch to smash into a thousand pieces in the yard below.

Late that day, Carey found Laurel in the grove sitting on the ground next to the limestone outcropping. Her knees were drawn up to her chest and her face lay buried in her folded arms. Her hair hung in tangled disarray down her back where it had fallen from its pins and combs.

"What's wrong?" Carey asked when he saw Laurel's disheveled appearance and swollen eyes. "All these tears can't be for me, surely."

"Don't tease me, Carey. Something terrible has happened."

He immediately sat down next to her. She threw her arms around his neck and began to sob all over again. When she calmed down enough to speak, she recounted the whole miserable story.

"Laurel, don't blame yourself. I don't care what that son-of-a-bitch uncle said to you. It wasn't your fault."

Laurel heaved a shuddering sob and wiped her nose on her sleeve. Carey leaned back against the limestone and pulled Laurel into his lap. He held her close and she rested her head on his shoulder. She welcomed this gentle intimacy.

"It might be my fault. I planted all those fears in Alice's head so they would let me have the tack room for my darkroom. If they hadn't just assumed Christine had swallowed poison–"

"Sounds to me like they were the ones who made the mistake, not you."

Laurel tried to smile. "Oh, Carey, how am I ever going to get along without you?"

"I'm gonna miss you, too."

"You are? You don't hate me?"

"Hate you? Hell, no. I mean, I know I've stayed away since...since–" He sighed and held her closer. "I've just felt so bad, so guilty since Mae's been gone."

"Guilty?" Laurel raised her face to look him in the eyes.

He nodded. "I just can't help thinking...I know this is going to sound crazy, but I just keep thinking God took Mae before her time...to punish me."

"To punish you? But what have you done wrong?" Laurel was almost indignant in her defense of Carey.

Carey's finely curved mouth creased in silent agony. "A man's not supposed love another woman than his wife, Laurel."

Laurel stared at him in confusion for several seconds before the true meaning of his words soaked into her stubborn brain. When the realization finally came, she simply whispered, "I love you, too."

He hugged her tightly and she began to cry again, this time from exhaustion and confusion. When she once again ran out of tears, they quietly watched the sun disappear, leaving behind an immense, gaudy tapestry in the sky. The low clouds along the horizon exploded with vivid hues of orange and purple. Over their shoulders, in the eastern sky, a full moon rose in the still-blue sky.

"It's nearly suppertime," Laurel observed. "You'll have to be leaving soon."

"I can stay as long as you need me. The girls are at the Taylors."

With a sad smile, she indicated her appreciation. They regarded each other carefully. Without removing his eyes from Laurel's gaze, Carey softly caressed the tender skin of her throat.

She leaned closer and he lightly kissed her cheek, her forehead, her eyelids. Then he abruptly pulled away.

"Don't stop," she whispered.

"We've got to."

She took his face in her hands and kissed him hard on the lips. He returned her kiss, then stopped again and took hold of her shoulders. "Laurel, we can't."

"I want you to."

"You don't even know what your saying."

"Oh, yes, I do." To emphasize her point, she began unbuttoning her blouse.

He closed his hands over hers to stop them. "But Laurel, it's just that there's no going back."

"Please, Carey? Please?"

"But I'm leaving tomorrow," he reasoned miserably.

"If you really loved me, you'd do this."

Carey had to grin. "That's the line men always use on women!"

"Does it work?" Her smile carried a wicked challenge.

"Sometimes. But the truth is just the opposite. If I really loved you, I'd want what's best for you. And that's not this."

She sobered for a moment. "But, it's just that...I don't want you to forget me."

Carey smiled sadly. "Laurel McBryde, don't you know I could as soon forget you as forget my own name? As forget my own soul?"

She hugged him for saying this. "I know you're leaving and that this won't stop you, but...at least I'll know that this night of all the nights of my life, you loved me. At least I'll have that."

He surrendered his protest and kissed her softly, then harder. He gently maneuvered her onto her back and feverishly kissed her lips, her face, her throat.

"Oh, Laurel, my beautiful Laurel," he whispered over and over.

She tenderly cradled his blond head in her arms and shuddered slightly as he kissed the soft skin peeking from the top of her camisole once her blouse was off.

She passively allowed him to remove the remainder of her clothing, surprised at his efficiency in this complicated endeavor, but grateful as well. When the last stocking came off, she languorously stretched herself out on the enormous, fluffy pile of discarded petticoats, wool skirt, muslin underskirt, bustle, silk blouse, camisole, corset, muslin chemise, drawers–the endless list of fashionable female attire. I am naked and I am not ashamed, she thought, blithely mis-quoting Genesis.

She gazed up through the trees at the turquoise and pink sky. Somewhere a log fire burned, pleasantly scenting the autumn air as it cooled with the approach of evening. Laurel felt curiously detached, much as she had when he had kissed her last summer. She heard the sounds of him frantically pulling off his own clothes and tossing them aside. Was he afraid she might change her mind if he didn't hurry?

Still, she fixed her gaze not on her lover, but on the leaves that trembled overhead forming a mystical circle around them. My gazebo, she thought. My summerhouse. *The oddest, most wonderful sense of privacy, even though none actually exists. A dazzling enchantment.*

He kissed and caressed her with increasing passion. The warmth of his skin next to hers delighted her. She felt lost, wonderfully lost, outside herself. In the seclusion of this grove, among the wild indigo and rustling poplar leaves, the real world seemed very far away.

He paused briefly and looked down at her in the fading light. His face hovered so close she could not focus on both his eyes at once.

"Are you sure?" he whispered.

She nodded, but with less conviction than before.

"Afraid?"

"No," she lied.

❧

Much later, Carey lay on his back against the pile of their clothing and held Laurel tenderly as he stroked her long, dark hair. "You gonna be alright?"

She raised her head from his chest to look at him. "Of course."

He smiled with a deep sigh. "I just care about you so much. Everyone says the first time is the worst time–for girls, I mean."

"I'm fine. Stop worrying." Despite her nonchalance, Laurel had been startled by the pain involved in losing her virginity. Her private parts felt like a raw, open wound at the moment. She wondered offhand how frequently married women were expected to submit to so much discomfort. Not that she had any regrets. She would do it all over again in a heartbeat, so fiercely did she love him.

She hugged him as hard as she could. *If I do not speak or breathe or think or move, perhaps this particle of time will last forever.* He kissed her forehead and they held each other in silence for a while longer.

Carey unexpectedly groaned. "I'm a terrible man."

"Why?"

"My wife is barely a month in her grave and here I am in the arms of another woman."

"It's not your fault. I insisted."

Carey laughed softly. She watched the muscles of his lean, hard stomach contract with each chuckle. She idly played with the wiry blond hair that grew down the center of his chest.

"Mmmm...Laurel, I've been dreaming about this moment since the day we met."

She raised her head. "But what about our friendship? I thought we were friends."

Carey shrugged. "That's just the way men are, Laurel. A man can't look at a pretty woman and not think about...this." He gently ran his hand up and down the curve of her bare back.

"But I'm confused," Laurel groaned. "Was our friendship just a fiction?"

"No, I'm not saying that. Just because I love you don't mean I can't *like* you."

Laurel remained unconvinced. "I'm quite certain my uncle doesn't think about women in those terms."

Carey snorted with derision. "You've got a lot to learn about men! Trust me, he thinks about it. With you in his house, I bet he thinks about it a lot."

"Don't be absurd. Uncle Jack is married." Though she considered her uncle a handsome man, always dapper and well-groomed, she never once thought him to be a romantic figure. Still, she now recalled overhearing a couple of young girls remarking on Jack Hartmoor's appearance at a social she had recently attended. She later saw the same two girls chatting with her uncle, all giggles and shy smiles. She remembered how her uncle had self-consciously grinned in enjoyment of the silly young girls' attentions.

"I'm talking about lust, Laurel, not love. Putting a wedding ring on your finger don't shut it off. All men, still breathing, have it. Some just stifle it better than others."

All this talk of lust made her uncomfortable. She turned her attention back to more immediate concerns. "Can we still be considered friends after doing what we just did?"

Carey shrugged. "I guess we'll find out."

"But I want us to be friends forever."

"If you insist," he chuckled. "Friends forever." He rolled her onto her back again and kissed her slowly, deliberately. Not a kiss between friends, despite his words. He smiled down at her, then plucked up her silver locket and ran his fingers over its engraved surface.

"You always wear this, don't you?"

She nodded softly. "I never take it off."

He did not tarry longer with the locket, the only item she now wore, the only link she now had with all her past life. She flinched with shyness as his hand found its way irresistibly back to her breast. But his touch was so gentle, at least at first.

She hid her face against his shoulder as she felt him sliding inside her again.

"Are you cold?" he asked afterward, holding her tightly.

"A little," she confessed, though she did not look forward to them getting dressed again. Basking in the delicious afterglow of their intimacy was too rich, too rewarding.

They sat up and she watched sadly as he pulled on his clothes. As discreetly as possible, she tried to see what she could. She had never seen an adult male naked before and she was plainly curious.

Once again, his physical beauty made her sigh just as it had the April before when she first watched him mending that fence. Surely Adonis, even golden-haired Apollo, could not have been more perfectly formed than this prairie farm boy. She studied the exquisite composition of muscle and bone that was his splendid physique. Would this be the last time she ever saw him? She ached at the thought.

She reluctantly pulled on her clothes, enough to be decent at least. As he tugged at his boots, she suddenly threw her arms around his shoulders from behind.

"I can't let you go," she whispered mischievously, but she meant the words as well. "I know I'm being selfish. I know the work you're going to do is important, but I just can't bear the thought of you leaving me."

He smiled at her over his shoulder. "Believe me, I don't wanna leave you."

"Then don't."

"Oh, Laurel, you're so spoiled. You don't even know how much. Only rich people do what they *want* to do. The rest of us do what we have to do."

He disentangled himself and turned to her with a sadder smile. "Still, I wish I could imagine a world where you and me could be together."

"There has to be a way. Under a sky so wide as this, there has to be."

"Laurel, you weren't meant to be the wife of a dirt farmer."

"Maybe *you* weren't meant to be a dirt farmer."

"Kinda beside the point," he shrugged. "I mean, the Hartmoors ain't never gonna welcome somebody like me into the family, no matter what my job is."

"I don't know why you say that."

"Face it, Laurel, the only relation the Hartmoors and the Fairchilds of this world are ever gonna have is landlord and tenant."

"But the world's going to change. We're going to make it change."

Laurel's face contorted with tears again and Carey pulled her into his lap. She cried quietly against his neck, thinking back on the dining room discussion of many weeks ago. How her grandmother had said no Hartmoor woman would marry that far beneath her. How Jack had said he would not invite Carey into his home much less his family.

"Shh, Laurel, come on. Don't cry now."

"There has to be a way. We're two intelligent people. We have to be able to figure out something."

"I'll try and save up some money, but–" He squinted into the distance.

"I'll inherit my house at Windrift when I'm twenty-five."

"When's that? I guess I don't know how old you are."

"That's four years from now." Four years sounded like an eternity.

He tucked his face down next to hers and whispered, "Do you believe in long engagements?"

She jerked her head with such a start she bumped his chin. "Are you asking me...are you–?"

He lifted her off his lap and made her turn and face him. They both sat back on their heels. He reached over and ripped a sprig of wild indigo from the clump that grew next to the limestone outcropping. He stripped off the leaves and petals until only the hardy, green stem remained. He took her left hand and tied the stem several times around her ring finger.

"With this ring, I promise we'll somehow be together. Can't say when or how, but as long as you have this, you'll know. Now I better seal this promise with a kiss."

He pulled her close and kissed her gently, without passion. The simple ceremony was complete.

The full moon hung in the prairie sky like a silent witness, so bright it cast shadows in the beige film of the night landscape.

Carey saw Laurel grimace as he pulled her to her feet.

"Sore?" he asked shyly.

"A little." She blushed in the moonlight.

"Sorry." He gave her a sheepish grin, then kissed her forehead.

They walked along holding hands.

"Oh, I forgot," Laurel mentioned as they walked. "I had a present for you. I left it at the house."

Carey grinned. "I think you already gave me something pretty special."

"Stop teasing me," Laurel begged. She playfully poked his shoulder. Why must he keep talking about it? "It was a picture...oh, never mind." The thought of the picture brought back glum memories of the tragedy. "I'm afraid to go home. It's going to be so awful. I feel so bad about–"

"Be strong. Don't let them put the blame on you. It was nobody's fault, just a terrible, terrible accident."

When the Hartmoor house came into sight, Carey prepared to bid Laurel good night and goodbye. He bent to kiss her when something caught his eye. "Someone's running towards us."

Laurel stiffened.

"Don't worry," Carey whispered. "I'll handle everything."

"Laurel? Laurel, is that you?" The voice was Cassandra's.

"Yes, Aunt Cassie."

"Where on earth have you been? We've all been worried sick. It's nearly nine o'clock."

"You went for a long walk," Carey whispered.

"I...uh...went for a long walk."

"Don't worry, Miss Hartmoor. Your niece is alright."

"Carey? Is that you?" Cassandra held up a lantern as she reached them.

"I found Miss McBryde out walking and I insisted on escorting her home. She really shouldn't be out alone after dark." He tossed an impudent wink in Laurel's direction behind her aunt's back.

"I suppose Laurel told you what happened."

"Yes, ma'am. A terrible thing." He followed the two women toward the Hartmoor house.

"This farm's had more than its share of tragedy this fall, hasn't it, Carey?"

"Yes, ma'am."

"How's Aunt Alice?" Laurel asked.

"The doctor's given her something to make her sleep. The funeral's been set for day after tomorrow."

"I'm sorry I won't be able to attend, Miss Hartmoor. My girls and I are leaving bright and early tomorrow morning."

Laurel felt an awful sinking weight inside her the moment he mentioned his departure. How could she get through the next four hours, much less the next four years, without him?

Cassandra and Carey chatted casually as they walked. Laurel wondered, somewhat irritably, how Carey could act as though nothing had happened between them. Had what transpired really meant so little to him? Then she had to remind herself that the act was a lot newer to her than it was to him. He must have done it countless times during his six-year marriage to Mae. The overwhelming specialness must wear off with repetition, she concluded.

Margaret stood on the porch, silhouetted by the lights blazing inside the house. Laurel felt a chill as they drew near the porch steps.

"So Mr. Fairchild has returned you to us, Laurel." The tone of Margaret's voice made Laurel go even colder. "To run off and worry us on such a day, child."

"I'm sorry, Grandmother. I walked too far to get back before dark. Mr. Fairchild was kind enough to see me home." Laurel mounted the stairs. Carey and Cassandra were still engaged in an animated conversation in the yard.

"I thank you for your efforts, Carey," Margaret called as she prepared to re-enter the house.

"Not at all, ma'am."

"Thank you just the same." She disappeared, closing the front door behind her. Laurel felt immediately more at ease.

Carey called goodnight to Laurel and her aunt, wished his condolences to the bereaved parents, then turned to leave.

Cassandra joined Laurel on the porch. She wished Carey good luck on his move. Then she put her arm around Laurel's shoulder. This casual familiarity surprised Laurel.

"He was such a nice neighbor," Cassandra remarked. "I'll miss him."

Laurel swallowed hard. She strained to see his receding form in the gray light of the full moon. What if I never see him again? She bit her lip to keep from crying and clutched the ring of wild indigo around her finger.

"Laurel, I feel just awful about what Jack did to your camera."

"It doesn't matter."

"It was a childish thing. Inexcusable. He was just so upset and your camera happened to be there."

"I missed supper," Laurel interrupted, desperate to change the subject.

"Let's go in the kitchen. We'll find something. Friends have already started bringing food by. Food and funerals–they always go together, don't they?"

Chapter Sixteen

Laurel walked to the grove the following day convinced she had not drawn a breath since she had left this sacred circle of trees the night before. The Hartmoor house was steeped in the requisite attributes of mourning. A suffocating gloom hung in the shuttered, dimly lit rooms, almost as if the very admission of the cool October sunshine into the house would somehow show disrespect for the tiny figure so carefully laid out in the parlor.

Laurel escaped the house the moment an opportunity presented itself. She was desperate to be free of the busy silence now enveloping it. Laurel knew she had been spared most of the work in preparation for the coming funeral. She'd overheard Margaret tell a neighbor that Laurel must blame herself for the accident, thus explaining her long and mysterious absence of the evening before.

Laurel wasn't sure whether she blamed herself or not. Sleeping in the room she had shared with little Christine was almost impossibly sad. After Laurel had undressed for bed she sat before Christine's prized doll house and idly rearranged the furniture a couple of times as she had watched her little roommate do on countless occasions. She then picked up Christine's favorite doll and gently brushed its hair, then placed its lacy hat upon its head. She thought Alice might want the doll buried with her owner, unless it could better serve as a keepsake.

Laurel's heart spun in chaos from both the appalling accident combined with her shocking new intimacy with Carey. Images of both horror and pleasure flashed in her brain all night, making sleep impossible. The images did not stop with daybreak, but came to her in unexpected moments no matter what she was doing. She tried not to think about Carey in deference to Christine's memory, yet every time she successfully curbed thoughts of the night before, the achy remnants of Carey's intimate intrusion would remind her all over again.

She had not planned on losing her virginity that night and she did not know how she ought to react to the experience. Did she look different to the casual observer? Could the Hartmoors tell somehow? At the breakfast table, she could not bear to look anyone in the face, so fearful was she that her very expression would betray her. A doctor would know. She was certain of this. The pain and blood would surely have left clear evidence.

She couldn't honestly say she had physically enjoyed the experience, yet she had loved the *idea* of it, the tenderness, the fondness, the memory of how happy Carey had been, the captivating, possessive smile he had worn. Every aspect of the event thrilled and delighted her when she recalled it.

She felt guilty for being unable to concentrate on any problems but her own. She knew in that single fateful night she had tossed aside the last remnant of the polite veneer the Hartmoor family had so labored to enshroud her.

She longed to confide in someone. She needed to talk about it, bring it into some kind of comprehendible focus, but how could she? She sensed even Lydia, easily the most liberal-thinking of the Hartmoors, would be shocked by what she had done. She feared that she had now so transgressed the boundaries of acceptable behavior, she had placed herself beyond all comfort and counsel. She clearly remembered her grandmother's admonition the day after the picnic: "*All a woman has is her reputation. If she loses it, she is despised.*"

Would the Hartmoor's despise her if they knew? If only she could talk to someone. The only person she could confide in now was Carey, her accomplice in this little social crime, and he was gone.

She arrived at the poplar grove slightly downcast that it was empty. She knew intellectually that it would be. She knew he had left before dawn with his daughters. Yet, she had longed for some miracle to have detained him, changed his plans. But the grove stood empty and silent.

Inside of two months she had witnessed two terrible deaths first hand. Both involved people of whom she had not been fond. This similarity had tormented her with every step she took. She could not understand or explain it, but she could not shake the thought away, just the same.

She walked over to the limestone outcropping and found an unexpected gift–the volume of Shakespeare. She opened it to read a farewell message.

"*Four years–not forever.*

Love, C."

Every word spelled perfectly. Laurel sat down on the hard limestone, hugging the book to her chest. The tears now fell with no prying Hartmoor to see them.

Eventually the sobbing slacked off long enough for Laurel to drink in the delicious autumn air in the bright October shade. The grove seemed more a paradise than ever. The very atmosphere was charged with a timeless, insulating delight she had not experienced since leaving the mystical terrain of Windrift behind.

She unbuttoned the top of her black dress just enough to allow her access to the top of her corset cover where she had hidden Carey's photograph. She pulled it out and stared at it until the tears dried away.

She unceremoniously wiped her nose on her sleeve, then carefully opened her silver locket where she had preserved the ring of wild indigo, sandwiched between the portraits of her parents. She placed the twig ring on her finger, then kissed it.

The cloudy, damp coolness of the funeral morning threatened rain. Barely audible thunder could be heard in the southwestern sky as the Hartmoor family drove towards the Presbyterian church for the service. Laurel sat next to Lydia in the carriage. She placed a comforting arm around Laurel's shoulder.

The Hartmoor family made a somber, elegant ensemble in their well-tailored black silk. Laurel sat with Lydia in the church pew. She tried to keep her mind on the service but could not. The church, chilly and smelling faintly of wet plaster, drifted in a slow mural of sights and sounds before her eyes. How could October have turned out so awful?

A photograph Laurel had made of Christine sat propped on top of the tiny coffin in an ornate brass frame bedecked with flowers. Laurel overheard several mourners remark favorably on the likeness, but Laurel was too grief-stricken and sick at heart to take any pride in their compliments on her work.

The brief service concluded and Laurel rose with the others to reassemble at the little graveyard outside the church. The mourners walked along in pairs of two. The air smelled of damp leaves and the ground had a spongy feel as they proceeded. Cassandra took Alice's place beside Jack, entwining her arm in his. Alice was at home in bed, unable to cope with the formalities of grief. Her mother had arrived in Wichita by rail the night before and she had traveled by coach with Lydia that morning. She stayed at the Hartmoor house, tending her daughter.

ꝭ

Weeks passed and still the fragile Alice refused to heal. Concern for her grew in the Hartmoor house. At first, her outbursts of despair were tolerated and accepted. A mother losing her only child could hardly be expected to bear the loss lightly. Additional allowance was made for the known fact that another child was not a possibility, dooming the unfortunate Alice to a childless future.

But Hartmoors were not expected to languish in grief indefinitely, no matter how sharp the pain or how great the loss. Alice's behavior soon reached unacceptable proportions. She refused to dress, to groom herself, to eat with any regularity.

She wandered from room to room, pausing occasionally to sigh or weep. Ordinary conversation seemed beyond her. The family openly voiced concerns about her sanity and secretly worried that she might try to take her own life.

Laurel tried to replace Alice in the normal routine of household chores as best she could. In the late afternoon though, she escaped the gloomy atmosphere of the Hartmoor house to fall into the dappled sunlight of the poplar grove.

With Carey gone, the grove took on a shimmering dream-like new dimension, more delightful and intoxicating than anything her ordinary existence had to offer. She could imagine him at will, she could relive the night in his arms over and over editing out any part she didn't care for.

She could not understand why he had not written to her. Perhaps he was too busy. She spent many hours inventing excuses for his neglect. She had his ring, after all. With an air of ritual, she carefully pulled it from her silver locket and placed it on her finger whenever she entered the grove, then placed Carey's photograph against the limestone outcroping.

Because she was so certain Carey would write and tell her of his travels and his new job, she had looked forward to Jack's arrival home each evening with the mail. He slapped the packet of letters down on the hall table every night promptly at six. More importantly, he would write to say how much he loved her and how he longed for the day they could be together.

She tried to appear casual as she dug through the letters, but each day she was disappointed. No letter arrived addressed to her in Carey's careful block printing.

After weeks of such letdown, she slowly began to dread the sound of her uncle thumping the mail down on the little table. Each night she grew less hopeful and more worried. Had he forgotten her? Each day without a letter seemed a more compelling evidence of this distasteful proposition.

A sick feeling pulled at her insides and she sought to cleanse her mind of these unpleasant imaginings. She could not allow them to intrude on her blissful memories, on her imagined ideal of Carey's feelings for her.

She seemed to have lost her appetite along with her virginity. From the day Carey left, the sight, even the smell of food repulsed her. She stopped coming down to breakfast because she wearied of explaining why she wasn't tearing into the eggs and fried potatoes with her usual gusto.

She found reasons for missing the noon meal, but family suppers were impossible to avoid. Nights on which Cassandra cooked were the worst. She took anyone's lack of appetite as a personal insult to her cooking skills.

"What's wrong with my chicken tonight?" she would explode on Laurel.

Laurel would shrug. "I'm sorry, Aunt Cassie, I'm just not hungry."

"Look at you, child," Margaret remarked on more than one occasion. "You're as thin as a rail. Don't tell me we're going to have to take those skirt waists in again."

Laurel had heard of the phrase "love sickness," but had never guessed such a malady actually existed. Still, every time she saw her hollow-cheeked face staring back at her in the little mirror above the washstand in her room, she began to wonder what was wrong with her. Love sickness–that had to be it.

✤

The Farmers Alliance grew as a force in the community. Laurel thought of Carey every time she saw their bright banners displayed at the Grange Office. One Sunday afternoon the organization held a picnic on the edge of town. All the farmers within a ten-mile radius of Chisholm gathered at the opposite end of town in their wagons and drove to the meeting site in a slow procession through Chisholm's main street. Many of the wagons sported banners with slogans like, "Death to the Monopolies" and "The Farmer is All."

Some parade wagons took a humorous turn. One filled with young children bore the signage, "Overproduction." Laurel was politically savvy enough to get the jibe. The remark took direct and satirical aim at the Republican claims that the farmers' current woes were entirely due to overproduction.

The turnout astonished and pleased Laurel. She lost count of how many wagons participated in the line somewhere after a hundred and eighty. A fine brass band brought up the rear of the parade.

Laurel and the Hartmoors watched the procession from their buggy just after church let out.

"*Kickers*," Jack muttered with contempt, but Laurel could tell by the tension in his voice that he felt increasingly threatened by the farm community's growing cohesion. Kickers, that's what they called them. Well, if Carey was a kicker, then she was one, too.

She strained her eyes hoping to see Carey in the throng of farmers, but he was not there. Undoubtedly, he was still in the western counties organizing similar events. She noted that the display lacked an overt political edge, though she knew from correspondence with Mrs. Lease's group that many hoped the Farmers Alliance would cast off the last pretense of its original non-partisanship and throw its growing influence into direct support of political candidates. Such a move would finally give the Republicans a serious challenge to their long-held and complacent dominance.

The following morning an editorial appeared in the Chisholm Courier condemning the Alliance picnic. The editor, a Republican and one of Jack Hartmoor's close friends, denounced the goals of the group and laid the farmers' problems entirely at their own door. He even raised the suggestion that Mr. Darwin's "survival of the fittest" doctrine should be applied to social situations and that the smartest and most "fit" naturally prosper, while the less able are doomed to failure.

This pompous pronouncement rankled Laurel to such a degree, she felt motivated for the first time in her life to write a letter to the editor. She carefully composed her thoughts on paper, then rewrote them several times until the letter satisfied her objectives. She wrote, in part,

"*To suggest that the principals of Darwinism should be applied to society is both self-serving and despicable. The "struggle for existence" may rightly apply to the natural world and the competition between species for survival against the elements, but to use this theory to exonerate, or even explain, the exploitation of one man over another is more selfish than any good Christian could possibly imagine. For the wealthy to oppress the working class and claim it is their "right" is not to be tolerated by any nation which purports to grant life, liberty, and the pursuit of happiness to all its citizens.*"

In a final bid to be taken seriously, Laurel signed the letter with the pseudonym, M.A. Blaine. She did not want the editor to know a woman wrote the letter for fear it would be attacked on that basis alone. Further, she feared to anger her uncle on the sensitive Farmers Alliance issues. She still essentially crept around him, worried that he blamed her for the death of little Christine, though he had never said a word to this effect since the dreadful day itself.

To Laurel's delight, her letter was published in the Courier the following day. Though the editor, in postscript, wondered who "M.A. Blaine" might be, he acknowledged that the writer had expressed "his" opinions well. The day after Laurel's letter appeared, six more letters were printed in response to hers. Half supported her, half agreed with the editor, but all speculated as to the identity of "M.A. Blaine."

Satisfied with her efforts, Laurel longed to share them with Carey. She wished she knew how to contact him. Surely he would be proud of her stand. Even Mr. Kellerman, the local Farmers Alliance leader, had praised her letter in print and had asked "M.A. Blaine" to come forward and join the Alliance.

Ironically, when Laurel timidly stopped by the Alliance office, now called the Grange Co-operative Store, to offer her services, she was coolly received.

"Aren't you related to Jack Hartmoor?" Mr. Kellerman had asked with an apprehensive frown. When Laurel nodded in the affirmative, Kellerman quietly observed, "I don't quite see how ladies whose families own banks can be too worried about our concerns."

Laurel had walked home glumly, smarting from Mr. Kellerman's snub. She was used to having her sex held against her, but to have her sincerity doubted because of her adopted family's social status left her bewildered and uncertain what to do next.

She finally decided to write to Lydia and ask if there were some way she could quietly involve herself in the Equal Suffrage Association.

❧

As October neared its end, the prairie turned a thousand shades of beige highlighted here and there with a faint burgundy hue from a maize field or amber from a ribbon of underbrush. The afternoons continued cool and sun bright.

One day, Laurel arrived at the grove to discover that the trees had lost the last of their leaves to a morning rain and an afternoon wind. The now-discolored foliage lay in damp heaps upon the ground. Through the empty branches, the western sky glowed with a strange purple and orange radiance of the setting sun.

Laurel smiled and kicked the leaves as she recalled for the millionth time what had happened there. A delightful tremor coursed through her at the mere thought of Carey, then was quickly replaced with the sting of his neglect. Where was he now? Why didn't he write to her? Why did he stop caring for her? Unbidden tears washed away the last remnant of blithe sentiments.

As the sun disappeared to leave only an ugly crimson stain behind, Laurel pulled Carey's photograph from its hiding place in her corset cover and very deliberately ripped it to shreds. With a sigh of bitter resignation, she tossed them into the chilly autumn twilight. October was gone. And so was Carey.

Chapter Seventeen

On the advice of Dr. Parnell, Margaret took Alice on a month-long visit to St. Louis to stay with her family. Laurel witnessed a surprising shift in the tone of the household the moment they left. Cassandra sometimes slept until noon and seldom came in from riding for luncheon, while Jack became much less surreptitious in his visits to the locked china cabinet. In the evenings, he openly enjoyed his whiskey at the table after dinner.

Cassandra and Jack seemed magically transformed back into their childhood selves. They became once again brother and sister–fighting, teasing, cajoling, expressing irreverent opinions they never voiced in the presence of their overbearing mother.

"These are the worst muffins I ever et in all my days," Jack proclaimed at breakfast one morning.

Laurel knew by his expression and the tone of his comment that his only motive was to tease his sister.

Cassandra took the bait. "Wear it, then!" She tossed a muffin at her startled sibling.

"I'll be damned, they *do* bounce!" He promptly retaliated with a return volley.

Laurel shrieked at the outrageousness of it all. She laughingly took cover under the table. She never imagined middle-aged people could act so silly. As the breakfast war continued overhead, Laurel suddenly felt ill. She rose too quickly from her hiding place and bumped her head.

When she got to her feet, she immediately vomited all over her place at the breakfast table.

"Oh, God," Jack cried in disgust.

"I'm sorry, I'm sorry," Laurel whispered hoarsely. She wiped her face on her napkin as Jack and Cassandra hurriedly picked up the breakfast dishes.

"I'll wash this," Laurel murmured as she folded back the tablecloth.

"You'll go sit down on the porch," Cassandra ordered. "Get some fresh air."

Jack left for the bank and Cassandra soon joined Laurel outside.

"Feeling better?"

"I'm sorry. I'm so embarrassed."

"Maybe you should see the doctor. You haven't been well for several weeks. You're looking so thin."

"I'm sure it's nothing," Laurel insisted, but she knew her aunt was right. She had lost a shocking amount of weight over the course of the autumn. Her arms looked downright scrawny and every single rib could be counted on sight. Thank God none of the family ever saw her without her clothes on. They had no notion of how thin she had actually become. She had taken to stuffing handkerchiefs down the front of her corset to make up for the lack of fullness in her breasts. Her thin hips could be cloaked in a second and even a third petticoat. She had begun to wonder if something more sinister were afoot than love sickness.

"I've just had my mind on a lot lately. I don't know, just nerves. A nervous stomach."

"Why should you be nervous?"

Laurel shrugged with a vague smile to change the subject. She could not divulge the true reason she was so on edge. "Is Uncle Jack seriously thinking of running for mayor?" Jack had mentioned nothing of this at the family dinner table, but an article in the Chisholm Courier had speculated that Jack Hartmoor was a likely candidate for the Spring election.

Cassandra shrugged. "He's talked about it on and off for several years. I don't know. I think the problems with Alice will keep him out of the race next year. Still, it might give him something new to do with his time. You know, take his mind off Christine and all."

"That would be grand," Laurel observed. "Just think, Aunt Cassie, we might be able to vote for him. The legislature is considering a bill this very term that would allow women to vote in municipal elections."

"Laurel, do you and Lydia ever think of anything besides suffrage?"

"I just think it's exciting, that's all."

"Well, if we get the vote, I guess I'll go vote for him, but I'm not kept awake at night by the prospect."

"Oh, I'd vote for him, too. I just wish we agreed on a few more issues, is all."

"Let's just hope Alice's health improves."

Laurel shivered with the mention of "health." The topic preoccupied her lately.

Cassandra sat in her mother's favorite chair, the white wicker rocker, that Margaret complained was a magnet for the prairie dust. She sipped her coffee and gazed out on the quiet fields, then pulled her woolen shawl more tightly about her shoulders. "This is the first year I can remember since we've lived here that we haven't attended the Firemen's Ball."

"I've heard so much about it, I have to admit I was curious." The Hartmoors would not be attending social events for the remainder of the year as was considered appropriate for a family plunged into mourning.

"Maybe next year," Cassandra said with a resigned shrug. "Jack leaves tomorrow for St. Louis."

"To bring Grandmother and Aunt Alice home?"

Cassandra nodded.

"I hope Aunt Alice is better."

"Don't we all?" Cassandra murmured. "Mother's letters haven't been encouraging. She said Alice hired a charlatan of some sort who claimed to be able to talk to the dead. And Alice's mother paid for it!"

"A spiritualist?" Laurel asked with interest. The occult fascinated her even though she didn't really believe in it. "Did they actually contact her?"

"Christine? They claimed to. Alice wept with delight, according to the last letter. Mother thought the whole thing to be blasphemous, I can tell you."

"I think I agree with her."

Laurel bided her time, hesitating to bring up a subject that had been on her mind a lot recently. "How is your friend, Hazel?"

Cassandra sighed. "Not well. Not well at all. Her fevers are more frequent and her coughing–so terrible."

"Coughing and fevers," Laurel murmured to herself.

"She's leaving soon, you know. Going to Denver. A sanatorium there is promising yet another miracle cure."

"You don't think they'll be able to help her?"

Cassandra shook her head with a frown.

"What were her earliest symptoms of the consumption?"

"I don't remember really. She's been sick for so long. At least two years. I think she complained of feeling terribly tired. No appetite. Why do you ask, Laurel?"

"No reason."

The first day of December brought the return of the Hartmoor family to Chisholm along with the season's first ice storm. At dawn, a clear, thin gloss coated the entire county and gave the tree outside Laurel's window a jewel-like glow as the sun's ray's reflected off its glistening branches. By noon, the ice had melted, leaving only a cold dampness in the air.

Jack, Margaret, and Alice arrived in the late afternoon amid as much noise and confusion as had attended their departure. Margaret snapped out orders with ruthless efficiency and the rest of the family marched in step, as always.

Laurel thought Alice appeared much improved. The color had returned to her pale cheeks. Cassandra remarked to her brother cheerfully on this change only to be met with a frowning acknowledgment.

When Laurel politely inquired after Alice's health as she helped her grandmother out of the carriage, Margaret only shook her head with a grumbled, "We'll see."

Laurel and Cassandra discovered at supper why Jack and his mother had been so reluctant to note Alice's improvement. As they sat around the table preparing to begin the meal, Alice, who smiled with a quiet, but almost eerie delight, announced it was time to say grace.

Laurel raised her eyebrows. In the Hartmoor house, grace was reserved for the large noon meal on Sundays following church. All bowed their heads in compliance with this pious request.

What followed stunned both Laurel and Cassandra. Alice's "grace" turned into a rambling, fervent conversation with the Lord that lasted nearly ten minutes.

After the first five minutes, Laurel looked up and cast questioning glances at the other diners. Jack sat with his head propped on one elbow. His visit to St. Louis had evidently prepared him for this onslaught. Margaret, too, sat back in her chair and gazed tiredly at the ceiling.

Alice continued her prayer in a devout monotone with hands folded, head bowed, and eyes tightly shut. Finally, without waiting for Alice to finish, Jack helped himself to the mashed potatoes, then the gravy. He passed the serving plates on to Cassandra, who looked to her mother for guidance. Eating while Alice prayed seemed to Laurel awfully disrespectful, but Margaret nodded to Cassandra, who then helped herself. Laurel felt ill-at-ease, but followed suit. Mercifully, Alice concluded with a heartfelt, "Amen," before the serving dishes reached her side of the table.

"Alice, dear, would you be so kind as to fetch me another fork from the kitchen?" Margaret asked her daughter-in-law. "I seemed to have misplaced mine."

"Yes, Mother Hartmoor, I'd be happy to." Alice rose from the table cheerfully. "Husband, do you need anything from the kitchen while I'm up?"

"No, thank you, Wife."

The moment Alice was out of earshot, Cassandra whispered, "What, in heaven's name, is going on with her?"

Margaret sighed. "She's been like this since the night of that...that seance."

Jack rolled his eyes. "I could just throttle my mother-in-law for promoting such nonsense."

"What's happened to Aunt Alice exactly, Grandmother?"

"Your aunt has become, what I would call *excessively* religious."

Laurel was not sure what this meant. "She seems so much happier."

"Oh, she's happy alright," pronounced Jack. "The question is whether she's also sane."

Alice returned to the table and the discussion came to an abrupt halt. She beamed with a luminescent glow. "I so look forward to the coming Christmas season. Laurel, what Christmas traditions did you and your father share at Windrift?"

"We never had much of a celebration, I'm afraid. I'm looking forward to joining in the Hartmoor traditions."

"In light of our recent loss, Alice, we needn't have a big to-do this year," said Margaret kindly.

"Nonsense. The Lord wishes us to celebrate his birth. My darling Christine will sing carols with the angels this year."

This was the first time Laurel could remember Alice bringing up Christine's name without bursting into tears.

After supper, Laurel helped Margaret clear the table.

"Jack tells me you haven't been feeling well, Laurel."

"Oh, a little stomach upset. It's nothing, I'm sure."

"He said you'd not felt well for several weeks. You look pale, child. And thinner."

"I'm sure it's nothing."

ꕥ

In the days that followed, the family's patience with Alice's new found religious zeal wore thinner. "Grace" lasted longer every night and soon the Hartmoors paid Alice no heed. They carried on with eating and even conversation over the fanatic monotone of her prayer offerings.

Laurel helped Alice all she could with the Christmas decorations and gift-making. Her holidays in the Flint Hills were nonexistent and her knowledge of holiday traditions came mostly from books she'd read. Their first activity was the selection of a tree to decorate. Only small, scrubby pines grew locally. Alice complained that they lacked the delicious scent of a fir, but were attractive to decorate nonetheless. On a bright, cold day, in the second week of December, Jack cut down a small specimen from the grove just west of the house at Alice's direction. They set it up in a little stand atop the tea table in the parlor.

When Alice left to foray in the attic for the many boxes of decorations, Jack surprised Laurel with an unexpected expression of gratitude.

"I want to mention my appreciation for your...tolerance of my wife's...eccentricities." He mumbled this statement without looking at Laurel. Seldom did he meet her gaze or look upon her in any direct way.

"I don't mind," Laurel offered, referring to Alice's non-stop preaching. Alice found religion in every single occurrence of the day, or seemed to. Laurel knew Jack was deeply self-conscious about Alice's recent behavior. "I want to help, Uncle Jack. I know this is a hard time."

Jack nodded. "I wanted to mention something else. I never apologized for...your camera."

Laurel tensed. She hated any reference to the terrible day of Christine's death. The subject was a silent, open wound in the Hartmoor house, everyone aware of it, but no one willing to speak of it directly.

"I'm sorry. I blamed your hobby, not you personally."

"I understand, Uncle Jack."

Jack nodded again, still avoiding Laurel's eyes. He abruptly left the room the moment Alice reappeared.

Alice and Laurel decorated the little pine with ribbons, candles, and a magnificent collection of glass ornaments. Every bauble seemed to have its own story and Laurel listened with delight as Alice told the history of each Dresdan, kugel, and sebnitz.

In a final flourish, Laurel and Alice hung glossy wisps of spun glass from every bough. The decorating did not stop with the completion of the Christmas tree. Every room of the Hartmoor house would feel the touch the season before Laurel and Alice completed their labors. Sprigs of greenery, red ribbon, and store-bought holly adorned the windows, mirrors, and picture frames.

Laurel's mysterious health problems did not improve during December. She found she often felt weak though she did not have any more public attacks of vomiting. She worried silently, but said nothing. Each day left her more convinced of the dreadful cause of her problems. Fear twisted in her stomach like a knife, often making the mere thought of food impossible.

Her fears did not escape the notice of Margaret.

"Child, what's bothering you?" Margaret asked as they worked together rolling cookies three days before Christmas.

"Nothing."

"It's not nothing. You've become so terribly thin. Now tell me what ails you."

Tears filled Laurel's eyes. She couldn't hold it in any longer. "Oh, Grandmother, I'm so afraid."

"Afraid of what? Now, now, calm down." She gently pulled Laurel close and let her sob into her broad, soft bosom.

Laurel wiped her wet face, took a deep breath, and whispered, "I think...I think I'm...*dying!*"

Cassandra accompanied Laurel to the office of Dr. Parnell. Margaret had promised to help decorate the church for the Christmas Eve service that would take place the following evening so she had drafted Cassandra to escort Laurel to her first-ever doctor visit.

"You're worrying for nothing," Cassandra said, as they made their way up the outside staircase of the town's only hotel to the second story doctor's office. A fall of snow the night before had blanketed the landscape like the powdery confections the housewives of Chisholm were concocting in their Christmas kitchens. "I'm sure you're fine."

Laurel nodded nervously when they reached the door. They entered a small waiting room furnished sparsely with the doctor's writing desk and bookcase full of medical literature. They could hear a baby crying in the examining room. They shook the snow from the hems of their skirts and sat on a simple bench near the pot-bellied stove while the snow on their boots dripped into little puddles on the rough-hewn plank floor.

"What on earth gave you the notion that you had the consumption, anyway?"

Laurel shrugged miserably in her heavy woolen coat. Her nose still ran from breathing the bitter cold prairie air. "I have many of the signs. Many of the signs you said Hazel Carmichael had."

"Poor Hazel," Cassandra sighed.

The door to the examining room opened and a young mother carrying the crying baby emerged. She smiled and greeted Cassandra as she passed.

"Merry Christmas, ladies," Dr. Parnell said jovially. He clapped his hands together. "What can I do for you this fine cold day?"

Cassandra opened her mouth to speak, but before she could utter a word, two men burst in the door to the office. One man supported the other whose knee gushed blood.

"Fred got hisself cut real bad, Doc. Chopping wood and missed."

"Bring him in here before he bleeds to death on my office floor. Sorry, ladies, this will take awhile," Parnell called over his shoulder as he helped usher the injured man into his examining room.

"Oh, well, do you want to stay here or go shop a spell, then come back?"

"I'll stay," said Laurel. Her mind was too preoccupied to enjoy a shopping expedition. "Why don't you go out and shop. I don't want to miss my turn."

"Suit yourself. I'll be back in half an hour."

The minute Cassandra left the office, Laurel dove into the doctor's collection of medical books. She searched the pages to seek out possible causes for her symptoms other than the dreaded consumption. Her eyes scanned the various indices for malaise, nausea, fatigue, and lack of menses.

The more she read the more nervous she became, but not because she thought she was consumptive.

Cassandra returned before the doctor had finished stitching up the bleeding man. Laurel snapped shut the large book on her lap the moment her aunt entered the office.

"I don't need to see Dr. Parnell after all," she announced.

"Why not?"

"I'm not consumptive," Laurel said decisively.

"Well, the family will certainly be relieved to hear that."

"Oh, I'm not so sure," Laurel said with a miserable expression. "When they find out what's really wrong with me, they'll *wish* I was consumptive."

Laurel rushed upstairs to her room the moment they returned home. She did not bother to remove her coat or boots.

Margaret poked her head out of the kitchen to see her swish by in a flurry. "Well, what did Emory say?" she called to Cassandra.

Cassandra hung her coat on the hall tree and walked into the kitchen. "We never saw him."

"What on earth?"

"Laurel thinks she knows more about medicine than the doctor, I guess. She read some of his medical books and up she stands and says she knows what's wrong with her and that she doesn't need to see the doctor."

"Well, that's the silliest thing I've ever heard."

"It gets better still. She says she doesn't have the consumption like she thought, but when we find out what's really wrong with her we'll wish she had consumption."

Margaret rolled her eyes and sighed in frustration. "As if we didn't have enough to worry about already."

"Living with the daughter of the Holy Ghost and all."

"Hush. Don't talk about your poor sister-in-law that way."

Laurel did not join the family for dinner, but Margaret was too busy with the holiday cooking to make a fuss. When Laurel chose to forfeit breakfast as well, concern replaced idle conjecture. She rapped sharply on Laurel's door.

"Laurel, what's ailing you? We haven't seen you since yesterday, child."

"I'm fine."

"Then why will you not come out of your room? It's Christmas Eve and Lydia is arriving on the afternoon coach. Don't you want to go into town to meet her?"

"No, ma'am. I'd prefer to stay home."

"Laurel, are you crying?"

"No, ma'am."

Margaret gave up momentarily. She had too many items on her holiday preparation schedule to tarry much longer at Laurel's door.

Jack picked up Lydia after the bank closed at three.

Margaret and Alice rushed out into the yard to greet their guest. They tried to embrace her without showering her in the flour that coated their aprons. As Jack unloaded Lydia's luggage and Christmas parcels from the carriage, the women departed the yard for the warmth of the house. Before entering, Margaret pressed Lydia's elbow to detain her.

"When Laurel stayed with you last summer, did she mention any special friends? Ones I might not know about?"

"Why...no," Lydia hesitated, recalling only too well the young man Laurel had said tried to kiss her. But Laurel had sworn her to secrecy. "I mean...uh...surely none that you would not know of, Margaret."

Margaret frowned at this equivocal response and took her daughter-in-law's arm in her own as the pair entered the hall. When Lydia had shaken out her wrap, she followed the others into the dining room where Cassandra was laying out the silverware for supper. She embraced her sister-in-law and exchanged holiday greetings.

"Any sign of Laurel?" Margaret demanded.

"Still up there–not a sound," Cassandra responded.

"Is Laurel ill?" Lydia inquired.

The whole family jerked to attention when Margaret marched up to Laurel's room. She rapped on the door, tried the knob, then shouted, "Laurel, enough of this foolishness! Come down to the parlor this instant!"

Few dared cross Margaret Hartmoor when she used that tone and no one was surprised when a humble voice on the other side of the door meekly replied, "Yes, Grandmother."

Laurel followed Margaret down the stairs, dressed in only her nightgown and a knitted woolen shawl. Her hair hung down her back to her waist like a dark veil and her bare feet looked almost blue with the cold as she entered the parlor where the rest of the family assembled near the crackling fire in the fireplace and brightly decorated Christmas tree.

Laurel gazed briefly at the circle of anxious faces. Lydia sat next to the fire and Jack stood on the other side of the hearth. Cassandra and Alice took seats on the settee in the bay window. Margaret stood in the center of the room like a small, stout mistress of ceremonies.

"Sit down," she commanded.

Laurel complied, taking a seat in a straight chair nearest the door.

"Laurel, I think it's high time you shared with us what has been troubling you. We're your family. We have a right to know."

Laurel made no attempt to reply, but instead looked away. She thought how pretty the frosty crystals on the bay window looked as they brightly reflected the late day sun.

"Laurel, would you be more inclined to speak if your uncle left the room?"

Laurel looked at her grandmother in guilty dismay. This expression only gave Margaret's suspicions more weight. Laurel quickly dropped her gaze to her lap. Her long hair closed around her, obscuring her face.

"Laurel, do think you might be with child?"

A shocked gasp rose from the ladies in the room.

Laurel lifted her head and glanced at her grandmother with a trembling lower lip. She nodded slightly and bowed her head again.

"Oh, dear," whispered Alice.

"I'll be damned," snorted Jack.

"Husband, such language," scolded Alice.

"Sorry."

"Who'd have guessed it?" murmured Cassandra.

Lydia sat quietly. She studied Laurel intently as she recalled Margaret's question on the front porch and now understood its implication.

"My next question is obvious, Laurel," Margaret continued. "Who is responsible?"

Laurel looked up at her grandmother blankly.

"The father, Laurel–who is the father of the child?"

Laurel dropped her head again. "I cannot say."

"Cannot or will not?"

This question inspired Laurel. "Cannot," she answered firmly. "A stranger...I was attacked."

A second shock wave passed over the little audience.

"When did this happen?" Cassandra asked with more curiosity than concern.

"In the fall," Laurel began extemporaneously. She was adamant in her desire not to mention Carey Fairchild's name. He had not written to her in all these months and she would not have him contacted now under these circumstances. Her pride would not bend on this point. "I was walking home from town one day–"

"You walked all the way into town?" Cassandra inquired. She could not imagine anyone walking if they had the opportunity to ride.

"Yes, and the weather turned sharply cooler and it started to rain. I didn't have a proper wrap, you see, I was getting terribly cold and wet. Miserably cold, in fact, and a man pulled up along side me in a carriage–"

"On the main road?" Cassandra interrupted.

"Yes. And he offered to drive me home."

"You spoke to a total stranger?" Alice asked, her pale gray eyes wide with shock.

"I know it was wrong. I know I shouldn't have accepted. It was foolish and stupid, but I was just so cold and wet. Anyway, he didn't drive me home. He drove me to an alley back in town and then he...." Laurel let her voice trail off melodramatically.

"In the rain?" Jack asked, dubious at this plot development.

"A shed, a covered shed in an alley. He threatened me with a knife and said he'd kill me if I tried to resist. I screamed, but no one heard me. Then I escaped and ran all the way home. It was a terrible experience." Laurel clenched her hands in her lap. She worried that her last words had tumbled out a little too quickly.

"Why didn't you tell anyone?" Cassandra asked.

"I was too ashamed."

"But the sheriff," Cassandra persisted. "He must be notified. This man should be apprehended."

"Well..." Laurel's mind raced for an explanation. "I think he was a stranger, just passing through Chisholm. I never saw him again."

A short silence followed, broken this time by Margaret. "That was a very interesting story, Laurel, but I would prefer you tell us the truth."

"That *is* the–" A single fierce look from Margaret told Laurel to continue was hopeless. She wished she had practiced this story in advance, perfected the detail, made the performance more convincing. "Wouldn't it be better for everyone if we pretended the story were true?"

"I'm afraid not. Now tell us the name of the man responsible."

"But why?"

"He must marry you, of course."

"No."

"You have no choice now, Laurel." Margaret placed her hands firmly on her hips in exasperation.

"Marriage is out of the question, I'm afraid." The thought of Carey forced into yet another marriage to a woman he didn't want was too humiliating to contemplate. That she could fall to the lowly estate of a Mae Fairchild–she could not imagine a worse fate. And yet she had no idea what fate might actually lay in store for her, now that she had so completely ruined her chances in life.

"Marriage or no, there are legal ramifications to all of this. You must tell us the man's name. He has placed you in this inconvenient position and it is his duty to extricate you from it as well. Now tell us his name!"

"No!"

"Laurel, whomever he is, I can assure you he does not deserve your protection. This man has greatly wronged you."

"Then I certainly do not wish to be married to a man who has 'wronged' me. But I don't wish to blame anyone but myself. What has happened is the consequence of my own choice."

"Then you are a selfish and wicked girl. Do you think the consequences of your wanton behavior affect only yourself?"

Margaret's words fell hard on Laurel. The thought that she had hurt others besides herself was a sobering new viewpoint.

"I'm sorry. I never meant to cause you trouble."

"You've disgraced yourself and you've brought shame to this family, child. Once this becomes widely known, your reputation will be quite permanently blackened."

Laurel recalled Margaret's words after the picnic once again: *All a woman has is her reputation. If she loses it, she is despised.*

"Please believe me when I tell you...I'm sorry." She tightened the woolen shawl as she rose slowly and left the parlor. She stole a single glance over her shoulder to see Cassandra shaking her head in surprise and disgust, Margaret staring at the floor in perplexed anger, Lydia looking directly at her in an unhappy confusion of guilt, and Alice benignly gazing out the bay window, preoccupied with distant thoughts. Jack abruptly left the parlor and proceeded directly to the locked china cabinet from which he withdrew one of his illicit bottles of whiskey to pour himself a drink. From the stairs, Laurel could see him bolt down the contents of the small glass and just as quickly pour another. Laurel had never seen him drink before supper, although he occasionally came home from Volunteer Firemen's meetings smelling of liquor.

When she reached her bedroom, she collapsed onto the bed, emotionally exhausted from the parlor scene and worn out from twenty-four hours of no food, no sleep, and sheer horror.

Soon enough she heard a soft knock at the door.

"Go away, please." She couldn't bear talking about it further. Since the moment she had returned from the doctor's office, she had retreated to the center of her bed, almost too dazed and confused to cry. As though in the eye of a whistling tornado, she had sat there quietly while blinding winds screamed around her, obscuring both past and future, imprisoning her mind in the single fact of the present.

Now she had to cope with the added humiliation of everyone *knowing* what she and Carey had done together that fateful night in October. The memory of her own wanton behavior shocked and shamed her. How could she have so thoroughly abandoned good sense and good morals that night?

"Laurel, I'd like to talk with you," came Lydia's voice.

With resignation, Laurel rose and crossed the room. She pulled the key from the knob and returned to her bed.

Lydia shut the door behind her and leaned back against it with her arms thoughtfully folded. "Are you absolutely sure about this? Have you talked to the doctor?"

"I read about it at the doctor's office. I'm sure."

"But Margaret and Cassie said you told them you thought you had the consumption."

Laurel smiled in embarrassment. "I was confused. You see, Aunt Cassie's friend, Hazel, she has it and Cassie told grandmother and me that she stopped having her monthlies and so I thought...I thought...oh, I feel so stupid."

"Have you told the baby's father about this?"

Laurel violently shook her head.

"Don't you think you should?"

"He's forgotten me," Laurel blurted out and started to cry.

Lydia rushed to her bedside and cradled Laurel in her arms. "There, there, poor girl. Hush now."

When Laurel paused to blow her nose and wipe her eyes, Lydia continued, "We'll figure something out. I'll help you all I can. I'd invite you to live with me, but I can't afford both you and a child in these hard times. It's all I can do to keep the store going. I could perhaps keep you through your confinement. But then you must make plans for the future."

"I'm grateful, Aunt Lydia. I suppose the Hartmoors don't want me anymore."

"Well, your condition poses something of an embarrassment to them. They are highly visible members of the local community, after all. I'm sure they feel they have a reputation to maintain."

"But what about *your* reputation?"

Lydia chuckled. "I suppose I don't have as much to lose."

Laurel tried to smile through her tears.

Chapter Eighteen

Lydia found the Hartmoor family assembled in the dining room, preparing to sit down to their Christmas Eve dinner. Lydia took her place with Jack, Cassandra, and Margaret. Alice had retreated to her room since the parlor revelations and had not yet reappeared.

Margaret sat a large, roasted goose on the table before Jack, who picked up a carving knife and fork.

"Well, Lydia, what did she say?" Margaret demanded. "Any hope for a marriage?"

"None, I'm afraid. The man involved has apparently abandoned her."

"That's unfortunate," Margaret sighed.

Jack shook his head with a bitter smile. "We worry for months because no man seems to like her, only to find out now that one liked her too well."

"*Jack*," his mother reprimanded.

Cassandra smothered a giggle into her napkin.

"Well, it's true, isn't it?" defended Jack with mock innocence.

Cassandra laughed out loud at this.

"Cassandra," Margaret hissed.

"I'm sorry, Mother, but he does have a point. I mean, who would ever have guessed?"

"I wonder who did the deed?" Jack asked rhetorically.

"I have to admit, the thought crossed my mind to ask if perhaps you–"

"*Mother*, how could you suspect me? I'm her uncle, for heaven's sake."

"I'm sorry, son. I didn't seriously consider the possibility. It's just that you had the oddest expression on your face in the parlor when–oh, never mind."

"And she's my ward. I'm legally responsible for her welfare until she reaches the age of twenty-five. This will undoubtedly reflect poorly on me, on my abilities as a guardian. And what if others in the community start scandalous gossip?"

"Let's concentrate on one problem at a time, Jack," interrupted his mother.

"My chances for becoming mayor just went down the well. That's for sure." Jack sighed. "If we knew who the rascal was, I'd...I'd–"

"Martin Simpson showed an interest in her last summer." Cassandra ventured.

"But he's married now."

"What about Jeffery Shaw?"

"Doubtful. I don't think he ever wanted to see her again after that time he came calling. I still can hardly look his father in the face. One of the Taylor boys, perhaps? They're never up to any good."

"What about Carey Fairchild?" was Cassandra's next guess.

"He's been gone since Mae died," Margaret interjected. "And I couldn't believe that of Carey."

"He was bold enough to take liberties at the Fourth of July picnic, Mother," Jack said.

"And he walked her home *after dark* the night of Christine's accident." Cassandra showed enthusiasm for this new theory.

"And look at the circumstances of his marriage," Jack added. "Old Man Brock had to beat the living daylights out of him to get him to do right by his daughter."

"It's hard to believe Laurel would be attracted to someone with so little education to impress her," countered Cassandra.

"And she was friends with his wife," Margaret mentioned.

"Laurel and Mae were friends?" Cassandra asked.

"Where is that wife of mine?" Jack wondered aloud. "This goose is getting cold."

"Laurel was visiting Mae the day she went into labor," Margaret explained. "She helped Dr. Parnell deliver the baby, remember?"

"Maybe it's catching," Jack grinned, but received a fierce look from his mother.

"Did she say how far along in her maternity she is?" Cassandra asked of Lydia.

"About three months, I think."

"How long has Carey been gone?" Cassandra persisted eagerly.

"Enough of this pointless speculation," Margaret snapped.

"But Mother," Jack continued jovially. "We must narrow the field of suspects. Haven't you ever read a detective novel?"

"Jack, stop this attempt at humor right now!"

"Oh, who could Laurel's sweetheart be?" sighed Cassandra.

"No one you know," Laurel announced upon entering the dining room. She considered her remark to be figuratively if not literally true. She wore a simple house dress, adequate for sitting at the table if not festive enough for the occasion.

Alice burst into the room. Her eyes blazed with a feverish delight.

"It's a sign from God!" she proclaimed.

"What is, Wife?" Jack asked in a tone of bored disinterest as he began to carve the goose.

"Laurel's baby–it's a gift from God!"

"I'm afraid you'll have to be more explicit with those of us not in personal contact with the Almighty, dear."

"Don't you understand? It's all so brilliantly obvious?" Alice's face shown with an eerie exultation. "Laurel took our child away and now she's giving it back."

"What?" Laurel cried.

Alice rushed to Jack's side. "Don't you see, Husband? Laurel took our darling Christine away, but now she's giving us another child. Isn't that thoughtful?"

"I didn't kill Christine," Laurel stood up in indignation.

"Sit down, Laurel," Margaret ordered. "You know we don't blame you. Alice be quiet. Christine's death was just a tragic accident."

"But it was God's will, just the same," Alice ranted.

"I suppose everything is God's will, one way or another," Margaret allowed.

"And Laurel's baby is part of God's plan. It's the answer to all my prayers. Jack and I will adopt Laurel's baby and raise it as our own. Doesn't that work out well for all concerned?"

"This is medieval," Laurel protested. "Uncle Jack, make her stop."

"Wife, be quiet," said Jack as he resumed carving the goose. He clearly resented Alice's embarrassing outbursts. There seemed no end in sight.

"I have it all planned out," Alice announced primly as she took her seat. "Laurel and I will go away together–we can stay with my mother in St. Louis. After her confinement, I'll bring the baby back to Chisholm and tell everyone it's mine. No one will ever be the wiser." Alice's face beamed with joy.

"Make her stop it," Laurel demanded, hot tears burned her swollen eyes once again.

Margaret sat back in her chair and then said, "Hmm."

This alarmed everyone.

"Mother!" Jack and Cassandra gasped in shocked unison.

"Alice may be on to something here," Margaret offered, while still lost in thought.

"What do you mean, Margaret?" Lydia asked.

"This might be a very convenient solution to everyone's dilemma. Alice wants a baby. Laurel doesn't. Do you, Laurel?"

"No, I guess not," Laurel answered in quiet confusion.

"We all certainly would like to avoid a scandal," Margaret reasoned. "A quiet, family adoption. It's not unheard of. It's been done before."

"This whole idea is absurd, Mother," snorted Jack.

"Oh, please, darling, please," Alice whined. She knelt by his chair with her arms around his waist. "It was meant to be."

"Think about it, Jack," said his mother sternly. "Alice wants a child desperately. Needs one. Adoption is your only alternative. And rather than adopt some stranger's child, here you'd be getting a Hartmoor child already. Probably a family resemblance in the bargain. Could there be a more advantageous resolution?"

"No one has asked me what *I* think," Laurel interrupted.

"Hush, Laurel," Margaret snapped. "We're trying to help you."

"I don't know," muttered Jack. He sat back in his chair and tried to disengage himself from his wife's embrace.

"And if we were all to participate in this little subterfuge–this pretense that the child belongs to Alice–where is the real harm? Who will be hurt? Perhaps Laurel will still be able to marry someday, if no one outside the family were to know the truth.

Her grandmother's ruthless efficiency at problem-solving almost made Laurel shudder.

"It's God's will," Alice whispered to no one in particular. She still knelt next to Jack's chair. "We must not ignore God's will."

"I don't know," Jack mumbled again, but his voice carried a detectable note of weakening which caused Alice to hold her breath.

"I'm certain the more you think about it, Jack, the more you'll come to agree with me," Margaret said with a quiet confidence.

Cassandra and Lydia exchanged perplexed glances, but said nothing.

Jack stared at the tablecloth, deep in thought. "I would have to know who the father was before making this decision."

Everyone at the table glanced at everyone else after this remark, for it meant the decision had essentially already been made. Now only details remained.

"She may refuse to reveal it," Margaret warned. "You know how stubborn she can be."

"I'm still in the room," Laurel said irritably. "I'd rather you didn't talk about me as if I didn't exist."

"Besides, what real difference does it make? Perhaps it's better that we don't know." Margaret turned to Laurel with a stern look. "Of course, we must be assured the man doesn't know about the child's existence. He doesn't, does he?"

Laurel swallowed hard. "No, ma'am."

"You swear to this?"

Laurel nodded. She ducked her head, feeling lost and abandoned and betrayed. How she hated Carey Fairchild at this moment.

"There, now." Margaret turned back to her son. "What do you say?"

"This is all so sudden," Jack sighed. "Perhaps a child would help Alice...."

Cassandra spoke up. "I think it's a fine idea if Jack and Alice want to adopt the baby, but I think this notion of Alice passing it off as her own natural-born child is just plain foolish."

"But how will we explain the child's sudden appearance in the house after a suitable absence by Laurel? If both were to leave, the family could be spared a great deal of unnecessary scandal. To my mind, everyone's best interests are served in this."

"How do you automatically know what my best interests are?" Laurel whined.

"But what if someone found out the truth later?" Cassandra persisted. "That would be awfully embarrassing."

"What chance is there of anyone making this discovery? Not even Dr. Parnell knows Alice is unable to bear more children."

"I still think it's preposterous," concluded Cassandra, but she was tiring of arguing the point with her mother.

"I'll consent if I'm told the father's identity," Jack said suddenly. "I just have to know."

"Oh, Husband, thank you, thank you," Alice sobbed with joy.

Margaret sat back in her chair triumphantly. Cassandra folded her arms over her chest with a frown. Lydia stared down into her lap uncomfortably.

Laurel witnessed the entire scene in a state of shocked disbelief. She cynically marveled at the Hartmoors' ability to so easily alter fate, change destinies, rearrange lives to suit their convenience. She turned and left the room hurriedly.

The family watched her flight with anxious eyes, then all turned to Margaret for guidance.

"Don't worry," she said in a cold, flat tone. "She'll come around. She has no choice, after all."

Christmas morning Laurel awoke from a surprisingly sound sleep. Despite the chaos of her life, she had slept deeply, not even dreaming of babies or disgrace or ostracism or Carey or any of the other hundred topics that had lately preoccupied her waking and dreaming life. Before falling asleep the night before, she had heard voices seeping up from the dining room. She could not make out the words, but the subject was not difficult to guess. Sometimes the voices were raised in argument, other times, only intense debate.

She pulled a smock on over her nightgown and quietly slipped downstairs. She drifted toward the parlor where the Christmas tree stood surrounded by gaily wrapped gifts. She spotted a box with her name on it. She knelt and slowly unwrapped it.

The removal of the wrapping paper revealed a sturdy wooden box. She sucked in her breath, almost afraid the box would not hold what she imagined–a new camera. Not a large view camera like her previous one, but rather the small portable snap-shot camera that came with its own roll of film. This was the very camera she had been so tempted to buy while visiting Lydia in Wichita the summer before. She had looked scornfully on this mass-produced item, still so new on the market that few owned one yet. She assumed they were purely for amateurs, not serious photographers like herself.

Still, this little camera was better than none. She removed and inspected the lens. She extended and retracted the small, leather bellows several times, marveling at the smooth harmony of its operation. She ran her fingers along the hard edges of the apparatus as gently as one might caress a lover's face.

She heard someone behind her and turned abruptly to find Alice standing in the parlor entrance, watching her. Her dewy, smiling face bore the same dream-like elation she had worn the evening before. Laurel mentally braced herself as Alice gracefully crossed the room and knelt next to Laurel on the floor.

"Laurel, I'm sorry if we upset you last night. You must understand we have your best interests in mind. After you retired, we all talked a great deal. Made so many plans." Alice paused when she noticed she was making little impression on her audience. She immediately changed her tack. "Of course, all these arrangements depend upon you, Laurel, dear. I mean, on your decision. It's all up to you now. We want this to be as easy on you as possible."

Laurel almost smirked at this remark. Did Alice really think she was supposed to believe the Hartmoors had no self-interest in the matter?

Yet she did not feel as though she had many choices open to her. A vivid, recurring image haunting her since learning of her pregnancy was that of Lizzie Fairchild, Carey's mother–a lonely eccentric trying to raise up a child all alone. Not a pleasant picture as it shimmered before her, taunting her.

"You and I can stay with my mother in St. Louis," Alice continued brightly. "You'll like St. Louis, Laurel. It's much bigger than Wichita and there are ever so many interesting things to do there–shopping and theater and concerts."

"Was the camera a bribe?" Laurel asked quietly.

Alice laughed uncomfortably. "Why no, of course not. We ordered the camera weeks ago. Jack was dreadfully sorry about what happened. He wanted to make it up to you."

"Thank you." She didn't want to appear ungrateful. The present was thoughtful, not to mention expensive.

"Jack says this camera comes with its own film already in it and you can mail away the whole camera back East and the company will develop all the pictures for you and send them back. Isn't that wonderful? You won't need that dreadful darkroom anymore."

"Very convenient," Laurel mumbled. She tried to keep the sarcasm out of her comment, but did not wholly succeed.

"You can take it with us to St. Louis and you can take a picture of the Mississippi River. Won't that be wonderful?"

"Aunt Alice..." Laurel disliked being talked down to like a sulky child, even though she might be acting like one.

"Oh, darling, what do you say? You will consent, won't you? Jack and I could love the baby so much, give it so much–"

"I won't say...I won't say who the–" Laurel's voice faltered. She bit her lower lip to keep from crying.

Alice smiled and opened her arms. "Don't worry, darling. We won't ask again. No one need ever know but you." She hugged Laurel tightly. "Oh, Laurel, God bless you. And God bless that precious child you carry."

Laurel buried her face against Alice's throat, crushing the stiff lace of Alice's dressing gown collar. She thought about how this was the most lucid Alice had been since the day she lost Christine.

When she pulled away from Alice's smothering embrace she noticed Lydia and Margaret standing in the arched parlor entrance. Lydia wore her dressing gown, like Alice, but Margaret stood fully dressed to meet the day. Laurel could not remember ever seeing her grandmother in anything less than full street clothes.

Alice turned to the two women and nodded triumphantly to answer their inquiring glances.

Christmas Day progressed as best it could. There was no formal opening of gifts. The presents were barely noticed or acknowledged, their purpose or custom seemed lost in the crisis Laurel's pregnancy had set in motion. Though Christmas dinner was large and lavish, the Hartmoors had no appetite for the feast.

Mrs. Collier, Alice's mother, was wired the following morning to inform her that Alice and her niece were to arrive soon for an extended visit, the details of which were to follow by letter.

Alice dutifully wrote a long letter to set the scene for the visit's necessity and the need for discretion. Margaret also wrote to Mrs. Collier. She not only felt it a courteous requirement, but she did not trust Alice to convey the proper message.

Laurel drifted through the days almost oblivious to the preparations and packing being made on her behalf. She stopped making ritual visits to the poplar grove. She no longer needed the grove to be reminded of Carey.

Jack still grumbled about wanting to know the identity of the baby's father, but he was always promptly hushed by his wife or mother. He never spoke directly to Laurel on the subject of the baby. He seemed even more uncomfortable in her presence than before.

Alice assured her that Jack's avoidance was not to be taken personally. Most men were simply uncomfortable with the topic of pregnancy in general and pregnant women in particular and Jack was no exception.

Margaret seemed concerned that Laurel might attempt suicide and insisted a mildly protesting Cassandra sleep in Laurel's room on Christine's old bed each night until they left. Laurel found this unnecessary, not to mention humiliating, but did not object. On their last night as roommates, Cassandra lay awake and surprised Laurel with an unexpectedly intimate interrogation.

"Laurel," came Cassandra's whisper across the dark, chilly room. "Are you asleep yet?"

"No, not quite." Laurel took a deep breath to try and rouse herself enough to be coherent.

"What was it like?"

"What was what like?" Laurel turned on her side and propped her head on her elbow.

"You know. When you were with...him...whoever he was. The one who got you in this fix."

"Oh." This was truly the last question she expected to be asked by anyone, much less her maiden aunt. She felt her privacy invaded by this question, yet, on some level, she longed to talk about it with someone. "It was...nice."

"*Nice*?" came Cassandra's whispered, unbelieving response.

"Well, yes. A little uncomfortable at first, though he tried to be as gentle as possible."

"Did you have to take off *all* your clothes?"

"You don't have to, but we did."

"Wasn't it terribly degrading?"

"No. When you love someone, you want to be with them like that. I can't explain it, you just do."

"So you really loved him?"

"I guess I must have." Laurel rolled onto her back and sullenly stared at the dark ceiling.

"Do you love him still?"

"No."

ஐ

The last day of the year was the appointed date of departure. Six inches of new snow fell the night before and heavy gray clouds threatened additional accumulation. Jack had the sleigh brought down from the storage shed and hitched to a pair of hardy mares from the winter pasture.

They would ride into Wichita to catch the train to St. Louis. Laurel kissed her grandmother's wrinkled cheek and climbed into the sleigh next to Lydia and Cassandra. Cassandra wanted an excuse to visit Wichita and Lydia was returning home to her store. Alice climbed in next to Jack. She was animated and conversing brightly, unlike the rest.

The somber-clad Hartmoors looked more like a mourning party than a holiday group as they pulled out of the yard in the large, painted sleigh with its incessantly clattering sleigh bells. They glided through the glistening winter landscape leaving scandal behind and Laurel hoped she could leave her memories, both good and bad, behind as well. She gave one last backward glance at the Hartmoor house. She saw her grandmother closing the front door under the big, carved "H." The "H" stood for "Hopeless" in Laurel's bleak view.

Chapter Nineteen

Cassandra waited until Jack left the breakfast table for work before sharing the contents of Laurel's latest letter with Margaret.

"If life gets any better for Laurel, we're going to have to stop referring to her as the 'poor, unfortunate girl.'"

Margaret frowned at her daughter's jesting remark but could not refute it. "She does seem to be milking this situation for all it's worth."

"Jack is going to have a fit when the bills for all this start rolling in."

"Alice is going a bit overboard, if I do say so myself. Don't repeat me, now. If your brother and his wife want to spend a fortune buying Laurel every little thing her heart desires, that's surely their business. After all, she is giving them a baby in return. Don't underestimate what Laurel is going through. You have no idea."

"But the *clothes*–all the new clothes! She'll never wear them again. She must be showing by now."

"Let's see–" Margaret silently counted on her fingers. "She's not that far along yet. I'm certain we can alter all the clothes to fit her once she gets her figure back. It's always easier to take things in than let them out."

"I suppose."

"It's hard for your brother to say 'no' to Alice when she's so obviously happy."

Cassandra shrugged with a noncommittal frown as she continued to read Laurel's letter.

Margaret picked up Jack's discarded Wichita newspaper to scan the obituaries.

"Oh, Mother, you'll never guess who's back in town."

"Carey Fairchild. Jack mentioned it last night."

"Well, isn't Jack the busybody? Anyway, he's working at the Grange Co-operative store. Staying at the Randall's boarding house with his girls."

"I don't think a boarding house is a proper environment to raise two little girls. I wonder why they didn't stay with the Brocks?"

"He didn't say. He was rather closed-mouthed about it. I never liked those Brocks. I didn't think Carey ever did either. Oh, well, I'm sure the Cyclones will be glad to have him back for another season."

"I shall have to stop in at the Grange today and say hello to him," said Margaret as she finished and closed the newspaper. "If it doesn't snow again."

Cassandra leaned close to Margaret and, with cocked eyebrow, added, "Carey asked about *Laurel*."

"Oh, Cassie, for pity's sake," Margaret frowned. "He was just being polite. Stop accusing every man who's ever said hello to the girl."

"But the suspects are so few in number to begin with," Cassandra complained. She was still upset that the identity of Laurel's seducer remained unknown and at large. "I say, guilty until proven innocent."

"What did you tell him?"

"The usual story. That she went to St. Louis with Alice because Alice needed a companion and so forth and so on."

"Good."

"He made an odd remark, though. When I told him about Alice being in a family way he said congratulations, of course, but then he said, 'That must have been a nice surprise for everyone.'"

Margaret's brow furrowed with concern. "Why would he make a strange remark like that? Surely, he had no way of knowing that Alice couldn't–"

"I asked him what he meant and he just said, 'Nothing,' like he hadn't said it at all, and then he got busy with another customer."

"We're undoubtedly too sensitive about all of this. We're reading too much into everything everyone says or does." Margaret rose from the table to begin her day. "I know it's uncomfortable having to lie to everyone, but it's certainly better than the truth for all concerned. Surely, the Good Lord will understand and forgive us."

St. Louis more than lived up to Alice's promises. The first weeks of the new year spun by in a dizzying whirl of activity for Laurel. Never had she seen so many shops, restaurants, theaters, and, best of all, a large library within walking distance from the house of Alice's mother.

Alice monitored Laurel's health with the same zeal she had once reserved for Christine. If Laurel so much as expressed the slightest fatigue–even the idlest remark–Alice made her go to bed for the rest of the day. Alice's mother occasionally suggested to her daughter that Laurel did not require quite as much pampering as Alice ladled out, but Alice ignored her.

She could not find fault with Laurel's eating habits, however. Laurel's appetite had returned with a vengeance. She couldn't seem to get enough food. Alice teased her about "eating for two."

"Two, Laurel, not seventeen," Alice would remind her playfully.

Laurel would grin in embarrassment and shovel in another mouthful. Soon her clothes no longer hung on her. In fact some were growing a little tight.

Laurel and Alice's residence with her mother, Mrs. Miranda Collier, was tense from its outset. Mrs. Collier made it known early on that she felt Alice's scheme to adopt Laurel's baby and pass it off as her own to be absurd and unnecessary. To her way of thinking, young girls in Laurel's predicament deserved little sympathy and even less protection. She let Laurel know at every opportunity that she felt she was getting off far too easily. That so many should conspire to cloak Laurel's sins for her seemed to mock the laws of God, according to her rigorous understanding of them.

Alice encouraged Laurel to disregard her mother's barbed remarks and, outwardly, she did. She liked the bedroom she'd been given. A pleasant room, scented by starched linen, oiled oak bedposts, and a large cedar chest that sat at the foot of the bed. Laurel could sit in the window seat and read or watch the passersby on the street below. The prim little room, with its walls of tiny red roses on an ivory field, matched the delicate, cloistered atmosphere of the household.

As a wet, grim January wore on, each shopping excursion with Alice brought an avalanche of gifts. As Laurel undressed one such evening, she idly gazed down at her bed, filled with silk stockings, imported underthings, a silver bracelet and matching earrings, three stylish hats, two blouses, a black fan fancy enough for a night at the opera, a dainty gray parasol, trimmed in pink ribbon rosebuds, and another new camera. She had shot up all the film in the first camera and sent it off to New York state, for developing. Alice replaced the camera with a new one. A hundred shots had lasted Laurel less than a month.

How strange, she reflected, to profit from such misfortune. She could not see any difference between herself and the prostitutes on the street who sold sexual access to their bodies. She, instead, sold the *aftermath* of intercourse, rather than the act itself. Carey had gotten that for the price of a smile and a few flattering words. And pale green, promise-colored eyes.

Carey.

She reflexively clutched the silver locket that still held the ring of wild indigo. She hadn't looked at the ring since leaving Chisholm. She pried the locket open to find the ring brittle and dry. She feared it would crumble to dust if she tried to remove it.

She snapped the locket shut. A lot of good that ring had done her. About as much good as Carey's promises. Where was he now, anyway? No word, no letter, nothing.

How could she have been such a fool as to think he actually loved her? Were all men so careless with their affections? She struggled to harden her heart. Love was a fool's game, a waste of precious time. She would learn to live without it. She would have to. She didn't need him. She didn't need anyone.

As she carefully unfolded the exquisite, lace-trimmed nightgown Alice had given her, she thought how a bride might wear such an elegant gown on her wedding night.

A bride, she thought sourly, something I'll never be. She often wondered if she would have so easily traded away her future for that one night with Carey, had she known what lay in store for her.

And then there were the nightmares. In the dark, quiet corners of the night, Mae Fairchild's screams became Laurel's. Her pain, her gushing blood, her dead little baby–all haunted Laurel. Worst of all, Laurel heard Mae's vicious epithet, "*Monster,*" over and over. Did this mean she might give birth to a monster? A hideously deformed creature with misshapen limbs and no eyes? Eleven fingers perhaps. Alice and Jack surely would not take the baby unless it was perfect.

Laurel tried to wipe these thoughts from her mind as she slipped off her drawers and kicked them into the corner where the little Irish servant girl picked them up each morning. Laurel quite enjoyed having servants. Her grandmother really ought to consider it. She had just pulled the elegant nightgown over her head when she caught sight of it: a bright red spot in the corner where her underdrawers lay in a heap.

She rushed over to examine it. She picked up the drawers and scrutinized the stain. There was no mistaking it. The spot was blood, bright, red blood.

She immediately ran to Alice's room and knocked. Without speaking a word, she held up the drawers for Alice's inspection.

Alice's thin lower lip trembled. "Oh, no," she whispered.

"Ladies, I have good news," announced the doctor after his examination of Laurel was complete.

Alice, whom Laurel requested be present, moved across Laurel's bedroom and sat next to her on the bed. She took hold of Laurel's hand and held her breath. She had not allowed Laurel out of bed since the night before when Laurel began to bleed.

Laurel had dutifully laid still as a corpse all night, not knowing what to hope for. How often had she prayed to be rid of this unwanted baby? And yet she had grown so fond of Alice in the weeks they had shared that she almost hated to disappoint her. Alice had nearly convinced her she was performing a public service of nearly celestial dimensions in carrying this ill-begotten child.

Unhappily for Alice, the morning found Laurel still bleeding and cramping, though not to an unusual degree had it merely been her normal time of month.

The doctor was summoned and arrived after breakfast. He poked and prodded and pushed on Laurel's abdomen until she flinched in pain, causing Alice even more distress.

"There is no evidence of miscarriage here," the doctor continued.

"Oh, praise the Lord," murmured Alice. "The baby's alright, then?"

"Baby? There is no baby."

"What?" asked Laurel, stunned. "There must be. I'm past my time by more than three months."

"Not any more, young lady." The doctor thoughtfully stroked his beard and opined, "It is not unheard of for a young woman to be so worried and troubled about the possibility of pregnancy that she disrupts her own body's natural rhythms to such an extent that she might believe herself with child when actually no such occurrence has befallen her. Do you think this might be the case, Miss?"

Laurel looked from the doctor to Alice's pained face and back again. "I guess so."

Chapter Twenty

Carey glanced out from the window of the Grange Cooperative Store to see Cassandra Hartmoor standing on the wooden sidewalk across the street in the bright, cold February sun. She obviously waited to meet the Plains Transit Coach arriving from Wichita.

Carey studied the situation eagerly. She had brought with her the large Hartmoor carriage, so she must be expecting a group. A group that would surely include Laurel McBryde.

The coach pulled up at five minutes past its time. Jack Hartmoor emerged first, then helped his wife down. The two Hartmoor women stood on the sidewalk and chatted somberly while Jack and the driver's assistant saw to the luggage.

Carey thought that for a homecoming, they did not look to be in much of a celebrating mood. Alice Hartmoor's figure, at least what Carey could glimpse of it below her fur-trimmed cape, looked as slender as ever. Not an expectant mother's shape to be sure. Perhaps that was the reason for the sudden return home with such glum tidings.

Carey debated whether to cross the street to greet them, thinking now might be an awkward moment, but the temptation to speak to Laurel again after so many months' absence proved irresistible. He ran across the Main Street of Chisholm, hatless and coatless in the chill February wind.

"Good day to you all," he called to the family and stretched out his arms to catch another of Alice Hartmoor's traveling cases being handed down from the top of the coach. Jack brusquely pulled the case from Carey.

"We're enough here without you, Fairchild."

"Just wanting to be of help, Mr. Hartmoor."

"When we need your help, we'll ask for it," returned Jack curtly.

"Good day, Ladies." Carey nodded to the two women and smiled broadly, ignoring Jack's incivility.

"Hello, Carey," said Cassandra with her usual friendliness. Alice merely nodded and then turned her pinched and pouty face away.

"And Miss McBryde, did she remain in St. Louis?"

Jack Hartmoor whirled round to face him directly for the first time. "Why do you ask?"

Carey shrugged with a somewhat awkward grin. "Just making conversation, I guess."

"Well, not all of us have time for idle conversation, Fairchild." Jack turned abruptly and helped his wife up into the Hartmoor carriage. "Now if you will excuse us."

"Yes, sir," Carey mumbled.

He looked to Cassandra Hartmoor, hoping for some further word but got only a penetrating frown in reply.

The Hartmoor family group had nothing further to say as they secured their traveling possessions and headed their rig for home.

Carey stood in the middle of the street and watched their departure with confusion and disappointment.

"Where's Laurel?" Margaret asked as Cassandra and Alice passed her on the front porch.

"Where she should be," answered Jack as he struggled to push Alice's trunk through the front door.

"That's not an answer," his mother snapped.

"We'll discuss the matter over dinner. I'm starved."

Margaret did not realize until all the family had assembled around the table to begin their noon meal that Alice had not spoken a word to anyone since arriving home.

"I'm receiving the silent treatment," Jack announced, by way of explanation.

"Are you speaking to the rest of us, dear?" Margaret asked of Alice.

"I have no quarrel with you, Mother Hartmoor." Alice's demeanor was even more prim than usual. She raised her pointed chin in a haughty gesture.

Jack rolled his eyes.

"I'm sorry things didn't work out as planned," Margaret said kindly.

"I don't wish to discuss it," said Alice.

"Well, I do," Margaret spoke up. "Where is my granddaughter?"

"Oh, Mother Hartmoor, you are not going to believe what your son has done–"

Jack angrily slammed his fist against the dinner table, causing all the china and glassware to clink precariously. "Wife, we have been over this and over this. The matter is closed!"

Alice jerked her head away from the table with a look of contempt pursing her thin lips.

"You still haven't told me where Laurel is, Jack. She's staying with Alice's mother still, I presume?"

"No, she is not," Jack announced in a clipped tone. "Mrs. Collier declined to keep our little slut for us, even for the generous sum we discussed before I left."

"Don't refer to your own niece by that awful word, Jack."

"What would you have me call her, Mother?"

"She's a young girl who exercised poor judgment."

"'Slut' is a lot shorter and to the point," Jack shot back with a thinly disguised smirk.

Cassandra giggled in spite of herself.

"Enough of this shameful attempt at levity. Where is Laurel?"

"I have placed Laurel in the Susan V. Bright School for the Moral Correction of Wayward Girls in Wichita."

"It's a terrible place, Mother Hartmoor. It looks like a jail," offered Alice.

"The girls who live there–all in the same state of moral depravity as our *dear*, little Laurel, who exercises poor judgment for which we all must suffer–are given food, shelter, religious counseling, and moral instruction. And it's not like a jail. It's the girls' *privacy* that's being protected with the shuttered windows and high walls. I made inquiries before choosing the place. Girls from some of the best families are sent there. They'd have to come from some kind of money to afford the tuition."

"I've heard of that place," Cassandra spoke up. "I thought it was just where unmarried girls went to have their babies."

"Such girls make up a large portion of the student body," said Jack as he spooned a massive helping of mashed potatoes onto his plate. "But the remainder are simply young women who have not demonstrated a proper moral outlook on life and need...correction."

"You should have seen the look on Laurel's face when she entered the hideous establishment," Alice countered. "She was too proud to cry, but I know she wanted to."

"I will not have her spoiling my chances to be mayor by bringing her shame and scandal into this house on the very eve of my election. It's not fair to me or to anyone in this family."

"A good Christian would place the needs of his loved ones before his almighty political ambitions." Alice pointedly did not look at Jack as she spoke this, though all knew him to be the object of her remarks.

"Just because I'm related to Laurel doesn't mean that I have to love her, Wife. She may return here after the election and not before."

"Carey Fairchild asked about Laurel *again*, Mother," Cassandra announced with a superior smirk.

"What's this about Fairchild?" asked Jack with more interest than he usually accorded his sister's remarks.

"Cassie thinks Carey is Laurel's secret admirer."

"Good Lord, I hope not," groaned Jack.

"I'm almost certain of it," Cassandra insisted. "I'm going to find a way to prove my theory, just you wait."

Jack threw his napkin onto the table and shoved his chair back. "That would be just too cruelly appropriate. I can practically hear Lizzie Carington laughing at me from her grave!"

He left the dining room in an unexplained huff.

"Lizzie Carington?" Cassandra repeated in confusion. "Do you suppose he meant Lizzie Fairchild?

Margaret shrugged with a frown.

"What kind of school is this?" Laurel asked as soon as she was shown to the dormitory. Her trunk was laid at the foot of an iron cot by two of the largest women Laurel had ever seen. The cot sat in a row of several dozen at the far end of the long, windowless room.

"The sort that teaches young girls such as yourself to make wiser choices," responded the tiny, shrill-voiced woman who had been assigned the task of getting Laurel "settled in." The elderly woman's back was so severely hunched that her head poked forward like a turtle, to Laurel's way of thinking.

"I don't understand."

"You will."

"And if I choose not to stay here?"

"The choice is not yours to make, Miss McBryde. Your guardian has made that decision for you."

"He's not my guardian. He's merely my trustee. He exercises control over my *property*, not my person! And I am twenty-one years of age. You can't keep me here against my will." Laurel was not a lawyer's daughter for nothing. She knew a thing or two about *habeas corpus* and would gladly educate these humorless women if the need arose.

"I'm afraid we can. And, trust me, someday you will thank us for it."

"You cannot! I'm not a criminal. I've committed no crime."

"Illicit sexual behavior is a crime in this state, Miss McBryde. Your uncle informs us you freely admitted to acts of fornication and showed no real remorse about them. We could summon the authorities if you wish and let them deal with you in the criminal courts, but I would not advise it."

Laurel sat down on the hard metal cot in shock. The bed made a loud creak with her weight that echoed through the empty dormitory. "I can't believe this. I've been sent here as *punishment*?"

"We do not use the word punishment at the Bright School. We prefer the terms *correction* and *enlightenment*. You will be taught humility, modesty, obedience, and, above all, godliness. Now, if you will put on this work smock, you will be set to your first round of chores."

"I will do nothing of the sort! I demand to see the headmistress. What was her name–Bright?"

The tiny woman narrowed her eyes, but did not lose her composure. "I see you are a willful one, just as your uncle implied. That sort of behavior will not be tolerated on these premises. I believe we will begin with some time in the Correction Room. Perhaps a day of silence and nothing to eat will stem this unwholesome streak of defiance." The woman nodded to the two large, red-faced young women who immediately lunged for Laurel over the far side of her cot.

Laurel kicked, struggled, and screamed, but was no match for the two women who effortlessly transported her down a dark stone staircase to the depths of the forbidding establishment. They half-carried, half-dragged her to the door of a small cell. She managed to bite one of the women on the shoulder and was struck in the face in retaliation.

Laurel was thrown onto the floor of the cell, still reeling from the blow. She had never been struck in the face before and she felt as though her nose had exploded. The metal door clanked shut and she was alone. She pinched her nostrils tightly to stem the flow of blood now gushing from them.

She looked about her, but could see little. The room was lit only by a tiny, high window apparently placed at street level, but too high for her to reach or peer out of. The brick walls of the cellar room wept rivulets of groundwater and spongy moss grew along the mortar.

The cell was entirely without furnishings. The toilet facility consisted of a hole in the floor in the corner, the stench from which not only assaulted her swollen nose, but stung her eyes as well.

The sudden, unmistakable sound of a scurrying rat sent Laurel bounding to her feet. She had never been particularly afraid of rodents–she had made pets of the field mice and prairie dogs that lived around her house at Windrift–but this retched, reeking atmosphere seemed so wholly unpleasant, so *unclean*, that she feared disease from these loathsome creatures.

She had no idea how many hours passed in the silence of the little cell. The sun went down and total darkness made the imprisonment even more frightening. She grew sleepy, but did not dare to sleep for fear of the rats. Her stomach groaned and ached with hunger. Unbearable thirst finally drove her to place her lips against the dank, weeping walls to catch a suggestion of moisture.

Sometime just after dawn, Laurel heard a loud commotion on the stairs outside her cell–voices shouting, a young girl crying and pleading. The metal door of her cell was solid, preventing her from seeing what was happening on the other side of it, but she noticed wildly flickering lamplight pouring underneath.

"No, no, not my hair!" screamed the young girl.

"Hold her more tightly," ordered a woman's voice. "You were far too vain about this hair of yours anyway, Anne. Vanity is one of the seven deadly sins, you know. Soon you'll have nothing left to be vain about."

Laurel heard more scuffling and crying, then the distinct metallic squeak of scissors chop-chop-chopping. The girl's cries drizzled into helpless moans and sobs as the cutting continued.

"Hand me the razor," said the woman.

"No, no, please no! Don't shave me. Please. I promise I'll be good. I promise! I promise!"

"We've heard those promises before, haven't we, Anne? Remember when we took your clothes away for a week to teach you the virtue of modesty? You had to display the shame of that disgraceful belly of yours to the whole world. And you swore you'd be good from then on if we would just let you have back your clothes? But you did disobey again, didn't you? At the first opportunity."

"But I mean it this time. I swear it! I'll swear it on the Bible if you want. Just don't shave me. Please. I'll never run away again."

"Oh, I'm certain you'll try again, Anne. Yours is the most pathological case of rebelliousness I've seen in a long while. But next time you try to run away, you won't get so far. You'll be rather easy to spot, won't you, with your new hairstyle?"

Laurel heard ugly laughter from other women, probably the ones holding the girl down. The girl started shrieking, then was silenced with a blow. Finally, Laurel heard the splash of water. A bowl of wash water being tossed out, she assumed. Then came the brisk tap of footsteps down the stairs.

"Are you almost finished?" asked a voice that Laurel recognized from the day before.

"Yes, just completed. Anne? Anne, are you listening? You are to clean up this mess. Do you understand? I don't wish to find a single hair on this floor when I return or you shall mop the floor with your tongue."

Laurel jumped in fear when the key in her door creaked. She stood against the far wall of the little room as the metal door swung open. The small, hunched woman appeared in the opening.

"Miss McBryde, have you undergone a change of attitude from your shameful display of willfulness yesterday?"

"Yes, ma'am," Laurel answered, trying to sound meek.

"Excellent. Then allow us to escort you to breakfast."

Laurel followed the matron out the door and beheld the girl named Anne. Anne toiled on hands and knees picking up the shorn locks of her long, reddish blond hair. Dressed in a torn and soiled muslin nightgown, the girl displayed an advanced state of pregnancy. She briefly glanced up as Laurel passed. Many bleeding razor nicks covered her bald head. Her left eye was nearly swollen shut.

Laurel quickly averted her gaze when she saw in the girl's eyes a look of pained disgrace. As Laurel followed the hunched matron up the cellar stairs, she thought she would tell the girl how all the queens of ancient Egypt shaved their heads and were considered quite beautiful. Maybe that news would give the poor thing some comfort. She would do whatever necessary to make a friend of this girl. She looked as though she needed a friend. Plus she must have ideas on how to escape.

Two weeks passed without a letter from Laurel. At Margaret's request, Lydia tried to contact her twice at the Susan V. Bright School, only to be sent away with the admonition that the girls were not allowed visitors.

Alice continued her reign of silence against her husband and refused to share a bed with him. She slept instead in Christine's old bed in Laurel's room.

Jack found himself too busy with his campaign to take a great deal of notice to his wife's indifference. The election remained only three weeks away.

Cassandra reluctantly helped out Jack's campaign to fill the gap created by the candidate's wife. This morning's assignment involved tacking up campaign posters all over Main Street, not easy work on such a breezy March day. After striking her thumb more times than she cared to count, Cassandra grew bored with her task and wandered over to the post office to see if the morning mail had been sorted yet.

The postmaster handed her a couple of advertisements, a fashion magazine for Alice, and one letter. She glanced at the envelope and quickly recognized Laurel's eccentric scrawl. So Laurel had finally decided to give up her solitude–of remorse, no doubt–from the outside world and communicate with her family again. The letter was addressed to Margaret, so Cassandra dared not invade its contents though she longed to know what was going on in that grim establishment to which Jack had so unceremoniously consigned Laurel. Cassandra had heard stories about the place for many years. Young girls were often threatened with it if they did not show the proper respect to their parents or guardians or if doubts had been raised about their virtue.

Just the thought of an establishment containing all those pregnant or otherwise unchaste girls filled Cassandra with a shiver of both disgust and excitement. To think that the results of so much sin could reside in one building. *Sin*–the word itself seemed to glitter with unholy and unsavory imaginings. Like the word *naked*, like the word *penetration*.

A broad gust of fresh-scented spring wind cleared Cassandra's head and returned her thoughts to more immediate concerns. She began to plot how best to utilize this letter to carry out her plan to uncover the identity of Laurel's seducer. Down the street from the post office, she spied the Grange. Carey Fairchild was occupied in some endeavor in front of the office.

She had only to find a way to confirm her suspicions about Carey. She needed to be stealthy. She could not afford to tip her hand, lest her hunch prove wrong. She liked Carey and wanted to keep his friendship, despite his animosity towards her brother.

She confidently marched towards the Grange office. Carey stood on the sidewalk in front posting several notices of items for sale on a large message board. He held small cards between his teeth as he worked, but removed them and smiled as soon as he saw her approach.

"Miss Hartmoor, what brings you to town this windy day? Oh, I see–campaigning for your brother, are you? You won't find much sympathy for your cause around here, I'm afraid."

"Can't a former neighbor say hello to another without political overtones being implied, Mr. Fairchild?"

"Of course." He extended his hand.

Now is my chance, she thought and pretended to drop her mail as she reached out to take his hand.

The wild March wind caught the posts and sent them soaring.

"Oh, no!" she cried in mock distress.

Carey, ever the gentleman, took off running after Cassandra's lost mail. She bit her lip anxiously as she watched him tear down the dusty street in hot pursuit. He quickly caught up with the magazine, but chased Laurel's letter nearly fifty yards.

"Don't worry about those advertisements," she called as loudly as she could to be heard over the roar of the Kansas wind.

"You sure?"

"Yes, yes, come back now, Carey."

As he walked back, she carefully watched and, to her dismay, he did not even glance at the mail in his hand. She thought quickly.

He reached her, still out of breath from his sprint. He handed her the magazine and letter with a smile as he ran his hand through his wildly disheveled hair.

"Oh, thank you so much, Carey. I would hate to have lost this...this letter from Laurel."

"A letter from Miss McBryde? How does she like St. Louis?"

"Just fine, I'm sure." She deliberately held Laurel's envelope against the magazine, clutching it to her chest in such a manner as to make it easy to read. But did Carey know how to read? Cassandra could not remember.

She bid him farewell and headed for home, uncertain whether or not her gambit had been successful. Well, she had dangled the bait before him. Whether he bit or not remained to be seen.

ꟸ

As Carey watched Cassandra Hartmoor mount her horse and ride away, his breath came quickly but not from the exercise.

So Laurel wasn't still in St. Louis, despite what the Hartmoors had told everyone. What did this mean?

What in hell was the Bright School?

He pulled on his jacket and asked Mr. Kellerman if he could have the rest of the day off. He told him he had urgent business and needed to go to Wichita that very afternoon. Kellerman sighed and frowned and looked put-upon, but granted him his request.

He caught the noon coach into Wichita and reached the downtown area by mid-afternoon. He had to inquire of a police officer directions to this Susan V. Bright School. He couldn't quite understand why the policeman chuckled when he asked about the location of the place.

"Got a sweetheart sent there, did ya, son?" asked the smirking policeman as Carey turned to leave.

Carey ignored the man's impertinence as he headed off in the direction of the School. He found it with some difficulty. A large brick wall surrounded the building and its name was designated by only a small brass plaque: Susan V. Bright School for the Moral Correction of Wayward Girls. He frowned at the odd name, the significance of which did not immediately occur to him.

Without hesitation, he rang the bell at the iron gate of the brick wall. A middle-aged woman wearing spectacles walked out to the gate.

"Deliveries are made in back," she announced in a cold, throaty voice.

"I'm here to see someone."

"No visitors allowed." She pointed to the sign that hung on the front door of the establishment. She turned and began to walk back to the building.

"I'm here about Miss McBryde and I insist–"

The woman stopped in her tracks and turned back to face him. She looked upset. "Miss McBryde?"

"Yes. I'm...I'm her brother."

"Oh, dear. Do come in immediately. I beg your pardon. I had no idea." She hurriedly unlocked the iron gate and led Carey up the steps and into the dark, square brick building.

The woman wrung her hands nervously as she led Carey down a dark hallway. Three pregnant girls passed them as they walked, then two more. Carey had never seen so many pregnant women in one place in his life.

Oh, God. He suddenly realized what sort of place this was and why Laurel must have been sent to live here. As they continued their hurried walk down the long hall, they passed rooms in which numerous young girls sat at large tables sewing at quilts, doing lace tatting, needlepoint, all manner of hand crafts. In each room, a stern-faced matron walked up and down the rows of seated workers and oversaw their work. Carey saw a frail-looking young girl of no more than fourteen receive a sharp blow to the back of the head with the matron's bible along with an admonition to keep her mind on her work.

In a third room, about seven girls, some pregnant, some not, stood around the perimeter of the room, each facing the blank wall in front of her, reciting aloud the Lord's prayer in unison.

At last they reached the end of the hallway and the woman briskly led him into an office of sorts.

"Mrs. Bright?" the woman called meekly as they entered.

A plump, hard-faced woman, also wearing spectacles, looked up from her desk. "What is it? I'm terribly busy."

"He's come about Miss McBryde, Ma'am."

"Oh." Mrs. Bright looked as startled as the woman who had met him at the gate. Why did the mention of Laurel's name elicit so much concern? Was she ill? Was she dead?

"Are you a detective, sir?" asked Mrs. Bright.

"I'm Miss McBryde's brother," Carey responded cautiously.

"But how did you find out so quickly? I sent a wire to Mr. Hartmoor in Chisholm barely an hour ago."

Carey didn't know whether to admit his ignorance or not. He decided to keep up the pretense. "I think the question is, madam, what are *you* going to do about the situation?"

"Well...well...nothing like this has ever happened at the Bright School. No girl has ever successfully escaped–I mean, left the School without permission before."

"Have you searched for her?" Carey demanded, relishing the role of outraged kin of the escapee. How like Laurel. Always the independent one. No passive victim, she.

"We've searched everywhere in the immediate neighborhood, sir. I've alerted the authorities. That's why I thought you were a–oh, well, never mind."

"I want all the details of my sister's disappearance."

Mrs. Bright sketched out the few facts known of Laurel's flight. She did not appear for breakfast on Wednesday morning, but no one looked for her immediately. So many of the pregnant girls missed breakfast, the matrons did not bother to count attendance. When she failed to carry out her assigned chores, then missed Bible Study, the head mistress was notified and a search of the premises was made. Her absence was reported to the local authorities on Thursday, but no trace of her had yet been found.

"Why wasn't my family notified the moment she was known to be missing?"

"We were so certain we would find her. A young lady in her situation, with no money. What are her options? I mean, besides the obvious?"

"The obvious?"

"Death or disgrace. Suicide or a life of degradation and sin, Mr. McBryde. Those specific avenues are being investigated as we speak."

Carey frowned at the woman's pious gall. "Well, there's no need for me to linger here."

"We're so sorry, sir. We've done everything in our power– "

"You may soon be hearing from my lawyer." Carey couldn't resist throwing this in. He watched the women glance at each other in helpless distress, then angrily stomped out of the office and headed back down the dark corridor towards the front entrance. Approaching him was a young girl with a wild mane of curly brown hair bouncing on her shoulders as she walked. She glanced at him with a faint smile as they neared in the passage. Her large belly preceded her. Carey nodded politely as they passed, almost brushing arms.

His eye caught a glint of a silver necklace on the young girl's plump bosom. She had already passed him when he realized that the necklace seemed singularly familiar. He stopped abruptly and turned.

"Miss?"

She halted and looked back at him warily. He observed the silver necklace in more detail, though, given the poor lighting, the task was difficult.

"Sir?"

"Might I inquire where you got the necklace you're wearing?"

The girl instantly tucked the locket under the loose gray smock she wore. "None of your business."

Carey drew a deep breath and with a pounding heart remembered where he had last seen that large silver locket with its scrolled engraving: hanging between Laurel McBryde's naked breasts.

ᘓ

On Saturday morning, with breakfast chores concluded, Margaret sat down on the porch in her favorite white wicker rocking chair and read Laurel's letter for the third time:

Dear Grandmother,

By the time you receive this letter, I shall have already left the Bright School. I write to you to allay your fears, not excite them. You must not worry about me. I have matured a great deal since you saw me last and I have spent much time deep in thought, making plans for the future. I will not trouble you further. I have already inconvenienced you more than you deserve.

Your "wayward," but loving granddaughter,

Laurel

Margaret placed the letter in her lap and wondered what to do. Her thoughts were interrupted by a man on horseback riding furiously for the Hartmoor yard.

"Why, Carey Fairchild, what brings you to my doorstep all dressed up like a Philadelphia lawyer?" asked Margaret Hartmoor. She frowned at the young man and studied him carefully as he dismounted and stood at the bottom of her steps trying to catch his breath.

"Laurel's run away from that...that *place* you put her in!"

"How did you find out about that?"

"Never mind. I know, that's all, and I'm going to find her. I don't care what you and your family think anymore!"

"Now, calm down. Come inside the house. I'd prefer not to discuss this matter in the yard, if you please."

Carey stomped up the porch steps and followed Margaret into the house. He quickly glanced around, wondering who else was about the place on this early Saturday morning.

Margaret motioned for Carey to seat himself in the parlor but he refused.

"I know where she is, I think, but I need your help."

"The Wichita authorities have been alerted. Surely, they will–"

"She's not in Wichita."

"How do you know this?"

"She told a girl that she was going to run away home. I figure that's gotta be Windrift."

"Why do you say that?"

"Because I know Laurel."

"Hmmmm...I think you perhaps know Laurel a little too well." Margaret frowned at the young man while trying to calm herself. She did not like losing her temper. Anger always proved to be an unnecessary distraction, diverting her from what needed to be done, but this betrayal by one whom she always favored was too wrenching to forgive. "Did you at least have the decency to wait until after your wife passed on before you completed Laurel's seduction, or is adultery within your catalog of sins, Carey?

"*After*, if you must know. What sort of man do you take me for?"

"The sort who would exploit the loneliness of a naive young girl."

Carey angrily gritted his teeth and refused to debate the issue. After several seconds of silent glaring, he said simply, "All I need from you is directions to her house in Chase County."

Margaret drew a long breath, impressed with his composure and his determination. In a moment she had made her decision. "I won't let the Flint Hills swallow up another one of my children. How I hate that place. You must bring her back here. I will give you directions and a wagon and food, money if you need it–just bring her back. Do you understand?"

Carey narrowed his eyes. "Will she be welcomed back here–scandal or not? I won't bring her home if you're gonna just send her back to that awful place in Wichita again."

"Scandal be damned!"

Carey almost laughed out loud. He'd never heard Margaret Hartmoor, or any woman of her station, swear before.

"But what about Mr. Hartmoor?"

"You let me handle my son. Just bring me my granddaughter back safe and sound. Do whatever you have to do, but bring her back." Margaret stopped her tirade long enough to smile at Carey.

Carey smiled back. "Yes, ma'am."

"God bless you." Margaret pulled Carey close and hugged him as though he were her own grandson. "What about your daughters?"

"They're with the Taylors." Carey looked suddenly troubled.

"I'll check on them and tell Imogene Taylor something. Now off with you!"

Chapter Twenty-one

Carey's voice startled Laurel so badly she dropped the muddy handful of wild orange crocuses she had just picked and was planning to arrange in a bowl on the kitchen table. The flowers were her small effort to brighten up her ruined home.

"Laurel...Laurel?" he shouted through the broken window next to the front door.

She knelt to the floor to gather the crocuses. She ignored Carey's pounding and shouting. She might be imagining him there. His sudden appearance on her doorstep at Windrift on a Saturday evening was so improbable and implausible, she had to be imagining it.

"Laurel, I know you're in there. Now open this door!"

He was real, alright, not an apparition. She sighed angrily.

"Go away, I don't want to see you," she called to her uninvited guest on the porch.

Carey stuck his head in the broken window and Laurel quickly turned her back to him.

"Laurel, let me in."

"No."

"Then come outside."

"No."

"Laurel, if you don't open that door right now, I'll climb in this window!"

She frowned. "Don't do that. You'll cut yourself."

As she walked to the door, she hurriedly attempted to wipe her face clean and smooth her hair. She hadn't bothered to pin her hair up or even comb it since her midnight escape from the Bright School. She had little use for vanity at Windrift. Reluctantly, she stepped out onto the porch.

"Why are you here and how on earth did you find me?"

"Hello to you, too."

"Why are you here?" she repeated irritably, jutting her chin out. She folded her arms across her chest.

He pulled his hat off. "I just happened to be in the neighborhood."

She smiled in spite of herself, then remembered how much she hated him. He looked so handsome, standing there in his business clothes and neatly groomed hair. And a beard. He'd grown a fashionably trimmed beard since she'd seen him last. He seemed very much a man of the world now.

He stared for some moments at her small waistline and looked profoundly relieved. "You're not...you're not–"

"Not what?" she snapped.

"Oh, nothing, never mind."

"Do you mind if we sit down?" she demanded, rather than asked. "I'm tired from digging debris out of my well all day."

"Of course." He took a seat next to her on the top step of the porch as there was no porch furniture in evidence. After a quiet moment, he said softly, "You look beautiful."

"Oh, you bet I do," she responded angrily. "I've never looked better!"

"I meant what I said." He reached over to smooth back a lock of dark hair from her flushed cheek.

"Don't." She jerked away from his tender gesture and looked out across the wide, rolling expanse of Windrift. The sun still hung high in the western sky. Evenings were drawing out longer now that March was here.

"I've missed you," he offered.

"Oh, really? Strange how you never found time to write and tell me that."

"I couldn't write to you, Laurel. You were in enough trouble when I left Chisholm. Getting letters from me wouldn't have helped you out with your family."

"You know I didn't care what they thought!"

"I told you I'd find a way for us to be together. I came back, but by then, you were gone. You gave up on me, not the other way around, as I see it."

"What do you mean?" Laurel narrowed hostile eyes at him.

From his vest pocket he drew out a familiar silver chain attached to a silver locket and dangled it before her astonished face. Laurel gasped.

She reached for it, but he jerked it out of her grasp. "It's mine. Cost me five dollars."

"I only got two for it," Laurel complained. She softened her tone, but only grudgingly. "Please give it back."

He casually tossed the necklace into her lap. She eagerly pried open the locket to discover with relief that the portraits of her parents and the ring of wild indigo were still safely contained inside.

"Are you still recruiting for the Alliance?" she asked to shift the subject to some territory less intimate.

"Yes, but I had to stop the traveling. Leaving the girls with Mae's parents...didn't work out. Something happened...never mind."

"Are you farming again?"

"No, I got a job working for the Alliance through the Grange when I'm not training more recruiters. The girls and me live at a boarding house in town. It's not a real good arrangement, but it'll do for a while, I guess."

They sat silently side-by-side for a while. Then Carey got up the courage to tackle the issue that bothered him the most.

"Why did you tell the Hartmoors about us?"

"They don't know about you, so you needn't trouble yourself." How she hated to admit the humiliation of the false pregnancy. Her pride would not let her even speak of it. "They have no idea about us."

"And that's why they sent you to a school for wayward girls? I mean, I always thought wayward was the least of it when it came to you, Laurel McBryde, but they must have had some notion–"

"Stop it!" She laughed in spite of herself. "All that happened is really my problem, not yours. Besides, I blame myself entirely for that night."

Carey grinned in disbelief. "Oh, really?"

"I remember it very clearly. You didn't want to, but I insisted."

"Didn't *want* to?" Carey laughed out loud. "Didn't want to *twice*? I'd only been living for that night since the day I met you! And re-lived it in my head every day since."

"But you said–"

"I believe we talked about what I *should* do, not what I *wanted* to do. God-in-heaven, Laurel, I'm sorry. I'm so sorry."

"Oh, Carey, let's not talk about it." Laurel placed her cold hands against her burning cheeks. "I just had a bad winter, that's all, and then to be incarcerated at that terrible place in Wichita. You can't imagine–"

"Oh, I can imagine, alright. I saw it."

"Oh." Laurel remembered that he must have been at the School to have retrieved her locket. "Would you like a bit of supper? You must be starving."

He nodded enthusiastically and pulled her to her feet. As they entered the front door, he couldn't help but remark, "Has your house always been in this condition?"

"Oh, I think there must have been a cyclone," Laurel answered in a matter-of-fact tone.

Laurel spoke at length of the damage to her home. Fierce prairie winds had ripped off half the roof, broken all the windows, damaged the windmill, and thrown all her plans into chaos.

"I'm glad you weren't here when it came through," Carey offered between bites of fried egg and bread.

"Fortunately, the house wasn't in the direct path, as far as I can tell. Otherwise, I wouldn't have a house at all."

The worse tragedy for Laurel had not been the cyclone damage, but rather the feast that the field mice had made of her father's enormous library. Nearly every volume showed signs of their gnawing ravages.

Carey nodded his agreement, then abruptly changed the subject. "Is there a telegraph office in Killdeer? I need to wire your family and tell them I've found you."

"Why do you have to do that?" Laurel set her jaw firmly.

"Laurel, they're worried. The authorities in Wichita are dragging the Arkansas River for you."

"I'm not going back."

"Yes, you are. I promised your grandmother."

"I'm not going back and, frankly, I'd *rather* jump in the Arkansas River than return to that so-called school."

"Your grandmother wants you back home in Chisholm."

"I don't believe that. I'm too much of an embarrassment to the Hartmoors. They consider me a fallen woman."

"It's me, isn't it? I know they think I'm not good enough for you and they're probably right."

Laurel dismissed this idea with a wave of her hand. "Oh, no. Don't think that. They know I had a lover, but they don't know who he was."

"I can understand you not wanting to tell them." He tried to sound philosophical, but the slight stung his handsome features.

"No, you don't," she insisted, instantly sensing he assumed she was ashamed of him. "I just didn't want to...trouble you." When Carey groaned at this, she tried to explain further. "I was afraid they'd contact you. The last thing on earth I wanted was for you to be coerced into marrying me the way you were forced to–" Laurel broke off. She could not bring herself to mention Mae's name. "And I didn't want to interfere with your new work."

"I do like my work. I won't deny it. For the first time ever, I feel like I'm doing something important. You can't imagine how much that means to me. You haven't spent your whole life feeling like dirt, and getting treated like dirt, and thinking it's never gonna get any better." His gaze skittered away. "Sometimes, I'm standing on the back of a wagon and folks would gather to hear me talk and I could see them hanging on my words. Really listening. I don't even get nervous anymore, 'cause I'm telling them things they need to know. I can see them being just like I used to be–ignorant, but wanting things to change and not thinking it's possible and not knowing how. When I get through talking, they come up and thank me, Laurel. Like I've changed their whole way of looking at the world. Like now, because of what I said, they realize that reform is really possible. It's exciting, Laurel. Really exciting. Do you know that in the last six months, the Alliance has gone from 25,000 members to over one *hundred* thousand? We've got fifty-two field organizers like me out there now. Over two thousand sub-alliances have formed this year in the state."

Laurel wanted to congratulate him on his success, but pride made the praise stick in her throat. That he could be so successful and productive without her did not flatter her still-wounded vanity.

After a long silence, she finally spoke. "I won't go back to the Hartmoors, Carey. There's no future for me in Chisholm. I'll have to make do here. I was always happy here. I should never have left."

"I swore to your grandma I'd bring you back. She says she don't–doesn't–care about the scandal."

"A Hartmoor not care about scandal? Don't be ridiculous. Those people *exist* for the sake of propriety."

"Your grandma said: 'I won't let the Flint Hills swallow up another one of my children.'"

Laurel dropped her cynical sneer. "She really said that?"

"Her exact words. She even said 'scandal be damned.' She actually used the word, 'damned.'"

"No!" Laurel laughed. "Not really."

"If I'm lying, may the Good Lord strike me dead."

In a sudden playful mood, Laurel looked heaven-ward and pretended to wait.

Carey laughed, then turned blindly serious. "I'd think you'd want to come back and vote for your uncle."

"Vote?" Laurel knit her brow in confusion.

"Haven't you read the papers this week?"

"I don't exactly get regular delivery out here."

"Well, the legislature got off their lazy backsides long enough to pass a bill giving women the right to vote in city elections."

"Oh, Carey," Laurel whispered with delight. "Are you serious?"

He held up his right hand, as though about to take an oath. "If you had a Bible here, I'd swear on it."

Laurel closed her eyes to savor this long-awaited success. "I knew it would happen. I just knew it."

Carey stood up and invited Laurel to take a walk before retiring for the night. The evening cooled as the sun disappeared. A pleasant breeze sifted through the tallgrass. The rolling seabed spread out before them in an almost mournful infinity. A light haze of insects hung in a ribbon-like band in the distance.

They walked to the top of the highest hill in silence side by side, but stopped when Carey noticed Laurel quietly crying. He pulled her close and kissed the top of her head, tangled hair and all.

"Hey, what's wrong?" he asked.

Laurel shook her head, refusing to answer.

Carey turned her around to face the vast, rolling, western horizon. He gently folded his arms around her slender waist and rested his chin on the top of her head as they both gazed out upon the undulating panorama. In the distance, a lonely hawk circled, then swooped down on some hapless field mouse or prairie dog.

"Bet you can see a thousand miles from here," Carey murmured with a touch of awe.

"More like eighty," she corrected, always one to be precise. A vague smile played at the corners of her mouth. This familiar vista had once given her so much comfort. Now all she wanted was to look into the face of her lover. The enveloping hues drained from the sky at a leisurely pace as the evening gathered around them.

"You're gonna reconsider, aren't you, Laurel? I mean about coming home with me."

Laurel sighed in confusion. "It would be...awkward."

"I won't embarrass you. We can pretend it didn't happen."

"It's the Hartmoors. They don't like me anymore. Especially Uncle Jack–not that he ever liked me. But now they don't...respect me anymore. All a woman has is her reputation. If she loses it, she's despised."

"Do you mean to tell me you're gonna let the likes of Jack Hartmoor keep you from casting your very first vote?"

Laurel turned her troubled gaze to the evening breeze and refused to answer. She had to admit, Carey's point was well taken.

Carey turned her round to face him and held her at arms-length by the shoulders. "Tuck in that pouting lip, Miss Laurel McBryde, and think what fine mischief it would be to stick a thorn in the side of that pompous jackass each and every day!"

Laurel giggled. "I hadn't thought of it that way."

"That's my girl! No more of that whipped puppy dog look for you. Go back and show him what *you* think of *him*!"

"Oh, what I think of him would not be ladylike in the least. After putting me in that terrible place in Wichita."

"Good for you! Now it's settled then. We'll leave at dawn."

She let him take her hand and lead her towards her house, then lagged behind. He turned back to her questioningly.

She debated how to broach a delicate subject. Laurel, being her own stubborn self, had to tackle it straight on. "There's only one bed at my house. Not even a bed. It's just what remains of a mattress, really."

"Oh. And I guess that's not an invitation to share it, right?"

"Well, it's just that–"

"Say no more. I know I don't have the right. I'll sleep in the wagon."

"I hate to ask you to sleep in that wagon."

"Well...I could sleep with you in your bed."

"I hope you aren't planning to start up where we left off, because that's out of the question. I just want to be friends now. That's all."

"I'll be good. I'll keep my hands–and everything else–to myself. I promise."

Laurel shrugged innocently. "Alright.

ℬ𝒶

"I've heard of a room with a view before, but I never saw nothing–anything–like this," Carey called from Laurel's bedroom. He looked up through the enormous, gaping hole in the roof over her bed and admired the stars of the March sky as he pulled off his clothes.

Laurel bashfully entered the room attired in the beautiful white lace nightgown Alice had given her in St. Louis, the one she thought should belong to a bride. The nightgown had been the only article of apparel Alice had bought her that she could not bear to part with. All the other fine linens and blouses and skirts and stockings she had sold to the other girls in the Bright School to gain enough money to make good her escape.

Carey turned round to face her in the moonlight. "You look like a vision. A beautiful vision."

Laurel groaned. "I haven't looked in a mirror in more than a month!" Only then was she close enough to him to realize he was naked. She glanced at the floor, embarrassed, but then looked again, unable to curb her curiosity. She immediately noticed his private part looked much different than the last time she had seen it just before he had pulled on his clothes last October. It now appeared all large and swollen and pointed straight up. She found it impossible to imagine such an enormous thing had been inside her. No wonder she had been so sore afterwards. At least she did not have to worry about that again. She had no intention of repeating her terrible mistake.

Carey laughed out loud he realized the target of her gaze and covered it with both hands in the same teasing pretense of modesty he had used the first day she saw him hold up his shirt and shout, "Don't look," as the Hartmoors passed him in their carriage.

Laurel felt such chagrin at being caught in her brazen behavior, she did not stop him from kissing her. The dizzying, delicious intimacy, this ancient ritual of lips and tongues and caressing hands. Six months had passed since last he kissed her and yet it seemed like an instant.

He pulled her down on top of him, then skillfully rolled her onto her back. Laurel did not think to object until she realized he had unbuttoned her nightgown and begun to frantically kiss and fondle her breasts.

"Carey?" No response. "Carey?" Still he ignored her, kissing and mouthing her breasts ferociously. As delightful as it felt, she grew more angry than aroused. How dare he think he can treat her like this, like his whore–to borrow his late wife's venomous assessment–after ignoring her the entire winter? Never so much as a postcard after the night they spent together.

"Carey!" She grabbed a handful of his curly blond hair and yanked.

"Huh?"

"We've got to stop. *You've* got to stop."

He broke their embrace and flipped over onto his back. He ran his hands over his face as he drew a deep breath and exhaled slowly.

"Carey, you promised."

"You're right. I did promise. Sorry. I got way too excited for my own good," he laughed. He lifted the covers and addressed something below his waist. "Down, boy!"

Laurel did not follow the joke.

"Tell me how on earth you got here from Wichita," he asked as they quietly lay side-by-side and stared up at the glittering dome of the prairie sky.

"Oh, it was fairly simple, really. I sold everything I owned to the other girls at the School. Took the train from Wichita to Emporia. Then a nice couple I met on the train drove me to my house, which was fourteen miles out of their way. That part was lucky."

"How did you get out of the School? They keep the gate locked like a prison."

"I climbed the wall. Another girl helped me. Her name was Anne. I told her she could come with me, but she got scared at the last minute and wouldn't follow me. She was due to have a baby almost any day, you see."

"You scaled the wall?"

"It wasn't that high." She would have climbed a mountain to get out of that terrible place. It was not so much the living conditions, abysmal though they were, but the oppressively melancholy atmosphere that not only made Laurel want to escape, but changed her whole outlook on her situation. She could have stood the hard beds, the meager food portions, the constant lectures on morality and the wages of sin. Rather, the helpless, hopeless attitudes of her fellow inmates made her long to rebel.

Daily, she observed the crying, pathetic girls wallowing in their own self-pity, drenched in the shame they had brought on themselves and their families. The whole world considered their lives to be ruined and they apparently agreed.

Their meek acceptance of this cruel whim of fate which had given them a baby rather than merely a memory, good or bad, seemed to Laurel profoundly unfair.

Carey had gotten off with just a memory. Carey didn't have to suffer away somewhere in a dismal institution getting daily lectures on wickedness and damnation. Carey did not have to work in the nursery of the orphans' asylum where the screaming babies lay three to a crib with no one to love them. Society's cast-offs, the human refuse of helpless women unable to support themselves or control their own future.

She became more determined with every day spent at the Bright School not to join the ranks of those helpless and hopeless women. Every day, she grew a little stronger and more resolved.

"Carey, it's not fair what happened to me. Men don't get sent off to places like that. All I did was love someone. I may be immoral, but I'm not wicked and depraved."

"Is that what they told you?"

"Each and every day. And you know what's worse? They exploit those girls. They make them work like slaves twelve–even fourteen–hours a day at various crafts–like lacework and finepoint and weaving–then they sell the fruits of their labor, but the girls never see a dime of it. It's legalized slavery, Carey. The girls are beaten or starved if they don't work. In fact, that so-called school makes money coming *and* going. They charge the families of the girls tuition as well!"

Carey groaned loudly through gritted teeth. "I hate Jack Hartmoor for putting you in that place."

"Not half as much as *I* hate him. It's not right, what he did. I know I did wrong, but I didn't deserve that. I didn't!"

"Of course you didn't!"

"But everyone in the world would agree with *him*."

"Then everyone in the world can go to hell. We're going to make a new world."

"Yes! Yes, you're right. A new world." She rambunctiously put her arms around him and snuggled close. How she loved the feeling of his strong arms, loved the scent of his skin as she pressed her face into the curve of his neck. Life seemed so much easier when you had someone to hold you.

The chastity of their embrace did not last for long. Before Laurel knew it, Carey's hands wandered to her breasts again and his body pressed itself against hers in an urgent fashion that mimicked what they had done in the grove last

October. Next she felt him gently insinuate his knee between her determinedly closed thighs.

"*Carey*."

"What?" he murmured, all innocence.

"Go sleep in the wagon."

With a resolute sigh, he sat up. "Yes, ma'am." He climbed off the mattress and grabbed the pile of his clothing from the floor and slowly left the room.

Laurel watched his moonlit form recede and could not help but admire once more the beauty of his muscular shoulders and back, looking as impressive as they had that first afternoon she had observed him mending the fence near the Hartmoor house.

Now she could admire all of him, the angular lines of his back drawing down to the tight waist, the hard roundness of his buttocks and the long, lean thighs.

She covered her face with her pillow and wished she could smother herself for the wildly indecent thoughts in her head. Perhaps she was wayward after all.

Chapter Twenty-two

Laurel found the long ride back to Chisholm tedious and anxiety-laden. Carey chatted endlessly about the Alliance and the Grange and the Pops–the growing political force of Populism churning through the wheatfields of Kansas.

Laurel tried to listen, but her thoughts were drawn again and again to Windrift and why she felt so melancholy. The partial destruction of her childhood home was not the source of her unhappiness. Houses could be repaired.

Her unease sprung from the difference she'd found in Windrift itself. She didn't understand how everything could have changed so profoundly when all had superficially remained the same. The air still held the same sweet scent, yet it failed to please her. The sky could still be as wild and ornamental, yet now seemed less impressive. How could the magic have left without a trace?

When they were more than halfway home, Carey suddenly remembered a present he had brought for her. "I found this in the wagon last night. I knew you'd enjoy it." He handed her a flyer entitled "Necessary Information for New Voters."

Laurel smiled with delight as she read the circular printed up by Aunt Lydia's suffrage group, the Kansas Equal Suffrage Association. The material instructed women–the "new voters" of the title, on how to best wield their newly found political power. A series of pointed questions were offered:

Do you not wish to have dram shops, gambling dens, and bawdy houses closed in your city forever?

Do you not wish to have your schoolhouses made wholesome places for your children?

Do you not wish to have your city's money spent as prudently as possible?

The pamphlet concluded with the warning that should women fail to do their duty on election day, the vicious elements of society were certain to triumph.

Carey and Laurel arrived at the Hartmoor house a little after seven in the evening only to find it utterly deserted.

"How odd for them to be in town on a Sunday evening," Laurel remarked as she returned to the front porch to say goodbye to Carey.

Carey slapped his knee, "There's a political debate in town tonight. I forgot this was Sunday. You want me to take you in to see it?"

"Yes, absolutely." Laurel eagerly climbed back up in the wagon, despite her weariness from the long day's journey from Windrift.

Carey snapped the reins and set the tired draft horses in motion once again.

"Do you think my uncle has a chance of winning the election?"

"A chance? I'd have to say he's a darn near shoe-in. The man running against him isn't much by comparison. The Democrats are backing Harry Johnson, the veterinarian. You wouldn't like him at all–he's totally opposed to women voting. And he's so quiet, he never even makes a dent in any of the political rallies he's spoken at. I think he just donated a lot of money to the Democratic Party and they wanted to do something nice for him. The Alliance isn't happy with either of the candidates. You *know* how they feel about bankers."

Laurel frowned with disappointment that Jack Hartmoor would so easily walk away with the mayor's race. This would no doubt make him more insufferable to live with than ever.

The March evening had turned off cool and fair. The winds had died down to a manageable breeze and the political debate had moved out of the limestone courthouse and onto the large lawn in front of it. Carriages and buggies lined Main Street on either side and an audience of about eighty had gathered to hear the candidates speak.

Jack Hartmoor and plump, bespectacled Harry Johnson stood on the middle level of the stone steps leading up to the courthouse to face the group. The four men running for the two open seats on the city council also stood by. A moderator, Laurel thought it must be Semper Cornwall, the grocer, stood between the two men to field questions from the audience.

Carey guided the wagon to the first open space he could find on the street, some two blocks from the courthouse.

As Laurel climbed down from the wagon, she wondered whether she and Carey should openly be seen together. If she was ever to restore her own reputation, not that she had ever lost it outside the confines of the Hartmoor parlor, she must make a clean break from the past. Carey would simply have to understand.

"Thank you for bringing me back to Chisholm, Carey. Perhaps we should part here for now. I don't think it would do for the Hartmoors to see us together, do you?" With that, she dashed off in the direction of the courthouse, leaving Carey alone as he tethered the horses.

He said nothing as she left, just watched her go. She felt a pang of remorse, but it quickly vanished when she recalled the shame of having seen Carey naked only twenty-four hours before and how he had tried to take advantage of the situation. She quickened her pace to nearly a run and arrived at the crowded courthouse lawn as the candidates were discussing the pros and cons of building a bridge over the West Jane.

She wandered to the front of the crowd, hoping to catch sight of her grandmother. She could not quite see the front row of the crowd even though most were now seated on the lawn.

Mrs. Elberta Maclean, the dauntless and imposing head of the Women's Christian Temperance Union, rose from the crowd like a ship of state whose ruffled prow preceded her by half a foot and asked in an almost threatening manner what the candidates for mayor would do to curb the illegal sale of whiskey in the town.

Harry Johnson eagerly stepped up to express his opinion. "Now you folks all know where I stand on this issue. While I don't condone drunkenness in any man, I do not agree that we should tell our fellow citizens what they can and cannot drink in their own homes."

This statement was greeted with an enthusiastic round of cheers and boos, in almost equal numbers.

Jack Hartmoor drew himself up and calmly broke in. "Temperance is the law of the land and I support it wholeheartedly. If elected, I would make it my business to see that the laws are rigorously enforced in Chisholm. Dramshops and saloons would no longer operate in the open and all would be done to see that they did not proliferate on the sly. The consumption of alcohol must be wiped out if we are to enjoy a truly Christian environment in which to live our lives and raise our children."

Elberta and the ladies of the W.C.T.U. nodded and politely applauded Jack's statement in support of their position.

A man who Laurel knew only as Dan, the butcher, stood up and asked the two candidates their opinion on the much-discussed initiative to require shopkeepers and other property owners along Main Street to build and maintain wooden sidewalks at their own expense.

Jack Hartmoor and his opponent did not differ sharply on this issue. Both thought the cost of building the walks should be shared with the town since all the citizens would benefit from the use of the sidewalks, though the prospect of raising a tax of some sort to pay the city's share was met with grumbling, especially from the Farmer's Alliance members who sat in tight solidarity in the far edge of the group. Laurel caught sight of Carey joining their number.

Jack shamelessly played to the female members of the audience by pointing out the necessity of wooden sidewalks to keep the lovely gowns of Chisholm's fairer sex dry and mud-free during rainy weather.

Was Jack actually courting the new female voters? The blatant hypocrisy of such an action would have been too galling to bear. Before Laurel's pounding heart could force her into silence, she took a deep breath, stood up, and asked in as loud a voice as she could muster, "I am interested to know the candidates' opinions on the recently passed legislation allowing women the right to vote in elections such as these."

Jack Hartmoor's mouth dropped open in shock to recognize his prodigal niece among the concerned electorate. Before he could answer, his opponent spoke up in a shrill voice, "I, for one, think it's a blasted shame and an unfortunate mistake made by our esteemed legislature this term. I believe that politics has always been the exclusive domain of men and should well remain so."

Mr. Johnson's remarks were met with a mixture of scorn from some and rousing approval from others.

Jack took this moment to collect his thoughts and then took the limelight. "I would be appalled to see any female member of my own family degrading themselves by voting come election day. Our women folk are too fine and fair to lower themselves into the cesspool of politics."

Jack's supporters applauded loudly to this statement.

"If politics is such a disgraceful and lowly mess–who is to blame for it?" asked Laurel, gaining momentum from the men's harsh remarks about suffrage.

"Good question!" shouted Delphinia Slidell, who served as Elberta Maclean's first lieutenant in the W.C.T.U. Elberta and the other temperance ladies applauded enthusiastically with their lace-gloved hands.

Laurel smiled and nodded her thanks to the ladies for supporting her.

When neither of the candidates seemed to come forth with a quick answer to Laurel's question, she decided to offer one of her own. "Maybe it's time someone cleaned up the 'cesspool,' as you describe it. And who is better at cleaning up than women?"

The crowd roared with laughter at this assertion and an unknown woman shouted from the back: "I been cleanin' up after men all my life!"

The audience not only laughed, but clapped their agreement with this remark.

Laurel beamed with the thrill of the moment. She felt the adrenalin shooting through her veins to be caused by excitement rather than fear.

She called to the chagrined candidates on the steps of the courthouse. "Women may or may not need politics, but I believe that politics certainly needs them!"

The women in the crowd, led by the ladies of the W.C.T.U., now jumped to their feet in a mass and wildly applauded. The Farmer's Alliance members joined them. The candidates and the moderator of the debate looked dismayed to have so completely lost control of the proceedings.

Jack Hartmoor stepped forward once again. "What next do you propose, Miss McBryde, a lady mayor?"

Everyone chortled at this absurd suggestion. Everyone but Laurel, who narrowed her October blue eyes at the man she despised most on earth. "I think the town of Chisholm could do a lot worse."

The steely, level tone of Laurel's voice brought a hushed silence to the onlookers.

Jack twitched his dark blond mustache to one side and arrogantly placed his hands on his hips. "Maybe you should put your name on the ballot, Miss McBryde."

Laurel was nonplused by this challenge.

"What's the matter, Miss McBryde? Unwilling to put your money where your mouth is? Don't you want to show us men the error of our ways?"

"This is all nonsense," Harry Johnson finally found his voice. "A woman is not qualified to be mayor."

A significant portion of the male members of the crowd mumbled their agreement with this remark.

"And precisely what would the qualifications be, then?" Laurel inquired with feigned politeness. "As I understand it, the main function of the mayor is simply to preside over the weekly city council meetings. Anyone with a nodding acquaintance of parliamentary procedure could easily fill the bill."

"The office of mayor requires experience and leadership," Jack announced pompously.

"Neither of you gentlemen has ever served as mayor before," Laurel pointed out with logic. "So neither of you can claim experience."

"The quality of leadership can be earned in many arenas," Jack insisted. "I have successfully run the First National Bank of Chisholm most of my adult life. That is an example of leadership."

Carey stood up with a slightly malicious grin on his handsome face. "Mr. Hartmoor has successfully led us all into debt!"

The Farmer's Alliance members roared loudly in approval of this remark and the rest of the crowd had to chuckle.

Jack's face reddened with emotion. "And...and I served my country in the War. That, too, is a show of leadership."

In a mockingly serious voice, Laurel asked, "And in exactly how many armed conflicts does the city council plan to engage during the next one-year term?"

Laurel brought down the house with this impudent remark, to her uncle's extreme chagrin. He glowered at her with a clenching jaw. Strangely, she did not feel threatened or cowed by his obvious displeasure. The howling crowd seemed to prop her up with invisible arms at every successful shot she fired. She never felt more exhilarated in her life.

Harry Johnson likewise frowned at the outspoken young woman in the audience who seemed bent on disrupting an otherwise perfectly respectable political debate. "Discussing a woman serving as mayor is a waste of our time tonight. The very idea of women serving in elective office is ridiculous. How would they manage to care for their homes and their children while holding public positions?"

"Are you suggesting, Mr. Johnson, that the demands of the mayor's office are so time-consuming that the mayor could not fulfill his other obligations? I guess that means my uncle will not be able to attend to his duties at the Bank. I hope this does not make too many of his depositors nervous."

"It means nothing of the kind," Jack sputtered. "I can assure everyone that I would never neglect my professional responsibilities. Why the town council meetings only require an hour, perhaps two, in a week."

Carey jumped to his feet again. "Sounds like Miss McBryde might be the perfect one for the job. She could probably devote a lot more time to it. Plus she's been educated by her father, a noted judge, Mr. Andrew McBryde. Some of you all might remember him. He helped start up the Hartmoor's bank. Miss McBryde's got more education than just about anybody in this town, as far as I know."

Mr. Kellerman, Carey's boss at the Grange stood up as well. "Plus she's a lot easier on the eyes than the two of you gents!"

Laurel blushed at this remark as the crowd chuckled and clapped in good humored approval. Laurel blushed even harder when a few of the rowdier young members of the audience whistled loudly.

Her eyes turned from Carey's smiling face to that of Margaret Hartmoor, whom she finally found in the crowd. Margaret sat with pursed lips, grimly staring at her granddaughter and slightly shaking her head in disapproval. Laurel knew she was probably cringing inside at the thought of a Hartmoor woman making such a spectacle of herself. Laurel realized at that moment that the one good thing about losing one's reputation was that one no longer bore the burden of maintaining it.

"Well, gentleman...and ladies," Jack said as contemptuously as possible, "we had better add Miss McBryde's name to the ballot."

Laurel's cheeks burned with the embarrassment of knowing she was being publicly ridiculed, but she decided on the spot that the only defense was a strong offence.

"Why thank you for the compliment, Uncle Jack. I would consider it an honor to share the ticket with two such esteemed gentlemen of this community."

A murmur of confusion and bemusement rose from the assemblage at this unexpected turn of events. No one seemed to know quite how to react.

Once again, Carey jumped to his feet. "I want to go on record as supporting Miss McBryde's nomination and offering her whatever support I can muster. This town would see its finest hour, should they choose to elect her."

The audience all talked loudly among themselves as everyone debated this point with their closest neighbors on the courthouse lawn.

Semper Cornwall, the grocer-turned-moderator, frantically waved his arms to quiet the group and restore order to the proceedings. When the clamor of the crowd dulled low enough for Semper to make himself heard, he spoke directly to Laurel. "Miss McBryde. The election of the mayor of this town is not a process to be mocked."

"No, sir, I agree," Laurel answered solemnly.

"Then I must know if your intentions in this matter are serious or not. If you are elected, will you serve?"

A lump formed in Laurel's throat big enough to choke her. She had not experienced so much fear and excitement ground together in equal measure since the night she let Carey relieve her of her virginity. *What am I doing*? Her mind silently screamed. *What am I getting myself into*?

Still a stronger voice spoke the opposite question: *What have I got to lose?*

"If I am so fortunate as to be elected by the people of Chisholm, I would be proud to serve."

ꕥ

The political debate adjourned in a frenzy of conversation as everyone present felt the need to comment on the sensation Laurel had created. Everywhere Laurel looked, eyes stared back at her. Some were contemptuous, some disapproving, but most were simply curious. She tried to push her way through the crowd to reach Carey and thank him for sticking up for her, but she soon felt her elbow roughly grabbed by her uncle who proceeded to guide her to the Hartmoor wagon whether she wished to go there or not. His fingers dug into the soft flesh of her arm with a determination that made her fear to look him in the eye.

Margaret, Alice, and Cassandra were already waiting there for them.

"Sister, would you take the reins tonight? I need to converse with my fellow candidate," Jack said as they arrived at their carriage.

Laurel drew a deep breath and swallowed hard as she allowed her uncle to help her up into her seat. Jack helped his wife and mother in after Cassandra and then joined Laurel in the back seat of the carriage. Margaret and Cassandra could not help but cast furtive glances over their shoulders as Cassandra headed the horses for home.

"Well, young lady, that was quite a performance you put on tonight."

"Thank you."

"Don't be impertinent with me, you little tramp. Tomorrow morning you will go into town and you will march to city hall and withdraw your name from the mayoral slate. Is that clear?"

"My running for mayor was *your* idea, Uncle Jack."

"Your running for mayor was a *joke*. Nothing more."

"Perhaps I don't see it that way."

"Don't be ridiculous."

"I'm of legal age. I have the right to run for office if I wish. The Kansas Supreme Court has spoken on the matter. What else is there to discuss?"

"You are not qualified to run your own life, much less the town of Chisholm."

"Obviously, I don't agree and neither did Mr. Fairchild."

"We all know what our Mr. Fairchild sees in you, my dear. A convenient skirt to get up." Jack nearly growled the last words and looked at her with a simmering contempt in his eyes.

"Jack," his mother warned. She turned a withering look on her son.

"Carey Fairchild will not be satisfied until he has destroyed this entire family," Jack muttered under his breath.

Laurel could not quite grasp her uncle's last remark. Still, she did not wish to discuss her past relationship to Carey, of which all the Hartmoors were apparently aware now. "We do not need to bring Mr. Fairchild into this."

"No, I can understand your reluctance on that score. The good people of Chisholm, Kansas, do not need a mayor who fornicates with field hands, do they?"

Laurel felt an excruciating jolt of panic in her ribs. Her breath came quickly and she tried to maintain her composure. She knew she would have to face this issue with Jack from the moment she left the solace of Windrift, but she had never anticipated having to deal with it in quite so public an arena.

"Uncle Jack, surely you would not reveal matters that are best left private."

"I will not hesitate...unless you act as I have suggested tomorrow morning."

Laurel seethed at this terrible threat. *I will not let him get the best of me. I will not let him triumph so easily.* Her thoughts raced for ammunition and just when she thought the outlook seemed hopeless, she recalled the existence of the locked china cabinet.

"If you are so cruel as to make public my past errors, I shall have no choice but to reveal the fact that you illegally possess whiskey and drink it on a regular basis. The good people of Chisholm, Kansas, do not need a mayor who publicly endorses temperance and privately laughs at the law."

"You wouldn't dare."

"You leave me no choice."

With their trump cards played, both candidates rode the remainder of the drive home in silence, with Laurel nervously twisting her skirt in her lap and Jack fuming in a stew of his own hypocrisy.

As they all disembarked in the yard of the Hartmoor house, Margaret was heard to say, "It's going to be an interesting three weeks."

The Hartmoor women entered the house and Laurel followed until Jack raced up the porch stairs ahead of her and blocked her entrance to the front door.

"You drive a hard bargain, Miss High and Mighty, but if you will agree to stay quiet on the subject of my little indiscretions, I will likewise cloak your unfortunate transgressions. Agreed?"

Laurel felt a triumphant smile spread across her face which she hoped the shadows of the covered porch concealed. "Agreed. May the best man–or woman–win."

Jack only harrumphed at this impudent remark and followed Laurel into the house.

Chapter Twenty-three

Laurel's mind raced through the night with the outlandish thought of what had so unexpectedly transpired the evening before. She knew in her heart she had no reasonable chance of winning and probably didn't deserve the honor, but when she thought of her two opponents, she couldn't see how they deserved it either.

She took a powerful deep breath before entering the dining room for breakfast. Another acrimonious encounter with Jack would only sour her stomach and weaken her resolve. Just when she thought she couldn't bear to face him again, Carey's words on the sunset knoll at Windrift came back to her: Think what fine mischief it would be to stick a thorn in the side of that pompous jackass each and every day!

She smiled to herself and entered the dining room with confidence. She sat down with a breezy arrogance and smiled at everyone present, Alice, Jack, and Cassandra.

Jack looked up from his newspaper warily. "I suppose it's too much to hope for that you might have magically recovered your senses overnight."

Laurel lifted her chin with a serene air. "No such luck, Uncle Jack. I'm more determined than ever. And...I want to thank you again for nominating me."

"I don't want your thanks or your insolence, you little slut."

Margaret entered the dining room with a steaming plate of fried potatoes just in time to hear her son's remark. "Jack, I will not tolerate such name calling at my table or in my house. If you cannot conduct your affairs in a civil manner, you can take your breakfast elsewhere."

All eyes widened at this rebuke. It voiced once again who really held power in the family and, by power, that was to say the controlling interest in the Hartmoor Bank.

"Excellent idea, Mother," Jack announced. "I'll eat my breakfast in town this morning and dine with people who share my outlook on life."

"You're dining at the jail?" Laurel asked with mock innocence.

"No, with the *voters*, Niece." With a sarcastic twitch to his moustache, he gathered up his Wichita newspaper and left the room.

Conversation did not resume for some minutes after Jack's departure, but Laurel finally found the nerve to ask her grandmother, "Might I get one new dress? I understand that since a year has elapsed since my father's passing, I need no longer wear mourning. And my birthday is just around the corner..."

"What happened to all the nice things I bought for you, Laurel?" Alice asked.

Laurel almost jumped at the sound of Alice's voice. She had not spoken at all since Laurel had returned the night before. Even more amazing was the fact that Alice slept on Christine's little bed in Laurel's room. Alice had retired to bed after Laurel and had risen before her that morning, so she had not yet gotten the opportunity to ask about the situation. She now wondered if she should inquire at all.

"They're just...gone." Laurel did not wish to explain in depth and did not want to speak of her weeks in the Bright School for the Moral Correction of Wayward Girls.

"I'm sure a new frock can be arranged," said Margaret. "We can go into town after the breakfast dishes are done and visit Selma Ann."

Laurel smiled with pleasure and anticipation. Selma Ann was the finest dressmaker in town and known for her speed as much as her skill. Laurel could already imagine the color of her new dress–October blue, her favorite, the color of her eyes.

"Would you like to look at some of my ladies' magazines, Laurel? They're filled with the latest fashions." Alice asked. "A candidate for mayor must look her best."

Cassandra and Margaret's eyebrows shot up at this unexpected endorsement from the opposing candidate's wife. Laurel, as surprised as the rest, but now realizing that it was somehow in keeping with Alice's choice of sleeping quarters, could only nod vigorously in reply.

"You have such a lovely figure, Laurel. The right cut of gown will set it off just perfectly. Heads will turn when they see you in one of Selma Ann's creations."

Laurel stood in her underwear behind a screen on a little pedestal in the back room of the dressmaker's shop as she got measured every which way.

Alice sat in a chair overseeing the work of the tiny, elderly woman whose talents with a needle had kept all the Hartmoor women clothed for the last decade.

"She does have a fine shape on her," said Selma Ann through a pencil between her teeth. "Small waist and nice and full up here."

Laurel blushed to hear the size of her breasts discussed in public, but as Selma Ann had just released her measuring tape from Laurel's bosom, she could not pretend they were referring to anything else. A sudden twinge of shame pinched her when she realized Carey Fairchild was the only person on earth who had ever seen her breasts uncovered. And not only had he seen them, but had wantonly kissed and fondled them. Why did such indecent thoughts about Carey have to keep popping into her head at every odd moment? Something strangely akin to a chill swept over her, causing her nipples to show beneath her muslin camisole.

"What color do you favor for this dress, Miss?"

"Blue, sky blue," Laurel answered without hesitation.

"No, dear," Alice interrupted. "Blue would not yet be thought appropriate."

"But I thought my year of mourning was over, Aunt Alice."

"It is, dear, but one does not jump back into bright colors immediately after wearing black. A soft gray, perhaps?"

"I've got a fine piece of the palest lavender taffeta, Mrs. Hartmoor," Selma Ann offered.

Laurel and Alice exchanged looks and nodded simultaneously in Selma Ann's direction while she completed her measurements.

"Are you the one they're all talkin' about, Honey?"

Laurel blushed even darker than before. "I guess so, if you mean the mayor's race."

Selma Ann turned to Alice. "And what do you think of all this, Mrs. Hartmoor? Your husband runnin' for mayor against his own niece."

Alice gracefully tucked away a coy smile. "I'm not at all sure, yet. The subject is too new. What are others saying this morning?"

Selma Ann packed away her measuring tape and grinned up at Laurel on her dressmaker's pedestal. "Don't mean to hurt your feelings any, but most folks are sayin' it's a lot of foolishness."

"I'm not surprised," Laurel remarked philosophically. She had placed herself, for better or worse, in the public eye and would have to endure whatever that entailed.

"So who are you going to vote for, Mrs. Hartmoor? Your husband or your niece?"

Alice smiled mysteriously. "I'm told that the content of a ballot is kept secret. I suppose my vote, should I actually choose to do such a thing, will only be known by myself and the Good Lord."

Alice made this statement in such a charming manner that neither Selma Ann nor Laurel could take offense. After the fitting was completed and the pattern and fabric chosen, Laurel and Alice left the shop and stopped in at the tea shop for sodas and dainty sandwiches.

"Are you really thinking about voting?" Laurel asked with a mischievous smile, as their lunch was served to them at a small, ornate white wicker table. Laurel recalled only too well how Alice had once informed her with authority that no decent woman would ever consider such an activity.

Alice shrugged. "I haven't made up my mind yet."

Laurel decided the moment was ripe to broach a sensitive topic. "Aunt Alice, why are you sleeping in my room? And why are you so nice about my running for mayor against Uncle Jack? In the year that I've known you, I don't think I've ever heard you even disagree with him in public."

Alice gazed out the window of the tea shop. The bell over the door of the shop jingled as two elderly women entered. They glanced at Laurel, apparently recognizing her from the political debate. They immediately whispered a terse exchange before finding a seat.

"Your Uncle Jack and I," Alice began slowly, "are not of like mind on some extremely sensitive issues."

Laurel ducked her head though she had no idea which issues Alice might be referring to. "I'm sorry."

Alice waved her hand delicately. "It's not your concern, dear."

"I don't mean to pry, but if I'm the cause–"

"No, it's not you. Well, it began with you, if you must know. Jack refuses to make any further discussion on the topic of adoption. His mind is utterly closed on the matter. You see, after we dropped you off at that...that school, I chanced to see–"

"The orphans nursery," Laurel guessed. She knew one look at all the abandoned babies and small children would cause Alice's heart to break.

Tears filled Alice's large eyes at the memory. "All those poor, homeless babes. Who could not come away from such a sight unmoved?"

Who, indeed? Laurel knew the answer to that one: her Uncle Jack.

Laurel decided she had better change the subject. "I'm glad you're not angry with me for this mayor situation. I won't do anything to embarrass the Hartmoors. I swear it."

"A young lady should not use phrases like 'I swear it,' dear."

"Yes, ma'am."

They finished their lunch and stepped out onto the blustery sidewalk. Alice opened her laced-trimmed parasol, only to have the March wind immediately turn it inside out. As she struggled to right it without destroying it, Carey Fairchild rushed up, breathless.

"Good day, Ladies." He pulled off his hat politely.

Laurel smiled faintly and was about to return his greeting when Alice grabbed her by the hand and jerked her away from Carey. She guided Laurel down the sidewalk at a furious pace.

"Laurel, you must not speak to that young man, now or ever again. He has ruined you and you must forget whatever attachment you once felt for him if you are to save yourself from further disgrace."

"Miss McBryde, I need to talk to you," Carey called after them.

Alice turned a haughty glance on Carey over her shoulder. "Miss McBryde is too busy to converse with you, sir." She did not even slow her stride.

Laurel looked back helplessly, confused about what she should do, if anything.

"It's about the mayor's race," Carey continued, undeterred.

Laurel halted. "I've got to speak with him, Aunt Alice. I'm sorry but I must."

Alice frowned with worry. "At least do not be seen speaking on the street alone with him."

Laurel nodded and motioned for Alice to accompany her back to where Carey stood. The wind kicked up a tantrum on the dusty main street of Chisholm, sending hats and newspapers and bits of trash racing down the thoroughfare.

"The members of the Farmers Alliance want to meet you, Miss McBryde. They asked me to invite you to their next meeting. It's Sunday afternoon. You'll come, won't you?"

"Tell them I'd be pleased to attend."

"I'll pick you up at noon."

"Just a minute," Alice snapped.

"We won't be alone, Mrs. Hartmoor. I can assure you Miss McBryde's reputation will not be endangered in any way. It's a picnic–food, lemonade, families. Your family is invited, too, of course. I just didn't think any of you would want to attend."

"Indeed not," Alice mumbled.

They exchanged terse farewells and Laurel rode home with Alice feeling excited by the prospect of Sunday's picnic. She wished her new frock would be ready by then, but there was no chance of that.

"You've turned me into another family scandal, I hope you know." Laurel made this remark only half-jokingly as the pair drove to the Farmers Alliance picnic on Sunday in a rig Carey had borrowed from his boss, Mr. Kellerman.

"Good," Carey laughed as he urged the horses on to a quicker pace. "A little scandal's good for the constitution. Stirs up the blood. The Hartmoor family could use a stirring."

"Well, we surely don't want any sluggish blood. Will I have to make a speech?"

"No, I think the speaking agenda is pretty full already. We've got two out-of-town speakers coming in to talk about farm issues. Mr. Kellerman just wants to introduce you to everyone and you might say a few words then. Most of the folks here don't live close enough to Chisholm to vote in the city elections. But some do, thirty or forty, at least, so you might get some votes here."

"Do you think I'm dressed alright?" She smoothed the plain black silk skirt of her outfit.

Carey looked her up and down. "I'd prefer you in nothing at all, but I suppose that'll do."

Laurel grew instantly furious. "Stop talking to me in that indecent manner. Don't you think I could die of shame about all of that. It's in the past now. Over completely. I want to forget it, but you won't let me!"

Carey turned a sullen face to the road ahead and jerked the brim of his hat down lower on his brow. "Sorry."

They did not speak again the rest of the journey.

Laurel watched with awe as they neared the picnic ground on the shore of the West Jane. Hundreds of farm families had gathered. The entire county seemed to be present. Several large canopies had been erected to shelter the group from the sun, or a sudden rain shower. A platform had also been built. She assumed she might be introduced to the gathering from such a place. She suddenly felt so overcome with nerves, she forgot to be angry with Carey for his lewd remarks and slipped her arm through his as he pulled the rig into a good spot to tie the horses.

He glanced at her entwining arm and then her face, but made no remark.

Mr. Kellerman rushed to greet them as Carey helped Laurel down from the buggy.

"Pleased to make your acquaintance, Miss McBryde," Mr. Kellerman offered. "Fairchild, here, has said some awful fine things about you."

"We've met before, Mr. Kellerman. Last fall. Do you remember?"

"I do recall it, Miss, and I believe I was a bit short with you. I had no idea just how serious you were. I mean, it's just that with your relation to Jack Hartmoor and all, it was hard to believe that–oh, well, you won't hold that against me now, will you?"

"Indeed not. I'm honored to be invited here today. And I want to thank you for the things you said last week at the political debate."

"My pleasure, I can assure you! Any time I see a body making Jack Hartmoor–or any banker–hot under the collar, I can't resist doing likewise."

"Let's get Miss McBryde some fried chicken before she starves to death, shall we?"

As Laurel strode arm-in-arm between Carey and his boss, she watched the faces of the farm families gathered there and wondered if they would be so easy a conquest as Mr. Kellerman. Disapproving glances met her curious gaze more often than not.

Chapter Twenty-four

"I think Mr. Kellerman likes me," Laurel remarked to Carey as he drove her home.

"He ain't the only one, you know." Carey leaned over and gave her an impetuous kiss on the cheek.

Laurel accepted his kiss with a blush, but when he tried to kiss her a second time on the lips, she pushed him away and scooted as far from him as the buckboard seat would allow. "No, we're just friends now. Why can't you accept that?"

He looked away, brooding and hurt. When his anger subsided, he quietly asked, "I know for a fact you loved me once, Laurel. Why did you stop?"

"I'm supposed to love a man who considers me some convenient skirt to get up?" It pained her to quote her uncle, but his spiteful words had given substance to all she feared the most.

"What the hell kinda thing is that to say?"

"Don't swear at me!"

"Then don't talk such dirt yourself."

She fixed her eyes straight into the vast expanse of prairie and tried to compose herself. The sun setting low behind their backs cast a golden glow across the newly green fields. "How do you expect me to love a man who could go off and forget me the day after–" The rest of the sentence caught in her throat. For all her sophistication, real or imagined, she still could not bring herself to verbalize the fact of their sexual intimacy. "All that time and not a single letter!"

"I couldn't write to you."

"Oh, yes, picking up a pen and writing a few lines is far too much to ask. I'm certain of that! If only you knew...knew about–"

"Knew about what?"

Laurel angrily sighed and tried to regain her composure. Her pride still stood stronger than an iron post and she could not admit the humiliation of her false pregnancy. "Nothing. It doesn't matter now. Something bad happened last winter. I don't want to talk about it."

"Well, if it's any comfort to you, something pretty bad happened to me, too. It was the lowest point in my life, 'cept Mae's parting, I guess."

"I doubt it compares to what happened to me."

"I was in jail a good part of the winter."

She glanced over at him with a skeptical frown. "Why were you in jail?"

"Attempted murder."

"Oh, really?"

"It's true!" He turned a furious face on her now.

"And who, pray tell, did you try and kill?"

"My father-in-law."

Her lips parted. "You're serious, aren't you?"

He nodded sadly.

"What happened?"

"It's not a pretty story. If you're sure you want to hear it, we've gotta go someplace totally private."

Laurel felt a queasy foreboding in his unnaturally serious manner. "Would you like to go to the poplar grove? It's where we always used to share our secrets."

"Sure."

"I knew I'd made a big mistake letting the girls stay with the Brocks almost right away." Carey stared straight ahead as he spoke, looking out beyond the circle of trees that sheltered them from the moist and warm March breezes. They sat side by side, leaning against the outcropping of limestone, just like the summer before.

"We never got on well and still didn't. They expected me to pay them to take care of the girls and whenever I visited, I had to sleep in the barn with the hired hands. Still, I was committed to my job with the Alliance so I tried to make it work. I hated the travel, though. I never hardly got to see the girls."

"That's terrible."

"That was the *best* part. What happened when I stopped to visit them Thanksgiving week...I'll never get over if I live to be a hundred." He propped his chin on his elbows against his knees.

The tone of Carey's voice made Laurel feel a gathering fog of apprehension. She'd never seen him so serious since the death of Mae.

"On the Sunday morning before Thanksgiving, I thought they'd all gone to church, so I let myself into the house to find something to eat. I'd overslept and missed breakfast." He stopped and covered his face with his hands. "I heard Rachel crying, so I went to her room in the attic."

He stopped speaking. He didn't seem able to go on. Laurel turned sideways to face him and reached out to place a comforting hand on his shoulder. He took her hand and kissed its palm, then held it against his face. She felt the wetness on his cheeks and realized he must be crying.

"He...he–"

"Mr. Brock?"

Carey nodded, swallowed hard, and tried to compose himself. "He was trying to take her drawers off her," he choked out.

Laurel clapped her free hand over her own mouth in shock. "That's vile. That's the most–"

Carey sniffed and wiped his eyes. "I went crazy. Like I had a storm inside my head. I grabbed him and knocked him to the floor and just started strangling him and beating his head against the wall 'til he was all bloody and Rachel was screaming and...and–" Carey choked back tears again. "I never thought I could kill anyone, but I wanted to kill him. I would have, too, if the rest of the Brock family hadn't of come home that minute. Mae's brothers pulled me off of the old man."

"But why were you charged with attempted murder? You were defending your daughter. Surely you had the right–"

Carey violently shook his head. "I couldn't tell them what happened. I couldn't make Rachel tell them. I couldn't put her through that."

"Oh, Carey."

"The Brocks told the sheriff about how him and me was always quarreling and the sheriff didn't have any reason not to believe them. Everybody knew we didn't get on. So the sheriff put me in jail to wait for the circuit judge to come for a hearing."

"Carey, that was so...so noble. Going to jail to protect your daughter. How did you get out?"

"The judge didn't come and didn't come and I sat in jail week after week. Then, just after Christmas, Old Man Brock, he took a turn for the worse. He was in a pretty bad way after the beating I gave him. On his deathbed, he told the doctor I had a good reason for doing what I did. He wouldn't come right out and say what, but the doctor and the sheriff got together and talked about it. And when the sheriff asked Mrs. Brock what she thought they oughta do, she said she didn't see no reason to hold me any longer." Carey turned on her with a face hardened by unspeakable bitterness. "Laurel, she *knew*. Mrs. Brock *knew*. I *know* she knew the truth. She knew about her husband. I could see it in her eyes the morning it happened. And why else would she suddenly think it's alright to let me out of jail?"

"That's so awful." Laurel had never heard such a terrible story in her life. "Do you think that Mr. Brock ever–"

"Got after Mae? I'm almost certain of it, now that I look back. The more I thought about it, the more I'm sure that the miserable old bastard did to her the same thing as he was trying to do to Rachel. It would explain so much. So much I didn't understand before. No wonder she begged me not to ask who got her into trouble."

"Poor Mae." Laurel had never cared for Mae Fairchild and yet now she wanted to cry on her behalf. The poor woman had suffered horrors Laurel could not even imagine. *Incest*. The word twisted in her stomach.

"If only I'd known," Carey continued, awash in misery. "If only she'd told me. Things would've been so different for us. And for *him*. That...that fiend! I would've taken care of him years ago!"

The violence in Carey's tone upset Laurel and yet, she, too, stumbled and staggered over her own outraged emotions. "How can such wickedness exist? Try to calm yourself, Carey. At least it's all over now."

Carey sighed. "It's not over. Rachel still has nightmares. And she blames herself for me going to jail. Thinks it's all her fault. She keeps saying, 'I'm sorry, Daddy, I'm sorry.' I can't seem to set her straight."

"Oh, Carey." In that one moment, Laurel forgot all the miseries she'd been through on his behalf. Her suffering seemed so impossibly trivial by comparison. The only thing she could think about was comforting him. She threw her arms around his neck and hugged him to her as tightly as she could.

"I never stopped loving you," she whispered. "I was just angry. That's all." She kissed his cheek, then his lips. "Do you forgive me?"

"Forgive you–for what?" He gazed at her with so much love in his eyes, she felt as if no time had passed at all since the last time they had visited the poplar grove together. He gently eased her onto her back. "Marry me, Laurel," he whispered between wet, feverish kisses.

"Yes, oh, yes." Laurel's moment of divine happiness was marred by the sensing of Carey's hand underneath her petticoat. She tried to protest, but every time she opened her mouth, he covered it with another kiss. By the time he had successfully slipped his hand into the open crotch of her underdrawers, she realized she had to take action.

She grabbed his shoulders and shoved him as hard as she could at the very moment she felt the intrusion of one of his fingers. "Stop it, Carey!"

He grinned down at her. "Stop what?"

"You know."

"This?" He roguishly wiggled the invading finger.

This action felt so strange she giggled in spite of herself.

"It feels good, admit it." His thumb now massaged a shockingly sensitive new spot. He was right. It did feel good, but still she tried to squirm away.

"We can't! We absolutely can't!"

"Why not? We love each other. We're going to be married."

"I'm afraid," she confessed miserably. "Afraid I'll get a baby."

"From my fingers?"

The sham innocence of his tone made her want to slap him. "Don't mock me! I know what comes next."

His handsome face dropped its wicked, jesting edge and he kissed her softly on the forehead. "Don't worry. I'll be more careful this time. Trust me. You won't get a baby, I swear it."

She had no idea what he was talking about, but with severe misgivings, she let him do as he wished. She braced herself for the worst, but was surprised to find out the so-called act of love no longer hurt at all. In fact, it felt almost...interesting.

Carey stayed true to his word and withdrew in time to splatter his seed all over her bare belly.

"You're certain this works?" she asked, once again apprehensive.

"Sure, it does. Well, most of the time. Mae and I–" He stopped suddenly and looked away. The mention of Mae's name cast a pall on their happiness. Laurel held her breath, wishing she could banish Mae's ghost from this sacred place.

He stood up and offered to pull her to her feet. "Let's go into town this minute and find a preacher. I want to change your name from McBryde to Fairchild before the day is out."

His sudden playfulness put her at ease once again. She smiled with relief, then frowned. "If we get married so suddenly, everyone will suspect the worst."

He raised his eyebrows provocatively and leaned forward. "They'd be right."

"Let's not get married until after the election, at least."

He groaned with mock despair. "You're going to make me wait a whole week?"

"Yes," she announced decisively. "But let's tell the Hartmoors tonight. Come home to supper with me."

Carey made a face like she had just asked him to dine on weeds and turpentine.

"It'll be fine, Carey."

"No, it won't. You know it won't. Let's tell them *after* the wedding, not before."

"Maybe you're right. Oh, alright. Let's get married tonight, but keep it secret until after the election."

"Fine with me."

As they climbed in the wagon, Laurel turned a pleading, nearly pouting face on her bridegroom. "Would you mind if I invited my grandmother to attend. It would really mean a lot."

"Only if I can bring my daughters."

"Of course." Laurel clapped her hands with childish delight, then her eyes widened. "Oh, my word, I'm about to become a stepmother. What will your girls say? What will they think about all this?"

"Only one way to find out," Carey said as he set the horses into motion.

"But I don't know how to be a mother."

"Trust me, the hard work's already been done. Or should I say, the *labor*."

Laurel was much too preoccupied to appreciate Carey's pun. "I want them to like me."

"They'll love you as much as I do. Now stop worrying."

As the Hartmoor house rose into view, another concern presented itself.

"Carey...do I look like I've just–"

"Been ravished? A little. You might want to smooth your hair a bit." He pulled a twig from her dark and tangled locks.

Chapter Twenty-five

"We are gathered here today to join this man and this woman in the bonds of matrimony," intoned Judge Marley.

Carey squeezed Laurel's elbow and the pair exchanged shy smiles. Margaret and Cassandra Hartmoor stood as reluctant witnesses in the poplar grove. The two women had still not quite recovered from the shock of Laurel running up the porch steps and bursting into the house, demanding that a preacher be sent for. The hired hand, Arthur, was sent into town to locate either a preacher or a judge and bring him to the poplar grove posthaste so that the wedding might be completed before dark.

Carey and his two little daughters were already waiting for them in the grove when the Hartmoor women arrived by buggy and the judge arrived on horseback, having been pulled from his supper table on the promise of a lucrative honorarium. The Hartmoor name was useful in such an instance.

Now they all stood in a quiet, joyful group. Cassandra held little Caroline on her hip so the child could watch the proceedings from a better vantage point. Rachel held Margaret's hand and looked on with a grave expression clouding her six-year-old face. She was not quite mature enough to fully understand the situation, but old enough to be confused by it. Surely she was no more stunned and surprised than the two Hartmoor women.

"Do you, Carey Fairchild, take Laurel McBryde to be your lawful, wedded wife?"

It's happening at last, thought Laurel. It's really happening. The sheer joy of the moment made her feel giddy. She took a deep breath to calm herself. She thought about the first time Carey had spoken to her in the grove–the day she fell from old Mona's back and landed ignominiously in the growing wheat.

She wished she had a nicer dress to get married in than her old black taffeta, still mourning-plain and unornamented.

Carey glanced at her with concerned eyes. So did the judge.

"Is everything alright, Miss?"

"Yes, Judge, I'm fine."

"No second thoughts?" Judge Marley teased, with a mischievous grin on his wizened face.

She smiled and shook her head vigorously. Everyone chuckled.

"You do have a ring?" Judge Marley queried the bridegroom.

"A ring? Uh-oh."

"Wait," said Laurel. "I have something." She pulled her silver locket up from the collar of her dress. She pried the compartment open and carefully extracted the twig ring.

Carey smiled down at her. "I'm a man of my word," he whispered.

Before the judge could continue, the small wedding party turned to the sound of an approaching horseman. A man rode astride at full gallop.

"What the–?" whispered Carey, with more than idle curiosity.

"It's Uncle Jack." Laurel felt a knot of fear grow in her throat.

"But how? Why?" sputtered Cassandra.

"Alice," said Margaret. "She was up sulking in her room when the young folks pulled up in the yard. She no doubt overheard everything we said on the porch."

"Someone else coming to join us?" asked the judge, amiably.

Jack reined his horse to a halt only yards from the party, startling everyone.

"What do you want?" shouted Carey, stomping over to where Jack dismounted.

"You can't do this." Jack, out of breath, gulped for air. He walked straight past Carey over to the judge.

"Good afternoon, Jack." The judge smiled broadly, still thinking Jack was just a late-arriving guest.

"This wedding can't take place." Jack's chest heaved, still breathless.

Carey confronted Jack with a look on his face that frightened Laurel. She deftly stepped between the two men to keep them separate. She would not have her wedding day spoiled by fisticuffs.

"Just get out of here. Leave us alone!" Carey demanded.

"You don't understand, Fairchild. You can't marry my niece." He raised his hands in a conciliatory gesture and his voice carried no anger, not even his usual condescending sarcasm.

"I can and I will. We're both single and over twenty-one. You can't stop us."

"Sounds good enough to me," reasoned the cheerful judge. "Just 'cause you don't like her intended's politics, Jack, doesn't mean you can really stop 'em from–"

"You don't understand," Jack repeated. "The marriage would be void."

"Jack, what are you talking about?" asked Cassandra.

"Why would the marriage be void, Jack? Don't you think I should be the judge of that?" Marley chuckled.

"Leave us alone, Hartmoor," Carey interrupted. "Just get the hell out of here!"

Carey made another threatening step toward Jack. Laurel laid a warning hand upon his chest. With a pleading look, she begged him to hold his temper.

"I wish I could," said Jack miserably. "I wish to heaven I could."

"Please, Uncle Jack. State your business."

"Spoken like a lawyer's daughter," Judge Marley grinned at Laurel. He was clearly the only person present enjoying himself.

"Judge, would you excuse us for a minute?" Jack asked uncomfortably. "This is a very private matter."

The judge shrugged and stepped away to allow the Hartmoor family some measure of privacy.

"Jack?" Cassandra repeated in an irritated whisper. "What is going on? Why would the marriage be void?"

"You see, you see...." Jack wiped his hand nervously over his face as though it were wet and he were trying to dry it. He sighed. "First cousins can't legally marry in this state–it's considered incest."

Laurel gaped horror and confusion. She could not believe she had heard the dreadful word *incest* spoken twice in one day.

Carey narrowed his eyes at Jack Hartmoor. "I knew it."

"Knew what? Knew what?" babbled an alarmed Cassandra.

"Oh, dear Lord," Margaret murmured.

"What your brother is trying to tell us, Miss Hartmoor, is that he is my father. Isn't that right?" asked Carey with his jaw still clenched in anger.

Jack stared at the ground, unable to speak.

"Isn't that right?" Carey bellowed, though the target of his question stood a distance of three feet away.

Jack raised his eyes and met Carey's ferocious stare. He nodded, first slowly, then more deliberately.

"Wait a minute," Carey was on the offensive again. "How do we know he's telling the truth?" He looked down at Laurel. "He'd say anything to keep us apart."

"This can't be happening," Laurel muttered. "It can't!" She pressed her lips together to hold back the tears. She felt as though the grassy prairie floor had opened in a gaping maw to suck them all straight to hell.

"I want this wedding to continue," Carey loudly demanded of the judge.

"But this is a serious charge, Carey," said Margaret. "We have no choice but to deal with it."

"He can't prove it," Carey insisted.

"I'm afraid I can," Jack said quietly.

"Please, let's not argue about this in front of your daughters," Laurel breathed into Carey's ear.

Margaret heard part of Laurel's remark and walked quickly to her side. "Let's all go back to the house," she said sharply to Carey. "We have a lot of talking to do."

The Hartmoor women made their way over to the buggy. Carey led his daughters to his borrowed wagon.

"Will you be needing me?" asked the judge.

"No," muttered Jack.

Judge Marley and Jack mounted their horses and rode off in opposite directions, while Carey and Cassandra headed their rigs for the Hartmoor house.

When they arrived at the homestead, Alice stood watching them from the porch. A strangely knowing smile creased her wan face.

"Good gracious, what's all this?" she called as Cassandra guided the buggy up next to the wide porch to allow the ladies to exit. Carey pulled up right behind and dashed over to help Laurel down. When she lowered herself into Carey's waiting arms, he hugged her close and pressed his cheek to her forehead.

"Don't be afraid," he whispered.

"I'm not. We'll figure something out. We've come too far to stop now."

"That's my girl." He smiled, but Laurel could see the concern in his eyes.

Arthur, the stable hand, dispatched by Jack, came loping into the yard to collect the horses and rigs.

Everyone seated themselves awkwardly in the parlor after Cassandra took Carey's girls to the kitchen for milk and cookies. Alice and Margaret sat together on the sofa. Laurel seated herself in the large red velvet arm chair while Carey solemnly stationed himself behind it.

All sat expectantly awaiting Jack's reappearance. He soon walked in the front door. Carey folded his arms across his chest with a defiant expression and waited with the rest for Jack to proceed.

Laurel's heart pounded as she waited for her uncle, her own mother's brother, to explain why her happiness and future would now be destroyed.

Jack drew a deep breath and exhaled slowly. Laurel noticed his hands shook slightly and he wiped them once again down his face. He cleared his voice twice.

"I'm sorry," he muttered, almost to himself. "This is very difficult for me."

"*Try*," said Carey in as cold and humorless a voice as Laurel had ever heard him use.

"I *am*," Jack protested, as though he felt everyone should pity him. He raised his head and looked Carey in the eye. "I met your mother during the War. Five companies of my regiment were dispatched to Douglas County. The officers were billeted with local families–those wanting to support the Union cause in any way they could. Another major and myself were quartered with the Carington family of Lawrence. Your mother's family. We met and...well...grew fond of each other, I suppose. I was twenty-years-old. I was lonely. I'd never been away from home before."

Jack became more agitated and visibly uncomfortable with each sentence he uttered. His audience remained silent but at times shifted in their seats, as uncomfortable as he was. Laurel sat rigidly. She refused to surrender her dignity to Jack Hartmoor with an outburst of girlish tears. She steeled herself, like a statue, and gripped the carved walnut armrests of the chair.

"We stayed in Douglas County seven weeks, then we were sent farther west, to Fort Riley. I promised to write to her. I told her I would come back for her after the War, but...I didn't."

Jack paused and looked at Carey briefly, then continued. "I didn't know...about you. I didn't see or hear from Lizzie for about five years, then she suddenly appeared in the yard one day with you by her side. For a moment, I didn't even recognize her. She was much altered in appearance–so thin. She was starving and so were you, I guess. She demanded that I marry her." Jack's face twisted in a torment of guilt. "I refused. I denied I was responsible. I said some terrible things, things I now regret."

"Scoundrel," Carey growled.

"You have to understand," Jack pleaded. "I was trying to make my way in the world. My father would have been furious, had he found out. Mother, you know how he was–"

"Oh, Jack," Margaret shook her head sadly. "Oh, Jack."

"It was the day of Sarah's wedding to Andrew," Jack continued. "I just panicked. I told Lizzie to take her child and wait in that old sod house. I promised I would discuss the matter further after Sarah's wedding. I gave her what money I had in my pocket and brought out some bread and cheese from the kitchen. The family was in such an uproar with the wedding preparations that no one really noticed.

"When I met with her later, she was impossible. Making all kinds of threats. Shouting one moment, crying the next. That was my first hint there was something wrong with her, that she was wrong in the head. I became afraid she would harm herself or you." He looked up once again at Carey. "Or me, for that matter."

Carey snorted in bitter derision at this, but Jack continued. His agitation had calmed somewhat. The more of his story he told, the more monotone his voice became.

"We finally struck a bargain of sorts. I agreed to let her stay on in the sod house and give her what money I could to pay for her keep. She promised she would say nothing of the matter and give no hint that I might be the father of...of–" With a sigh it was clear he could not even bring himself to say Carey's name.

"I had no idea," said Margaret. "When she came to me and asked to stay in the soddy until she found work–"

"We concocted that story together. It was all by careful design that you thought it was your decision, Mother. I'm sorry for the deception."

"I feel like such a fool," Margaret mused.

"That makes two of us," Carey whispered under his breath. He rested his hands on Laurel's shoulders over the high chair back. She patted his hand reassuringly.

Jack hung his head. Silence filled the room. Carey and the Hartmoors sunk into a rediscovery of the past, a relearning of their own family history.

"Where does this leave us?" Laurel asked quietly.

"You cannot marry this man," Jack explained. "He is your cousin. I consulted a lawyer about this issue weeks ago. As soon as Cassandra started guessing that Fairchild was your lover. I feared just this circumstance. I don't know what else to say. I...I'm sorry."

"Wait a minute," Carey snapped to life, angry once again. "We still have no proof. Nothing but your word. How do *you* even know for certain?"

"Why would he make up such a terrible story?" Margaret asked.

"Because he hates me, Mrs. Hartmoor. Because he doesn't think I'm good enough to marry into your precious family."

"Oh, Carey..." Laurel began, almost as a reproach.

"I think I have proof," Jack interrupted, looking more miserable than ever. "Excuse me just a moment." He left the room and went upstairs to his bedroom. He returned quickly, holding something small in his right hand.

"The timing of your mother's suicide was not a random moment," he said to Carey.

"Did you have something to do with her death?" Carey demanded. Laurel felt his hands clench with rage upon her shoulders. She held her breath.

"Oh, good lord, no. But...the announcement of my impending marriage to Alice precipitated it, I believe."

Laurel caught a shocked look cross Alice's thin face. A trembling hand fluttered to her lips. For a fleeting moment, Laurel pitied Jack. To have his wedding spoiled by the suicide of a former lover. Perhaps Lizzie Fairchild or Carington or whatever her name was, finally exacted upon him the revenge she required for his earlier cruelty to her.

"Read this." Jack handed a yellowed piece of paper to Carey.

Laurel assumed this must be Lizzie Fairchild's suicide note, written to Jack. She longed to read the note herself and wondered if Carey would share its contents. The whole room watched as Carey scanned the faded handwriting of his mother's last words. The tension of the room hung on Carey's distraught face. Laurel could see he was holding back tears. She knew him well enough to recognize that particular tightness in his jaw and angle of his brow that accompanied his strongest emotions.

"I need some fresh air," Carey stated in a low voice and left the room. Laurel rose to follow him, but Margaret bade her stay with a wave of her hand. On a moment's reflection, Laurel agreed with her grandmother that Carey might need to be alone.

Margaret went into the kitchen to see how Cassandra was getting on with the two little Fairchild girls. Alice rose abruptly and disappeared upstairs without a word to her husband.

The two candidates for mayor sat silently on opposite sides of the deserted parlor.

At last, Jack spoke again. "I'm sorry, Laurel."

"I'm not the one you should be apologizing to."

"You're right."

He reluctantly stepped out onto the porch to find Carey sitting in the porch swing with the brittle, yellowed paper in his lap.

Laurel stepped over to the open bay window to see what would transpire next.

Jack walked behind the swing and placed a comforting hand on his son's shoulder, a tender act that Carey promptly rejected, jerking away with an almost violent disgust.

"*Don't.* Don't try to play father to me now. You're about a quarter of a century too late!"

"I know," Jack replied quietly. He wandered back towards the door. "Would you like a shot of whiskey?"

Carey sullenly nodded and Jack quickly returned with a bottle and two glasses.

"Now would the purpose of this beverage be medical, scientific, or mechanical? Being as how all other uses are a crime in this state." Carey sounded slightly arrogant.

Jack smiled ruefully. "Medical, surely. Wonderful for calming the nerves. I bought this stock years ago before the county went dry. It's much finer than those awful concoctions they sell at the drug store. I suppose becoming a father, however belatedly, qualifies as a special occasion."

"A grandfather, as well. I have two children."

"Oh, yes, of course. I never really thought about that before."

Laurel continued to deliberately eavesdrop. She somehow felt she had a right to know what they said to each other. At some point, Alice returned to the parlor and joined Laurel in the bay window. Two women watching two men that they felt belonged to them.

Carey took the glass of whiskey Jack poured for him. He gulped down the contents, wincing slightly as he swallowed. "My wife died in childbirth," he remarked as though telling Jack something he didn't already know.

"Yes. Bad luck. This farm's seen a run of bad luck in the last year."

"I was sorry to hear about your daughter," Carey offered with perfunctory courtesy. He swallowed another large gulp of whiskey and tried not to grimace as the fiery liquid seared his throat.

The two men each drank down another glass in a silence punctuated only by the chirping of the crickets in the spring grass as darkness closed in on the wide horizon.

"I'm...I'm sorry about your mother."

Carey's hostility instantly returned. "Sorry? Sorry that you made her your whore and then despised her for it?"

"That's not how it was. That's not ever how it was."

Jack remained surprisingly calm, Laurel observed as she continued to eavesdrop.

"When you hear people talk about the 'grand and glorious War,' you must guess they are men who never saw battle," Jack continued, waxing glumly nostalgic. He stared into the middle distance and shook his head. "Before I was transferred to the frontier, I served in Pennsylvania briefly. I saw a man's head once, lying on the ground. Just his head. Torn clean off by artillery fire. I remember his eyes, still wide open, looking a little surprised, but only a little. Couldn't get that sight out of my mind. Then I came out here, met your mother." Jack smiled faintly with the memory. "Such a pretty girl. So cheerful. Lovely singing voice. When I was with her, I didn't have to think about death and war and dead soldier's faces."

Carey said nothing, so Jack continued. "I contacted your mother's family after her death. I made a discreet inquiry through my lawyer to see if they would be willing to take you in."

"What did they say?"

Jack frowned and shook his head sadly. "My lawyer got a one sentence response from Mr. Carington, her father. He replied that he did not ever have a daughter named Elizabeth and not to trouble him further."

Jack poured them another shot of whiskey and they quietly drank again.

"I never wanted to be your father," Jack suddenly broke the silence. Laurel could hear a perceptible note of sadness in his voice. "In fact, God forgive me, but I hated you, despised you. You were the living reminder of the terrible thing I'd done. Every time I looked at you, I hated myself more. I didn't like to think of myself as a liar, a seducer, a man who could callously ruin a young woman's life. I never *meant* to do that. I was just young and careless and made promises

I never meant to keep. I blame myself entirely. Your mother loved me and trusted me and I betrayed that trust so grievously."

"I suppose you're hardly the first man to make promises in the dark," Carey conceded with a sigh. Jack's anguish seemed so real, so genuine, Carey found it hard to remain completely unsympathetic. But then he remembered his mother's anguish. "Still, you could have redeemed yourself. You *could* have done the right thing. But you didn't."

"No, I didn't. I wanted to hide my mistakes, not own up to them. That's what a terrible man I am."

"You're not a terrible man," said an unexpected voice.

Both Jack and Carey jumped at the sound. Alice now stood in the doorway

"You're not a terrible man," Alice repeated. "Just a flawed one." She crossed the porch unsmilingly and stood directly behind her husband where he sat in the porch swing next to Carey. She rested her hands delicately upon his shoulders.

Jack rose from the swing and turned to look upon Alice with a hopeful uncertainty. He placed his arm around her waist and the pair entered the house. They retreated to the bedroom they had not shared since Christmas.

Laurel joined Carey on the porch swing. She placed her hand on his forearm in a soothing gesture.

"He used to come around once a month when I was a kid. He never looked too happy about it. My mother would always send me outside, even in winter. Give me some chore to do to get me out of the way. After he left, she'd be all tearful and melancholy for days. I never knew why. I just thought when he came it was a landlord coming to collect rent from a tenant. I never dreamed that the money was going in the opposite direction."

"What happens now?" she asked.

Carey drew a deep breath, then slapped his knees. "We need to focus on the election. We only have a week left. Right now I have to drive the girls back into town before it gets any later. And I'll need to think of some way to explain this to them. Poor kids. They were confused enough *before* this happened."

Laurel could not quite grasp his change of mood. She found herself at a complete loss for words with the man she had planned to be married to before nightfall. She felt too miserable even to cry. She looked up at the big, carved "H" over the door. It surely stood for "Heartbreak" on this godforsaken night.

She silently watched Carey load his little girls into the wagon and drive off into the twilight and felt as empty as the Kansas landscape.

Chapter Twenty~six

Cassandra and Laurel were the first to rise the following morning. They sat in the dining room and ate toast and coffee.

"You know, I never until last night thought of how Lizzie Fairchild's death and Jack's marriage to Alice were so close in time. I remember how odd and upset he was then. We thought he was just nervous about getting married. We even teased him about it. You know, accusing him of cold feet. Good heavens, if we'd only known what was really bothering him." Cassandra shuddered. "Oh, listen to me go on."

Margaret entered the room looking older than Laurel had ever seen her. She walked at a slower pace than ususal and her pale, creased skin seemed to hang more loosely than before. Laurel had never in the year since she had come to the Hartmoor's house, known a day when her grandmother was not the first one up in the morning.

Margaret took her place at the table and Cassandra offered to fill her cup with coffee.

"Are you feeling alright, Mother?"

"I got very little sleep last night." Margaret took a sip of her coffee.

"I doubt any of us slept well after Jack's little announcement," Cassandra observed.

Without warning even to herself, Laurel burst into tears.

"Oh, Laurel, poor thing," Cassandra said in the kindest voice she had ever used in addressing her sister's child. She rose and circled the table to offer Laurel a comforting pat on the back. "Come on now, future mayors can't cry. It's not dignified."

Laurel wiped her wet face on her napkin and tried to smile through her tears as Jack breezed in the room and seated himself at the table as if nothing were the matter at all. He poured himself a cup of coffee, opened the morning paper, and began to read without a word to anyone.

All three Hartmoor women present collectively glared at him.

When Jack finally noticed the silence his entrance had occasioned, he reluctantly laid his newspaper on the table. "What?"

"Jack, I've spent a great deal of time thinking about last night," Margaret began.

"I'm sorry about that," Jack offered, though he seemed far less contrite than he had been the night before. "I'm sorry it had to come out at all. I would never have revealed the sordid details had I not been forced to." He looked pointedly at Laurel when he said this as though it were her fault somehow. "What then? Why do you all look at me as though I were some sort of criminal?"

Bitter silence met his question.

"My behavior has been beyond reproach in this matter."

"That's debatable," said Cassandra.

"I fulfilled my legal obligations to the fullest. No one can say I didn't. I supported Lizzie and her son all those years.," Jack argued.

"What about your moral obligations?" Cassandra countered.

Jack set his jaw and defiantly folded his arms across his chest like a sullen little boy, refusing to grant an inch.

This action incensed Margaret. "Jack, you have always counted on this family for support. But I'm afraid you have done nothing to earn it."

Jack frowned more deeply, but just the slightest bit uneasy. "What are you getting at?"

"I have decided upon this moment that on Election Day, I will cast my first vote and that it will not be for you, Son."

"*What*?"

Though Laurel did not shout "what?" with her uncle, she was nearly as amazed as he. All eyes turned to Margaret.

"Mother, you can't be serious!"

"Oh, but I am, Jack. I intend to cast my vote for Laurel, here, and I intend to encourage all my friends to do the same."

"Oh, Grandmother," Laurel whispered, wide-eyed.

"This is completely absurd." Jack's face turned in to a mask of outrage at this maternal betrayal.

"Absurd or not, I'm joining the group," said Cassandra. "Laurel, you'll have my vote, too!"

"But Laurel is just a...just a young girl who–"

"Whose moral fiber I have less doubt about than yours at the moment, son."

Laurel drew a deep breath and turned to her uncle with a superior smile. "It's too bad there's not a School for the Moral Correction of Wayward Bankers."

Cassandra hooted with laughter at this, though no one else found Laurel's remark funny.

"My own family betraying me?"

"Which family would you be referring to Jack? The family you chose to acknowledge, or the one you sought to hide?" asked Margaret pointedly.

Jack stood up in a fury. "I'm going to get my breakfast in town this morning and I just hope that you will have come to your senses by the time I return this evening or–"

Margaret narrowed her dark eyes at her grown son. "Or what, exactly?"

Jack nervously met his mother's fierce gaze and realized he might at last have gone too far. He stalked out of the room and slammed the front door behind him.

Laurel turned to Margaret, sharing some of Jack's shock and surprise. "Do you really mean it, Grandmother? Are you really planning to vote for me?"

"Of course, child. You ought to know me well enough by now to know I never make idle remarks."

"You don't think my candidacy is a joke?"

"Hartmoors do not joke. And you, dear, are a Hartmoor as well as a McBryde and I expect you to live up to our standards even if your uncle has not."

"I want to make you proud of me, Grandmother. More than anything on Earth."

"You don't need to be mayor to make me proud of you. But I'm going to spend the next week doing everything in my power to help you achieve that goal. If any woman should be the nation's first mayor, I want it to be you."

"Me, too," Cassandra added. "You can count on me. For your sake...and for Carey's."

Now Laurel fought back tears of joy. "I don't know what to say."

"Don't say anything," Margaret commanded. "We need to finish breakfast as swiftly as possible. We have a great deal of work to do."

The membership of the Women's Christian Temperance Union was to be the first target of Margaret's new-found political zeal. Margaret drove the Hartmoor buggy, something she rarely did and headed the horses straight for the homestead of Elberta Maclean.

Laurel knew that Margaret was acquainted with Elberta, though the two were not close since most of Margaret's friends came from her church circle and Elberta was a Catholic.

Elberta and a hired girl were washing the laundry in the back yard when they arrived. Both Margaret and Laurel held on to their hats as they struggled against the buffeting March winds and made their way around Elberta's modest farmhouse. They interrupted a gathering of chickens who squawked and flapped at their brisk intrusion.

"Margaret Hartmoor, what brings you out on such a windy day?" called Elberta Maclean cordially.

"A matter of fine importance, Berta."

"Well, let's all go into the parlor, shall we?" Elberta unrolled her sleeves and gave some instructions to the hired girl, then ushered her visitors into the house.

"Tea?" asked their hostess.

Margaret nodded and she followed Laurel into the small parlor. They seated themselves on a flowered blue sofa and waited for Elberta to return from the kitchen.

"Forgive us for coming unannounced, Berta, but our mission couldn't wait a second," Margaret began when Elberta brought out a tray of gingerbread and sat it before her guests on a small tea table.

"Whatever is the matter, Margaret?"

"You are acquainted with my granddaughter, Miss McBryde?"

Laurel smiled stiffly and tried to look composed.

"I heard her speak up quite smartly at the political meeting last week. You acquitted yourself most admirably, my dear."

"Thank you, ma'am."

"I've come to ask for your vote on Monday, next, Berta."

"Your son already has my vote, Margaret. You know my WCTU ladies and I would never consider a vote for a 'wet.'" She referred to the Democrat Harry Johnson.

"My granddaughter is also running. It's her that I'd like you to consider."

Elberta looked so astonished by this request, she seemed at a loss for words. The kettle sang in from the kitchen as though to punctuate the moment and

Elberta dashed off. She returned quickly with a silver tray bearing the teapot with a fine set of china cups and saucers decorated with delicate pink cabbage roses.

"You are serious, then, Miss McBryde?" Elberta remarked sharply as she poured tea for her guests. "We all thought the menfolk were simply having some rude fun at your expense."

"No doubt they saw it as that," Laurel returned with a confident smile. "I can assure you, Mrs. Maclean, that I have never been more in earnest."

"Elberta, let me put it to you plain. It's time we ladies showed the men in this town a thing or two."

"Well, you know I'm all for that." Elberta Maclean sipped her tea and scrutinized Laurel closely. "McBryde...is that an Irish name?"

"Yes, ma'am, I guess so."

"Would you, by any chance, be a Roman Catholic?"

"No, ma'am, I'm afraid not." Laurel did not wish to reveal that her father, though baptized a Catholic, had parted company with his faith long before she was born and that she had been raised with very little in the way of traditional religious teaching.

"Elberta, can we count on the ladies of the WCTU to support my granddaughter? I can guarantee she will advance your policies more vigorously than either of the men running against her."

"I must say she impressed me at the political rally. We all spoke of it afterwards and would have invited her to join our group, but your family left rather abruptly."

Elberta studied Laurel so intently, Laurel felt inclined to squirm, but resisted the urge.

"Chisholm has the chance to make it into the history books, Elberta. I, for one, would be proud to say I had a hand in it."

"Indeed. I will bring this up at our regular Tuesday meeting tomorrow. Would you like to come and meet our membership, Miss McBryde?"

"Very much, Mrs. Maclean. I'd be happy to attend."

"I'll send my coach for you at about 6:30. That alright?"

"Yes, ma'am. I'll look forward to it."

As Margaret and Laurel climbed back into their buggy, Margaret remarked with a twinkle in her eye, "You're halfway there, child."

During the course of the following week, Laurel attended not only the scheduled meeting of the Women's Christian Temperance Union, but a quilting bee, a baby shower, a choir practice of the Presbyterian Church, a dance recital, a reading club, a Bible study, and, on the Saturday afternoon before the election, a "New Voters Tea" hosted jointly by Margaret and Lydia. Lydia brought some of her suffrage friends up from Wichita to lend Laurel their moral support. All were enthusiastic supporters of Laurel's bid, though few voiced confidence in her success. All found it amusing that Jack Hartmoor had fallen into his own trap by suggesting Laurel run against him.

Jack made himself scarce during this week, still reeling from his mother's defection.

Laurel met, in those few days, every single woman in the town limits of Chisholm known to Margaret Hartmoor, and Margaret Hartmoor knew them all. If nothing else, she enjoyed the distraction from her misery of losing Carey once again, though she knew she was only postponing the pain, rather than dealing with it.

Monday, April 4, 1887, dawned cloudy and threatened rain. The Chisholm Courier issued a special edition with an editorial encouraging women to exercise their newly granted franchise. They endorsed Jack Hartmoor, to Laurel's disappointment though not to her surprise. What irritated her was the fact they failed to even acknowledge her candidacy. Her name was not mentioned once in the paper.

The ladies of the WCTU decided to organize a carriage service for all women wanting to vote. They would ride up and down the streets of Chisholm and past all outlying farms within the voting jurisdiction and offer to drive women voters to the polls.

Their first stop was the home of the candidate herself. Delphinia Slidell presented Laurel with a bouquet of spring crocuses. Delphinia kissed Laurel's cheek and whispered how brave they all thought she was. Laurel wore the new lavender dress created by Selma Ann. She felt like a queen being escorted to her own coronation as she rode in the brightly decorated wagon adorned with streamers and signs that proclaimed: "For country, for home, for liberty." Coronation or beheading, she laughed to herself. Either way, she had experienced the wildest, most exhausting week of her life. One so filled with activity that she had not had time to see Carey at all. She was fairly certain this had been one of her grandmother's motives in keeping her so distracted. She was almost glad of it. Seeing him again so soon would have broken her heart.

Cassandra and Margaret followed them in the Hartmoor buggy. Alice, feeling newly conflicted towards Laurel's opponent, stayed home to please him.

Newspaper reporters from around the state lay in wait for them at the polling place–the schoolhouse.

"I see no signs of public drunkenness," Elberta Maclean remarked approvingly as she guided the wagon to a halt in front of the polls.

"It's only nine in the morning, Berta," Delphinia sniffed.

Laurel quietly smiled. The Temperance ladies seemed doubtful the election day would not devolve into the usual stag party of prior years. The day looked quiet enough as it began. The presence of the female sex on the electoral scene just might clean up the "cesspool" after all.

"Oh, look, there's old Mrs. Green. Poor dear. Looks like she's wandering around lost," said Elberta. "Yoohoo, Mrs. Green. Can we be of assistance?"

Tiny Mrs. Green stepped to the edge of the wooden sidewalk and waved to acknowledge Elberta's hello. She wrung her hands in a nervous confusion. "I came to vote, but I'm not sure how."

"There's nothing to it, my dear," said Delphinia. "I'll walk in with you. You simply take a ticket and mark it as you please, then hand it to the election clerk. You are registered to vote, are you not?"

Delphinia climbed down from the WCTU wagon and took the elderly woman's arm. As soon as Laurel alighted, a small group of men rushed towards her with such ferocity she blanched.

"Are you Miss McBryde?" demanded a tall mustachioed gentleman Laurel had never seen before.

"I am, sir. Who wishes to know?"

All the men chuckled at Laurel's naiveté.

"Stanley Cross, Miss, of the Topeka Journal. Is it true you will serve if elected?"

"Of course, sir. I would not mock the electoral process in any manner."

"What would be your first order of business, should you be elected, Miss McBryde?" asked a short, plump gentleman who chewed a short stub of a cigar. "Oh, Marshall Briggs of the Kansas City Star."

Laurel nodded graciously at this terse introduction. "I suppose my first order of business would be to call the town council meeting to order." She smiled coyly to indicate to the reporters she intended this remark to be flippant and most of them dutifully smiled back.

Then she thought better of her light-heartedness. Women already had enough trouble being taken seriously in this brave new arena. No need to compound the problem by creating the impression she considered her candidacy as big a joke as some others did, most notably her opponents.

"Seriously, gentlemen, I plan to conduct the affairs of this city in as dignified a manner as they deserve and will try my utmost to see that the interests of prosperity, security, and the welfare of all Chisholm's citizenry are protected and respected in our halls of local government."

"Is it true you are the niece of your opponent, Jack Hartmoor?" The question came from yet another reporter from out of town.

"Yes, sir, that is correct." Questions about Jack made Laurel nervous. She now realized she stood amidst a crowd of nearly twenty people. In addition to the reporters, various voters on their way to the polls and curious passersby had now gathered about her.

"Doesn't that cause a good deal of family strife, Miss McBryde? Isn't Mr. Hartmoor your guardian?"

Laurel opened her mouth to reply to these awkward questions, but before she could respond, a familiar voice answered for her.

"Miss McBryde is engaged to be married, gentleman."

"Carey!" She turned to find him at her side.

"Are you the lucky gent?" asked the Topeka reporter with a grin.

"Indeed, I am. Now if you will allow this lady to step up to the polls she will be able to cast her first vote."

Laurel stared at Carey with speechless amazement as he deftly led her through the crowd towards the door of the schoolhouse. Why was he speaking of marriage as though nothing had interfered with their plans?

"It's my first time to vote, too, you know," Carey whispered in her ear.

"Your first time, too? How could that be?"

He continued to whisper. "Couldn't read, remember? Until a sweet girl I know taught me." He gave her gloved hand an affectionate squeeze.

"Who will you vote for in the mayor's race, Miss McBryde?" one of the reporters called after her. She turned with a ready answer for him. "As it is considered inappropriate to vote for oneself and since I cannot, in good conscience, support either of my opponents, I shall regrettably be forced to leave the ticket blank as to the office of mayor."

This reply satisfied everyone in the crowd to such a degree, they applauded and Laurel curtsied on the schoolhouse steps. She turned once more to enter and met both Margaret and Cassandra as they were emerging.

"Well, we did it, dear," Margaret announced with a relieved smile on her ancient features. "Easy as falling off a log."

"And not half so painful," Cassandra chimed in.

"I told you so!" Laurel winked and gave them each a kiss on the cheek. They had apparently gone ahead and voted while Laurel stood prisoner to her entourage of reporters. She felt grateful that the women had not overheard Carey's curious remark that he considered them still engaged.

As Carey ushered Laurel toward the desk of the election clerk, she whispered, "What did you mean out there? About our engagement?"

Carey grinned down at her. "Tell you later. Now go vote, lady!"

She gave him a smile of mystified distress as he backed away and the throng of onlookers swallowed him.

"You seem awfully calm and composed for a candidate on election day," Cassandra observed as she drove Laurel and Margaret home from voting. The WCTU ladies and their decorated suffrage wagon had gone on about their mission to round up women voters and escort them to the polls.

"Oh, I don't have anything to be nervous about."

"That certain of winning, are you?" Cassandra raised a skeptical eyebrow at such confidence.

"No, I'm that certain of losing, of course. I've known all along I had no chance. Still and all, I'm glad I did it."

"Don't be so certain of the outcome, child," said Margaret with a serene and distant expression in her dark eyes.

Laurel felt a strange, tingling sensation on the back of her neck.

Chapter Twenty-seven

"I convinced the election clerk to let me deliver this in person," Carey announced as he bolted up the steps on the Hartmoor house to where Laurel stood waiting on the porch.

Laurel eagerly ripped open the envelope and read aloud its contents:

"Madam,

You are hereby notified that at an election held in the city of Chisholm on Monday, April 4, 1887, for the purpose of electing city officers, you were duly elected to the office of Mayor of said city. You will take due notice thereof and govern yourself accordingly.

R. J. Michaels, Clerk"

Laurel looked up from the notice with a breathless smile. Laurel had known of her election since midnight when the final count of the votes was made public. The tally had racked up 392 for Laurel, 196 for Jack, and a dismal 73 for Harry Johnson, the Democrat. Nearly all of the 270 women voting had cast their ballot for Laurel.

Until this moment, however, it all seemed blissfully surreal, a strange, prairie dream she had yet to wake up from. Now the certifiable truth lay in her hands. She read the letter again, for good measure.

"Can you handle some more good news, Miss Mayor?"

Laurel threw her arms around his neck and planted a breezy kiss on his cheek. "I'm not at all sure."

"I talked to my boss at the Grange, Mr. Kellerman. I asked him–very discreetly, of course–if he ever heard of first cousins getting married. I pretended I was curious because a friend of mine wanted to marry his cousin. He said 'sure,' they do it in Texas all the time. It's downright commonplace in the Southern states, according to him. He's from Texas, so he ought to know."

"Oh, Carey, does this mean we can actually, legally marry?"

"As far as I'm concerned, it does."

Suddenly perplexed, she bit her lip. "Are you sure you still want to marry me? Knowing what we know now?"

"Have your feelings changed?"

"No, not at all, it's just that–"

Carey placed his hands on his hips with a defiant frown. "As far as I'm concerned, I think Jack Hartmoor's a lying son of a bitch. He don't, I mean, he doesn't have any proof of what he said happened twenty-five, no, twenty-six years ago."

"But what about the letter?" Laurel still felt vaguely slighted that Carey had not shared the letter's contents with her.

"My mother was never right in the head in all the years I knew her. I loved her, God bless her poor soul, but I'm not gonna throw away everything we have based on her rantings and ravings in that letter she wrote. She always told me my father was a soldier named Robert Fairchild who got killed in the war and that's good enough for me."

Laurel remained distressed and not the least convinced by Carey's blithely convenient discounting of Jack's shocking confession. "You're certain we're doing the right thing?"

Carey put his hands on his hips and adopted his fiercest frown. "You once promised me your first born child. You gonna go back on the deal?"

"Stop making jokes, Carey. This is serious."

"Then give me a serious answer, Mayor McBryde. What do you think about going to Texas and marrying me?"

Laurel drew the deepest breath of her life. "I think it's wonderful."

He pulled her close and hugged her tightly. "Wonderful, if we can locate some money for the trip. Don't worry, though–I'll rob a bank if I have to." He grinned at her and his pale green, promise-colored eyes twinkled with merriment. "In fact, I'll rob the *Hartmoor* Bank if I have to.

She did not return his smile, but narrowed her own eyes. She looked far away, but she gazed into the future, not the distance. "I don't think you'll need to do that."

After Carey left to pick up his daughters, Laurel returned to her room to rest and digest the impossible news that she had both won the mayoralty and a husband on the same day. To think that one year ago, life as she had always known it had ended and fate had given no hint of what was to come. Her father, dead one year now...how proud he would have been of her. Tears filled her eyes with the sad regret that he did not live to see her day of small glory. Yet, had he lived, she would still be at Windrift. None of this amazing year would have transpired at all. This paradox left her powerfully confused, but she lacked the time to dwell on it.

A discreet knock on her bedroom door signaled Laurel's next wellwisher–Cassandra. She wore her riding habit and smelled of saddle soap and horse flesh.

"My brother's lost his mind, I hope you know." She smiled as she said this, seeming more perplexed than upset by the situation. "You missed an interesting scene by sleeping through breakfast, Lady Mayor. Jack's like a different person entirely. First, he comes to the table without his collar and jacket on and when Mother asks him why he's not dressed for work, he tells her he's not going in to work. In fact, he announces he's staying home all week. And when Mother asks if he's sick, he laughs out loud and says he's never felt better in his life."

"That *is* odd."

Cassandra looked out the bedroom window into the yard below. The sounds of lumber being lifted and dropped filtered up. "Look at him out there," Cassandra mused. "He's got it into his head to build something. I bet he hasn't swung a hammer in twenty years."

Laurel joined her aunt at the window and studied the Hartmoor yard. A large pile of new lumber lay in a heap. Jack picked up one board, then another, and laid them in a circle of sorts. She had never seen him with his shirt sleeves rolled up before. A lock of his dark blond hair, free of pomade, for once, hung carelessly on his forehead. Alice watched her husband with a delighted smile on her face, her hands clasped demurely to her bosom.

"He's building her a gazebo," Laurel whispered.

"A what?"

"A gazebo. A summerhouse. He promised to build her one when they got married, but he never did."

Jack had laid the circle out exactly where Alice had told Laurel she thought it ought to be.

"Aunt Cassie, I need to talk to Uncle Jack. Do you suppose we're on any kind of speaking terms?"

"I don't know why not. He doesn't seem bothered by losing to you in the least. In fact, he seems thrilled with all the attention it's brought to Chisholm. He thinks a lot of—what did he call them?–venture capitalists, that's it, are going to be interested in Chisholm, with all this free publicity."

"You mean he's not still mad at me?" Laurel was dumbfounded by Cassandra's revelations.

"Oh, he probably is, but he's hiding it well. You know Jack, as prideful as the day is long, but it would kill him to admit his disappointment. What's so important that you look all worried?"

"I need Uncle Jack to sell Windrift for me."

Cassandra frowned. "Are you sure you want to do that?"

"Oh, yes, I'm certain."

Jack knocked at Laurel's door just before suppertime.

"Come in, I'm decent."

Jack cautiously poked his head in the door. Then he entered and immediately apologized for his disorderly appearance. He quickly explained that he was just on his way to wash and dress for supper. Laurel had to smile. Never had she seen her prim and proper uncle in such a state. Dirty, sweaty, his sleeves rolled up, his hair disheveled. He smelled of raw lumber and spring grass.

"Cassie said you wanted me to sell Windrift."

"Yes, I need money, Uncle Jack. Carey and I plan to take a trip to Texas. We're going to be married there. It's perfectly legal in that state, so we won't need to lie."

"I...I hope you're doing the right thing," Jack responded awkwardly. "But I've learned not to offer opinions to you or your intended spouse."

"Don't worry. We're never going to tell anyone the true reason we need to go all the way to Texas to get married."

Jack waved a hand and shook his head to silence her. She could tell in an instant, he did not wish to discuss the matter. He rubbed his chin and contemplated her request for a moment. "About your property–I've already had an inquiry on it. I didn't take the offer seriously at the time because I thought you had no interest in selling. The house and acreage is, after all, your father's only legacy to you. You realize what little capital he had at the time of his demise went to settle the debts of his estate?"

"Yes, I understand. You've actually had an offer on the property?"

"Yes."

"How much?" Laurel asked eagerly, afraid to hope for too much.

Jack paused for a moment, then drew a mournful breath. "Ten thousand dollars."

"Ten *thousand* dollars?" The sum was incredible, unbelievable. She swallowed hard. "That's at least ten times what I expected. Who on earth made such an offer?"

"You wouldn't know him," Jack said quickly. "Do you wish me to respond?"

"Of course. By all means. As soon as possible."

Jack was nearly out the door of Laurel's room before the truth of the situation came to her in a sudden rush, why the sum of ten thousand dollars had such a familiar ring. She called him back before he could close the door. He stuck his head back in.

With a kind and grateful smile she said quietly, "I guess Chisholm will have to wait a little while longer to get telephone service, won't it?"

His dark blond moustache twitched, but he said nothing and closed the door.

Laurel stunned Carey with the news of her good fortune concerning the sale of Windrift when he came to drive her to her maiden town council meeting. Nervous tension made the day nearly unbearable and three times longer than it should have been. She was no good at chores around the Hartmoor house, so preoccupied was she with the events of the coming evening. Two reporters, both from the East, had called upon her in the afternoon and she gave them an impromptu interview along with cake and lemonade on the Hartmoor front porch. They would be reporting on her conduct at her first council meeting along with numerous other reporters. The Chisholm *Courier* had wondered in print if the town council hall could suitably hold the expected throng of curious onlookers in addition to the usual crowd having legitimate business with the council.

She spent two hours getting dressed and letting Alice curl her hair at the kitchen stove. Alice had even offered subdued congratulations on her impending nuptials with Carey. Laurel could not quite read Alice's reaction to the relation of Carey and Jack. Alice didn't speak of it at all, though her decision to reunite with her husband seemed more in character for her than her quiet rebellion ever had.

"They offered you *how much*?" Carey asked again when Laurel announced the selling price of Windrift.

"Ten thousand. I was surprised, too."

"What a sucker," he exclaimed in disbelief. "No offense, but who would pay that kind of money in these hard times? Oh, well, his loss is our gain."

Laurel smiled to herself, grateful the true identity of the anonymous buyer had not occurred to Carey. She feared he would not accept the money if he knew it came from Jack Hartmoor.

"With the resources we now have, you'll–we'll–be able to carry on our political work, won't we, Carey?"

"Sure. If you want to, I mean."

"Of course, I want to."

"But it's your money, Laurel."

"Once we're married, it will be *our* money. And I can't think of a better way to spend it than on something we both believe in." How odd and ironically fitting, she thought, to use a banker's money to further Carey's populist agenda.

He smiled over at her and shook his head as though amazed that anyone could be so generous to him. He put his arm around her shoulders and tucked her in as close to him as driving a wagon would allow. "I think first off, we're going to buy someone a new camera, and a darkroom–and a house to put them in."

Laurel squeezed Carey's hand with delight and kissed his cheek.

"It'll have to be a pretty big house," he continued with a straight face. "Especially if it's going to hold all nine children."

"*Nine?*" she nearly screamed.

"Our own baseball team," he explained.

"Oh!" She pulled his loving arm off her shoulders when she finally realized he was teasing. "Well, you've already got two, so that leaves only seven to go."

"Girls can't play baseball, Laurel. Baseball's a man's game."

Laurel tilted her chin provocatively. "They used to say that about politics."

Carey grinned. "I guess you're right."

With a kiss on the forehead from her future husband, the mayor of Chisholm entered the crowded and noisy council chamber. Laurel blanched at the sight of so many staring faces all looking to her with penetrating curiosity. Some almost seemed apprehensive, as though contemplating some new species of being, unsure of what to expect. Whispers rose to a low roar as all felt the need to comment on her. Was it her clothes? Her youth? Her demeanor? Her audacity at this very unlikely undertaking? Her nerves calmed when she caught sight of Lydia's smiling, serene face in the crowd. She must have taken the last coach from Wichita after her store closed to make the meeting in time.

Laurel returned her smile, her confidence restored. Then she saw Margaret and Cassandra sitting next to Lydia. Margaret looked concerned. The fret lines in her creased face seemed twice as deep as usual. Did she worry her granddaughter would make a perfect fool of herself in front of half the town?

And wonder of wonders, who sat next to Margaret, but Jack with Alice in tow? Laurel decided Cassandra knew her brother pretty well. His appearance at the meeting must surely be to prove to all he didn't care a whit about losing, lie though it was.

The clamor dropped to a low rumble as Laurel walked confidently to the front of the room. The six councilmen rose to greet her. She seated herself at the head of the council table, spread her notebook before her, and called the meeting to order:

"Gentlemen, shall we commence?"

Historical Note

The nation's first woman mayor was elected in the tiny southern Kansas town of Argonia on April 4, 1887. Her name was Susanna Madora Salter. She was twenty-seven years old and married with two children. Her name was placed on the ballot without her knowledge by some men wishing to ridicule the idea of women in politics.

When asked on election day if she would serve, if elected, she surprised everyone by announcing she would. A sizable group of people, angered by the prank, formed a voting block and elected Dora Salter by a two-thirds majority, attaining international fame for tiny Argonia. Dora Salter didn't find out until years later that two of the men on her city council were among the pranksters who had placed her name on the ballot. From all accounts, they behaved themselves during her one-year term of office.

ABOUT THE AUTHOR

Michelle Black was born in Kansas. She studied photography at the Brooks Institute in Santa Barbara prior to graduating from law school with honors. Her first novel, NEVER COME DOWN, won first place for fiction in the 1997 Colorado Independent Publisher Book Awards. She currently lives in Colorado with her husband and two children. Readers may contact her by email: michelle13@compuserve.com.

ACKNOWLEDGMENTS

The author wishes to thank all her early readers and editors, among them, Paige Marshall and Carol Gates. Thanks also to Maxine Holden of the Argonia Chamber of Commerce for providing information on Dora Salter and to Dr. Patricia Duletsky, for all her help on matters medical.